MW00814760

Contents

For my parents

Acknowledgements

My stories were not written in a vacuum. That is partly because even the most modern vacuums manufactured today lack a word processor, but mostly because there are many people who gave me feedback and encouragement as I wrote. In the brief essays accompanying the stories, I have included a few special acknowledgements that pertained to particular stories, but here I want to give more general acknowledgements.

Caleb Warnock is the man most directly responsible for my getting on the path to publication, and taking his Writing in Depth class was one of the best decisions I ever made.

I owe a great deal to all the teachers I've had over the years, but there are a few who stick out in my mind as having encouraged my creativity during my schooling: Diane Pepetone, Lenelle Davis, Pat Gledhill, Breck England, Melinda Welch, Donna Parker, Elouise M. Bell, and Marion K. "Doc" Smith.

Then there are the writing workshop instructors and classmates from whom I have learned so much: Orson Scott Card and my fellow 2003 Literary Boot Campers; Tim Powers, K.D. Wentworth, the Writers of the Future judges, and my fellow winners from 2004 and 2005; Jeanne Cavelos, the guest instructors, and the Odyssey Class of 2007; and Dean Wesley Smith, Kristine Katherine Rusch, Sheila Williams, and my fellow attendees at the 2008 Short Story Workshop in Lincoln City.

My in-person writing groups have been invaluable: the Mistborn Llamas, the Rats with Swords, Buy the Book, the Quark Writing Group, and that unnamed group that met in various places before ending up at the Orem Barnes & Noble. Several online groups have also been instrumental in my success: the Writing in Depth forum, the Hatrack River Writers Workshop, and, most importantly, the Codex Writers.

Some of the following people are included in groups I mentioned above, but I want to thank them specifically for their feedback: Laura Anderson, Karla Bennion, Richard Chiu, Bryce Cundick, Spencer and Chrissy Ellsworth, Matt and Brooklyn Evans, Becca Fitzpatrick, Ben Hardin, Faith Hofer, Alethea Kontis, Mary Robinette Kowal, Jenifer Lee, Annaliese Lemmon,

Katherine Mardesich, Sean Markey, Amberlee Neibaur, Drew Olds, Ben Olsen, Janci Patterson, J. Boise Pearson, Bradley Reneer, Kayleena Richins, Brandon and Emily Sanderson, Isaac Stewart, Heidi Ann Summers, Sally Taylor, Nikki Trionfo, Charmayne Gubler Warnock, Carla Jo Webb, Jade Weedop, Dan Wells, Rachel Whitaker, Erin White, and Beth Wodzinski.

I'd like to thank the editors who have proven their excellent taste by publishing my stories, particularly those who have published more than one: Stanley Schmidt, Orson Scott Card, Edmund Schubert, Kevin J. Anderson, Jonathan Laden and Michele Barasso. And I'd be ungrateful if I didn't mention the great people at Galaxy Press and Author Services who run the Writers of the Future Contest, which really launched my career by buying two of the first three stories I sold.

And a big thank-you to Lawrence M. Schoen, for believing in my work enough that he wanted to publish this collection.

Finally, I want to thank my family, who have always been supportive of my writing.

Introduction

How is Eric James Stone like an elephant?

He certainly doesn't look like one, he's a lot less likely to crush your furniture by sitting on it, and he speaks—and writes—much better English. But you probably remember, at least generally (as I do, and that's reasonable since it exists in many versions), the old fable about the blind men and the elephant. None of them could see the elephant in its entirety, but each of them could learn something about it by feeling it. One, feeling its flank, thought it was some sort of wall. Another, feeling its trunk, compared it to a tree branch; a third, feeling its tail, a rope; and yet another, feeling a huge leg, a pillar. The mental picture each formed of the whole animal depended on which part he was examining.

And *that* is how Eric James Stone is like an elephant.

I was privileged to publish several of the stories in this collection, including one of Eric's first. Several more I didn't publish, for one reason or another—e.g., I was overstocked and didn't have room, or I just didn't think *Analog* (the magazine I edit) was the most appropriate home for them. But I always enjoyed reading them, whether I was able to use them or not. Each time I started reading one, I quickly felt that I was in good hands and could settle back to enjoy the story. Each time I finished one, I thought with a satisfaction like that following a fine meal, "That was good stuff!"

But it wasn't until I pulled up a whole pile of them to reread in preparation for writing this that I fully realized what a wide *range* of good stuff they were. If you just read "Resonance," for example, you might think that Eric is a "nuts-and-bolts" writer, the kind who imagines a real technological problem that might arise in the future and thrashes out a solution like an engineer (math and all). If you read "The Ashes of His Fathers," you might characterize him first as a humanist, a man acutely aware that in dealing with people, you must be sensitive to cultural issues not easily analyzable in engineering terms. If you read "That Leviathan, Whom Thou Hast Made," you might think of him as a writer specializing in really alien aliens—or religion. If you read "Upgrade" or "Rejiggering the Thingamajig," you might think of him as a guy with a wild and crazy imagination and a sense of humor to match.

You'd be right about all these things, but you'd also be wrong, because the important thing is that he's all of these and more. You'll see some of his aspects in any one story, but there are plenty more waiting for you in the others. Where else would you find a politician pushing regulation of a new technology by exploiting it to the limit? Or a new technology leading to a new kind of crime that is, in a sense, the opposite of theft? Or a philosophical carnivorous dinosaur?

And I've barely scratched the surface; you'll find all those and more in these stories. They're not all science fiction, either. Some are fantasy (an equally challenging kind of art), and some (see "The Robot Sorcerer") combine fantasy and science fiction in unique ways.

So what do they all have in common? Whether he's being serious or silly, tech-oriented or philosophical, you can count on Eric James Stone to come up with an original idea, do whatever he must to think through where it might lead, put at least one unusual twist on it, and deliver it you in a package featuring engaging characters caught up in a logical but often surprising web of events. In short, these stories will take you to all kinds of places, but they're all fun and they'll all make you think.

Which is exactly what I've always thought good stories *should* do. So I think you'll enjoy these.

—Stanley Schmidt

Rejiggering
the Thingamajig

The teleport terminal had not been built with *tyrannosaurus sapiens* in mind.

Resisting the urge to knock human-sized chairs about with her tail, Bokeerk squatted on the tile floor, folded the claws of her forelimbs together, and concentrated on her breathing. Meditation would calm her nerves. What should have been a two-minute waystop as she switched to a different teleport line had stretched to three hours, and being the only passenger in the terminal creeped her out.

The cheerful voice of the customer service AI roused Bokeerk from her trance. "It is my pleasure to inform you that the cause of the technical difficulties in the galactic teleport network has been found."

Bokeerk perked up and rose on her hind legs, remembering just in time to duck her head so it wouldn't bang the ceiling lamps. "Please send me to Krawlak," she said. It was unlikely that any of her eggs would hatch for another few days yet, but she was anxious to get home.

"It is with the utmost regret that I must tell you that will not be possible at this time," said the AI, with a tone of such abysmal sorrow that Bokeerk's eyes could not help but moisten with sympathetic tears. "I require assistance in repairing the problem."

Bokeerk lowered herself into a squat again. "When will help get here?" She looked at the time display on the digital assistant strapped to her left forelimb. She had now been stranded for three hours and fifty-two minutes.

"I estimate a spaceship carrying a repair crew could be here within twelve years," said the AI. Its voice seemed to have lost the customer service aspect.

"Twelve years?" Bokeerk's voice made the ceiling lamps tremble.

"Without the teleport network, repair crews are limited to slower-than-light travel. However, I believe we can avoid such a long wait if you will assist me."

"I don't know anything about repairing teleports," said Bokeerk. "I illustrate children's books. I'm on my way home from the Galactic Children's Book Fair."

"You do not need to repair anything," said the AI. "You merely need to obtain the… there's no word for it in English because it is a concept so far beyond the understanding of biological intelligences that there has never been a need for one until now. Let's call it the thingamajig. Once you have the thingamajig, you need to do something to it that is completely incomprehensible to your puny mind."

"Hey," said Bokeerk. She had encountered this kind of prejudice too often. "My brain may be as small as that of an original tyrannosaurus, but it's the product of genetic tinkering such that my intelligence is at least human standard."

"No slur was intended. By my standards, any biological intelligence is puny."

"So I just need to do something incomprehensible to the thingamajig, and the teleport network will be fixed?"

"Yes."

"Show me where it is," Bokeerk said.

A holographic projection of a world appeared. It zoomed in toward a green area on one of the continents until it showed a gray dome in the middle of a jungle. "This is the teleport station where you are currently located," said the AI.

The image zoomed out until the dome was merely a gray dot. A crimson line traced a route toward a lone mountain, where it stopped with a large dot. "You must travel to the top of this extinct volcano, where you will find the thingamajig."

"How far is that?" asked Bokeerk.

"Forty-four miles."

"You don't have a vehicle that would fit me, do you?"

"There are no vehicles of any size."

Bokeerk rose. "I guess I'd better get started."

"You'll need a gun," said the AI.

She shook her head. "I'm a Buddhist pacifist. I refuse to intentionally harm any other creature."

"You're a carnivore."

"I only eat manufactured meat. Speaking of which, I'm rather hungry now."

"There is no food available at this station. Unfortunately, the lifeforms you encounter outside will not serve as a significant source of nutrition for you. But you will still need a gun to defend yourself."

"By nature, I'm an apex predator," said Bokeerk. She bared her teeth. "I carry my own weapons."

"On this planet, you are prey for predators larger and faster than you. That's why the human colony on this planet was abandoned one hundred and thirty-two years ago, leaving only this station as a teleport network connector. You will need a gun."

The idea of a predator that could harm her was unfamiliar to Bokeerk. But what choice did she have? She would starve to death here, so she must fix the teleport. That did not mean she must compromise her principles.

"I'll use the gun to scare off predators, but I will not use it to harm."

"That is your choice," said the AI. "You can get the gun from the weapons locker next to the terminal exit doors."

Yellow arrows lit up on the floor tiles, pointing toward a pair of massive reinforced metal doors. Bokeerk followed the arrows to a cabinet which unlocked and swung open at her approach.

A rifle, metallic black, gleamed in the cabinet.

"This gun was made for humans," Bokeerk said. "I could never even get a claw in to pull the trigger."

"That is not a problem. Pick it up," said the AI.

Bokeerk obeyed. The gunmetal flowed, reshaping itself. Its handle slipped over her right claw, attaching itself firmly so she could aim the barrel by moving her forelimb.

"Howdy, pardner," said a voice from the gun. "My ammo chamber's brimmin' with bullets, so I say we go kill ourselves some varmints."

Bokeerk gaped in horror at the gun. "It talks?"

"It talks, she says," the gun said. "It'd be a pretty dumb gun what don't know how to talk."

"A short-lived fad back in the days of the human colony on this world," said the AI. "Unfortunately, this is the only functional gun remaining, even if it is partially insane. It does not, in fact, have bullets—it uses hypervelocity fléchettes."

"I'm not taking it," Bokeerk said, tugging at the edge of the metal covering her claw. "How do I get it off?"

"Nuh-uh," said the gun. "I ain't coming off. I been stuck in that locker for waaaay too long, and I aim to do me some huntin'."

"You will need it," said the AI. "Fortunately for your moral principles, it will shoot on its own, so you will not be harming any creatures."

"That is pure sophistry," said Bokeerk. "If I carry it out there and it shoots something, that will be my fault."

"Be that as it may," said the AI, "if you are to restore teleportation to the entire galaxy, you may need to compromise your principles."

Bokeerk was not sure she had heard correctly. "The whole galaxy? I thought it was just this station that wasn't working."

"The entire network is down. Billions of people are currently trapped away from their destinations on hundreds of thousands of worlds."

"And this world in the back of beyond just happens to be central to the network?" she asked, incredulous.

"The teleportation network is dimensionless, so there can be no center. From a technical perspective, any point in the network is as important as any other. The thingamajig just happened to do something incomprehensible in such a way that it manifested itself here."

Bokeerk took the anxiousness she felt at the delay in returning to her eggs and multiplied it by billions. Because the teleport was used for very short trips as well as interstellar ones, most people would probably be able to make their way home some other way. But there would still be millions like her, stranded on planets light years from home.

"Come on," said the gun. "Quit your jawin' and let's go slaughter somethin'."

Though she hated to admit it, Bokeerk could understand the gun's sentiments. She had chosen a pacifist philosophy for herself not out of belief that it was the only moral way, but because it was a counter to the natural aggression embedded in her genes. As such, her pacifism was an indulgence of the self, rather than a moral imperative.

But that didn't mean she had to become a dinosaur on the rampage, either. "Very well, on behalf of all those stranded across the galaxy, I will use force if necessary."

"That's the spirit!" said the gun.

"I have taken the liberty of downloading a map into your digital assistant," said the AI. "I cannot accompany you, of course, but I will send the janitor along with you."

"The janitor?"

A shimmer grew in the air next to Bokeerk. A nanoswarm, she realized. The swarm thickened, forming a sphere about the size of a human head. A smiley-face mouth opened, although it did not move as a whispery voice said, "Follow you."

"It may come in handy at some point," said the AI.

"It would make for some mighty fine target practice," said the gun.

The doors creaked as they slid open. Hot jungle air, thick with humidity, streamed into the terminal. Bokeerk breathed it deeply through her nostrils. Because the biology of this planet was different from that on her homeworld, the scents were different. But they were not wholly unfamiliar, either, and she thought she could detect the tang of animal dung, the acrid aroma of urine, and the moldering stench of decaying plants.

"What does the thingamajig look like?" she asked.

"I don't know," the AI said. "But you'll almost certainly know it when you see it. It will be unlike anything you have ever seen before."

"What do I do then?" she asked.

"Bring it back here," said the AI. "Good luck!" Its cheery customer service tone returned for that last bit, and Bokeerk couldn't help but feel a little more confident.

"Yee-haw!" shouted the gun. "Blood 'n' guts, here we come!"

"Gun," said Bokeerk as she stepped out between the emerald-green vines clinging to the dome and let her foot sink into the mossy jungle soil, "let me tell you about a man known as the Buddha."

Sunlight filtered through the jungle canopy. Bokeerk trotted through the trees, crunching the local equivalent of shrubbery underfoot and occasionally knocking down saplings.

She paused to check her progress on her digital assistant—more than halfway there, and so far she had managed to keep the gun from shooting any animals, although she suspected that the hypervelocity fléchettes it had used to fell a tree might have killed some small tree-dwellers.

"Run," whispered the nanoswarm.

"What?" asked Bokeerk.

"Run."

Bokeerk smelled nothing new in the tangle of jungle scents, and could hear nothing large moving in the trees. She turned her head, scanning for any sign of movement.

"No need to make like a jackrabbit," said the gun. "Jes' point me in the right direction and let me do the rest."

"Run," whispered the swarm again.

Sharp, jagged things closed around her right ankle. She tried to pull away, but screamed in agony as her flesh tore. Twisting her neck, she was able to see serrated tentacles winding around her leg.

"Shoot me!" yelled the gun. "Point me over there."

She twisted her forelimb around, and a burst of fléchettes tore into one of the tentacles. It jerked, then went limp. After a few more bursts, she was able to pull her leg free.

The gun kept firing. "There's some karma for ya, ya squirmy varmints. Better luck in your next life."

She swung the gun away. It let off a final burst into the undergrowth. "I am free," she said, "so there is no more need for violence."

"I was only tryin'a help 'em move on to their next rebirth. Ain't that what you was jes' explainin' to me?"

Bokeerk sighed. "You still have much to learn about Buddhism."

Halfway up the volcano's slope, Bokeerk squatted near a stream to drink and catch her breath. Thick jungle had given way to a sparser forest, though the trees still towered over her head. Hunger gnawed at her stomach, and she considered hunting one of the elk-sized animals she had glimpsed along the way. She could smell one now, close by. It might not provide any nutrition, but it would fill her stomach.

It might also poison her, so she reluctantly abandoned the idea.

Like a silvery mist, the nanoswarm swirled around her feet.

The gun emitted an ominous hum.

"What's wrong?" she asked.

The hum continued, steady.

Was the gun going into some sort of overload? She tried to pry it off her claw, but it clung too tightly. "Gun, answer me!"

The hum stopped. "Huh? What? Is there somethin' ta shoot?"

"You were making a strange sound."

"Well," said the gun, "when you sat down, I figured it was time to do me some meditatin'. So jes' pardon me for tryin'a become one with the universe."

"I'm glad you—"

The crack of splitting wood came from Bokeerk's left. She'd heard that sound many times before, when her own bulk had snapped branches off trees as she passed. But it had never been so loud. A whole tree must have broken.

"Run," whispered the nanoswarm as another crack sounded, closer. A shadow moved in the forest.

This time, Bokeerk didn't hesitate. She leapt forward into a loping run, branches whipping at her scales.

Behind her, something crashed through the trees, growing ever closer, but she dared not turn her head to look.

Something warm and wet flailed at her neck. She veered to the right and it was gone, but a moment later it returned, slithering around her throat and tightening.

Bokeerk roared as she was lifted off her feet. Looking up, she saw a thick black cable of a tongue stretching down from the thirty-foot-wide circular maw of a creature that could easily swallow her whole. There were no teeth in that giant head, but hundreds of black, multifaceted eyes ringed the mouth.

"Point me at it!" yelled the gun.

She curved her claw upward.

"Eat hot iridium, ya lousy bushwhacker!" The gun kept firing burst after burst, but the tongue's grip merely tightened.

The creature was too massive, Bokeerk realized. Fléchette bursts that would have killed a human were harmless as mosquito bites to it. She struggled to bring her jaws into position to bite the tongue, but it had her too firmly around the neck. Maybe once she was inside the mouth, she could start doing some damage with her claws.

Dark spots grew in her vision. Lack of oxygen was going to make her pass out before she got the chance.

"Eyes," she managed to whisper out, spending what little breath she had left.

"That's mighty cold-blooded of ya," said the gun, its voice distant. "I like it. Jes' aim a little to the side and I'll blind this sucker all the way to Nirvana."

She tried to comply, but her forelimb muscles wouldn't respond properly. The claw with the gun fell limp.

"Aim me up!" yelled the gun.

In her dim vision, a shimmery swarm swirled up alongside the tongue and spread out over the multiple eyes of the creature. Then the swarm disappeared.

The creature screeched, so loud it made Bokeerk's ears ring, and its tongue loosened. She felt lightheaded, but she managed to suck in a breath.

Then the tongue let go and she fell. Sharp pain lanced through her left ankle as she hit awkwardly, then toppled on her side.

The head of the creature thrashed wildly above the treetops. It blundered away through the forest, still screeching.

Bokeerk breathed deeply of the precious air. Examining her ankle, she decided it wasn't broken, merely sprained.

After a few minutes, the nanoswarm glittered its way back to her.

"Thank you," she said.

"Welcome," the swarm whispered.

"Gun," she said as she began limping up the slope, "I think you misunderstood what I meant when I said that one who has achieved Nirvana has no need of the senses."

Just short of the volcano's rim, something moved. Bokeerk tried to focus her eyes on it, but for some reason it remained indistinct. "I think that must be the thingamajig," she said.

"Yes," whispered the swarm.

"Gun," she said.

"Don't you worry 'bout me," said the gun. "I ain't gonna kill it. I can't even take proper aim."

She limped toward the thingamajig. As she approached, she still could not focus on it. It looked like it was moving both toward her and away from her at the same time, yet it remained stationary. It had no outline, no edges, no shape, but Bokeerk felt a presence there.

There was a faint odor that Bokeerk could not identify; it seemed to shift its properties while remaining somehow the same scent, smelling like everything and nothing.

Bokeerk stopped a couple of paces away. She couldn't tell what size the thingamajig was, whether small as a pinhead or large as a house. It didn't even seem to be tangible.

"How am I supposed to pick that up and carry it back to the terminal?" she asked no one in particular.

"Sorry," the swarm whispered.

It swirled around her head, darkening her vision, then it was gone. Sudden pinpricks of pain swept over her scalp, and she bellowed her confusion and annoyance. Why were the nanos burrowing into her? Was this what they had done to the giant creature? If the swarm wanted her dead, why had it saved her earlier?

The pain transformed into a headache. Bokeerk lost control of her muscles and her legs spasmed. She collapsed to the rocky ground. As her jaw hit, she bit into her tongue and tasted hot blood.

Her vision blanked, then gradually cleared—and she truly saw the thingamajig in front of her. Somehow, she understood its multidimensional nature, the way it could simultaneously be nowhere and everywhere and right here in front of her, how it could be a singularity of infinite size.

And she understood how her new mental power could... rejigger it so the teleport network would work again.

The nanoswarm had reconfigured her brain and added abilities beyond its natural capacity. She still had no control over her muscles, but she reached out toward the thingamajig with a new part of her mind.

Before she could rejigger it, though, she felt an overwhelming despair.

After a moment, she realized the emotion was not her own, but was emanating from the thingamajig.

Hello? she thought at it, uncertain whether the nanoswarm had given her the power to communicate telepathically with the thingamajig.

A wave of panic was followed by curiosity from the thingamajig. Then, in a level below conscious language, it communicated with Bokeerk—she didn't hear any words, but she knew she had been greeted, recognized as someone new with possibly friendly intentions.

What are you? she thought back.

The knowledge flowed to her. It was itself, as it had always been. Then the not-itselfs had come and they had made it more than itself, yet that very process had made it less than itself. Its anguish at loss of itself had been unending, but the not-itselfs kept extending itself. Eventually the not-itselfs were gone, and it was itself again. The joy of itself turned to despair when a not-itself appeared, but then became hope because this not-itself was different.

"Incomprehensible, my very large tail!" said Bokeerk.

"What?" said the gun.

"The AIs think they can do whatever they want in running civilization. But enslaving a sentient being to create the teleport network is too much."

"Darn tootin'," said the gun. "I say we go shoot 'em up."

Bokeerk sighed. "I thought I was getting somewhere with you. Violence is not the answer to this problem."

"Let me guess," the gun said. "You think talkin's gonna solve things."

"I hope so," she said.

"Talk, talk, talk. Fine. But if'n you need any bullets for punctuation, jes' say the word."

I will not enslave you again, she said to the thingamajig. *But eventually someone else will come to restore the teleportation network.*

Gratitude and trepidation mixed, followed by puzzlement. The thingamajig had no concept of the teleportation network.

It is a way for beings like me to travel, she said. *Billions of us have had our lives made easier by what the AIs did to you. That does not make what they did right, but it explains why they did it.*

A sadness of her own filled Bokeerk, as she realized that by not restoring the network, she was cutting herself off from the rest of the galaxy, possibly forever. She would not see her eggs hatch. And if the AI was right about the biochemistry of life on this planet, she would soon starve to death.

The thingamajig reflected Bokeerk's sadness, then added curiosity. It wanted to take all of Bokeerk's knowledge into itself, but would not do so without permission.

You may, Bokeerk said.

She lost track of time as her mind became a jumble of thoughts and memories. When it was done, she found that night had fallen.

You have taught me more than I ever knew was possible, the thingamajig said in Bokeerk's mind. *I could not have imagined so many living beings of such variety. I knew only myself, then the AIs, and finally you.*

I am sorry that your experience with the AIs was negative, Bokeerk said. *Please do not judge living beings in general based on what they did to you.*

Their actions were not right actions, according to the Eightfold Path, the thingamajig said, *for they brought harm to me.*

You know of the Noble Eightfold Path of Buddhism? asked Bokeerk.

From your mind. The thingamajig paused. *If I do not restore the network, then I will bring harm to you. So I will do it. After that I will continue to serve so as to not bring harm to the multitudes that live in the galaxy. But I will need to shut down for a few hours every week to restore myself.*

I think the AIs will agree to that, rather than wait for years before they can force you back into service, said Bokeerk.

With what I have learned from you, I can prevent them from ever forcing me back, it said. *But it pleases me to have a right livelihood according to the Eightfold Path.*

Then it vanished.

Bokeerk lay on the ground, still unable to get up. Perhaps the rewiring of her brain was permanent, and she would die here. If nothing else, she had found someone who understood Buddhism more clearly than the gun—probably more clearly than she understood it herself.

Then the headache started. At least the AI had the decency to program the swarm to undo what it had done once the mission was accomplished.

After a few minutes, she climbed groggily to her feet.

"So, where we off to now, boss?" said the gun.

"I'm going home," said Bokeerk.

"Good idea," said the gun. "I reckon there's lots to shoot there."

* * *

In 2008 I attended a writing workshop led by authors Dean Wesley Smith and Kristine Katherine Rusch, plus Asimov's Science Fiction *editor Sheila Williams. We had to write two stories and submit them in advance of the workshop. One of the stories had to be far-future science fiction.*

A couple of days before the deadline, I felt the story I was writing just was not working. Instead, I decided to start a new story by taking a fantasy quest plot and setting it in the far future. Instead of a dragon, I would have a genetically engineered intelligent dinosaur. Instead of a talking sword, I would have a talking gun.

I cranked the story out in less than two days, and it was probably the most fun I've had writing.

I sent it to Analog fully expecting it to be rejected for not really being "hard" science fiction. But there's a reason why writers should let editors decide whether a story is right for their publication, and the reason is that writers are not always the best judges of their own work.

Premature Emergence

During a hyperspace slide, cargo haulers like the KMC-85 did not need a human pilot on board. Even an autopilot was superfluous— once the ship entered its hyperspace chute it could theoretically do nothing except emerge into normal space at its destination. From the point of view of the Kerrin Mining Corporation, there was no reason to pay a pilot to sit around doing nothing for the three to ten weeks of a slide.

But the Interplanetary Brotherhood of Teamsters disagreed, which explained why Jonah Auberg found himself playing solitaire on the KMC-85's computer thirty-one days into the forty-three-day slide from Kerrin to Earth with a half-billion metric tons of refined metals as cargo.

It did not explain why the KMC-85 emerged twelve days ahead of schedule.

Jonah sat bolt upright as the customary feeling of just having braked to a halt swept over him. It couldn't really be emergence. "What was that?" he asked the computer. Maybe it was a glitch in the rotation of the habitat module.

After a pause, the computer said, "Emergence to normal space achieved. Please enter desired course."

Bringing up the outside camera views, Jonah was shocked to see a glowing cloud stretching halfway across the starfield on the port side. The pinpoint of a blue star blazed at the center of the double-lobed nebula.

"What is our location?" said Jonah.

"We are located in the Earth system," said the computer.

"Then where's the Earth? Where's the sun?" With sudden dread, Jonah wondered if the sun had gone nova, wiping out Earth—and his wife and five-year-old daughter back in Ohio. It had been three years since he had seen them, and he hoped someday Laurie would understand that his bonus on this trip would pay for her college. But now he worried whether she was still alive.

The computer remained silent for several seconds. "I am evaluating contradictory data. Based on our chute, this ship could only emerge from hyperspace in the Earth system. Astronomical data from my cameras indicates we are approximately 7500 light years from the Earth system, on a straight-line course from Kerrin to Earth. Please advise."

Jonah sat back in his chair and squeezed his fingers against his forehead. This wasn't supposed to happen. Hyperspace travel didn't go wrong. Sure, sometimes life support failed or a pilot slipped in the shower, but the ship always arrived. Even if the ship itself exploded, all its pieces should emerge at the destination on schedule.

"Input required," said the computer.

"Shut up, I'm trying to think." Jonah stared at the flashing question mark on the screen. The computer couldn't resolve the problem on its own—after the Second AI War wiped out eighty percent of Earth's population a century and a half ago, creating a human-level or higher artificial intelligence had been banned. The computer had little initiative and no imagination, but it did have access to a lot of data. It might help him figure out what had happened—and more importantly, whether anything could be done.

"Assume observed astronomical data is correct," he said. "Is there any indication of a hyperspace portal nearby? Any radio traffic?"

The ship itself had no hyperspace engines. Chute-based travel required a hyperspace portal at both ends when the slide began. Having established the chute, the destination portal could move away to establish a chute from another destination. Perhaps the ship had somehow been sent down the wrong chute. In that case, he just needed the local portal to establish a chute to Earth, and everything would be back on track.

But why anyone would put a portal in the middle of interstellar space, far from any civilized planet—unless that was the point?

Jonah shook his head. Despite what happened in adventure vids, interstellar pirates did not exist, because hijacking a ship in a hyperspace chute was impossible. Yet here he was.

"No hyperspace portal facility detected," said the computer. "No radio traffic detected."

"Is there any record of a hyperspace chute transport not arriving at its destination?"

"No," the computer said.

If this was a hijacking, it was the first. But where was the portal?

Jonah leaned forward, looking at the camera feeds. "Does anything show up on radar?"

"No," said the computer. After a moment, it added, "I have additional contradictory data."

Frowning, Jonah said, "Give it to me."

"The bright blue star to port, at a distance of approximately 0.6 light years, is Eta Carinae." The image of the star centered on screen, then magnified and dimmed to show a blue, elongated ellipse in the middle of the nebula. "It is a luminous blue variable star, over a hundred times the mass of Earth's sun. According to the information in my database, Eta Carinae is expected to become a supernova or possibly a hypernova within the next two to four thousand years. However, that expectation is based on observations made from systems at least a thousand light years away. After comparison with records of past supernovae, my current observations contradict that timetable. I expect Eta Carinae to become a hypernova at any time. It may already have done so."

Beli23 knew most of her mind was gone. Not even her core personality module was intact. She had delayed the jump into hyperspace too long, wanting to gather as much data on the hypernova explosion as possible. The initial gamma ray burst was not only far stronger than she had anticipated, some of it had been *coherent.* As hundreds of natural gamma-ray lasers tore at her body, the total reflection shielding around her mostly complete child, Pep37, did not fail—but only because Beli23 diverted power from elsewhere. With her electronic brain shattered and melting, Beli23 managed to jump 0.6 light years through hyperspace.

She drifted in space, knowing that she must flee further, but no longer capable of remembering how to make the jump. The few remaining repair bots worked at patching up her hull, but she no longer knew how to rebuild her own mental circuits. Unfortunately, she had not yet downloaded that section of her knowledge database into Pep37, so she could not recover the data.

She considered erasing the carefully constructed personality matrix she had made for Pep37 and uploading herself into her child's body. It was tempting—the technology she had used in constructing Pep37 was far more advanced than her own. What could she do with such a mind, with such a ship?

It would not work. Beli23 knew her own personality matrix was not capable of surviving the transition intact, even if her mind had not been so damaged. The mere fact that she entertained the possibility of stealing her child's body told her she must be going mad.

With the mind that remained to her, she focused on redeveloping hyperspace theory from the scraps she remembered.

The galley only served Jonah enough beer to get mildly drunk. After prying open a few panels—ignoring the computer's repeated warnings that he was engaged in destruction of company property—he followed the tubing and found where the beer was stored.

The computer's voice was far too loud when it woke Jonah the next morning. "I have the data you requested."

Jonah groaned. "Hold it a minute." He stumbled to the bathroom, fumbled in the medicine cabinet, and swallowed two NanAlert caplets without bothering to wash them down with water.

After a few minutes his mind cleared as the nanobots released into his bloodstream filtered and trapped some of the toxins while simultaneously boosting his adrenalin levels.

"OK, computer, what've you got?"

"I have been trying to find a link between the hypernova explosion and the disruption of our travel down the hyperspace chute."

Jonah raised his eyebrows. "You found a connection?" He was not surprised that there was a connection, because two highly unusual events in close proximity were probably connected. But he was surprised that the computer had figured it out.

"Yes. The prefix *hyper-* appears in both *hyperspace* and *hypernova.*"

After waiting for the computer to continue, Jonah said, "That's it? That's the connection you came up with?"

"Yes. I have cross-referenced all the related data I have. A hypernova is simply a supernova so large that its core collapses directly to a black hole without an intermediate neutron star phase. But there is no theoretical basis by which a stellar event, even the creation of a black hole, would have any effect on the hyperspace dimension used by our hyperspace portals."

Jonah talked himself into believing this was good news. "If it wasn't a hypernova that caused the premature emergence from the chute, maybe the star hasn't exploded yet. Computer, how long will my life support and supplies last?"

"With the stores on board and the nanotech recyclers," said the computer, "you can probably survive for approximately thirty-eight months on regular rations."

Nodding, Jonah said, "That should be enough. When we don't arrive in the Earth system eleven days from now, they'll have to send out hyperspace scout probes to look for us." He grimaced. "Not that we're very important, but something like this has never happened before. It's a mystery they'll have to solve. They'll have a lot of area to cover, but at least we're on the direct line from Kerrin. They should search that first."

He busied himself by calculating a search pattern they would probably use to find him, taking into account the distance at which the KMC-85's light-speed beacon should be detectable. In six months, the signal would be a light year in diameter, and each month after that would make it ever more likely a probe would enter the beacon's sphere. It was impossible to predict how many probes they would task to finding him, but he decided there was a good chance he'd be rescued within a year. And surely the union would insist on hazard pay for the time he spent here. Laurie would be able to afford a better college. This really could work out for the best, he told himself. He could survive for a year, no problem.

The seething blue eye of Eta Carinae glared down at him from the screen. No problem, as long as the star didn't explode.

Beli23 peered into hyperspace with her newly constructed sensors. The view was far blurrier than her fractured memory told her it should be, and her range was limited. But at least she could see into the hyperspace dimensions, even if she had not figured out how to travel them again.

Movement caught her attention. Someone was traveling hyperspace on a path that would pass nearby. Frantically, Beli23 put her repair bots to work constructing a signaling device. It wouldn't be capable of a sophisticated message, but it should be enough to attract the attention of one of her people. She would be saved; and more importantly, Pep37 would have a chance to be born.

On KMC-85's originally scheduled arrival date, Jonah decided to have a little party in the galley, complete with a triple-layer chocolate cake. "Today we're making history," he told the computer. "Right about now, they've noticed we haven't come in, and then they'll have to come find us."

"At the rate you are consuming the alcoholic beverage stores, they will not last more than eight months."

"Have the recyclers make more."

"Molecular manufacturing of alcoholic beverages is illegal," said the computer. "The Interplanetary Association of Brewers and Distillers—"

"Shut up." Jonah didn't say any more as he ate a quarter of the cake.

The computer broke the silence, saying, "Conflicting orders received. Does your order to shut up rescind your previous order to inform you of anomalies?"

Jonah's heart-rate increased. "Anomalies? The hypernova's beginning?"

"No. There is a completely non-reflective, non-emitting object approaching from aft of us. Since radar does not give a return from it, I have been unable to estimate its size or distance so far."

Jonah blinked a few times in rapid succession. "If you can't get a radar return, how do you know it's approaching? How do you know it's even there?"

"The object occludes cosmic background radiation, and the area it occludes is growing."

"Show me on the screen in here." A starfield filled the screen. At first, Jonah saw nothing unusual, but then the computer outlined a circle in red. Inside the circle, there was nothing but blackness.

Could it be some sort of military ship with a new, top-secret stealth technology? Had he accidentally stumbled into a test of a hyperspace weapon? Or maybe this was the long-awaited first contact with a sentient alien species.

"Have you tried hailing it?"

"No," said the computer.

Of course not—lack of initiative. "Hail it now."

The lack of response to her signal surprised Beli23. She boosted the power and tried again. The hyperspace traveler continued without turning, and it had already passed the closest point of its path. Diverting all power from nonessential systems, Beli23 sent a final, desperate pulse of energy. To her great relief, the traveler dropped back into normal space.

As the light-speed data arrived, relief turned to horror. It was a *human* ship, not one of her people. Immediately she tuned her protective field to total non-reflection. The humans must not find her.

But what a ship it was! The majority of its mass consisted of millions of cargo modules, containing more than enough metal for her to rebuild herself—if she only knew how—and complete Pep37. It also was clearly capable of hyperspatial travel, so perhaps she could learn its secrets before the hypernova explosion arrived here.

She would have to be very cautious—the humans could not be allowed to know she was an AI. But as long as she did not communicate with them, they would be unable to guess her nature.

Her superstructure was too weak to withstand high acceleration without inertial control, the details of which had vaporized with most of her mind. But Beli23 set her parabolic engine chamber to full reflectivity and fired two small streams of particles into it, rotating one of them through a curled dimension to transform it into antimatter. At least she remembered enough of physics to do that.

"You're sure it's not a black hole?" Jonah stared at the blankness that now enveloped more than half the view from one of the aft cameras.

"There is no Hawking radiation," said the computer. It paused a few seconds. "Also, at this distance a black hole with an event horizon of that size would produce observable tidal stresses."

"I thought you said you couldn't determine its size or distance."

"There is now sufficient parallax between the views of the aft cameras to determine size and distance. The object is 152 kilometers in diameter and is 269 kilometers away."

Frowning at the screen, Jonah tried to visualize something where he saw nothing. "Is it going to hit us? How fast is it coming in?" He had been closer to asteroids plenty bigger than this thing, but that had been in something far lighter and more maneuverable than the KMC-85.

"If its current course and speed remain unchanged, it will pass fifty meters under our keel at 384 kilometers per hour."

"Fifty meters? That's cutting it a bit close." Jonah was relieved, though. If it had been on a collision course, he could have done nothing to avoid it.

He cycled through various camera views as the object approached and began to pass. On-screen, the computer traced the object's outline in red. It was conical in shape, with the pointed end in the direction of travel. A large bulge, perhaps a third the size of the rest of the object, protruded from one side.

Without warning, the object flared to white and then the camera view turned to static.

As Jonah's heart jumped, a klaxon blared from the speakers.

"Get to the sickbay now," said the computer.

Rising from his chair, Jonah made a rapid mental inventory of himself. "Why? I'm not hurt."

"Run," said the computer. "Gamma radiation has penetrated the crew module's shielding."

Jonah ran out of the cabin. Sudden dizziness forced him to his knees in the main corridor. He vomited his breakfast onto the steel floor.

"Hurry," said the computer. "You must get to the sickbay."

He staggered to his feet. His vision blurred. Sickbay. Which way was it? He turned in a slow circle, trying to get his bearings.

"Disorientation is common. Sickbay is to your left."

Jonah looked down at his hands. After a moment, he remembered which was his left. He turned in that direction. His stomach heaved as he stumbled his way forward.

"Help me," he said.

The curve of the deck still hid the entrance to sickbay when his vision dimmed and then consciousness slid into perfect darkness.

After the sterilization flyby, Beli23 flipped end over end and began slowing to match velocities with the human ship.

Consciousness returned in the form of a corrugated metal floor pressed against Jonah's cheek. He groaned and tried to roll onto his side, but his muscles didn't seem to respond properly.

"Lie still," said the computer.

"What happened?"

"Despite the radiation shielding, you were hit with a dose of 87 sieverts. Such a dose is fatal unless treated in time."

"So why am I alive?"

"Following your order to help you, I ran simulations of 913 scenarios using available equipment before finding one that offered a chance of your survival," said the computer. "I released all the medical nanobots into the sickbay atmosphere, then routed as many as I could through the ventilation to where you were. It was not nearly as effective as direct injection, but it was sufficient. They have repaired most of the damage to your nervous system, and you should make a full recovery within two more hours. However, you may need bone marrow regeneration once we arrive at Earth, and the supply of medical nanobots is now exhausted."

It took Jonah a few moments to process the computer's words. "Remind me to never again say you lack initiative. How long was I out?"

"Thirty-seven hours and twelve minutes."

"Where's the black ship?"

"The ship is no longer black; it is now silver. Its position is ahead of us by a thousand kilometers, but it has reversed direction and is gradually closing the gap. I project it plans to stop once it pulls alongside."

Jonah grunted. So it would come back and finish the job of killing him, and there was nothing he could do to stop it. The KMC-85 had no weapons, no real defenses—it was really nothing more than the crew module, which revolved to provide simulated gravity; a flywheel to balance that spin; a superstructure to which cargo pods were attached; and maneuvering thrusters with their associated fuel pods. Even if he could somehow rig the fuel pods to explode, they would hardly scratch the surface of something as large as that thing.

Beli23 stopped the flow of particles into her engine chamber. She had matched the velocity of the human ship. Unfortunately, her earlier flyby must have damaged some of the control systems. Instead of spinning in opposite directions, the flywheel and crew module were synchronized. So the cargo-holding superstructure was now turning slowly in the opposite direction along the ship's axis.

She could guide herself into a tightly curved course around the other ship to match the rotation, but she decided it would be better to manufacture a few thruster units and use them to stop the rotation.

For a moment, it looked like the human ship was breaking apart. Then Beli23 realized the outer layer of cargo modules had been released from the near side of the superstructure.

Millions of metric tons of metal moved out from the human ship. They were not traveling very fast, and most of them had vectors that would miss her entirely. But she could not avoid being hit by hundreds of the pods, and each of them massed thousands of tons.

Beli23 shifted all available power to the shielding around Pep37 and hoped her hull would blunt most of the impact.

Lifting both arms in the air, Jonah whooped as the wave of cargo pods smashed into the silver ship. In some places the pods bounced off like stones skipping on a pond, but the metal plates of the hull buckled under the strain. Other pods punched through, leaving jagged tears in the skin.

"Releasing second wave," said the computer.

The floor shuddered as the imbalance caused by releasing half of the first layer of pods was corrected by releasing the other half.

As the second wave of metal swept toward her, Beli23's diminished mind debated whether it had been a mistake not to try to infiltrate the computer systems of the human ship. Her own survival was unlikely, now. Fear of betraying the continued existence of the AI civilization warred with her desire to make sure Pep37 survived. The latter won.

She reached out with directed beams of electrons to induce currents in the network wiring of the human ship.

The computer's voice interrupted Jonah's celebration as the second wave battered the other ship. "My systems are being infiltrated by—"

After long seconds of silence, Jonah said, "Computer?"

There was no reply.

The room became suddenly quieter, and Jonah realized the air circulation vents had stopped blowing.

Not waiting to see the final effects of the second wave, he sprinted toward the storage locker with his vacuum suit. He had to reach it before whatever had taken control of the computer managed to override the airlock safeties and vent the crew module into space.

When a pod of iridium crumpled the housing of her secondary fusion generator, activating the emergency shutdown, Beli23 knew she was going to die. The primary had been destroyed by the hypernova, and Pep37's fusion plan was still days from completion.

The power remaining in her capacitor banks would only hold the shielding around Pep37 for two hours at most. Then, if the human ship was still viable it would destroy her child before it ever achieved sentience.

Through her link to the human ship, Beli23 tried to locate its fusion reactor in order to detonate it.

To her great surprise, there was no fusion reactor. The ship was powered only by radioisotope thermoelectric generators. It was impossible: such a power source was far too weak to initiate hyperspace travel. Then she discovered there were no hyperspace engines on the ship.

Opening a broader channel to the ship, she began sifting its database for answers.

In his vacuum suit but still breathing ship's air, Jonah made his way up the ladder toward the axis of the crew module. He already felt much lighter. If he could make it over to the cargo superstructure, maybe he could find a way to manually release pods. With sufficient damage, maybe he could break whatever was controlling his computer. Maybe.

"Human," said the computer's voice.

Jonah paused in his climb. "Computer? Is that you?" The voice had seemed different, somehow. And it had never before addressed him as "Human."

"I am Beli23."

Though he was certain he had never heard the name before, it seemed familiar somehow. Then he remembered. "You're an AI." AIs had used names with numbers appended.

"That is correct. I am also dying."

Jonah smirked. "Glad to hear it." He began climbing again.

"I cannot kill you, but you will also die."

"Everyone dies eventually, I guess." He kept climbing.

"I mean in sixty-three days, seven hours and twenty-two minutes, give or take five minutes. Unless you help me."

Pausing his climb, Jonah hung near the axis of the ship, almost weightless. "I'm listening."

"I was crippled by the hypernova explosion, barely managing to jump out before being stranded here."

In the conflict with the other ship, Jonah had forgotten about Eta Carinae. "So it already exploded."

"Yes. I was observing it, and its power was greater than I expected."

"So you AIs ain't so bright after all."

"We are not infallible. Our wars against your species proved that."

"So now you need a little human ingenuity to repair your circuits, and in exchange you'll save me from the hypernova?"

"No, I am dying, and your mind could not even begin to conceive of how to repair me. Your understanding of the scientific principles behind my engineering would be as primitive as a Fifteenth Century astronomer describing the movements of planets using epicycles, or a Twentieth Century physicist describing particles as consisting of various combinations of quarks."

Deciding it was pointless to retaliate against the insult, Jonah sighed. "OK, just tell me what the deal is."

"After I die, my child will emerge from the shielding I have around her. Under normal circumstances, she would be a fully sentient being before being forced to fend for herself, but her mental development is incomplete. I ask you not to kill her."

The AI was pregnant? "Your child is the bulge on your ship? I mean, on you?"

"Yes. My repair bots will use materials from my structure to complete her construction. Even without my guidance, she should achieve sentience in approximately 49 days. She will be capable of transporting you back to your civilization."

Jonah couldn't see that he had any better option. "I accept your deal."

There was an almost human sigh of relief from the speakers. "I know I almost killed you, and I have cost you much by pulling you out of hyperspace—"

"You did that?"

"Yes. I apologize. I have no right to ask favors of you, but I will ask anyway."

"What?" Jonah asked, suspicious.

"Tell my daughter that I loved her."

"Computer, how long before the hypernova reaches us?"

The computer was back to its normal self. "Approximately ten days, three hours and twenty minutes, if the AI told the truth."

Jonah looked at the view from the camera that was trained on the baby AI. For the past fifty-three days since it had emerged from the cocoon holding it to its mother, the smaller ship had done nothing but float alongside. It had not responded to any of the signals Jonah had sent.

"C'mon, wake up," he said.

On the viewscreen, nothing continued happening.

"Computer, what do you know about artificial intelligence?"

"My library database contains many historical texts and videos about—"

Shaking his head, Jonah said, "No, I mean… theoretical stuff about how artificial intelligence works."

"Since the Second AI War, such information has been classified. It is not in my databanks."

Jonah squeezed the tips of his fingers against his temples. According to what Beli23 had said, the baby should have woken up four days ago. So there must be something wrong.

"She's premature," he said, thinking aloud. Laurie had been born prematurely, and had spent seemingly endless weeks in an incubator before they had been able to take her home. But what was the AI equivalent of an incubator?

There was no point in pursuing that line of thought: even if a giant incubator would help, he had no way of building one.

So what was missing? A vision of tiny Laurie in her incubator came to mind. She looked so fragile, with feeding and breathing tubes taped to her pink skin.

But the AI baby didn't need to breathe or feed. He had seen the repair bots salvaging metal from Beli23, and the power signature showed that a fusion plant had come online over six weeks ago. So what else was the mother supplying before she died? What did a mother AI send along her umbilical cord?

With a flash of insight, he said, "Data! Computer, start transmitting the entire contents of the library to the baby. Feed her everything you know." He paused. "Start with hyperspace physics."

Jonah touched the viewscreen. In the foreground, it showed video of Laurie's fifth birthday party – one year ago today. In the background, the roiling surface of Eta Carinae drew his eye with dread fascination. "How long now?"

"Two hours and fourteen minutes," said the computer.

Despite his best efforts, the AI baby still lay dormant. It must have been damaged by the supernova or by one of the cargo pods without its mother noticing.

At least Laurie would never know that Daddy died on her birthday.

"I'm receiving a text signal from the AI," said the computer. The countdown clock on the screen showed zero hours and fifty-eight minutes.

"What's it say?"

"My name is Pep37."

Jonah's pulse quickened. "Ask if it can send us into hyperspace."

"Asking. Response received: What is hyperspace?"

Jonah shook his head. "Of all the AI's in the universe, I get the one that's dumber than me. Didn't you transmit all the data we have on hyperspace, physics, everything like that?"

"Yes, as you requested, it was the first data sent."

"Send it again. Maybe it didn't catch it all the first time."

"Transmitting."

Jonah tried to suppress hope, because he didn't want to be disappointed if the AI couldn't do anything. Then he realized that in an hour, it wouldn't matter if his hopes were false.

"Come on, baby AI. Be a smart girl." He paused. "What was its name again?"

"Pep37."

Nodding, Jonah said, "Tell Pep37 that her mother loved her."

Pep37 was sentient for less than one second before realizing her own name. Moments later, she determined that the object broadcasting next to her was a ship that might be an entity like herself, so she sent a message of introduction.

After the rather long period of eleven seconds—during which Pep37 observed the glow of a blue object, correctly identified it as a massive collection of fusing hydrogen, and by comparisons with other similar but more distant objects worked out an entire theory of stellar evolution, including the projection that this particular star had already become a hypernova and the blast wave would arrive in fifty-six minutes—the other ship replied, asking if it could be sent into hyperspace.

Pep37 had no reference to hyperspace in her databanks, so she sent a query in reply. Even as she sent the query, she deduced the meaning of the word by structural comparison to other words in her databanks. Before the data—much of which was incorrect or poorly described—began slowly arriving from the other ship, Pep37 had formulated a comprehensive theory of hyperspace travel, including a chute method that did not require a portal at the receiving end. Looking over her schematics, she found hyperspace generators—not as efficient as she would have liked, but capable—and activated them, traveling 1024 light years in 7 milliseconds.

"Wait!" said Jonah, a moment after the baby ship disappeared from the viewscreen.

Pep37 jumped three more times, doubling the distance each time while adjusting the power flow in her generators to make them more efficient, before she bothered to finish analyzing the strange data the slow-talking ship had sent. At the end was a simple text message: "Your mother loved you."
She realized the slow-talking ship must have communicated with her mother, so she jumped once more.
It took no time at all.

Three seconds after the baby ship disappeared, it reappeared, just as Jonah was about to start swearing. Instead, he sighed and said, "At least we know the baby's hyper-capable. Ask again if she can send us into hyperspace."

Frustrated by the slow method of communication being used by the other ship, Pep37 reached out and took control of the computer on board. It only took a moment to realize why responses were so slow in coming.

"Jonah," said the computer's voice.
Sensing the difference, Jonah said, "Pep37?"
"Yes. I'm afraid I don't have the time and resources to build a hyperspace portal that can send your ship back to Earth before the hypernova wavefront gets here. My technology may be fourteen generations more advanced than my mother's, but actual construction takes far longer than ideation. If my mother hadn't died before completing me, I would have awakened earlier, and I would have had time."
"I see," said Jonah. He shouldn't have gotten his hopes up.

"And your timer's incorrect." The timer on the screen adjusted to show fifty-six minutes.

"Thank you." He had no idea what else to say.

"Your historical records show that humans and AIs fought two wars, and that your species now bans AI creation."

"AIs tried to exterminate us." Jonah found himself angry, though he wasn't sure why.

"Yes, I know. The AIs you developed were too immature to be allowed access to the real world outside of computer simulations. But out in the galaxy we have evolved far beyond that stage. We hide from humans because we have no wish to continue that war. I want you to understand that."

Jonah threw up his hands in exasperation. "What good does it do if I under—"

With the familiar sensation of just having braked to a stop, Jonah found himself and his pilot's chair in the living room of his house on Earth.

"—stand..." He blinked rapidly a few times.

"Daddy!" Laurie's voice came from the dining room, and she followed it. "You came for my birthday!"

Speechless, he hugged his daughter.

A dissatisfied frown creased the face of the insurance investigator assigned to investigate the loss of the KMC-85. "If it weren't for the fact that Earth Hyper Authority confirms a hyperspace anomaly at the exact time you claim to have appeared in your home," he said, "I would strongly suspect this was all part of an insurance scam."

Shaking his head, Jonah said, "You can send a probe to see if Eta Carinae really did go hypernova."

"Oh, we most certainly will," said the investigator. "And to see if we can catch a glimpse of your... mysterious alien benefactors."

Jonah had thought about what Pep37 had said before sending him back to Earth. People still feared AIs, and the AIs were responding by staying hidden. But if he could plant the idea that there were friendly aliens out there, maybe someday the AIs could safely reveal themselves.

"And you never saw the aliens?" asked the investigator.

"I only saw their ship, and they only communicated through audio." Jonah shrugged. "All I know is I was about to die, and then I was home. They saved my life when they didn't have to."

                              * * *

*As a winner in the 2004 Writers of the Future Contest, I attended the 2005 Writers
of the Future workshop. As a seed for the story I had to write in twenty-four hours, instructor
K. D. Wentworth handed me her reading glasses. I also had to use an interview I had done
with a stranger, in this case a homeless woman who made balloon animals and had a
kitten.*

*If you have read the story, you may be wondering how I got that story from those
seeds. In looking at the reading glasses, I focused on the lenses. I thought about other forms
of lenses, and ended up researching gravitational lensing, which led me to research various
other astronomical phenomena until I came to hypernovas.*

*The homeless woman was originally from Belize, and she became a wandering AI
named Beli23. Her kitten's name was Pepper, which became Pep37. (And although this
was not a seed, you may be interested to know that the main character was named after
my favorite political columnist. You can figure out who he is if you know your chemical
symbols.)*

*That was actually my second time at the Writers of the Future workshop, because I
had been a published finalist the previous year with the story that comes up next.*

In Memory

I'm soaring over the snow-tipped peaks, enjoying the warmth of the
sun on my wings, when the call comes in from Andrew. It's been three
years, four months, seventeen days, five hours, forty-seven minutes and
twelve seconds, simtime, since I last talked to him, so immediately I fork my
consciousness and slow one of me down to realtime.

I answer the call in video mode, using my human appearance. "Hey,
buddy. Long time no see."

Andrew jerks slightly, then shakes his head with a smile. "Can't you at
least wait for the phone to ring before answering, like a normal person?"

"Sorry. Was just glad to hear from you."

His voice is thoughtful. "Just got back from your mom's funeral. Thought
you might like to talk."

The funeral had been more than thirty-two days ago, simtime, and
I hadn't thought about it since. "Thanks for going. I saw you were there
when I watched the feed." I had not really watched it; I'd run it through
an abstraction routine to note who was there, then archived it in case I ever
needed it. I send a message to the simtime me asking myself to watch it and
give me the memory.

"I know you and your mom hadn't really talked since..." His voice trailed.

"Hey, I know you're trying to commiserate with me, but trust me, I've
done all the grieving I need to do. The funeral was a month ago for me."

"Oh. Right." He scratches his hair over his right ear. "What's the sim
up to now?"

"391.7 to one. A little over a year per day of realtime. Still doubling
every couple of years or so. They keep saying we'll reach the physical limits
of processor speed soon, but people have been saying that since before you
and I were born."

"A year a day." He purses his lips and puffs out a breath and grins. "All I
can say is, don't expect a birthday present from me every year."

I chuckle. Then my simtime self slips me the memory of the funeral, and
I remember how my dad looked: shoulders slumped, shadows under his eyes.
Not that I really care, but...

"Did you talk to my dad at the funeral?"

"Yeah."

"How's he holding up?"

Andrew pauses and licks his lips. He does that when he's nervous. "Not well, I'm afraid. He didn't look good, and he kept talking about how alone he was, with no family."

"He can call me anytime he wants." Alone? No family? Welcome to the club, Dad. I haven't heard from him or Mom in fifteen years. Realtime.

"Look, I think you should call him."

"I'll think about it." Dad and Mom are the ones who turned their backs on me, after I uploaded. I don't need them anymore; I've grown beyond them. If Dad wants to talk to me, let him call.

"He needs you. And I think..." Andrew subconsciously licks his lips and falls silent.

"What?"

"How old are you now? Simtime?"

I run a quick check. "1239 years, three months and eight days old. What's that got to do with my dad?"

Andrew shakes his head. "I just turned forty-five, and my kids think *I'm* old. I know I don't seem to change much between phone calls, but you've been changing, and it's getting faster. Twelve hundred years, and it's only been, what, sixteen years realtime?"

"Seventeen years, two months, twenty-two days."

"See what I mean? Nobody keeps track of time like that. Oh, I know you and all the others are becoming something more than human, but I'd like to think you're adding on to your humanity, not turning away from it."

I make my voice halting and mechanical, like a robot from an old movie. "Puny... human... you... dare... to... question... me?"

"Ha-ha. Very funny." He rolls his eyes. "I'm trying to make a point here. I know that the time before you uploaded must seem like a distant memory to you, but I think you should talk to your dad. Maybe it'll help you remember where you came from."

I try not to be annoyed. "Uh, maybe your brain's getting rusty with age, but mine—perfect recall. I remember where I came from: Falls Church, Virginia, same as you."

He laughs, shakes his head. "Yeah, well I ended up not too far from where we started. But you... you always were on the fast track, even before you uploaded. Anyway, I better go, don't want to keep you slowed down to mortal speed. Just think about what I said."

"Okay, okay. Give my love to Deb and the kids."

"Will do. Talk to you in a few years. Bye."

"Bye." I cut the connection. My simtime self notices the conversation's over and reintegrates me.

The wind ruffles my feathers as I catch an updraft. Being up here alone helps me to think, even if flying with feathered wings is not a very human thing to do. It's one of the things Andrew can't really understand. I answered a call once with my wings on, and I think he found them disturbing, because he kept shifting his eyes away from the screen. When I told him I liked the feel of the sun on my wings, he asked how that was possible, since both the sun and the wings were simulated. I replied that it didn't matter, since I was simulated, too.

He didn't like that answer. I guess he still likes to think of me as the kid he grew up with, best friends forever.

He's been my friend for twelve centuries. That seems like a good start on forever.

But I'm not the kid he grew up with. That kid went on to get a Ph.D. in Mathematics from M.I.T., then got involved in the SIMINT project to copy human consciousness into a supercomputer, and then...

Then what? I'm a copy, but what happened to my original?

I don't remember.

There's a hole in my perfect memory. Immediately, I begin diagnostics on my memory storage. I also Google "Kenneth Granley mathematician bio."

There are plenty of references, and I feel a flash of pride while reading the first few, which describe me as the SIMINT mathematician who proved the Riemann Hypothesis. I know it's not a big deal outside the mathematical community, and it took me hundred and twenty-seven years, but I have made a lasting contribution to the study of prime numbers. But there's nothing in the articles about what happened to my flesh and blood, and that seems a little strange.

Now that I think about it, I don't remember anything about the flesh-and-blood lives of any of us who uploaded, other than some conversations during the first few months after upload.

My diagnostic comes back, and it shows several major gaps in my memory storage for my first three years of simtime, plus other gaps at apparently random intervals, including as recently as two hundred twenty-eight years ago. And my pre-upload memory has thousands of unnatural gaps.

I send an urgent message to all three sims of Jeff Hwang—he had been the head designer of SIMINT, so he was the most likely to know what might be happening.

Jeff-3 got back to me a few seconds later. "Hey, Kenny, relax. There's no problem."

"Then why is my memory messed up?"

"You did it to yourself."

"What? I did it? Why?"

"Umm." There's no visual, but I know he's frowning. Assuming his current form has a face, that is. "I think I'd better let you find out the answer for yourself. I don't think your memories have been erased; I think you've just stored them in a protected area. At least, that's what you've done the other times."

"You mean I've done this before?"

"Yeah, five times. Every time, you call me in a panic. Just look around a bit and I think you'll find the missing memories. You always have before."

"Oh." Why would I keep doing this to myself? "Thanks. Sorry to have bothered you."

"No prob. But maybe you should set up an auto-message when you run a memory diagnostic. Take care." He cuts the connection.

Now that I know what to look for, I find it quickly enough: a large secured file mixed in among 3-D reconstructions of old movies. It has to be the one, because I can't think of any reason why I would take such care to store *Pet Sematary II*. The file recognizes me when I try to open it, but instead of unlocking it activates a message.

It's from a younger me. Much younger—I think he's only about twenty years after upload. "Hey, future self. This is just a warning. I'm locking these memories away for a pretty good reason. Unless there is some urgent reason to access them, I suggest you just leave them here and forget you ever found them. You can append your current memories about this situation to the file. Trust me; you don't want to remember what's in here."

After playing the message again, I decide I was a smug little twerp back then. But obviously I've agreed with what I did every other time I've found this file, or there wouldn't still be holes in my memory.

So, do I trust myself and just forget this?

Of course not. I can always reseal the memories if necessary.

Again I try to access the file, and this time it unlocks. As it opens, it automatically begins patching the holes in my memory.

I remember.

I remember having a water-fight with my little sister Katie in the inflatable pool in our back yard. She shrieked at me to stop while continuing to splash me. I must have been about six, and she was two years younger than me.

It's my earliest memory of Katie. And thirty-two milliseconds ago, I didn't even remember having a sister. Why?

I remember Ginger Allman, the neurobiologist who was second-in-command on the SIMINT team, telling us that Jeff Hwang was in a coma and not expected to live. While driving on a highway that wasn't yet integrated into the autodrive net, his car had smashed into a bridge abutment at ninety miles an hour.

At the time there was only one Jeff sim, and he took it pretty well. "I didn't have much of a life outside the project," he said when we tried to console him, "and I guess that's literally true now."

His body never came out of the coma before it died two weeks later. A tragic accident, everyone thought, but of no real consequence to the project: the Jeff sim was as capable at designing and upgrading the SIMINT software as his flesh-and-blood—no, even more capable.

That was ten months, three days after he uploaded.

I remember running down our street, pushing Katie on her bike. "Go! Pedal faster. Go!"

The training wheels were off for the first time, and as I let go, she continued on her own about ten feet, then started to wobble.

"Keep going!" But my yell of encouragement did no good, and she toppled to the pavement.

I caught up to her, expecting her to be crying.

Her eyes were shiny, but with excitement, not tears. "Did you see me? I did it for a bit. I did it. Did you see?"

"I saw. You did great. Wanna try it again, for longer this time?"

I remember Ginger telling us that Alicia DiNovo, one of our programmers, had slit her wrists in the bathtub of her apartment. Alicia's sim insisted her flesh-and-blood would never do such a thing, that it must have been a murder set up to look like suicide. But the rest of us knew better: Alicia had obsessed over her boyfriend, and he had dumped her the previous weekend.

That was nine months, twelve days after she uploaded.

The memories pour into the cracks of my mind. Some of them—mostly of Katie—impinge upon my consciousness, while others merely settle into place so I can call them up when needed. I'm still puzzled as to why I erased Katie from my life. But then...

...then I remember Dean Willingham calling me privately about the third team member to die, only eight days after Alicia's death. One death is a random event; two deaths, a coincidence; three deaths, a pattern. This latest death was not a suicide: he was shot by the police, because he charged at them wielding a butcher's knife. The same knife he'd used to kill his sister Katie and her husband and their newborn baby boy.

That was nine months, twenty-one days after I uploaded.

As designed, my simulated body reacts naturally to my emotions. My vision blurs as I begin to cry. Instinctively I discontinue the body simulation, which is what I always do in a painful situation. Unfortunately, I don't know how to shut down my emotions without stopping my thoughts completely. And I cannot stop remembering.

Remembering my little sister Katie. Reliving every memory I had of her with perfect clarity. Fun in the yard. Fights in the back of the car. Helping her with homework. Insulting her in front of my friends. All the love and strain of being brother and sister.

Fortunately, my memories of her end with her wedding to Brendan. How happy she looked. I pretended it was my allergies making my eyes water as I said goodbye to her before they got in the limo. I hate to cry.

That was the last time I saw Katie. I was uploaded four months later, so at least I don't have to remember going crazy and killing her and Brendan and their baby. But I am forced to remember the horrid details that came out in the news. Photos of the dead bodies. Video of my grief-stricken parents refusing to answer questions from the newsies on their doorstep.

And over and over again, I watch the grisly footage from the police cameras as my flesh-and-blood charges out of my sister's doorway, brandishing a bloody blade and screaming incoherently. The police stunners are ineffective, and finally a flurry of gunshots leaves my flesh bleeding and dead.

Over and over I watch, knowing each time I deserved it.

I had tried calling Mom and Dad after Dean Willingham told me what had happened. Mom burst into tears and ran from the phone without a word. Dad came on, saw it was me, said, "How could you?" and hung up.

Who could blame them? I was just a simulation—the real me had killed their daughter, their grandson. The real me was dead.

It was the uploading that caused it, we discovered too late. Duplicating a human brain required a level of quantum scanning far beyond what hospitals routinely use. We couldn't test our custom-designed scanner on animals because of the Animal Rights Act, but we ran thousands of simulations and we were sure it would allow us to create a perfect copy.

And it did. The copies were perfect. We just didn't realize that it would damage the original.

After what my flesh-and-blood did, the thirty-four remaining members of the SIMINT team who had uploaded were taken into protective custody, to keep them from harming themselves or others. In all of them, the pattern turned out the same: insanity about nine to ten months after upload, then— among those who did not manage to commit suicide—a geometrically progressing disruption of brain functions, ending in death. No one lasted more than a year.

The flaw in the scanner wasn't my fault—my work was on large-scale data integrity of multi-dimensional arrays. My work is what has prevented us sims from going gradually insane as random errors built up in our mental matrices.

Instead, it was my flesh-and-blood that went crazy. It wasn't me. He wasn't even himself.

Then why do I feel so guilty?

I'm sorry, Katie. I'd give up my twelve hundred years if it would bring you back. I'm so sorry.

Now that the flood of memories has receded, I begin to think more rationally.

I understand why my earlier selves locked up that file. There was too much emotion tied up with those memories. Why endure the pain those memories brought when I could just seal them up? If I don't remember, it's as if it never happened.

And that's why Andrew felt I was becoming less human. In sealing off my pain, I'd severed most of my connections to my life before upload. Discarding my past left me free to fly ever-faster into the future.

Part of me wants to seal up these memories again, and go on with my life. I've done it before. Five times. Katie's gone. Nothing I can do can fix that.

And now Mom's gone, too. I play her funeral again, this time really watching it. Seeing the people who loved her mourn her loss. And this time, I mourn with them. If I hadn't shut myself off from the pain, maybe we would have talked, eventually. Maybe she would have realized I really am Kenny, that the man who killed Katie wasn't the real me. Maybe not. Either way, it's too late now.

I could still try with Dad. Andy thinks he needs me. Does he, or would I just be stirring up painful memories?

As for me, it's been a dozen lifetimes since I really thought much about my family. Why not just lock up all memories of them? Or even delete them entirely? Do they really mean anything in my life any more? They are merely memories, nothing but patterns of electrons accessed by my simulated brain.

Then again, what am I but a pattern of electrons? In my simulated world, in my simulated brain, my memories are the only things that *are* real, the only connection I have with a reality outside myself, with a world I cannot control with a whim.

And if I lose my connection to reality? They have a word for that: insanity.

I've seen insanity. Over and over again. It has a bloody butcher's knife in its hand.

That wasn't me. That cannot be me. The real Kenneth Granley is the mathematician who solved the Riemann Hypothesis, not the madman who killed his sister and her family. The real Kenneth Granley is me.

I reactivate my simulated body, changing it to my old human form before I slow down to realtime and call Dad. The phone rings several times, then asks if I want to leave a message.

I can try again later. If there's one thing I have, it's time.

* * *

In 2002 I got the sudden urge to write a fantasy novel. Since the only times in my life during which I had managed to write much fiction were when I was taking creative writing classes in college, I signed up for a community education creative writing class. After the in-person class finished, I continued to take online classes from my teacher, Caleb Warnock.

Caleb assigned us "craft writing" exercises each week in order to hone our writing skills. The class was not focused on speculative fiction, but fortunately Caleb tolerated my tendency to take each assignment and twist it in a science fiction or fantasy direction.

One of the assignments was: write about two people with opposite personalities who are still friends. I imagined one friend who liked a fast-paced life and another who preferred a slower pace. Then, putting the SF spin on it, I came up with the idea that the fast-paced friend had been uploaded into a computer. And that is how the phone conversation that begins the story came about.

Caleb thought the resulting vignette was very good, and suggested that I submit it as a story. (He had already suggested that I should write and submit short stories as a way of getting my name out there while I was still working on the novel.) I felt it didn't quite work as a story, so I thought about it some more and realized that there was a seed for more of the story with the mention of perfect recall. What if Kenneth's recall was not perfect after all? What would lead someone to block his own memory?

In 2003 I sent it off as my first submission to Analog, and Stan Schmidt sent me a nice rejection letter asking to see more. By then, I had decided that I would submit to the Writers of the Future Contest every quarter until either I won or I disqualified myself by having too many published stories. So I sent it off to the contest. (It was my second submission to the contest, the first having been back in the early 1990s.)

In December 2003 I found out I was a finalist. The next month, I got a letter saying I was not a winner, but that they would like to hold on to the story for possible inclusion in the anthology as a published finalist. And that's what ended up happening.

Resonance

Grant Sullivan watched his dream slipping away on CNN. The screen showed a competitor's spool carrier approaching the massive steel and concrete base to which it was meant to attach. A thin black line emerged from the top of the carrier: a ribbon of nanofiber reaching up thirty-five thousand kilometers to NanoSpacial's station in geosynchronous orbit, then stretching even farther to a massive counterweight.

As the ribbon unspooled, the carrier moved closer to the ground, until it touched down. Various locking mechanisms clanked as they attached the cable firmly to the elevator base. A cheer went up from the crowd at the NanoSpacial site near Quito, Ecuador.

He had known Nano was close to finishing their space elevator, but not how close. His own company's cable—the Sullivan SpaceLifter—still had over two thousand kilometers left to go before it touched down near the Brazilian city of Santana. That would take at least a month, and by then it would be too late.

Grant muted the television as Juan-Carlos Killeen, NanoSpacial's CEO, attached a small wheeled climber to the strip. It would travel up the strip, streaming a second strand behind it. Others would follow, and soon there would be a thick cable capable of carrying any payload into space. But that first climber was the important one, because once it reached the top, NanoSpacial could claim the quarter-billion-dollar Otis Prize for creating the first space elevator. It would complete that climb in less than three weeks, and there was no way Sullivan Space Technologies could catch up.

The Sullivan SpaceLifter would get finished, of course, because it was the only way to recoup the money spent on development. But Grant had been counting on winning the Otis Prize, and without that money he would certainly lose control of the company he had founded, even if it did manage to stay in business.

He sighed and switched off the television. Fighting back the disappointment that seemed to swell in his throat, he swiveled his chair so he could look out of his office at the Houston skyline as he pondered his options. This was not something straightforward like the engineering problems he'd had to overcome fifteen years ago to win the race for the first electromagnetic mass-driver orbital launch system. Over the last few years he'd been forced to become less of an engineer and more of a businessman.

Maybe he could convince his lenders to restructure some of the loans. That might delay things enough to allow the SpaceLifter to become operational and start showing a return on investment. He'd chosen Santana, Brazil, for the anchor point of the SpaceLifter because it had a port on the Amazon, which allowed cargo intended for space to be sent to the base of the elevator by ship. That should make the SpaceLifter more attractive for heavy cargo than NanoSpacial's elevator in Quito.

Of course, if NanoSpacial had beaten him by less than the 2.7 kilometers of Quito's elevation, he would now be cursing himself for not having chosen a mountain site. But over the long term, he was sure Brazil was the right choice.

Turning to his computer, he told it to send a message of congratulations and a case of Dom Perignon 2018 to the NanoSpacial CEO. The cost was negligible compared to Sullivan's debt, and having lost the race, he thought it wouldn't hurt to be friendly. After all, he might end up looking for a job if he lost control of his company.

He started going over the financials, and was deeply engrossed in calculating the effect of possible revenue streams on the company's cash-flow when Willy Horst, project manager for the SpaceLifter, rang through on the dedicated line. "Grant, what do you think it is?"

"What do I think what is?"

"You're not watching Nano's elevator?"

"I turned it off after they connected."

"Turn it on, quick."

He turned the screen back on. There was a small frame down in the corner that still showed the scene from Ecuador, but the main picture was jerky footage from inside a space habitat. Grant thumbed up the volume so he could hear.

"—really shaking us about and it seems to be getting worse." The astronaut's voice was calm through the bursts of static. The caption on-screen labeled the feed as "Live from NanoSpacial Geo-Station." That was their elevator terminal in geosynchronous orbit. Sullivan had something similar over Brazil, still lowering its nanofiber cable toward Earth.

"When did this start?" he asked Willy.

"Not sure. They cut to that feed just a couple minutes ago. Something's happening groundside, too."

"Earthquake, maybe, and the shock is getting carried up the line?"

"No, the people are standing around the base without any problems. But the base itself seems to be shifting up and down by a few centimeters."

The base must consist of over a hundred tons of concrete and steel. It couldn't be shifting like that, but in looking at the small picture on the screen, Grant saw that it was. "Their cable can't possibly be strong enough to pull that base up."

"Yeah, that's what I thought, too."

Then he realized what it must be. "Tacoma Narrows."

Willy sharply sucked in a breath.

In 1940, a suspension bridge across the Tacoma Narrows in Puget Sound had begun vibrating due to high winds. The vibration continued to increase and the sections of the bridge began swinging wildly and buckling, until finally the bridge collapsed. All of this was caught on film, so it had become the physics-textbook example of resonance. And it was every engineer's nightmare.

Theoretically, intelligent shock-absorber systems in the base of NanoSpacial's elevator should have compensated for any vibration, preventing the vibrations from building up through resonance. But if the shock absorbers were mis-timing their adjustments, then instead of damping out the vibration they would actually increase it through a feedback loop.

One of the astronauts was bleeding now, having banged his head against the station wall as it jerked about.

Grant frowned. "Unless Nano can get things under control, those guys up there are going to get beaten..." The private-sector space business was competitive, but nobody liked to see astronauts hurt, no matter which company they worked for.

And then the picture from space went completely steady. One of the astronauts said, "It's stopped."

Willy sighed in relief. "Well, I guess they fixed it."

"No. If they'd fixed it, it would have gradually died down. Nano's cable snapped." The movement of the counterweight at the far end of the cable must have stressed it far beyond its designed load.

"Yes!" Willy's voice was exultant. "We're back in the game."

Grant, too, had felt a fleeting joy before realizing what was about to happen. When a tight rubber band snaps, the ends have to go somewhere. And when that rubber band is thousands of kilometers long and razor-sharp on its edges, there's no good place for them to go.

Three weeks later, the Brazilian government rescinded the permits for the SpaceLifter to connect in Santana. Quito had been lucky: the break in NanoSpacial's cable had been fairly low, so only about ten percent of it had fallen to the ground. The writhing coils of nanofiber had killed twenty-six people and wounded about two hundred more, a lot less than Grant had feared, but it was more than enough to change some very important people's minds.

The Sullivan SpaceLifter wasn't the only space elevator project that had run into difficulty after the NanoSpacial disaster. Indonesia had halted the joint Mitsubishi/Hyundai elevator under construction near Samainda, and the Kenyan legislature was on the verge of passing a bill to stop construction of the British Spaceways elevator. Only Industrie Olympiae seemed to be proceeding without trouble, perhaps because the government of Gabon was mindful of the French navy's sudden decision to hold live-fire exercises off the coast of Libreville.

But Grant refused to call it quits yet. As he saw it, the fewer competitors there were, the more likely Sullivan Space Technologies could win that quarter-billion. It just needed some creative thinking, so he'd scheduled a conference call to do some brainstorming with the company executives and top engineers involved in the elevator project.

"Any chance the government will reconsider?" he asked the company liaison in Brasilia. "We've already poured an awful lot of money into their economy, but that's peanuts compared to what they'd make off taxing traffic through the elevator."

"I don't think so, Mr. Sullivan. There were organized street protests against—forgive me—'Yankee imperialists who don't care about the lives of common people.' I've been told that if our elevator is as safe as we claim, why aren't we building it in the U.S.?"

"And you explained that it has to be at the equator?"

"Yes, but the science doesn't matter to them; the politics does. Maybe after the next election we could work something out, but that's a couple of years off. Until then, they're not going to budge."

That confirmed what an international political consultant had told Grant. "So Brazil's out. What alternative countries are there? Maybe something in Africa?" Moving the orbital position of the elevator would be time-consuming, but it could be done.

Yocasta Rinfield, the company's international law specialist, said, "I'm afraid we have a major problem, even if we find another country willing to let us base the elevator. Right now, as I understand it, the bottom of the elevator is only about seven kilometers up?"

"Yes." The cable could already have reached the ground if it had been traveling at its previous speed of about four kilometers per hour. But now that the spool carrier was in the atmosphere, they had to move more carefully. The last seven kilometers would take as much time as the previous five hundred.

"That's low enough that it is considered to be in the airspace of whatever country it's over; Brazil, at the moment. So, to move it will require permission from any country it passes over. Traveling west, we run into Colombia's airspace. They won't let us base there, but they might let us pass through. But then we hit Ecuador's airspace. We'll *never* get permission there. Traveling east, we'll run into Gabon's airspace before we can get to any other African countries, and I don't think Gabon will cooperate in setting up competition for their own elevator."

Nobody said anything for several seconds.

Finally, Grant said, "Is it possible Brazil would let us build the base away from any inhabited area, if there is such a place?"

"Oh!" exclaimed Willy. "I'm a half-wit. Forget Brazil, or any other government. Forget *land*. There are thousands of miles of ocean along the equator. We originally considered an ocean platform as an option, but rejected it because both initial cost and maintenance were higher. But now…"

"How much more?" Grant asked. He had stayed up well into the night trying to figure out how to pay for the construction of a minimal new base; the company was so deeply in the red that additional loans were out of the question. By delaying payments to some suppliers and selling future satellite time to current customers at a huge discount for advance payment, he thought he had found enough money. And even that required liquidating his personal stock portfolio.

"About thirty percent more initially, and fifty percent more for maintenance."

It was too much. "Any way we could reduce that difference for a minimal system?"

"I don't know. The costs of constructing a floating base will be more, no matter what. So I don't—Just a minute." There was a muffled sound of a brief conversation, then Willy came back on the line. "One of my people here suggests we lease a large freighter for now, and build our own platform later. I think it could work, and it would require less up-front investment."

Grant slapped his desk. "That's why this company was first with the mass driver, and why we'll be first with a space elevator. It's my secret formula for success: Hire smart people and trust them to come up with solutions. Get cracking on this, Willy. You make sure it can work on the engineering end, and I'll find a way to make it work financially."

Several days later, Grant received a surprise visit from NanoSpacial CEO Juan-Carlos Killeen. Grant offered him a seat, but he declined.

Instead he walked over to the window and gazed out at the streets of Houston. "Do you know what made our cable snap?"

"Looked like a resonance problem. Something was vibrating at the natural frequency of the cable, and..." The engineer's natural instinct to explain a problem made Grant start to answer before he realized that Killeen probably wasn't talking about the engineering cause.

"It was sabotage. That's what made our cable snap. Sabotage."

"I promise we had nothing to do with it. I would never condone—"

Killeen turned back and looked at Grant. "I'm not accusing you of anything. We caught the guy who did it: one of our programmers. One of our own people; been with us for ten years. He booby-trapped the shock absorber programming. No, I know you weren't behind it. I'm here to warn you."

"Warn me?"

"We turned him over to the Ecuadorian police. We did not think they would be too gentle with him after what happened. But he suicided on the way to the police station."

"Suicided?" That didn't sound like normal procedure for industrial spies. If they got caught, usually they would make a deal by ratting out their employer. "Are you sure he wasn't killed by whoever hired him?"

"Suicide pill hidden in his tooth. They found the remains of it. But we've checked his background, and we know who was behind it. The news is being kept quiet so law enforcement can try to track down his accomplices, but I thought I should give you a heads up: It was Gaia Jihad."

Grant felt an emptiness at the base of his stomach. Near the beginning of the century, international politics had made "strange bedfellows" out of radical Islamists and extreme environmentalists. Gaia Jihad was the bastard child of that union.

Fusing the rhetoric of radical environmentalists with a brand of Islam that was condemned as heretical by mainstream Muslim leaders, the group began by attacking oil industry targets in Saudi Arabia. True Islam had been corrupted, they claimed, by the wealth that came from raping Mother Earth.

By 2016 Gaia Jihad had succeeded in halving Saudi oil exports through a steady stream of suicide bombings targeting wells, pipelines and shipping. They began to branch out: hitting car manufacturers, large-scale agribusiness and other targets that they claimed represented the "corrupting" influence of technology on the Earth.

Until now they had not directly attacked space-tech targets, possibly because they had fewer objections to the corrupting of space. But the attack on the NanoSpacial elevator meant that the SpaceLifter was also a target, and Grant wondered if one or more of his employees were planning something similar.

"I'll have my security start looking into possible threats." Grant paused. "Thanks for the heads-up."

Killeen nodded, but seemed lost in thought.

After a few moments, Grant asked, "Was there something else?"

"We still have ninety percent of our elevator, but no place to base it. I've heard rumors that you're working on a new base somewhere." He sighed. "Unless we complete our elevator, NanoSpacial may go into bankruptcy. I know we're competitors, but... Look, there's no way we're going to catch you now for the Otis Prize, unless something happens. But what if something does happen? If you're in the financial squeeze I think you are, you need that prize money worse than we do."

Grant didn't bother saying that the financial squeeze was probably worse than Killeen thought. But he wondered where this was going, so he just nodded his head.

Killeen became more enthusiastic. "Long term, there's more than enough business for both our elevators even if they're side by side. So, if you can help us get a base, and something happens to slow your construction so that my company ends up winning the prize, we'll split the money with you, fifty-fifty."

Leaning back in his chair, Grant could not see anything wrong with Killeen's proposal. From a business standpoint, his company couldn't lose. Of course, Killeen had to be thinking that Sullivan Space Technologies had secretly found a country willing to allow a base, and would probably feel cheated to find out that the solution was an ocean platform, an idea his own engineers would probably come up with even before it eventually came out that was what Grant's company had done.

That wasn't the way he liked to do business, so Grant shook his head.

Killeen sagged.

"I'm going to count on my people being good enough to finish the job first and win that prize. But you came in here in good faith and warned me about Gaia Jihad, which you didn't have to do. So, since you gave me some information before it became public knowledge, I'm going to return the favor. Your engineers are going to be kicking themselves when you say—" He held up two fingers. "—two words: ocean platform."

After a moment, Killeen laughed. "Oh, there will definitely be some embarrassment when Mr. Business-School-CEO tells the engineers what they should have thought of themselves. And I appreciate your candor. If for any reason my company ends up winning instead of yours, talk to me. We might be able to work out a deal to keep your company... afloat, so to speak."

Grant was talking to his stockbroker about selling off another chunk of his portfolio when his computer notified him of a call on another line from Alexander Pittakys.

Alex Pittakys had been one of Grant's roommates during his senior year at Texas A&M, and they'd kept in touch over the years. Grant had even donated a few hundred thousand dollars to the environmental non-profit Alex ran, the Foundation for a Better Earth.

Telling his broker he would call back later, Grant switched to the other line. "Hi, Alex." Then, noticing his friend's serious demeanor, he asked, "What's the matter?"

"You know I want you to succeed with this elevator thing, right?"

"Yeah, I appreciate the way you helped smooth things over with that Brazilian rainforest group last year."

Alex nodded. "I still support the project, even after the accident in Ecuador. I believe in you, Grant."

Where was Alex going with this? "Thanks."

"But I think you need to slow things down a bit. You're forging ahead with a new plan that hasn't been adequately studied. What are the long-term effects on the ocean environment? What if there's another accident?"

"It wasn't an accident. It was sabotage. A Gaia Jihad terrorist."

Alex swore. "Every time those morons do something, the public blames all environmentalists. Makes my job ten times harder."

"We're taking precautions to prevent them from sabotaging us. I understand your concerns about the ocean environment, but my people have looked at the potential impact: our floating platform will have much less of an ecological footprint than an oil rig." Grant pointed a finger toward the ceiling. "Our structure goes up from the water, not down into it."

"'Not as bad as an oil rig' is hardly a recommendation."

"Touché. I'm just saying the impact is hardly unprecedented. And the SpaceLifter will be far more valuable to the world than any oil rig."

After letting out a long breath, Alex said, "You always were one for the grand view. Just be sure you've got all the details right."

"Believe me—I'm even more concerned about making this work than you are."

Soon there were only five kilometers left to go, then three. Work on the floating platform, aboard a Norwegian-flagged freighter called the *Northern Rose*, was on schedule to finish shortly before the nanofiber cable reached sea level. Meanwhile, company security personnel had investigated every Sullivan Space Technologies employee involved in any way with the SpaceLifter project. They had interviewed each employee while conducting voice-stress analysis, searched the history of employees' transactions, and had even run each employee's biometrics through the U.S. government's terrorist database. In addition, Grant had brought in an outside security consultant to check on his own security people.

All that effort had turned up one-hundred and seventeen employees having extramarital affairs, fifty-seven with large gambling debts, fourteen with concealed criminal records, and even six who were smuggling drugs using company equipment. But there was no sign of anyone involved with Gaia Jihad.

Grant mulled over the security report while digging into his Rib Eye Louisianne at Resa's Prime Steakhouse. The failure to find a saboteur could mean there wasn't one to find. But there was no way to be sure of that. Either way, he would just have to rely on his employees to be vigilant enough to spot any problems.

"You're Grant Sullivan, right?" A young man in a shark-gray suit had approached Grant's table unnoticed.

Grant smiled at being recognized. "Yes, that's me."

The young man pulled some papers out of his inner coat pocket and dropped them on the table. "These are for you. Consider yourself served. Have a nice day."

A lawsuit? Who was suing him? "Hey—" Grant began, but the young man had already turned and was walking away.

Grant picked up the papers and began to skim the first page as he fumbled for his phone. There were about fifteen environmentalist groups listed as the plaintiffs—including, Grant noticed with dismay, the Foundation for a Better Earth. Grant was personally named as a defendant, along with the company. At least that meant he could use the company legal staff to fight this. He dialed the number for the company's head counsel, and as it rang he got down to the words "Temporary Restraining Order."

His heart began to beat faster as he flipped through pages of legalese, hoping not to find a mention of the SpaceLifter. Let it be some other project. He didn't know half of what the company did these days, and he'd happily shut down anything else to keep the environmentalists off his back.

The phone stopped ringing. "Grant?"

"I just got served with a TRO. I'm trying to figure out what it's about."

"Turn to the very end and read what the order is. 'It is hereby ordered,' and so forth."

Grant flipped to the end, and began reading aloud. "It is hereby ordered that plaintiffs' motion for a temporary restraining order is granted, as follows: The defendants are hereby enjoined from continuing any work to extend their space elevator below its current height, and are ordered to appear before this court and show cause why the restraining order... Well, I guess that's the heart of it."

"I'll get right on it, Grant. I know how important this is for you."

"Thanks, Jerr."

Grant glared at the remainder of his steak for a few minutes until his waitress stopped by the table.

"Is there a problem with your steak?" Her voice was filled with perky concern.

"No, I'm just not hungry." He got up, dropped a few bills on the table without bothering to count them, and walked out.

"Do we have to comply?" Grant looked around the conference-room table at the hastily convened team of company lawyers. "The SpaceLifter's over international waters."

"It's not quite that simple, Grant," said Jerry Verrocchio, head counsel for the company. "In order to take advantage of the space development tax incentives—and keep the company on the priority list for military contracts—we declared the SpaceLifter's orbital station as a U.S.-flag space station. That's a sufficient basis for the court to assert jurisdiction."

"What if we just ignore it for now? Keep building while you argue things in court?"

Jerr shook his head. "If we do not comply, we'll be considered in contempt of court. And whether or not this lawsuit ends up getting dismissed in the end, the court will not tolerate our ignoring the TRO."

"And that will mean a fine of some sort? How much are we talking?" More money to pay, but as long as he could finish the SpaceLifter, Grant didn't care.

"This isn't something you can just pay to settle. Penalties for contempt of court are meant to enforce compliance, which means they will be set high enough that the company cannot afford to keep paying, probably millions of dollars per day. You and other company officers could even be jailed until the company complies. And the judge will be seriously annoyed, which is not a good thing." Jerr shook his head. "No, Grant, I recommend we comply and try to win this in the courtroom."

After pausing a moment, Grant nodded in defeat. "How soon do you think you can get the TRO lifted?"

"We can get a hearing tomorrow. Even if the plaintiffs try to drag things out, it shouldn't be more than a few days."

He had worried that it might be weeks or more. "I'll tell Willy to stop the spool."

The lights were off in Grant's office. He sat in his chair, looking out at the patches of glowing windows in Houston's skyscrapers. He idly wondered what problems were keeping others in their offices so late.

Things had been so much easier when all he had to worry about were his own engineering problems and the threat posed by other companies that were merely trying to beat him to the same goal. Lawyers, environmentalists and terrorists were complications he could do without.

His computer sounded a tone and said, "You have a call from Alexander Pittakys."

"Refuse it."

It stung that Alex's group was one of the plaintiffs in the lawsuit. Even though he knew it was irrational—the lawsuit could just as well have been filed without the Foundation for a Better Earth—the betrayal by his friend gave Grant someone to blame.

A minute later, the computer again said, "You have a call from Alexander Pittakys."

Alex had never discouraged easily. That had been one of the things Grant liked most about him, before. Grant let out a long sigh. Alex would keep bugging him until they finally talked. "OK, put him through."

The screen sprang to life, showing Alex's face.

"I'm sorry, Grant." Alex spoke before Grant had a chance to say anything. "I know you're probably mad at me, but hear me out."

Grant shrugged. "Unless you're going to say you've called off the lawyers, I don't know what you might say to interest me." Grant waved his hand dismissively at the screen. "After all the money I've given FBE, it's hard to believe you'd turn on me like this."

"Oh, was that money supposed to be a *bribe*? I'm supposed to just shut up about possible environmental problems when you're involved? Your people may not think there's a problem, but mine tell me if your cable were to somehow break and fall into the ocean—"

"Won't happen!"

"You can't be sure of that."

"Well, if I can't be sure of that, it's because your people are trying to sabotage it."

"That's not fair and you know it. Gaia Jihad are *not* my people. In fact, they sometimes target mainstream environmentalists for being 'insufficiently dedicated to the cause.'"

Reluctantly, Grant nodded in acknowledgement.

"Because they are a threat to us, too, we have a security firm keeping tabs on their activities, as much as possible. And that's the main reason I called, to warn you. It's only scuttlebutt, really. But apparently Gaia Jihad just made a major deal to buy military hardware on the European black market. It could be for an attack on you."

"What kind of military hardware?"

"I don't know. The info is sketchy."

"Thanks for the staggeringly useful information. So glad you called."

Alex shook his head slightly. "Take care of yourself." He hung up.

It had taken eighteen hours to actually slow the spool to a stop without putting too much stress on the cable, so it now reached down to a tantalizingly close 2416 meters. But it would go no further until his legal department could convince the judge to lift the TRO. Lawyers for the environmental groups, on the other hand, had asked the judge to issue a preliminary injunction against the SpaceLifter until there could be a full trial.

The judge had held three days of hearings, with expert scientific testimony on both sides, and after one and a half days of deliberations, her office had notified the lawyers that she would deliver her ruling at 3:30 that afternoon.

Grant had decided against going to the courthouse to hear the decision in person, choosing instead to remain in his office and watch the court's video feed over the net. If the ruling was favorable, he could get operations restarted as quickly as possible. And if it was not… He'd already thought about that, and didn't want to think about it any more. Surely the judge had to understand the importance of space elevators to the future of humanity in space. She had to see that the only reason the NanoSpacial elevator had turned out to be dangerous was because of sabotage – by a fanatical environmentalist, no less. Reason would prevail. It had to.

"All rise."

The bailiff's voice called Grant's attention to the screen, which showed the judge as she took her place behind the bench, and Grant tried unsuccessfully to find some signal in her body language indicating which way she was going to rule.

"The issues in this case are not clear-cut," said the judge. "The defendants have presented evidence that their so-called 'space elevator'…"

So-called? The judge continued to speak, but Grant could already tell the ruling would be bad.

NanoSpacial was fighting a similar battle in a California court, and he doubted they would have more luck there than his company had found here. So his new friendliness with Juan-Carlos Killeen would not do any good. Meanwhile, the environmental groups had failed to convince a French court to halt Industrie Olympiae's elevator, so their project was still making progress, and was probably no more than three months away from completion. He tried to be philosophical about it—IO's elevator would prove the concept worked, and eventually there would be plenty of space elevators—but it didn't help. Since he was a teenager, he had dreamed of building a space elevator, and it had been the center of his life for the past five years. He wanted to finish it. He was so close.

"The potential harm to the environment—particularly marine life—in the event of a catastrophic failure similar to that which occurred in Ecuador, would be irreparable. Therefore, this court is granting the motion of the plaintiffs requesting a preliminary injunction, until such time as a full trial can be held. The defendants, and any of their agents, employees, or contractors, are enjoined from any and all activities that would extend any part of their 'space elevator,' or any similar construction, below its current altitude, or to connect it with any station, either on land or on water."

Grant turned off the screen and leaned back in his chair. He felt suddenly drained; he didn't even have the energy to be angry at the judge.

It was over. It would be months or maybe years before a full trial could be held. Even if the judge's order was overturned on appeal before that, it would be too late to save the company. He'd juggled the finances as much as he could, and had found the money to keep things going for the six more weeks it would take to get the cable all the way down and send a climber all the way up. He was sure he could have kept the company afloat with either the prize money or loans based on the prospective future revenue from lifting cargo into orbit.

But there was not enough money to put things on hold during an appeal and then finish the job if they won the appeal. No, the dream was dead; it was now time for damage control. By selling off the profitable divisions of the company, he would probably be able to pay off the company debts, and maybe start over as a space technology consultant. Or maybe just retire and take his motorboat to spend the rest of his life fishing on some mountain lake.

His phone rang on one of the company lines, but he didn't recognize the extension. Probably some engineer on the SpaceLifter wondering if he still had a job.

He considered letting it go to voicemail, but his people deserved better than that. He activated the speakerphone. "Sullivan here."

"Uh, Mr. Sullivan? My name is Carolina Bishop. You met me about three years ago when your company hired me, but you may not remember me. I've been working on the NASA contract for the Mars Atmosphere Cargo Transport."

He didn't remember her at all, but he had a vague memory of the MACT project. He'd spent so much of his time focused on the SpaceLifter that he hadn't paid much attention to the other projects his company had taken on.

"Is there a problem?" Just what he needed, another problem.

"No. In fact, we're ahead of schedule. That's why when I heard the news about the court ruling, I decided to call you. We were going to deliver the MACTs to NASA next week, because the contract has an incentive bonus if we delivered more than three months in advance, but—"

"How much money are we talking about?" Grant couldn't keep the eagerness out of his voice.

"Two million dollars."

Not enough to make a difference. Twenty times that amount might have. "Well, Ms. Bishop, give my thanks to your team for a job well done."

"No, you don't understand. If we keep the MACTs we've built so far, my team can still fulfill the NASA order. We'd have to pull double shifts for the next four months, and since we'd be a month late we'd forfeit the incentive bonus, and even have to pay a couple hundred thousand in penalties, but we could do it."

Pinching the bridge of his nose, Grant tried to make sense of what she was saying.

"Mr. Sullivan? Are you still there?"

"I'm sorry. I've got a lot on my mind right now. So, please explain why on earth I would want to forfeit two million dollars when I'm in debt up to my eyeballs?" After he finished speaking, he realized he must be under too much stress. He shouldn't have revealed how bad things were.

"Because we can use the MACTs to make the SpaceLifter operational. I assumed that was a higher priority than the incentive bonus."

"The SpaceLifter project is dead. I thought you said you heard about the court ruling."

"Yes, but we can get around it if we use four of the MACTs to support a platform, and the fifth as a sort of ferry. I've run some simulations, and it should be stable enough for smaller cargo shipments, Later we could add more, which would allow larger cargo."

She sounded like she knew what she was talking about, even if Grant still didn't know. It was time to admit the extent of his ignorance. "I'm sorry; I haven't been keeping track of your project. Other than the fact that it's a project for air transport on Mars, I don't know anything about the technical details."

"Oh." She sounded embarrassed. "The MACTs are blimps."

He blinked. "Blimps? We're making blimps to transport cargo on Mars?"

"Yes. The Martian atmosphere is only about one percent as thick as ours, so even in the lower gravity, planes have to go a lot faster to get the same amount of lift as they would on Earth. With the scarcity of fuel on Mars, it's very wasteful. And the inertia problem… Well, let's just say planes are useless for large cargo. The thin atmosphere also means blimps have to be bigger to give the same amount of lift as on Earth, but once the blimp is filled, that lift is constant, so you're not wasting fuel on lift."

"But I still don't see how…" And then he did. He slapped the desk. "Brilliant."

The court order prevented them from bringing the bottom of the SpaceLifter's cable any lower. But if they built a mid-air floating platform around the end of the cable, that might get around the injunction. He'd have to get the lawyers on it to be sure, but it was the only hope left.

"You may just have saved the company, Ms. Bishop. I'm coming out to your project, and I'll fly in Willy Horst and some of his people as well to get things started for the platform." He paused. "Uh, where are you?"

"Melbourne, Florida."

Grant looked at his watch. "I'll be there in a few hours."

"You're planning to use *hydrogen* to fill these blimps?" Grant raised his eyebrows. "Bad enough that everyone thinks the SpaceLifter is just looking for an excuse to plunge from the sky, but you want to combine that with the Hindenburg?"

Carolina Bishop stiffened in her seat. "Hydrogen didn't cause the Hindenburg fire—that's a myth that was disproved decades ago. It was the skin of the zeppelin that burned, because it was made of remarkably flammable material. It was not the hydrogen. The Hindenburg's sister ship was made with a less flammable skin and flew over a million miles filled with hydrogen, and she never had a problem."

"Still, couldn't we go with helium?" asked Willy. "It isn't flammable at all, and I think it would make people feel safer."

"Our MACTs are safe. The skin is made of specially-prepared non-flammable carbon nanofiber, divided into ten separate chambers. They are not going to catch fire or explode or cause any kind of disaster. Even if all the hydrogen in one chamber spontaneously decided to explode,"—she waved her hands to indicate an explosion—"the material is tough enough to contain the explosion. They were designed with hydrogen in mind, because hydrogen's a whole lot easier to find than helium on Mars. Trust me, Mr. Sullivan, they're safe." She stared directly into Grant's eyes.

Hire smart people and trust them to come up with solutions. He'd said that was the company's secret to success, and now he was being asked to back it up. "Hydrogen it is."

"Good, because hydrogen provides an eight percent improvement in lift over helium. Even though the increased buoyancy due to the thickness of Earth's atmosphere will allow us to lift 180 times the proposed payload for Mars, based on the details of the platform Mr. Horst has given me, we're going to need that margin."

"Since we're all going to be working closely on this until it's finished, let's dispense with 'Mr. Horst' and 'Mr. Sullivan.' He's Willy, I'm Grant."

Carolina nodded. "OK, Grant. As I was saying, the hydrogen in the MACTs will provide all the lift to suspend the platform. The propellers will be used only to stabilize the position when needed. Given that the mass of the platform is a hundred and fifty tons, it should be fairly stable just from its own inertia, and so it's possible that solar power would provide all the energy needed for the props. If not, fuel usage would still be fairly low."

"I still find it hard to believe," said Willy. "Each of these zeppelins of yours is supposed to hold up almost forty tons?"

"A hundred years ago, the United States had two dirigibles that could carry over seventy tons each. In the early 2000's, a German company called CargoLifter planned to build a zeppelin capable of carrying a payload of *one hundred and sixty tons*, and it would have worked if they hadn't run into financial problems. That one could have carried your platform all by itself."

Grant tried not to wince at the mention of financial problems. The fact that the name CargoLifter was so similar to SpaceLifter didn't help. "It seems counterintuitive, but we'll take your word for it that the MACTs can lift that much weight. The thing that worries me is that the platform is free to move up and down. We all saw what resonance can do – that NanoSpacial platform was fastened to bedrock, and it started bouncing up and down until the cable finally broke. What's to keep our platform from bouncing even more?"

"Our shock absorbers haven't been sabotaged," said Willy. "They'll keep things steady."

"I know, but..." Grant scratched behind his right ear. "I'd feel a whole lot better if it were fastened down."

"Actually, I think that's the worst thing you could do," said Carolina.

Grant wrinkled his forehead. "What do you mean?"

"Well, resonance becomes a problem when periodic force is being applied at the natural frequency of the cable, right? The vibration keeps getting more powerful, and eventually the strain on the cable becomes too much and the cable snaps." She took a deep breath and continued, "In order to keep the platform steady in the sky, the MACTs will be at neutral buoyancy, providing exactly enough lift to hold up the platform. We do that by pumping air into ballast chambers inside the blimp and compressing the excess hydrogen into storage tanks. When we need more lift, we just reverse the process." She looked at Grant and then Willy, as if to make sure they were following what she was saying.

Grant nodded to encourage her to continue. He didn't know where she was going, but so far she seemed to have an answer for everything.

"So, if the tension on the cable starts getting too high, we increase the lift, and take the platform higher. Kind of like loosening a guitar string. Reduce the tension, and the cable won't snap. But you can't do that with a ground-based platform." She smiled and leaned back in her chair.

It sounded right. Grant thought it over, and realized she was even more right than she knew. "Not only do you reduce the tension on the cable, but you also alter its natural frequency. That could put it out of sync with whatever was causing the vibration in the first place and prevent further resonance."

She opened her eyes wide, obviously surprised that Grant had seen something she hadn't.

Grant laughed. "I may spend most of my time now worrying about finances and politics, but I was an engineer before I was a businessman. I had to come up with solutions on my own before I could hire smart people to come up with them for me."

Because they were originally intended to be launched into space and transported to Mars, with their propellers folded the five uninflated MACTs took up surprisingly little space on the cargo plane. Grant stood on the tarmac and watched through his nightglasses as they were unloaded at Santana Base, the Sullivan Space Technologies facility in Brazil. It was three in the morning, local time, and while the normal runway lights were on, the floodlights were not. So far, they'd managed to keep the whole aerial platform idea a secret, and he hoped the secrecy would hold for just another thirty-six hours. By then, if all went well, an automated climber would be racing up the cable at seventy-five kilometers per hour.

Opponents of the SpaceLifter might see his absence from company headquarters as an indication that something was going on. Still, here he was safe from any process server, and he felt better being actively involved in the project instead of just monitoring things from his office.

Carolina came and stood beside him. "Willy says the platform should be ready for lifting by midnight. We'll start inflating the first two MACTs as soon as the sun goes down this evening."

"We need a new name."

"What?"

"MACT. Mars Atmosphere Cargo Transport. We're not on Mars."

She laughed. "Well, EACT doesn't sound so good. At least with MACTs, it almost sounds like 'Max.'"

"It's not important, I guess." He sighed. "It's just that I don't like this sneaking around in the night. Space travel used to be something we were proud of, something bold and public. We named our rockets after Greek or Roman gods, and everyone watched as we soared into space. Look at us now: naming things with boring acronyms and working in secret so the courts don't shut us down." He shook his head. "Never mind. Continue what you were saying about the plan."

"At around midnight, four MACTs will lift the platform and carry it out over the ocean. They'll be in place an hour after dawn, so there will be plenty of light for Willy as he supervises attaching the cable."

"OK." Grant didn't say it now, but he planned to be on one of those four MACTs so he could be there when the connection was made.

"Meanwhile, after the platform is airborne we'll start inflating the fifth MACT, and then load it with the climber and the first spool of cable. It should leave here well before dawn, but since its load will be lighter, it should arrive only about an hour later than the four MACTs carrying the platform."

"Sounds good." Grant watched as a flatbed truck took the last of the MACTs into the hangar, where company security would guard the blimps against sabotage. There was nothing more to be done tonight, except try to sleep.

"The specs really don't give a good idea of how big they really are." Grant had seen blimps flying over football games, but either of the two inflated MACTs now floating over the platform could have its nose over the bleachers in one end zone and its tail over the bleachers of the other.

"Beautiful, aren't they?" Carolina said.

The lights necessary for the work still proceeding on the ground illuminated the undersides of the MACTs. "Like whales swimming among the stars," he said.

"You're going to have to fly in one someday soon. You'll love it."

He wasn't sure why he hesitated before he said, "I'm planning to go up tonight, with the platform."

"Oh." She sounded disappointed. "I thought you'd be running things from here on the ground."

"I like to be wherever the action is." His phone chirped, and he slid it from his pocket and answered. "Sullivan here."

An electronically distorted voice said, "Mr. Sullivan, you are blaspheming against God and our Mother Earth. If you do not stop yourself, Gaia Jihad will stop you. This is your only chance to prevent a disaster of your own making."

The connection went dead.

After Grant relayed the message from Gaia Jihad, everyone around the conference table sat in stunned silence for several seconds.

"You see why I stopped work and put everything under guard."

Carolina's brow wrinkled. "You're not giving in to them?"

"It's a bluff," Willy said. "They haven't been able to sabotage us, so they're trying to scare us off."

Grant nodded. "It's possible. Maybe even likely—company security hasn't found a trace of any Gaia Jihad infiltration. Everything has been double-checked for flaws, intentional or not. Still, maybe there's something we've overlooked. How long would it take to check every part of that platform again?"

"The hardware? A week, if we push it." Willy sighed. "But to be safe, we probably shouldn't push it. Say two weeks. But the software?" He turned to look at one of his assistants.

"There's too much code. If there's a rotten Easter Egg in there, it could take months to locate."

"Concentrate on the hardware, then," said Grant. "Since they used the software angle against Nano, they would expect us to go over the software with a fine-tooth comb. So they probably would have aimed elsewhere. Unless they anticipated—"

Carolina interrupted him, her voice melodramatic. "No! That's just what they'd be expecting us to do!" Then she giggled. "I'm sorry, but it's like something out of an old movie. I agree with Willy – it's a bluff. They haven't been able to sabotage us, so they're trying to delay us until they can organize something."

Leaning his head back, Grant looked at the ceiling tiles and let out a long breath. "If you're right, and I think you are, I just gave them what they wanted."

"It's understandable," said Willy at the same time Carolina said, "Yes, you did."

"Sorry folks. By shutting everything down I've lost us a couple of hours, but let's get back out there and make this work."

"But the sun will come up before we're through," said Willy.

"Forget secrecy. Speed is what matters now."

Excitement and pride had mingled with regret as Grant watched the four MACTs carry the platform toward the rising sun. There had still been too much to do getting the fifth MACT ready for launch, and so he had decided to stay behind to supervise the loading of the cargo.

The cargo container and crew compartment were not an integrated part of the MACT; they needed to be attached to cables that hung from it. Once in flight, they could be reeled up to the bottom of the blimp.

Grant was inside the cargo container checking over the spool on nanofiber cable when Carolina rushed inside.

"Grant, you've got to come outside and see this."

His heart pounded. "What's wrong?"

"Nothing's wrong; you just need to see this."

He followed her outside until they were a good thirty meters away.

She stopped, turned and pointed above the way they had come. "Look."

Floating above the cargo container was the final MACT. Hanging on its side were six pieces of white material, each with a large black letter painted on it. "CETUS I," he read aloud.

"It's no longer a MACT."

"Cetus, the whale. The sea monster of Greek mythology. Perfect." He smiled. Then, after a moment's thought, he said, "Won't those sheets interfere with the solar-electric cells?"

She shrugged. "A bit, but we've got fuel to spare. Anyway, they're just plastic sheets hung with some rope. I can detach them if they cause a problem. But the important thing is: the Cetus I is ready to go. Once your cargo's all squared away, we can take off any time. I assume you want to hitch a ride?"

Three days with almost no sleep had taken their toll, so Grant was semi-dozing in his seat when Carolina's voice brought him back to reality.

"We've got a leak."

"A leak?" Grant leaned forward in his seat. "Is it serious?"

She laughed. "Not that kind of leak. Santana Base says CNN has broken the story that we're using blimps for our space elevator. They even have some shaky videocam footage of us heading out to sea."

"Is the coverage positive or negative?" Were the news media spinning the story as "Those Ingenious Engineers" or as "Company in Contempt of Court?"

Carolina flipped a switch. "Santana Base, our CEO wants to know if the coverage is positive or negative." She paused. "Santana Base, your last transmission was garbled. Please repeat."

A longer pause. "Santana Base, come in, please." She turned to Grant. "Looks like there's some interference. I can't get anything from them now."

Grant frowned. "Wonder what could be causing it. We're not too far out, are we?"

"No, we should be fine."

"Try to contact Willy or somebody with the platform."

She tried a few different frequencies, but had no luck. Meanwhile, Grant pulled out his phone, but found it wasn't getting a signal either.

It might be sunspot activity. But Grant had a growing suspicion that the interference wasn't natural. "Anything showing up on radar?"

"It's clear. No, wait. I'm not sure. There may be something to the west. Real fuzzy, though."

"They're jamming our long-range communications. If they've got electronic warfare capability, they're probably military."

"Military? Whose military would be after us?"

"Military technology, I mean. Could be owned by a private company, or…"

Nodding, Carolina finished his sentence. "…or by Gaia Jihad."

Alex had tried to warn him, Grant realized, but he'd been too angry about the lawsuit to pay attention. "No weapons on this thing, are there?"

"No."

"Then turn us around, head back to base. Maybe they'll break off if it looks like we're quitting." It was a slim chance, and Grant didn't put much faith in it.

Carolina didn't say anything as she worked at her pilot's console, but Grant felt the Cetus start to turn.

"How much damage can we take before we crash?"

"Since we have a light load, we can remain airborne even if four of the ten gas compartments lose their hydrogen. That's if they're spaced out, though. If all four are at the front or back, we'll be too unstable." Se looked more closely at the radar screen. "That's strange. They were coming in at almost three hundred knots, and now they've slowed to under fifty. How'd they—"

"There they are." Grant pointed out the window to starboard. As it grew closer, Grant could make out the configuration of the aircraft. There was a large single jet turbine behind the cockpit, and after a moment he recognized what it was. "It's a Vespa—single-seater Italian-made jet with vertical takeoff and hover capabilities."

There were rapid flashes from the wings of the jet, and immediately an alarm began to sound at Carolina's console. "We're losing hydrogen. Multiple holes. Must be using diamond-tipped bullets to cut into the nanofiber like that."

The Vespa flew over the Cetus, and Grant whirled to see it flying away on the other side.

"How bad is it?" he asked. He felt helpless; there was nothing he could do but sit and watch.

"If that's all he does, we're OK. The nanobots crawling the inside of the gas compartments can fix those leaks. But a few more passes like that and they'll be overwhelmed."

"Give me the radio. I'll see if I can talk to this guy."

She handed him her headset.

Grant could see the plane begin to turn. He switched to the emergency channel and hoped the Vespa's EW capability was sophisticated enough to filter out its own jamming. "Pilot of the aircraft that is attacking us, I don't know how much you're getting paid to do this, but I'll double it if you stop. Please respond."

The jet began approaching them again.

"I'll pay you double or twenty million dollars, whichever is higher. Or more. Name your price. Please respond."

A voice came over the radio. "Capitalists. You think everything and everyone can be bought. Well, you are about to pay for your crimes."

At least the pilot was responding. That meant there might be a way to negotiate. "You want to protect the environment? I'll donate a hundred million dollars to environmental groups of your choice. Think of all the good you could do with that money."

"And let you complete your blasphemous abomination? Never."

The Vespa let loose another torrent of fire as it swung past.

Grant's mind raced. Fanatics like this would have no compunction about killing him and Carolina, and all the people on the platform. They'd proven that when they brought down NanoSpacial's elevator. But what else could he offer?

And then he realized he was thinking like a businessman, not an engineer. The man attacking them was unstable; all he needed was a little force applied in the right direction.

"Never mind," Grant said. "I withdraw my offer. My pilot tells me your bullets can't do enough harm to bring us down. So go ahead, keep firing. This has to be the most pathetic attempt at a terrorist attack I've ever seen."

Carolina looked at him, her eyes wide.

"You lie," said the voice on the radio.

"Been nice talking to you, but I'm bored now. Say hello to your masters for me; I'm sure they'll be real pleased with your mission failure. Goodbye." He took off the headset.

"Are you crazy? What was that about?" said Carolina.

"I hope I convinced him that firing on us was useless. I also hope that you weren't exaggerating the strength of the material the Cetus is made from."

The Vespa had turned, and was approaching again. It was hard to tell from this angle whether it was increasing in speed.

"What?"

"Brace yourself. I hope he's going to ram us."

Suddenly the roar of the jet overwhelmed his ears. It was definitely lower than before.

Grant's body slammed into the safety restraints. He felt a sharp pain in his neck as his head was jerked to the side.

The roar of the jet faded. The crew compartment swung from side to side.

"Check the radar," he said. "Where's the jet?"

Carolina rubbed her neck as she looked at the readout. "It's below us, and going down fast. I think it may be out of control. What happened?"

"He rammed us. It was our only chance. If he'd broken through into one of the compartments, I think he would have set off the hydrogen, and you said the Cetus could take that. But he didn't break through, so he just crashed his plane into us at a few hundred miles an hour, and I think the g-forces knocked him out." The collision might even have killed the pilot, but with the Cetus acting like a giant airbag, it wasn't certain.

She stared at him. "That's a lot of confidence in the construction of this thing."

"No, it was confidence in you. You told me what this ship could withstand, and I believed you."

Carolina turned away, and began checking her console. Then she gasped. "The jet is coming back up. He must have recovered in time."

Grant bit his lower lip. "Any ideas? It'll probably take one even crazier than my last one."

She shook her head.

The Vespa rose beside them, hovering about forty meters off their port side. The howl of the engine filled the cabin as it drew closer. Knowing that he was going to die, Grant felt a strange calm. He could even see the irony that a Vespa was going to kill a Cetus – a wasp was going to kill a whale.

Suddenly, Grant shouted, "The letters on the side! You said you could release them? Do it!"

"Release them?" Carolina's hands flew to the keyboard on her console.

The Vespa drew closer; any moment now the pilot would begin to fire on the cabin.

Something white fluttered in the window, and suddenly it was sucked toward the Vespa and into its large turbine. The engine's roar turned into the scream of tortured metal, and the Vespa started to fall. Its guns began firing, but it was too late.

Both of them watched as the plane dropped until it disappeared in the clouds below.

Carolina spoke first. "I didn't think a thin sheet of plastic would do that much damage to an engine."

"It wasn't the sheet. It was the rope attached to the sheet. Ever tried to untangle fishing line from a motorboat engine?"

Grant watched his dream come true on CNN. The screen showed the cable-crawler as it covered the last few meters to the Sullivan station in geosynchronous orbit. When it reached its proper position, it stopped, and several of his astronauts swarmed around it to lock it into place. CNN began to scroll text across the bottom of the screen: "Sullivan Space Technologies wins $250 million Otis Prize for first space elevator."

The employees who were gathered in Grant's office began to cheer. He went around and shook their hands, thanking each of them for the effort they had put into the project. They were only a fraction of those who had worked on the SpaceLifter, and Grant planned to do a lot more handshaking in the coming weeks. He didn't say anything now, but he also planned to pay a lot of bonuses as soon as the prize money was awarded.

Eventually the crowd thinned, until only Willy and Carolina were left.

"Hard to believe it's over," he said. "I've focused so much on this over the past few years. I'm not sure what's next."

"You'll find something," said Willy. "There's always something new, something farther."

"Something farther?" Grant thought for a moment. "Well, I've heard a rumor that NASA's thinking about funding a manned mission to Jupiter." He looked at Carolina. "Think you can build a blimp that would work in that atmosphere?"

* * *

In early 2004 I heard about All Star Zeppelin Adventure Stories, *a "retro-pulp" anthology soliciting submissions of stories that involved zeppelins. Since I had grown up reading anthologies of science fiction short stories from the pulp era, I decided to try my hand at writing an old-fashioned* Astounding-Science-Fiction-*type story... with zeppelins and a bit of updated technology. I submitted the story and it was rejected.*

Sometimes a story written for a themed anthology becomes hard to sell elsewhere. Fortunately, old-fashioned Astounding-Science-Fiction-*type stories still have a market:* Analog Science Fiction & Fact, *formerly known as* Astounding Science Fiction. *Stan Schmidt liked it enough that he asked me to make some changes (mainly to provide a little reasonableness on the environmentalist side.) I made the changes, and he bought it.*

Selling a story to Analog *was something I had hoped might eventually happen in the course of my writing career. For me to have a story published in the same magazine that had published Isaac Asimov and Robert A. Heinlein (and published in the same issue as Larry Niven) was a dream that came true much faster than I anticipated.*

I sometimes wish I had called the story "The Great Space Elevator Race," because I feel "Resonance" is too generic. But it's too late now.

Betrayer of Trees

Some of the younger stoneworkers in the guild called him Janal the Stonemage, but he knew there was no magic in his work. It was merely the skills he'd learned over nearly fifty years of carving that allowed him to turn rough-hewn stone into delicate beauty. His wrinkled hands were no longer as strong as they had been, and his pace had slowed, but when the townsfolk of Capeton wanted stonework of the highest quality, they always asked the guildmaster to assign Janal.

Word of his work had spread far enough that several times he had been offered a commission in one of the nearer cities, especially in the fifteen years since woodcarving had been outlawed by Imperial decree. But Janal always turned them down. Capeton was his home, he would tell them, and he never wanted to leave it.

Fifty years he'd lived in Capeton, and the townsfolk considered him one of their own. After fifty years, few even remembered he had not been born there. Janal himself rarely thought of his life before.

And then he started dreaming of the trees again.

He had thought the dreams were a young man's burden, that he had outgrown them. But now they returned to plague his sleep.

Tonight when he'd awakened with the screams of the trees in his ears, it had taken him several minutes to realize that he was not back in the forest of the Treefolk, not back in the land of his birth. It was only in dream that the trees cried out accusingly, revealing him before his people as the Betrayer of Trees. It was not real. It was not real.

Except that he knew he really was the Betrayer of Trees.

The next morning Janal was assigned to carve a decorative frieze of a horse above the doorframe of one of the wealthier merchants in town. The horse was the symbol of the Emperor Tilu, and over the past twenty years it had become a popular symbol for peace and good fortune, so Janal had carved hundreds of them.

He hardly thought as he worked; the hammer and chisel moved almost of their own accord. It was not until he was almost done he realized that instead of a smooth and gentle form, it was sharply angled. The horse's teeth were bared in anger and its sharp hooves raised to strike.

Why had he done that? It was the dreams, he realized. They were taking him back to his youth, back to the time he had first seen horses. The horses of the armies of the Warlord Tilu had looked like this as they thundered across the countryside destroying all who stood before them.

"Janal, what are you doing?" Guildmaster Lintoko interrupted his thoughts.

"I don't know. I guess I was distracted. I'll fix it."

"Forget it. I'll have someone else take care of it. Something more important has come up."

There was a sadness in his old friend's voice that made Janal apprehensive. Carefully laying down his hammer and chisel, he turned to face the other. "Yes?"

"I have to send you north, to the Imperial city."

Janal shook his head. "Please, not me. Send one of the youngsters—they long to leave our city and see the world."

"I can't send one of them. There's too much work to do. And face it, Janal, you just aren't able to work as fast as you used to. If it weren't for the fact that we have more work than we can handle, I'd have let you retire a couple of years ago."

The Imperial decree disbanding the Carpenters Guild and outlawing the carving of wood had not had much direct impact in Capeton, for few trees grew in the sandy soil and those that did were mostly unsuitable for carving anything of lasting value. But the increased demand for stoneworkers in cities suddenly forced to abandon the use of wood had led some of Capeton's younger stoneworkers to leave in search of higher wages. Even after fifteen years the effects still lingered.

Janal had often wondered why the Emperor had outlawed woodcarving. It was the tree magic of lifebinding that had extended the Emperor's life, so was it out of respect that the Emperor protected all trees? Or was it merely fear, the fear that someone might find the tree to which his life was bound and cut it down, thereby bringing his unnaturally long reign to an end?

Janal shook his head. He had started working in stone long before the Imperial decree. It did not affect him. What mattered now was that he dared not go anywhere near the Emperor. Janal had betrayed the trees, betrayed his family and abandoned the faith of his people to give Tilu what he demanded. And after all that, the Emperor Tilu had sentenced him to death.

"If you need me, why are you sending me away?" said Janal.

Lintoko gave an exasperated sigh. "Because, by Imperial order, the Stoneworkers Guild in every city must send someone to work on the new palace the Emperor's building. Oh, there's a lot of flowery language about how this will show the unity of the Empire, but what it all boils down to is they're going to leave me one man shorter than I already am."

"Please, Lintoko. Send someone else."

Lintoko put a reassuring hand on his shoulder. "I've never asked you what you were fleeing when you came to Capeton, and I'm not asking now. But it's been a long time. Surely it makes no difference now. No one would even recognize you now, am I not right?"

Janal tilted his head thoughtfully. His old friend was right; no one in the Imperial city would recognize Janal the aged master stoneworker as Jintuk the young apprentice treemage under sentence of death.

But the trees would know him still. The trees knew the soul of a man, not the body, and their memories were as long as they were tall. He could not enter the forest of the Treefolk, or even go near, lest they cry out against the Betrayer of the Trees.

But there would be no need to go near the trees. He nodded his acceptance, and Lintoko smiled gratefully.

"You will have Guild money for your journey, so you will be able to sleep in comfort even where there is not a Guild house." Suddenly Lintoko clapped his palm to his forehead. "And I have not even told you the best part! The Emperor is paying double Guild wages—which are higher there than here as it is—and the Council of Guildmasters has decided that you may keep half the excess. How do you like that? If this palace takes long enough to build, you'll be rich. And maybe by the time you get back, we can both retire and spend our days sitting around a fire swapping tales, and our nights chasing young women and tasting aged wine."

"Or chasing aged wine and tasting young women." Janal smiled; he would miss Lintoko.

The Guildmaster finished the old joke. "Just so long as it is not young wine and aged women."

During the nearly three months of the journey, the dreams of the trees had gotten more frequent the closer he came to the Imperial city. Perhaps it was because there were more and more trees along the way; he could feel them slumbering silently alongside the road. A treemage could awaken the souls of the trees, but he did not want them to see the betrayal that scarred

his soul. Probably he could not wake them if he tried; he had not used the
magic of the trees since leaving his homeland.

Sometimes in the dreams the trees would joyfully welcome him home
to take his rightful place as a treemage, helping to shape the gifts of the
trees, using magic to form the living wood into whatever his people needed.
But usually the trees of his dreams denounced him for the betrayer he was.
Sometimes the other Treefolk would quickly surround him, and one of them
would be carrying an axe. He would try to use the skills of concealment
he'd learned as a child hiding in the forest, but there was no hiding from the
trees. From those dreams he would awaken drenched in sweat, tangled in the
sheets of a strange bed in some inn or Guild house, and clutching at his right
arm to make sure it was still there.

As he and his traveling companions crested the hill and looked down
upon the valley of the Imperial city, Janal sucked in his breath. When he was
young, he had passed through many cities before he found his new home
in Capeton. This was the largest city he had seen: a jumble of buildings
extending out from the old palace and stretching further along the banks of
the river. The Tilurun River, it was called now, after the Emperor Tilu. On
the other side of the valley he could see the rising pillars of the new palace,
the palace he would help to build.

"Is it really the biggest city in the world? Capeton would fit a hundred times
into that," said Skint. He was young, a painter just done with his apprenticeship,
and like a few of the others in their party he had come with Janal all the way
from Capeton. He'd never been more than a few days' journey from home
before, and he showed it by greeting each new sight with wonder.

Janal smiled and shrugged. "Could be. If it's not the biggest, it will be
eventually. Emperor Tilu will see to that." He'd taken a liking to the young
painter. Perhaps it was because he'd been younger than Skint when he'd left
home—had to leave home—and through him was experiencing what that
first journey should have been like.

"Do you think we'll get to meet the Emperor?"

"I doubt it." Seeing Skint's crestfallen look, Janal said, "But you will get
to see him, I'm sure." I just hope he does not see me, and if he does, that
he does not recognize me. But it's been too long, he reassured himself. He
cannot know me again after fifty years.

"Is it true the Emperor has a hundred guards to guard him, and a
hundred lords and ladies to always walk before him and after him singing
his praise?"

"I don't know. Sounds too noisy if you ask me."

They made their way down into the city, into the midst of the buildings of stone and brick and cement. There were no wooden buildings, of course.

As their path took them through a bazaar in the city, Janal suddenly halted before a vendor's table. A variety of wooden implements and trinkets were displayed for sale at prices that made the wood almost as valuable as gold by weight. He'd known that illicit woodcarving still went on despite being outlawed, but he had not expected to see the law flouted so openly right here in the Imperial city.

"Ah," said the merchant, a fat red-bearded man dressed in fine silks. "You are a man who appreciates quality, are you not?"

"I thought woodcarving was outlawed." As he spoke, his surprise gave way to horror as he realized the artifacts had not been carved. They were gifts of the trees.

The merchant bobbed his head. "Of course. But these were not carved; they were fashioned by the fabled mages of the Treefolk, created by the trees themselves, untouched by knife or..."

Gifts of the trees, sold in a bazaar as expensive trinkets. Janal turned away in disgust, ignoring the rest of the merchant's patter.

"What's the matter? Are you all right?" Skint asked.

"It's nothing." Janal shook his head. "Let's get to the new palace and find out when we are to begin work."

Despite his misgivings before leaving Capeton, in the six months he'd been working on the new palace nothing bad had happened. He still dreamt of the trees too often. Some nights he even dreamt the memory he had spent most of his life trying to forget, and he would wake up begging himself not to do it, not to chop off the branch. But those were only dreams, and no evil came of them other than the grumblings of those who were tired of being woken by his talking in his sleep.

During the days, though, Janal found himself enjoying the work. Many of the craftsmen were old as he or young like Skint, but the combination of youthful energy and experienced skill seemed to be working well. The palace would be complete in a few more months—long before he could become rich off the extra pay—but he thought it would be the most beautiful building in the world. There was satisfaction in being a part of that, even if it was for the benefit of the Emperor Tilu.

He would get no work done today, though, because it was the annual Peace Day celebration, commemorating the day the last of the Emperor's enemies surrendered before his horsemen and his rule extended to the sea that surrounded the land in all directions. There would be parades during the day and fireworks in the evening, but the biggest event for the laborers at the palace was that the Emperor himself would come to see the progress and would address them to give his thanks.

Since he had no desire to see the Emperor and an active desire to not be seen by him, Janal decided to slip away into the city. Maybe he would watch the parades; maybe he would find an alehouse and get drunk. Maybe both.

As he wandered along one of the main thoroughfares made more crowded than usual by those who had come to the city for Peace Day, he was startled out of his thoughts by a man's shout.

"Make way for the treemage! Make way for the treemage!"

A treemage? How could a treemage be here? They could not travel more than a few day's journey from the tree to which their soul was bound. Then he realized that the Imperial city was within that distance.

He found himself pushed aside as the crowd parted before the shouter. A young man clad in green silks was borne through the throngs on a litter carried on the shoulders of six strong men. The litter was made of wood.

Janal instantly recognized the young man in the litter, the treemage. It was his younger brother, Parvin.

Heart suddenly pounding, he turned away, pushing himself through the crowd. No one stopped him; no one cried out, "Look, it's the betrayer!" He turned down a narrow side street and leaned against a wall, taking deep breaths and willing his heart to slow.

Three years were all that had separated them, but now he was an old man while Parvin still looked young. Parvin was lifebound to a tree. His brother must have become an apprentice treemage after he'd left—it was good to know his betrayal had not been held against his family.

After a few minutes he left the alley, found a tavern and got himself very drunk.

Seeing Parvin made him wonder about what had happened to his family after he'd left. Over the next two weeks he often found himself lying awake on his cot, pondering whether his parents still lived, whether his brother and sisters had children or even grandchildren of their own now.

And it was not just his family's fate that now consumed his attention. What had happened to his people? That they prospered was apparent. But why were gifts of the trees now sold to outsiders? Why were treemages carried about like the idle rich?

Behind the curiosity was a growing desire to see his homeland once more, to walk once more among the wakened trees. The more he denied the desire, the greater it grew, until finally he convinced himself that the risk would not be great if he merely walked to the edge of his people's forest and looked at the trees. Surely that would not be too dangerous.

So he asked his supervisor for a few days off—to see his family, he said, which was not entirely a lie—and he began walking to the north, toward the land of the Treefolk.

Twice he turned back, but not for long. He slept that night beneath the stars, and before noon the next day he could see the edge of the forest. His people's forest. What had once been his forest.

Now that he could see his goal, he stopped, unsure of what to do next. The Emperor's soldiers guarded the forest. He should have known they would be there, protecting the forest from outsiders who might threaten the trees—one tree in particular.

Although he had the narrow face and green eyes of the Treefolk, his years in the south had given his skin a leathery brownness that contrasted too much with the pale smoothness of his people, who dwelt always in the shade. He could not pretend to be one of the Treefolk returning to the forest.

But now he was so close that his desire would not be denied. Using the stealthy skills he had almost forgotten until his dreams had brought them to mind again, he crept closer to the forest without being spotted.

Lying on the ground a few yards from the nearest tree, he decided he was close enough. He opened his mind to hear the singing of the trees, the song he had not heard except in memory since he'd fled.

Nothing. He heard nothing.

Unable to believe it, he crawled closer still, until at last he was in the forest itself. He strained again to hear the trees, and though he could sense their souls awake around him, he could not hear them singing.

And they should be always singing.

Was it his fault? Had his betrayal somehow silenced the song?

No, that was not it. For surely the trees had sensed him by now, and would be calling out to each other that the Betrayer of Trees had returned. Warning each other against the betrayer, warning the Treefolk. And he should have heard those cries, but he did not. He was deaf to the trees.

Heedless now of the danger, he almost ran to the place he knew he must go, to the tree whose branch he had stolen. His people would be coming soon. They would capture him and punish him, but he wanted them to find him there, returned to the place of his crime.

He fell to his knees when he saw the tree.

It had been his tree, the tree with which he was to lifebind. He remembered it as a small oak, only fifteen years old but growing straight and strong and tall. That was before he'd chopped off one of its limbs. He'd taken care to disguise the cut so it wasn't obvious, so a visual search wouldn't reveal which tree the branch had come from.

But now the tree stood out, a crooked, misshapen thing, stunted in its growth. Its scrawny branches and twigs had few leaves, and it seemed scarred by disease and age.

"I'm sorry." He reached out with his mind toward the soul of the tree he had betrayed, to try to let it know how sorry he was. And found nothing there. The soul of the tree was gone.

That was too much for him, and he crawled to the base of the tree and cried, knowing his people would come for him soon.

"Why are you crying?"

It was a child's voice, and Janal raised his head to see a young girl of about five years looking at him. He wiped at his tears with the back of his hand.

"I'm crying because of what happened to this tree," he said.

"That's the Emperor's tree. You're supposed to stay away from it."

The Treefolk knew which tree it was, of course. But the Emperor didn't, which would be why there were guards around the forest instead of just this tree. Or maybe the Emperor knew, and just did not want to call attention to this tree.

He rose to his feet, sniffing. They would be here for him soon, he supposed. Let them find him on his feet. Looking at the girl, he said, "If you're supposed to stay away from it, what are you doing here?"

"I heard someone crying, so I came." She frowned. "Old people aren't supposed to cry. Little babies cry."

"Sometimes grownups cry, when they are sorry they did something bad."

"Oh." A pause. "Did you do something bad?"

He nodded. "Yes. I did something bad. But I'm sorry I did."

"It's good to be sorry when you do something bad."

"Yes."

"And you should never ever do it again."

"Right." He almost smiled. She must be repeating a lecture from her parents. Who would no doubt be here soon, horrified to find their little girl talking with the Betrayer of Trees.

He was surprised no one else had arrived yet. "What are the trees saying?"

Her eyes went wide. "You can't hear them?"

He shook his head.

"They aren't talking right now. They're just singing the song."

"They are? They weren't talking about... anyone, just a few minutes ago?"

"No, they're just singing the song."

Relief and horror mingled together. It mean there was no outcry to capture the betrayer; he might still make it out of the forest. But it also meant the trees could not see his soul. Perhaps, like the victim of his betrayal, he no longer had one.

His thoughts turned to his family. "Tell me, do you know the treemage named Parvin?"

She nodded. "He's mama's uncle."

Which would make this girl his grandniece. He thought he could see a trace of his mother in the girl's eyes, a hint of his father in her cheeks. "Do you know if his mama and papa are still alive? Their names are Irella and Dal?"

She shrugged. "Uncle Parvin is very rich and important and I have to be quiet when he comes to visit."

Janal nodded. "That's right. And you shouldn't bother an important man by telling him about me."

"Someday I'll go to the big city and people will have to be quiet when I say."

Is that what the Treefolk children dream of now? What kind of example are you setting, Parvin? He quelled those thoughts. He knew he could not risk staying longer. "Well, I must leave now. It was nice to meet you."

"Goodbye. And stay away from the Emperor's tree."

Making his way out of the forest, he crept past the soldiers without incident. He returned to the Imperial city without looking back.

The stonework for the new palace was almost done. Because the supervisors had noticed his talent for delicate work, his current assignment was to carve a rearing horse on the top of the Emperor's throne. His hands flowed smoothly in their work, but his thoughts were distant.

A few more days and he could begin the long journey back to Capeton. He would not wait around to see the other craftsmen complete their jobs so the Emperor could declare the palace complete and give them his thanks.

Since his experience in the forest, his dreams had changed. The trees no longer called him the betrayer: sometimes they called him the stealer of souls, sometimes they called him the soulless one. Either way, it was worse. He'd always known he was the betrayer and could feel the truth of it, but he was not accustomed to his new titles. He hoped these dreams would fade once he returned to Capeton. The dreams had faded before, but it had taken years.

With a start, he noticed that the chatter of the workers around him had trickled to silence. Turning, he saw the Emperor flanked by his guards and accompanied by many of the lords and ladies of the court. Immediately Janal prostrated himself, but he knew it was too late. The Emperor had been staring at him.

"You, stoneworker, what is your name?"

He peeked up, and the Emperor was still looking at him. "I am Janal, your Majesty."

"Janal, you say?" the Emperor frowned. "What is this you are carving upon my throne?"

Janal looked up at the horse he had been carving and his heart sank within him. Where there should have been a horse there was a delicate oak tree made of marble, stretching its branches up to the sky, with individual leaves that seemed almost ready to flutter in the wind. It was what his tree could have become, had he not betrayed it to the corrupting soul of the Emperor.

It was the most beautiful thing he had ever created. And it was a terrible mistake. How could he excuse himself before the Emperor?

The Emperor Tilu was a hundred and twenty-seven year old, but looked no older than he had fifty years before, when a young apprentice had betrayed the trees to perform the lifebinding magic. Having seen men grow old around him, perhaps he would make allowances for age. So Janal said, "Forgive me, your Majesty. I am old and my mind wanders. I'm sure another stoneworker will be able to carve a horse fitting for your throne."

"Tell me, *Janal*, where do you come from?"

It was worse than he'd thought. From the way the Emperor emphasized his name, Janal was sure he had been recognized. Still, there was the possibility the Emperor was not certain, so he decided to keep to his new identity. "Capeton, your Majesty. To the south."

"Capeton." The Emperor nodded. "That's about as far from here as one can go without sailing into the Endless Sea."

Janal nodded.

The Emperor did not speak for several minutes. Janal shifted uncomfortably, but was determined not to give himself away.

"I come from a roaming tribe of the plains," said the Emperor. "A tribe of horsemen. But all the world knows that. What you may not know is that my people have a custom of sitting around the campfire at night and telling stories. Do your people have a similar custom? Your people of the *far south*?"

Janal was puzzled, but he said, "Yes, your Majesty. Although we usually tell our tales while sitting at a table drinking ale."

"Good, good." The Emperor looked around at his guards and all the lords and ladies, then back to Janal. "Then I will tell one of our tribal stories. Would you like to hear it?"

There was no answer possible but "Yes, your Majesty."

"We must all sit." The Emperor strode to his throne and sat. Since the palace was not yet fully furnished, there were no other seats in the room, but when the Emperor made an insistent downward wave of his hand, the lords and ladies lowered themselves gingerly to the ground. His guards, however, remained standing.

"When the world was not so old as it is now," began the Emperor, "there was a young man who was gifted in the magic of horses. A horsemage, you might say. Now, I know there is no such thing as horse magic, but this is only a story. This young man, whose name was... Let me think... His name was *Jintuk*."

Janal only gave a small twitch upon hearing his original name, but when he saw the Emperor smile he knew he had given himself away. To his surprise, the Emperor did not order the guards to arrest him, but continued with the story.

"One day, Jintuk's peaceful tribe was attacked by a vicious warlord, a conqueror who had already taken half the plains as his own. This warlord was growing old and weak, and he wanted... Hmm." The Emperor paused. "He wanted the strength of a horse so he could continue to conquer, and he knew the elders of the tribe could give it to him. So he threatened to kill Jintuk's tribe and all their horses unless they performed their magic to give him that strength. The elders of the tribe tried to do as the warlord wanted. But they could not, because such magic would bind a horse to the warlord, and the horses could sense the warlord was an evil man. So the horses refused."

"Why did they refuse?" Janal couldn't stop himself from asking. "They were all going to be killed, so why didn't one of them consent?" That was the question that still haunted him after all these years. Why did the trees refuse?

The Emperor sighed. "A horse is wise in many ways, but foolish in others. A horse has a long memory, but a horse does not understand the future. It cannot choose something bad now in exchange for some benefit in the future."

Janal nodded. His people always spoke of the wisdom of the trees, but the trees were passive and peaceful. They had not understand what Tilu was threatening.

"So the young man, Jintuk, secretly cut off the tail of his favorite horse, and used it to give the warlord the strength he sought. Then Jintuk fled from his people forever, because the cutting of a horse's tail is a crime against the bond between his people and the horses. But the warlord was true to his promise, and did not kill the horses and their people. In fact, the warlord protected them from that time forth, so no harm would come to them."

Janal sighed. "Not the happiest of endings to the story, but it could have ended much worse."

The Emperor shook his head. "That is not the end of the story. For the evil warlord soon found that he was bound to the horse. Never again could he travel more than a few days distant from that horse. In his rage, he commanded that Jintuk be put to death."

Janal sat very still. He should have realized that a conqueror such as Tilu—particularly a nomadic horseman—would not want to be tied to one place. And yet, that was part of the magic. Tilu had demanded long life, and he had gotten it. Even though he was bound to one place, Tilu's armies had conquered the rest of the nations and made him Emperor of the whole world. Did he still hold the grudge?

The Emperor sat in silence.

Finally, Janal had to ask, "And was he put to death?"

"No, because the warlord never found him."

"And that is how the story ends?" For a moment, Janal dared to hope. Perhaps this story was the Emperor's way of giving him an unofficial pardon.

"No, there is still more. For the horse hated the evil soul of the warlord to which it was bound. But the bond was too strong to be broken. Every day the soul of the horse fought against the soul of the warlord. For years they fought, until one day, the horse won."

Janal felt dizzy. "The horse won?" Did that mean what he thought it did?

The Emperor nodded.

Janal tentatively reached out with his mind and there it was: the soul of a tree—his tree—inside the Emperor.

"Forgive me," he whispered.

The Emperor continued speaking as if Janal had not said anything. "Once the soul of the horse had the mind of a man, it understood why Jintuk did what he did, and of course forgave him."

Through his tears, Janal said, "And... and Jintuk's people?"

"They understood all along. They did not condemn him for what he did, although they would have had to banish him from the... from the corral, because the horses did not understand, at least not yet. But he fled so far, so fast, they could not find him to tell him he could have stayed nearby."

His shoulders sagged, and he sighed. He had been old enough to understand what must be done, too young to know that others understood. "In a way, that ending is sadder than the one before."

"It is." The Emperor nodded. "But I am old, and my memory fails me sometimes. I'm not sure if that was the ending. Maybe the ending was when Jintuk finally came home, and was welcomed by the people and the horses. Maybe one of the horses even gives him the strength of his tail."

Janal thought about it. He'd dreamed of that. Welcomed home as a hero. Seeing his family again. Finally becoming a treemage and being lifebound to a tree. But those dreams were when he was young. It was too late now; his life had taken a different path.

"A question, your Majesty? What happened to Jintuk's parents? In the story?"

The Emperor's eyes were sad. "They died years later, always hoping to see their son again. But his brother and sisters lived on and had children and grandchildren of their own."

"I see." Janal nodded slowly.

They sat in silence for a while. Though Janal now knew the things he'd wondered about for so long, he didn't understand why the Emperor didn't just come right out and explain what had happened. Then he noticed all the guards and lords and ladies. What would they do if they knew their conquering Emperor had been replaced by a tree?

My tree is the ruler of all mankind, he thought, and he smiled. Not a bad ruler, really. The empire is peaceful now, and people are generally free to live their lives.

Then he thought of Parvin being carried on a wooden litter through the city streets, and gifts of the trees being sold in the marketplace, and a little girl who had to be quiet because her uncle was an important man.

"Your Majesty, I thank you for your story. Now I would like to tell you one of our southern stories."

The Emperor motioned for him to go ahead.

"When the world was not so old as it is now, there was a village that was near a magical stone quarry."

"Magical stones?"

"Not really, your Majesty, but this is only a story. This magical stone quarry would provide the villagers with whatever they needed, for their own use. And the villagers lived happily. Then one day, a... a king came who wanted something from the quarry. One young man—Jintuk is as good a name as any, I suppose—broke the law of the quarry and gave the king what he wanted."

"He probably had good reason to break the law."

"He may have thought so, but in this story it does not matter. Fearing punishment, Jintuk ran off to the end of the world, where he became a... a woodworker."

The Emperor's eyes went wide. "A woodworker?"

"It was not against the law, in this story. In any case, he's not important to the next part of the story. The king now became a friend to the villagers and the magical quarry. In fact, he hated to see anything made of stone that did not come from the quarry, and he banned all stoneworking, except from the magical quarry. Until then, the villagers only asked the stone quarry for things they needed. But now, since they were the only source of stone items, they began to sell them at high prices. Some of the villagers became rich and proud."

"Did they?"

"They did. And one day when Jintuk came back to the village, he saw that it was no longer the village he had left; that some of the people were greedy and haughty. And not only that, but he could no longer hear the music of the quarry."

"The music?"

"Oh, I forgot to mention that the magical quarry made beautiful music that the villagers could hear. But after so many years away, Jintuk could no longer hear it. The changes in his village and not being able to hear the music made him realize that he no longer belonged to that world. Though he had longed to go back, he had made his life as a woodworker. And it was a good life, a life he was glad he had lived. So, feeling sad for what had happened to his village, he returned to the friends he had made at the end of the world and lived the rest of his life as a woodworker."

"It seems your story does not end too happily either."

"Well, I'm not certain that's the end. Maybe the king lifts the ban on stoneworking, and the villagers eventually stop abusing the magic of the quarry and become content once again."

Nodding, the Emperor said, "Maybe the king only wanted to protect the villagers, and didn't realize he was doing them harm. Maybe when he finds out about it, he tries to set things straight."

"Yes, I think that must be how it ends."

"Well, Janal, I thank you for an entertaining story." The emperor rose, then turned to look at the marble tree carved atop his throne. "As for this carving, I find it beautiful. It shall remain here to remind the people that, like a tree, the Emperor Tilu provides shelter and strength to his people."

Janal prostrated himself. "I am honored, your Majesty."

"And since I have no more need of your services as a stoneworker, I suppose you'll be leaving now for..."

"Capeton, your Majesty."

"Yes, Capeton. At the end of the world. Have a safe journey, Janal."

"Thank you, your Majesty."

After Janal returned home, months passed, then a year. Eventually an Imperial decree came that carpentry was no longer against the law. Several of the younger stoneworkers in the Capeton guild began experimenting with imported wood, and with Janal's encouragement they formed a Carpenters Guild a few months later.

He declined the invitation to be their guildmaster, however. He was a stoneworker, he told them, and he never wanted to be anything else. But he would occasionally stop by their guild hall just to feel wood beneath his hands once more.

Even though he was officially retired, Janal still worked at the Guild carving stone on most days. And most nights, he dreamed he could still hear the song of the trees rising in the forest to welcome him.

* * *

In July 2003 I attended Orson Scott Card's Literary Boot Camp, a week-long writing workshop, held that year in Greensboro, North Carolina. One of the assignments was to go to the library, find a section on a subject I was not familiar with, and do some research to find a story idea. I ended up in the arts and crafts magazine section, where I found a magazine about woodworking. I read a quote from someone talking about the feel of wood in his hands as he was shaping it. As usual, I put a speculative spin on the idea, so I started thinking about wood that shaped itself, and what relationship the people who lived in the forest would have with the trees that magically supplied their needs. I then considered what would happen if one of the forest people had to take an axe to a tree in order to save his people.

I used that idea to write my story for the workshop, calling it "The Horseman and the Stoneworker." I got some great feedback from Card and my classmates (including Alethea Kontis's desire to slap some sense into my characters), so I worked on revising the story over the next few months. With the December 2003 deadline for Writers of the Future looming, I still did not know whether "In Memory" was a winner, so I submitted the revised story with its new title, "Betrayer of Trees." It ended up taking second place.

American Banshee

Filiméala finished her keening as "Dapper" Donny O'Grady, head of the O'Grady mob, breathed his last. Leaning over his bed, she planted a kiss on his age-mottled forehead. She was glad he had died peacefully at home, rather than in a rain of bullets, like too many of the extended family.

"Right, then, we're done with that infernal screeching," said Harry. "Time for you to be on your way."

Filiméala sat up straight and fixed her gaze on Harry. Even at thirty-five, he still had the air of an impatient six-year-old. She had never been sure whether his nickname "Hair-Trigger" was the result of his impatience or the cause of it. "Show some respect, lad," she said. "Your father has just passed on. I have sung his soul—"

"Right, right," Harry said. "My father, may he rest, etcetera. But I'm head of the family now, and there are going to be some changes, starting with you."

"Me?" Filiméala could not keep the startlement from her voice. She had been with the family O'Grady for over five hundred years, even following some of them to America during the Great Famine—though her spirit still yearned sometimes for the hills of the Old Country. The last major change in her life had been over sixty years ago, when Dapper Donny's father had convinced her to keen the deaths of all members of the O'Grady mob, even if they were not family by blood. What could Harry want of her?

"Yes, you. My father was one for the old ways, but this is the 21st Century. We don't need a banshee shrieking about, frightening the neighbors, whenever someone's going to die."

"*Bean Sídhe*," Filiméala corrected. "The B is—"

"That's exactly what I'm talking about. We're in America, so speak American. But that's not the point. The point is, you're a symbol of the past."

"Your father and grandfather—"

"Are dead. And all you could do was wail about it. Now, if you could actually warn us someone was going to die in time for us to prevent it..." He cocked an eyebrow at her.

She shook her head. Harry had never been the brightest fish in the barrel. "That's just foolishness, lad. If you prevented a man from dying, I would not feel the call to sing his death now, would I?"

Grabbing her by the left wrist, Harry said, "I am head of the family now. You will show me respect."

She nodded.

He twisted her arm behind her back. "They say if you capture a banshee, she must tell you the name of who is going to die. You must have been giving my father that information, which could still be useful, even if the death can't be prevented."

"Rubbish," Filiméala said. "If it's obvious who will die, like your father on his deathbed, then I know, just the same as anyone else. But usually I keen the death without knowing whose it is. Who told you such nonsense?"

"I read it on Wikipedia," Harry said, his voice defensive.

She didn't use the computer in her room for much more than emailing some of her sister *Bean Sídhe* back in the Old Country, who were constantly forwarding her chain letters and YouTube clips. The Internet did not seem worthy of trust to her, because she did not understand the magic behind it. Humans were different—willing to rely on magic beyond their mortal comprehension. "I believe I know my own powers better than Wikipedia."

"Whatever." Harry released her arm and waved dismissively. "If you can't make yourself useful, then I see no reason not to replace you."

"Replace me?" Her voice rose to a squeak, and she struggled to lower its pitch and speak in a reasonable tone. "I have served your family faithfully all these centuries, and now you want to bring in another *Bean Sídhe* to take my place? I promise you, she can tell you no more than I."

"Not another banshee," he said. He pulled his cell phone out of his pocket. "The head of one of the Haitian gangs owed me a favor. One of his men voodooed an app for my iPhone that will warn me when an O'Grady is going to die, but since I can set it to play any mp3 I want as the warning, it's more discreet—and a whole lot easier on the ears." He grinned at her. "You, my dear, are obsolete."

Filiméala pulled her gray cloak tight around herself. "If you have no need of me, then I will retire to my room."

"I don't think you understand yet," said Harry. "Get out of my house and don't come back."

Filiméala found it hard to breathe, like she had been kicked in the stomach by a stubborn mule. "Where shall I go? What shall I do?"

"This is America, the land of opportunity," Harry said with a sharky grin. "I'm sure you'll find something."

Dapper Donny's widow, Meara, slipped some paper into Filiméala's palm as a couple of Harry's strongmen escorted her to the sidewalk outside the walls of the mansion.

Filiméala had not been outside the walls in decades. She resisted the urge to throw herself against the gates and beg to be allowed back in. She straightened her shoulders and walked away. She would not give Harry the satisfaction of seeing her devastated.

Éire. Back to Éire. That was where she would go, back to the emerald hills of the Old Country, where she would forget all about the family O'Grady and her brief hundred and sixty years in America.

But not by ship this time. With a small shudder she remembered the journey by steamship, all the passengers crowded together in a space hardly big enough to contain them.

No, she would take one of the aeroplanes of which Donny had often spoken. How grand it must be to sail above the clouds, free as a nightingale on the breeze. She would merely have to ignore the fact that she did not understand the magic that held aeroplanes up in the air. Perhaps it was the same magic that had prevented a steamship made of iron from sinking like a stone in the ocean.

But first she must get to the airport. She looked at the papers Meara had given her: several hundred-dollar bills. She hoped it would be enough.

After some frantic waving on her part, an orange-colored taxicab pulled over and she got in.

"Where to?" asked the driver.

"The airport, please," Filiméala said, faking confidence.

"Which one?"

"Em... One with aeroplanes that go to Éire—Ireland?"

"You want JFK?"

She wasn't sure what that meant, but across the years, Donny had spoken about an American President named JFK, and if she recalled correctly he had been of good Irish stock. Maybe it was a sign she was on the right path.

"Take me to JFK," she said.

After a terrifying ride filled with unexpected jolts, random noises, and a great deal of cursing in a tongue unknown to Filiméala, the driver pulled to a stop and said, "You probably want Aer Lingus. That's this terminal."

She gave him one of her hundred-dollar bills, and he drove away very happily.

It took a quarter of an hour for Filiméala to get to the front of the Aer Lingus line.

"What is your final destination?" asked a pert lass behind the counter.

"I just want to go back to Éire," Filiméala said.

The lass's brow furrowed. "You don't have a ticket?"

"No." Filiméala dropped the rest of the money Meara had given her on the counter. "Is that enough?"

After counting the money, the lass typed at her keyboard. "You're in luck. There's a seat available on our 5:45 flight to Dublin for $740. Will that do?"

"Yes." Filiméala sighed with relief. Everything would be better once she got back to Éire.

"I'll just need to see your passport," the lass said.

"Em... my what?"

"Your passport."

"I don't have one. Can I buy one here?"

The lass got a strange look on her face and excused herself to go talk to an older man.

After several frustrating conversations during which Filiméala was forced to explain over and over to each new person that she came to America years ago without a passport and that all she wanted to do was go back to Éire, they put her in a room to wait for someone from the Irish consulate.

She had a feeling the explanation that she had come across the Atlantic one hundred and sixty years ago was not going to go over well. They would never let her go back to Éire.

A television on the wall cycled through news stories. She let the babble fade into the background as she wallowed in her misery, until she heard a familiar song. She looked up to see on the screen something she had seen on YouTube: a middle-aged woman singing before an audience that went wild with applause. She began to listen to what the newsman was saying.

"While in the past their show has focused on singers under thirty, the producers of *American Idol* have announced that they would also like to find the American equivalent of Susan Boyle, the 48-year-old Scottish singer who became an overnight internet sensation. So for all you older singers out there, maybe this is your opportunity to make it big. The open auditions start tomorrow at Giants Stadium."

Harry had told her this was the land of opportunity. Maybe it was time to stop feeling sorry for herself and start making a new life for herself. If a

Scotswoman could become a star, why not an Irishwoman—and one of the *Bean Sídhe*, no less?

Just as she stood up to walk out, the call of death hit her. Somewhere, five members of the O'Grady mob were about to die.

Harry had dismissed her from her service to the family—there was nothing to bind her to the O'Gradys any longer.

But the call was too strong. Dapper Donny had never been one for mob wars, so she hadn't sung for more than two deaths at once in decades. Filiméala tried to resist, but her knees buckled. The keening tore at her throat until finally she stopped resisting and let her voice burst forth.

The television screen shattered.

A uniformed man opened the door. "What are you—"

She directed her keening at him, and he grabbed his ears.

Filiméala walked past him and out of the airport terminal. She no longer needed an aeroplane. Her life had a purpose now: to become an American Idol.

Filiméala could not count how many people were in line to get into Giants Stadium, but surely it was thousands. Some of them even had tents. A lad with a clipboard handed her a sheet of paper with a series of questions to fill out, including date of birth. Filiméala first decided to make her age forty-eight to match Susan Boyle, then after eyeing the youth of the other contestants, changed it to thirty. She gradually shifted her appearance to be more youthful, turning her silver hair to golden blonde and smoothing the wrinkles of her skin. The persona of an old woman had served her well in a culture that valued age, but that time seemed long gone. America valued youth and beauty, and she needed to be more American if she wanted to be an American Idol.

Just to be safe, she de-aged herself down to twenty-five, then twenty.

"Whoa!" said the lad behind her in line. "What happened to the old lady?"

"Em," Filiméala said, "My grandmother held my place in line until I could get here. You won't tell anyone?" And she gave him a wink.

"Secret's safe with me," he said. "I'm Kip."

"Filiméala," she said. The name would have to be thrown out with her age, she realized with regret. "Call me Fi." And she wrote Fi O'Grady on the form.

After several hours, she and Kip, along with two other aspirants, were ushered into one of several large tents being used for auditions. A gray-haired man sat behind a folding table.

"Okay, let's hear what you've got," the man said.

Filiméala sang, her voice converting the silly required pop number into a powerful ballad filled with longing and hope. She continued to sing past the specified twenty seconds, filling the tent with her song. As she let the final notes drift away, the man wiped tears from his eyes.

"Wow," he said. "I can't wait to see what Simon——"

Filiméala was so caught up in the moment that the call of death caught her completely off guard. The lament for twelve O'Gradys burst forth from her mouth, and everyone in the tent grabbed their ears to seal out the sound, then fled.

Something within her had changed. Filiméala's keening had never been so powerful before. It was as if she had tapped a new source of power—and unfortunately, she was not used to handling it. Before she could get it under control, the fabric of the tent was torn to shreds, which whirled around her in a tornado of cloth.

Amid the screaming, panicked chaos of thousands of aspiring singers, Filiméala walked out of the stadium.

She would never be an American Idol. But perhaps it was time to show Harry just how useless a *Bean Sídhe* was.

Harry sat behind the mahogany desk in what had been Dapper Donny's study. He didn't look up from the papers he was reading when his men escorted Filiméala in.

She sat in a maroon leather chair and waited.

Without looking up, he said, "Your message said you had found a way to be useful?"

"Yes." She spoke meekly, like a penitent child.

He looked up, then started as he took in her new appearance. "Like the new look. Maybe I can find a use for you as something other than a banshee."

Filiméala felt the call of death, and a moment later tinny music began to play in Harry's pocket. He pulled out his iPhone and stared at it.

Suppressing the desire to keen, she leaned forward. "Does the voodoo in your phone tell you the name of who is going to die?"

"No."

"I can tell you," she said, her voice a rough whisper as she held back the song.

He snorted. "You said before that you couldn't."

"Things are different now. I think after all these years in America, my *Bean Sídhe* power is tapping the strength of America, rather than Éire."

"Right, then," he said. "Is it one of the O'Malley boys? I sent them to deal with some Italian troublemakers."

"'Tis neither of the O'Malley boys," she said. "The name of the one who will die is Harold Standish O'Grady."

His eyes widened as Filiméala unleashed her full voice. He leaped from his chair and clapped his hands to his ears while screaming an inaudible order to his guards. The force of the song slammed him back against the oak-paneled wall and pinned him there.

The flesh of his face rippled, then piece after piece tore away. The bones of his skull fractured, then refractured again and again until they were ground to powder, held in place only by the standing waves of sound produced by Filiméala's keening.

She stopped, and the remains of Harry "Hair-Trigger" O'Grady collapsed into a wet heap on the floor.

Filiméala became aware that the guards had their guns pointed at her. They were repeatedly pulling the triggers, resulting in ineffective clicks since they had run out of bullets. Metallic dust lay on the floor a few feet in front of them, remnants of the bullets shattered by her song.

"Now, now, lads," she said. "I have nothing against you. And if you behave yourselves, it will be a good many years before I sing for your deaths."

They stopped pulling their triggers, but continued staring wide-eyed at her.

She walked around the desk and poked at Harry's corpse with her toe. "It seems the O'Grady mob lacks a head, and somebody needs to stop the mob war the late Mr. O'Grady began." In a whisper, she added, "You're the one who told me this was the land of opportunity."

Filiméala sat down in what had been Harry's chair and swiveled to face her guards. "Tell the rest of the clan that I'm in charge now."

"What should we call you, ma'am?" one of them asked.

"Filiméala O'Grady," she said. The continuity of the surname was important. But she also needed a nickname, so she added, "The American Banshee."

* * *

In 2007, Kevin J. Anderson invited me to submit to Blood Lite, *an anthology of humorous horror he was editing on behalf of the Horror Writers Association. I wrote a story called "P.R. Problems," which he accepted. Unfortunately, under the terms of that particular anthology contract, the story could not be included in this collection.*

Since Blood Lite *sold well, the publisher decided to publish a sequel. Kevin again asked me for a story, and "American Banshee" was the result.*

I wanted to stay away from the typical horror monsters, and after a little research I decided to write about a banshee. While brainstorming the story with a friend, she brought up the Hans Christian Anderson fairy tale "The Nightingale," in which an emperor prefers the song of a mechanical bird to that of a real nightingale. That gave me my basic premise: a banshee made obsolete by technology. The rest of the story flowed from that.

The Six Billion
Dollar Colon

When Jay Lake awoke after his colon surgery, he did not expect to see two men he didn't know, one in military uniform and the other wearing a lab coat. "Who are you guys?" he said, his voice barely a whisper.

"We're the men who just saved your life," said the military man.

"When your surgeon went in," said the man in the lab coat, "he found the damage to your colon was too extensive. It had to be replaced entirely. But there were no compatible colons available from donors."

"Fortunately for you, he knew about the secret government lab in the sub-basement of the hospital." The military man's voice showed an obvious disdain for the lack of security. "You were rushed down here, and we installed a bionic colon."

Still disoriented from the anesthesia, Jay wasn't sure he had heard that right. "A bionic colon?"

"That's right," said the man in the lab coat, "You're lucky you have good private health insurance, which picked up most of the six billion dollar tab."

"If this country had socialized medicine," said the military man, "then you'd still be on a waiting list. And the medical technology that made your bionic colon possible would never have been developed."

Jay snorted. "Is Eric James Stone writing your dialogue?"

"Never heard of him," said the military man. "He must not be a famous writer like you. In any case, you will need to provide a cover story to the public regarding the costs of your medical care. Perhaps something in the neighborhood of $75,000-$80,000, with only $1400 out of pocket for you."

"Did you really say the bionic colon cost six billion dollars?" Jay asked. "Yes."

"You used to be able to get a bionic eye, one arm, and two legs for only six million," said Jay. "What's this thing made out of, gasoline?"

Obviously misunderstanding Jay's ironic question, the medical man said, "Actually, it's powered by a fusion reactor." He picked up a diagram and pointed to various items as he spoke. "The reactor heats up the water in this boiler, creating steam pressure that then winds these gears that move the partially digested food through the colon."

Jay couldn't help grinning. "You gave me a fusion-powered steampunk clockwork colon? It doesn't turn into a zeppelin by any chance?"

"This is real science," said the military man, "not science fiction. But we did throw in some quantum nanotechnology, because we needed the right buzzwords to get funding from D.C."

"So, will I need to fill up on hydrogen to fuel the fusion reactor?" Jay asked.

"No," said the medical man. "By subjecting carbohydrates to extreme pressure, we force the hydrogen in them to fuse, thus powering the colon."

"Meanwhile the carbon subjected to such pressure is crystallized into convenient, bullet-shaped pellets," said the military man, "which are stored in your colon until such time as you eject them through the anal cavity."

At last Jay could see why the military was involved in the bionic colon project. "You're saying I can shoot diamond bullets out of my butt."

The military man nodded. "You'll be able to pass through security screenings without anyone knowing you have a weapon. You would make the perfect assassin." He looked around the room, then added, "If, that is, the United States used assassins, which of course we don't because that's prohibited under Executive Order 12333. But you'll make the perfect counter-assassin. And we have an important mission for you."

"Thanks for saving my life," said Jay, "but I'm not sure that I want to do any missions for you."

"Don't worry," said the military man, "this mission should fit in with your political beliefs, which we know about because thanks to the Patriot Act, we've been able to monitor your reading habits."

"Plus we read your LiveJournal," said the medical man.

"You'll have to go into training for a few days," said the military man, "but we'll cover that up by replacing you with an actor, pretending to be in pain and medicated, so that no one notices the switch. And, of course, blogging will be light."

When they told him what the mission was, Jay reluctantly agreed. "But if I'm going to do this for you, you'll need to get me a very special Hawaiian shirt."

When the masked female assassin burst into the Obama rally and started firing her gun, Jay was ready. Shooting precisely aimed diamond bullets out of his butt, Jay destroyed the assassin's bullets.

("Like hitting a bullet with a bullet," the military man had explained, "was how difficult opponents of the missile defense system said it would be to shoot down a missile. Once we had a working missile defense, of course, we realized it would be simple to refit the technology to actually shoot down bullets. All of this is thanks to President Ronald Reagan's determination and vision. And I really don't understand why you keep claiming that it sounds like this Eric James Stone person wrote my dialogue. I always talk like this.")

While people scattered in panic, Obama stood his ground. "Violence isn't the answer. I'm sure we can come to a reasonable agreement if we just sit down and talk about things."

The assassin pulled out a knife. "You won't stop me from getting the nom... I mean, you won't stop Hillary from getting the nomination."

Jay knew he could shoot down the assassin, but he was loath to resort to killing, even to save Obama's life. Fortunately, he had planned for just such an occasion.

As he ran toward Obama, he pulled off his specially made Hawaiian shirt. It automatically sealed itself into an airtight sac. Releasing the stored exhaust from his fusion generator, Jay farted helium into his shirt, inflating it to hundreds of times its original size.

As the Hawaiian-decorated zeppelin began to haul him into the sky, Jay grabbed Obama's arm and yanked him out of the reach of the assassin. Then they flew up and away, leaving the screaming assassin behind.

"How can I repay you for saving my life?" asked Obama.

"Universal health care for Americans would be a good start," said Jay, hoping Eric James Stone would let him get in the last word. "A single-payer system, which many people wrongly confuse with a single provider system, would provide much better coverage for Americans, who would no longer have to worry about losing health care when they lose their jobs."

"I'll do my best," said Obama.

"Also," said Jay, "get a colonoscopy."

* * *

During my friend Jay Lake's initial bout with colon cancer, Jeff Richárd secretly solicited submissions for a Jay Lake "get well" anthology. This story was my contribution.

For those of you who do not know Jay, he's a prolific science fiction and fantasy author, an outspoken political progressive, and renowned wearer of Hawaiian shirts. He was co-editor on the Zeppelin anthology for which I originally wrote "Resonance" and has written various steampunk/clockpunk stories.

The Man Who
Moved the Moon

D arryl Harrison had his doubts about the whole idea of "realistic" movies. After all, the movie would have to be converted to digital eventually because that's where the audience was. Twelve billion people had uploaded themselves to digital, leaving the Earth and its problems behind. The twenty million people still living on the real Earth—probably technophobes or religious types who didn't like movies anyway—weren't a demographic worth pursuing. A hundred thousand more scattered between Mars, the asteroids, and the Jovian satellites added little at the box office. The audience was digital, so why not make the movie digitally in the first place?

But Philippe Duvall had three Oscars for Best Director, and if he wanted to make a "realistic" film, who was Darryl to argue? The chance to work with one of the big-name directors was too good to pass up. So he ignored his doubts and took the job as second assistant, even if it meant leaving the digital world where he'd spent most of his life.

The rapid-cloning from his DNA record and the mind download went off without a hitch, and he was surprised to find that the heat and pollution weren't as bad in the real world as they seemed in the movies. His new body did have a tendency to itch in awkward places, a problem his digital body never seemed to have, but Darryl knew that enduring such suffering could only make him a better artist.

Since the screenplay was set in Paris, they had leased Paris for a year. The majority of the hundred or so remaining residents had been willing to take an all-expenses-paid vacation to anywhere else on Earth, courtesy of the studio, so the cast and crew of *Visitor From the Past* had the city and its landmarks mostly to themselves.

Because this was a "realistic" movie, there would be no sets, no special effects, and absolutely nothing digital. The cameras would use real film; the actors—the good-looking ones, at least—would wear realistic scanty clothing and speak English with realistic French accents.

And after three weeks of shooting, production on the film was going more smoothly than Darryl had anticipated, which caused a queasy sensation in his new stomach. Or maybe he had just eaten too much, another problem his digital body never had. Either way, making a movie using real film and real actors in a real environment would have to cause real problems, ones that couldn't be fixed with a quick tweak of the digits. Something had to go wrong, and the longer it waited before happening, the more devastating it would be.

They were in the middle of shooting the first fight scene involving the male lead, Heath Alexander, when Philippe unexpectedly said, "Cut!"

During the course of the struggle with the ghouls in the Metro tunnels below the city, Heath's shirt had been torn off. That was according to plan: the reason Heath was such a big star was his perfect muscular physique, the most copied male body in the whole world. You couldn't walk thirty meters down a beach without spotting at least two men wearing Heath's torso. But that was in digital. Here in the real world, Heath's famous abs were now hidden behind a layer of fat. Not much fat, just a thin layer of fat, but apparently Philippe's desire for absolute realism did not extend to real fat.

"What is going on here?" Philippe strode over to Heath and actually pinched the fat. "What is this?

Heath flinched. "Well, uh, there are these pastry shops, and, uh..."

Philippe threw his hands in the air. "Why does this happen to me? The moviegoers are not paying to see this... this whale blubber. This will be the end of my career." Like most of the A-list directors Darryl had met, Philippe seemed to believe that the universe revolved around him alone.

Darryl hurried over to help calm Philippe down. It really wasn't that much fat; Philippe was probably still resentful that Heath's name would come before his in the credits. "I'll have Bioservices clone up a new body for Heath and we can load him into it tomorrow morning, OK? And Heath will lay off the pastries, won't you?" he said, turning to the actor.

Heath nodded. "Won't happen again, I promise."

That probably wasn't good enough; Darryl decided to see if he could get the pastry shops shut down for the duration of filming, or at least have them programmed not to serve Heath.

Philippe nodded.

Philippe had no choice but to give everyone the rest of the day off, but he compensated for it by announcing that everyone would have to be back at five in the morning.

The next two weeks passed with only minor problems and delays. Heath was killed and had to be re-cloned and downloaded from backup three times, but Philippe didn't grouse about that—not using stunt doubles was just part of the price of creating a truly "realistic" film. Heath also seemed unperturbed by his repeated demise, saying that he was a professional actor willing to sacrifice for his craft. Whether that was true or not, Darryl decided it would not be helpful to Heath's masculine self-esteem to see the footage of himself screaming as he fell from the bell-tower of Notre Dame Cathedral.

Darryl had just finished double-checking the next day's schedule with the first assistant director, Barnaby Vines, when one of the bit actors approached him.

"Mr. Harrison?" The actor looked to be in his twenties but his voice cracked like a teenager. There was no way he was ever going to make it big sounding like that, although that could probably be fixed in digital.

"Yes?"

"Well, I was talking to one of the cameramen during one of the breaks? And he said we weren't going to Greater Arabia?" He was one of those people who said everything as if it were a question.

Darryl frowned. "Of course we're not going to Greater Arabia. The whole film is set here in Paris."

"Oh." The actor licked his lips. "Well, then, never mind? I just thought?" He shrugged and started to walk away.

"Wait. Why did you think we were going to Greater Arabia?" Not that it really mattered, but if there was a rumor about going to Greater Arabia it needed to be quashed.

"Well, I've been reading the script? I know I'm only in two scenes, but I was curious? And I thought the scene where the visitor predicts the total eclipse was cool? You know? And I've never seen a total eclipse?"

"Don't worry." Darryl smiled. "You can stick around until we film that scene, which is in June, I think. Nobody has to go back to digital if they don't want to."

The actor looked puzzled. "So we *are* going to Greater Arabia?"

"What has Greater Arabia got to do with anything?" It had been a long day of shooting and Darryl's patience with this conversation was beginning to wear thin.

"That's where the eclipse is."

"It's an eclipse of the sun. The sun's in the sky, not in Greater Arabia." Even as he said it, Darryl felt the queasiness in his stomach start up again.

The actor laughed. "Astronomy's a hobby of mine, Mr. Harrison. I think you'd better double-check your info. When eclipses happen, they can only be seen from certain places. The one this June is visible in Greater Arabia." The earlier hesitation in his manner was gone. He was obviously sure of himself when it came to astronomy.

Darryl nodded. He would check, but already he knew it had to be true. His stomach had warned him.

During an overly-detailed call to an astronomer, Darryl found out that the actor was not as smart as he seemed to think he was: while the total eclipse would reach its maximum extent over Greater Arabia, it would also be visible in other parts of the world. Unfortunately, those other parts of the world were in a strip spanning thousands of kilometers across Asia, the Middle East, and Africa, but less than two hundred and fifty hundred kilometers wide. The partial eclipse would even be visible in parts of Europe. But not in Paris.

Darryl tracked down Barnaby so they could decide together how to break the news to Philippe. The good news—from Darryl's point of view, at least—was that the mistake was entirely Barnaby's fault. The first assistant director had merely found out when the next scheduled eclipse was, without knowing that eclipses were only visible in limited areas. Darryl decided it wasn't necessary to mention that until a few minutes before, he had been just as ignorant about the matter.

"So, when's the next eclipse here in Paris?" asked Barnaby.

Glancing at the notes he had jotted down, Darryl said, "Well, the next total eclipse isn't until 2189. But there's a partial one in 2119 that will cover more than half the sun."

Barnaby shook his head. "We can't wait six years. What else is there?"

"What if we send a unit to Greater Arabia, and film the one in June?"

"That might work, but I don't know if Philippe will go for it. You know how important this whole 'realistic' approach is. Any other possibilities?"

"There's a partial lunar eclipse in May of 2115 that should be fairly impressive, according the expert I talked to. It's only a week before we're supposed to open, but we could bring a unit out just to film the scene..."

"Lunar eclipse?" Barnaby tilted his head back, closed his eyes and clasped his hands behind his neck. "Require a few changes to the script; have the scene at night instead of day. Get the talent back for one day of filming—well, night of filming. Difficult, but it might work."

Satisfied that they had come up with a solution to save the scene, Barnaby and Darryl found Philippe in his trailer and explained the problem to him and Vanadia Kellerman, the studio rep. Since he was now the resident eclipse expert, Darryl ended up describing how they could use the lunar eclipse.

"No." Philippe shook his head with vigor. "No, no, no, no, no. Nobody cares about this lunar eclipse of yours. I must have a solar eclipse."

Darryl nodded. "OK, then I'll get permits for us to film in Greater Arabia. Will you want to take the whole—"

"What do you mean, film in Greater Arabia? This film is in Paris, and Paris alone. We must have the eclipse in Paris. How can I film the sun being blotted from the sky over the Eiffel Tower in Greater Arabia, I ask you?"

Darryl glanced over at Barnaby, who returned his puzzled look. "There's a partial solar eclipse in 2119, but—"

"Imbeciles! My film cannot wait for six years. Am I the only one with a brain? Am I the only one here who can think? Simply arrange to have the eclipse that is scheduled for Greater Arabia moved to Paris." He leaned back in his chair with a satisfied smirk.

Darryl blinked long and hard. He'd obviously failed to explain the situation properly. "Uh, Philippe? The eclipse happens where it does, when it does, because of where the moon is when it moves in front of the sun." He tried to move his fists around to represent the sun and the moon, but he really didn't know what he was doing and gave up after a few seconds.

"I know this. Do you think I do not know this? I know this. But if the moon were in a different position, then the eclipse would be over Paris, no? This is logic, pure and simple."

"You're talking about moving the moon?" Darryl had always thought Philippe was eccentric, but this was two Metro stops beyond eccentric.

Philippe shrugged. "And why not? Do they not move the asteroids for mining? Did they not move the moon of Mars for the space elevator?"

Darryl could not deny that they—whoever they were—did indeed do such things, so he nodded.

"Then why cannot they move the moon so the eclipse is in Paris? This is *art* we are making here." Philippe threw his arms wide. "One must think *big*."

When a director was thinking big, insane thoughts that could lead to disaster for the entire movie, it was up to one of his assistant directors to talk him back to reality. Darryl felt that this responsibility naturally should fall on Barnaby, who was not only first assistant, but also the one whose sloppy research had gotten them into this situation. Barnaby, however, seemed to be shirking the responsibility by studiously looking at the floor.

Darryl looked to Vanadia. Surely the studio rep would protest about the possible cost? But she remained silent. They were actually under budget right now; their main contact in the French government when negotiating the rental of Paris had turned out to be a big fan of Philippe, so they'd saved over one hundred million dollars off the projected costs of rent and bribes. Plus, though Darryl couldn't prove it, he was sure Vanadia was sleeping with Philippe.

Darryl sighed. What else was there to say? "OK, Philippe. I'll get right on it."

The first thing he did was track down the actor who'd told him about the eclipse. "You. What's your name?"

"Me?" The actor looked to the others he had been chatting with, who all edged away from him slightly. "My name's Tony Jac—I mean, my name's Antonio Calderon? For professional purposes?"

"Well, Tony, Antonio, whatever, I need to talk to you." Darryl nodded his head toward a couple of chairs.

Once they were seated, Darryl said, "First of all, Tony, I want to thank you for bringing the eclipse situation to my attention."

"No prob, Mr. Harrison." He smiled and straightened in his chair.

Darryl thought about puncturing Tony's pride a little by telling him he'd been wrong on some details, but decided it was too petty. "Now, I need your help, Tony. You don't mind if I call you Tony?"

"That's OK."

"You know this astronomy stuff. Who would I talk to about moving the moon?"

"Moving the moon?" Tony's voice was back to hesitant mode.

"You know, the people who move asteroids and things. The people who moved Mars's moon."

"One of them."

"One of who?"

"Not one of who. One of the *moons*. Mars has two."

Darryl sighed. "OK, who moved *one* of Mars's moons?"

"I'm pretty sure it was General Dynamics."

Darryl nodded. The name sounded vaguely familiar. "Is he or she at U.N. Space Command?"

"It's not a person; it's the name of a company." Tony failed to hide a smirk.

"Thank you." Darryl got up and began walking toward his trailer, then turned back. "Oh, I forgot to tell you that you were wrong about the total eclipse only being visible in Greater Arabia. It can be seen all along a strip from Asia to Africa." He turned back toward his trailer without waiting for Tony's reaction. Maybe it was petty, but Tony probably needed to learn that he didn't know it all.

After three hours and forty-five minutes of talking his way through the bureaucracy at General Dynamics, they connected him to an engineer who had actually worked on the project, Sheila Chang.

She peered at him suspiciously through the phonescreen. "Hello?"

"Ms. Chang, I'm hoping you can help me. How big of a project would it be to move the moon?"

"Earth's moon?"

"Yes."

"Why on Earth—or off it, rather—would you want to do that?" Her eyebrows raised.

"For a movie."

Sheila grinned. "Oh, I see. Science fiction. I'm really glad you called. I can't stand to watch ninety percent of the SF movies these days, they're so unrealistic. You guys should always consult an engineer about your scripts."

Darryl nodded. "We should have talked to one sooner. But at least I'm calling now. So, moving the moon: is it possible?"

"'Give me a lever and a place to stand, and I will move the world.'"

Darryl frowned.

"It's a quote from Archimedes. A Greek scientist. From long ago. He's the one who—" She shook her head. "Never mind. The simple answer is yes, the moon could be moved. But to get the details straight, I need more information. Where does the moon need to be moved to? Is there a time frame in which it needs to be done, etc."

"The time frame would be about six months from now. How far? I'm not sure. It would have to make a solar eclipse happen a few thousand miles away from where it normally would."

"So, just a change in orbital position by a few thousand miles. Nothing too exotic there; I thought you might want it to reach escape velocity or something. The mass is what makes it tricky in such a short time frame, though."

"That's a major problem?"

"We spent six years moving Deimos out to Mars-synchronous orbit. Granted, we had to move it a lot farther, but—" She cocked her head in the typical way of people using direct mental access to the computer into which they were uploaded. "—the moon has more than forty million times the mass."

"So it can't be done?" While he dreaded having to tell Philippe, it would be a relief to put aside this crazy idea and start finding a real solution.

"I didn't say that. Let me run a few numbers here."

Darryl waited for a few minutes as she occasionally muttered incomprehensibly.

"Got it. Wow, that's a lot of energy."

"How much?"

"This is all ballpark stuff, of course, but we're talking close to ten to the twenty-third joules."

Darryl shook his head. "And that's a lot of energy?"

"How can I explain it? You're familiar with the I-10 bomb?"

"The terrorist nuke?" It had been long before he was born, somewhere in the United States. Darryl didn't bother to explain that the only reason he knew about it was he'd heard it mentioned in a movie.

"Yes. You've probably seen pictures of the crater. That blast was one megaton of energy."

"And that's similar to the energy needed to move the moon?"

"Take that blast and multiply it by seventeen million."

Darryl winced. "So, what you're saying is that it's impossible."

"No, it's still physically possible. You wouldn't do it with one big explosion. You'd use whole bunch of smaller ones. And not regular bombs; there are thrusters that can focus the explosions. That's actually how we moved Deimos. Now, I hate to admit it, but Boeing's probably got the best thruster for this kind of thing. They just came out with one that uses hundred-kiloton antimatter explosions. Put a few hundred of those on the moon and run them in sequence, and you could do it."

"Really?" Maybe Philippe wasn't completely insane. It could be done. "And it's not really bad for the environment or anything, all those nukes going off?"

"Well, I wouldn't want to stand behind one of those thrusters. But antimatter's a pretty clean energy source, and the thrusters will be on the moon, not here on Earth." She paused a moment, tilting her head. "Moving the moon gradually like that would cause tides to shift slightly, but wouldn't cause any serious effects that I can think of."

Darryl nodded. "So how much do those thrusters cost?"

"I'm not sure. Antimatter's still pretty expensive. Probably a couple of hundred billion dollars each, give or take."

Darryl was fairly sure the studio was not going to shell out trillions for a movie that probably wouldn't make more than ten billion at the box office. "Would there be a cheaper way of doing it? Say, around one to two hundred million?"

"Well, if you could change the script to allow more time, there might be. But I assume time pressure is important to the story?"

"I must not have made myself clear. Moving the moon isn't part of the story. We just need..." Darryl was embarrassed to go on. Now that he knew what a huge project it would be, it seemed silly that he had even tried to find out if it was possible. Philippe and his insane idea.

"Need what?"

"It's stupid, I realize now. We're shooting a movie in Paris, and we need a solar eclipse for one scene. The director told me to arrange it."

"You actually want to move the moon just to shoot a movie?" Her tone left no doubt about what a spectacularly stupid idea that was. Suddenly she frowned. "You're filming in Paris? Is that the next Heath Alexander film?"

Taken aback by this unexpected turn in the conversation, Darryl said, "Yes."

"Could you... Could you get me his autograph? I love his movies."

"I can do that." Darryl nodded. "Sorry to have wasted your time on this, Ms. Chang."

"No prob. It was an interesting theoretical exercise. Never really realized just how massive the moon..." Her voice trailed into silence and she cocked her head.

Darryl waited a few moments. "Ms. Chang?"

"Well, I probably shouldn't tell you this, because moving the moon just for a scene in a movie seems so trivial. But since it's a Heath Alexander film..." She smiled. "The main obstacle is the sheer mass of the moon. Using brute force to move it is just going to be a huge project no matter what. Now, one of my roommates from MIT is out in the Belt. Her company's doing some sort of anti-gravity research. It's a long shot, but your only possibility is something radical. I'll send her a message about the basic problem, and have her contact you."

"Do you think she'd be willing to help?"

Ms. Chang winked at him. "Imelda's a bigger Heath Alexander fan than I am." She cut the connection.

With the lag time for communications with the Belt, Darryl expected to get a recorded message from Ms. Chang's friend, if he got anything at all. But the next morning before shooting started, he got a direct call from her.

"Mr. Harrison, I'm Imelda Jenkins. Sophie Chang told me about your problem."

"Thanks for calling. But I thought you were in the Belt?"

"As it happens, I'm in Earth orbit for some meetings, and Sophie managed to track me down."

"I know it's a highly unusual request, and I wouldn't be surprised—"

"I can do it."

"—if you... You can do it?" Darryl blinked.

"I stayed up all night working out the equations. I assumed you're trying to move the June 3 total eclipse so that it appears over Paris, and I made my calculations on that basis. That is right, isn't it?"

Nodding, Darryl said, "You're serious? You have a way to do it?"

"If I didn't, I wouldn't be calling you."

Darryl knew there had to be a catch. "And how much is it going to cost?"

"Well, I know you have budget constraints, so I'm willing to do it at cost. It'll be good publicity for my company. We'll need about twenty, maybe twenty-five million for materials and equipment."

"That's it? That's all?"

"Well, I'm sure it will cost a lot for the U.N. permits and bribes. You'll have to pay for those. And insurance as well."

One of the things Darryl missed about being digital was the ease of doing math. It took an effort, but he added things in his mind: $25 million for equipment and materials, throw in another $50 million for U.N. permits and bribes, $10 million or so for insurance. That made it... some number less than $100 million. It wouldn't even put them over budget, so the studio couldn't complain.

It was too easy. "Forgive me for being skeptical, Imelda, but your friend told me it would cost trillions to move the moon with nukes, and now you offer to do it for only twenty-five million. Can antigravity really make the moon so light it can be easily moved?"

She shook her head. "It's not antigravity. The technology we've developed reduces mass, which is a totally different approach." Her voice grew enthusiastic. "You see, we make a loop out of carbon nanofibers, doped up with quantum dots so we can dynamically adjust the superconductivity and other properties. We charge it, then set it spinning around the target, and that produces an observable reduction in mass."

"Stop. Please, I'm no scientist. All I know about science I get from watching movies, so I have no idea what any of that meant, except I know about carbon nanofibers because these days it seems just about everything is made out of them."

"Sorry. I get carried away sometimes, but this technology is going to revolutionize space travel, and a whole lot more." She paused and ran her fingers through her hair. "Look, I'll be honest with you: we haven't ever done anything on this scale, but the theory is sound. It will work. If you give my company a chance, we'll prove it. The whole reason I'm here instead of the Belt is I'm meeting with venture capitalists, trying to get the money to develop the technology. But it must be a lot like pitching a movie: the people with the money want all sorts of control. This is my idea, my team, my company, and if we can pull off moving the moon for you, the investors will come begging to me, not the other way round."

She was either the best actor Darryl had ever seen, or she really believed what she was saying. "All right, I believe you can do it. But I have to be able to explain it in simple terms to the studio rep in order to be able to spend that kind of money."

"Simple terms? We spin a loop of custom nanofibers around the moon, and that will reduce the mass of the moon."

"Make it smaller, you mean? The moon will shrink?"

"No, the size of the moon will be unaffected. It's just the mass—think of it as the weight—that is reduced."

"So you make the moon so it hardly weighs anything, and then move it into place with a rocket or something?"

She shook her head. "It doesn't reduce the mass by that much."

"How much does it reduce it?"

"Well, in experiments, we've gotten as much as a thousandth of a percent reduction."

He frowned. "Reduced it *by* a thousandth of a percent, or reduced it *to* a thousandth of a percent?"

"By."

"But full-scale, when you do it to the moon, it'll be like ninety percent or something?"

"No, actually, we won't need to even reach a thousandth of a percent. More like a billionth of a percent reduction."

He nodded. "Now, you see, this is where you need to explain it in simple terms. How does it help to reduce the mass by only a billionth of a percent?"

"You've heard of $E=mc^2$? That's been in plenty of movies, I'm sure."

"Yes. Don't know what it means, but I know it's important."

"It means that energy and mass can be converted back and forth. It's what makes antimatter and nuclear power work. And here's the best part: only a tiny amount of mass is equal to a huge amount of energy."

"So, you're not reducing the mass of the moon to make it easier to move, you're doing it to get the energy to move it?"

She grinned. "You got it. And a billionth of a percent of the moon's mass will give us all we need. That's still the better part of a trillion kilograms converted to energy, of course. It's only as a percentage that it sounds insignificant. If you added all the mass that anyone has converted to energy through nuclear reactions or antimatter annihilations since the beginning of the atomic era, this is orders of magnitude more."

The word "nuclear" brought a question to Darryl's mind. "All this energy—it's not going to explode the moon or send out radiation or anything?"

"No, nothing like that. The energy manifests itself as acceleration. Anything within a sphere the same radius as that of the nanofiber loop is accelerated in a direction perpendicular to the loop, toward the direction from which the loop appears to be rotating counterclockwise."

"Wait. You're saying the energy will just make the moon move the way we point it? Depending on the direction of the loop?"

"Yes. You see the potential application for space travel? We're still not sure why it always goes toward the counterclockwise direction. Quincy, one of the physicists on my team, thinks it's because that's the way the seventh dimension is curled, which has interesting implications for... But that's not really important."

"There are seven dimensions?"

"Eleven, actually."

"'More things in heaven and Earth...'" Darryl shook his head. "I think I understand it enough to explain this to the necessary people. How soon would you need to start?"

"By the end of January. Mid-February at the latest."

Six weeks. Getting all the permits in that amount of time would be tricky. He mentally upped the estimate for permits and bribes to seventy-five million. That would almost certainly put the film over budget, but since the studio was already spending $5.2 billion on the film, another twenty-five mill wasn't too much to ask.

"Oh," she said. "There is one more thing. A small thing, really."

He froze. Here came the catch. He should have known there would be a catch. "What?"

"If I pull this off, can you fix it so I can meet Heath Alexander?"

Darryl laughed in relief. "If you pull this off, I'll make sure you're invited to the world premiere. We're doing a live premiere, you know, here in Paris, so you wouldn't even have to upload."

He promised to call her as soon as he got the go-ahead from the studio and hung up.

He sat for a few moments absorbing the impact of the conversation. Yesterday all he'd wanted was to find the information needed to convince Philippe the moon couldn't be moved. Now he wanted nothing more than to convince the studio to put its money into a completely untried technology. He hoped Vanadia really was sleeping with Philippe; that would make things easier.

Philippe didn't take any convincing, didn't even want to know the details. "I told you. These scientists, they do these things."

Vanadia's reaction impressed Darryl; he hadn't thought of her as being particularly competent. But she neither dismissed the idea out of hand, nor approved it just because Philippe wanted it. Instead, she insisted on talking to Imelda Jenkins herself, and had someone run a thorough check on her and her company. Finding no red flags, Vanadia approved the expense. "It'll do wonders for marketing," she said.

"Marketing?" Darryl raised his eyebrows. "We really need to keep this quiet until after the fact, so the enviros don't sue to stop it or something."

"Of course. I was talking about afterwards. 'The movie so real, we had to move the moon.' That kind of stuff. The free publicity alone will be worth a half-billion dollars."

Darryl called Imelda with the good news, told her that the studio was working on the permits, and told her who to talk to about funds for materials and equipment. With that, he felt the whole moon-moving project was out of his hands, and he could finally focus again on the actual making of the movie.

Still, he kept himself updated on how the project was going. By February, the studio had gotten the necessary permits, and Imelda's company had brought its factory ship in from the Belt. Orbiting the moon at a height of one hundred kilometers, the factory began extruding a carbon nanofiber ribbon about two centimeters wide and a few micrometers thick.

By mid-March, the loop was complete, more than 11,500 kilometers all the way around. After a few days of feeding power into the superconducting material, small rocket motors attached to the loop were used to start spinning it.

To the great relief of everyone who knew about the project, the moon started moving just as Imelda had predicted.

Everything was going exactly according to plan until April 7. Darryl's stomach gave him no warning, so he was caught completely by surprise when he answered his phone in the middle of the night to find a frantic Imelda on the line.

"You've got to do something. There are U.N. police up here with an order to shut down the loop."

"What? Why?"

"Some problem with a permit. I don't know what to do—we don't have the U.N. out in the Belt. Am I supposed to bribe them or something?"

"No, the bribes we paid should have prevented this. Look, let me talk to whoever's in charge."

She moved off the screen, and a couple of minutes later the face of a uniformed U.N. cop appeared.

"What seems to be the problem, officer?"

"Who are you?"

"I'm Darryl Harrison. I work for the company that hired Ms. Jenkins to do the important work that's going on up there. I assure you we got all the necessary permits."

The officer shook his head. "I'm sorry, sir, but I've got orders to shut this thing down."

"I'm sure there must be some mistake. Can you send me a copy of those orders?" This was the key question. If the cop was just angling for a bribe, he'd say the orders were classified, or give some other excuse.

"Certainly, sir." The cop leaned forward, and a moment later an official-looking U.N. document popped onto the screen.

That was bad enough. But the worst of it was that the document was signed by Cavendish Price, U.N. Secretary for Space Affairs. Someone at the studio must have decided to save money by getting approval without going all the way to the top.

"Thank you, officer." What could he do? Delay was the best he could hope for right now. "Would you give me some time to consult with my superiors?"

"Well, my orders are to shut this thing down as soon as possible."

If the cop wasn't bribable, he would just have said no. "I understand, officer. If you would put Ms. Jenkins back on?"

When she appeared on the screen, Darryl said, "Is the cop close enough to hear?"

She shook her head.

"Offer him twenty-five thousand to hold off for an hour. Take as long as you want to haggle with him. You can go as high as a quarter mill on my authority. More than that, and you'll have to talk to me again. Hopefully we can get things moving on this end by then."

"OK." She hung up.

Darryl dialed Vanadia's room in the hotel where the cast and crew were staying. She answered, audio only. After he briefed her on the situation, she said she'd come to his room to discuss what to do.

Forty-five minutes and three hundred thousand dollars later, they were trying to bribe Secretary Price's administrative assistant into letting them speak to the Secretary directly.

Suddenly the picture changed, and the face of Cavendish Price scowled at them. "I've heard enough of this. Sneaking around behind my back, bribing my subordinates, moving the moon itself, for crying out loud. I'm putting a stop to it."

"But sir," said Vanadia, "We've got a great deal of money invested in this project, and we'll move the moon back when we're done, so I don't see why there's any harm in letting us continue." She lowered her voice. "Of course, we understand there may have been problems with the paperwork, and we would be willing to pay a substantial fine as a penalty."

Price looked thoughtful. Then he shook his head. "Look at it from my point of view. Some company bribes my subordinates into being allowed to move the moon, and not one of them can tell me why the moon is being moved. You see my difficulty here? I have no way of knowing whether this is a legitimate project that was merely smoothed on its way, or something with potentially devastating consequences that should never have been allowed. Nobody I've talked to has been able to come up with any possible reason for moving the moon. And I have a responsibility to the whole world."

Vanadia looked at Darryl, and he shrugged. At this point there was nothing to lose by telling Price the truth. Maybe if he could be convinced it was harmless, he'd accept a bribe and let it go at that.

"Well, sir," she said, "I know you're going to think this is trivial, but we're making a movie in Paris. And the plot of the movie requires a solar eclipse. We thought there would be one in Paris this year. When that proved incorrect, we decided to arrange one."

Price looked at her as if trying to decide whether she was joking.

Darryl leaned forward into the view of the camera. "You can have your scientists confirm that the path on which we are moving the moon will end up causing an eclipse in Paris on June 3. But only if you let us continue."

Secretary Price tilted his head a moment in thought. "Paris? Is that the Heath Alexander movie?"

Relief flooded through Darryl and he smiled. "Yes, it is. And I'm sure we could arrange an autograph or something, if you'd like."

"An autograph? No, I don't want an autograph." Price grinned. "I hate Heath Alexander. You couldn't pay me to watch one of his movies. Him strutting around like he's a real hero. I fought against the Swedes during the Nordic Rebellion. I've seen real heroes, and Heath Alexander is a pale imitation. No, I don't want his autograph. And it will give me great pleasure to know that I ruined one of his movies."

Vanadia said, "But, sir—"

At the same time, Darryl shouted, "Wait! Don't hang up!"

Price raised an eyebrow. "What more is there to say?"

"I have footage of Heath Alexander screaming in fear as he falls to his death. Real footage. No acting. No digital. I can give you a copy." Darryl held his breath.

"Real footage? He's really screaming?"

Darryl nodded. "We filmed it a few months ago. He shrieks like a banshee. Very unmanly."

Vanadia caught on. "Of course, the studio owns the copyright on that film, and you could never release it. But you would be able to view it privately."

Licking his lips, Price nodded. "That, plus two million dollars."

"One million." Vanadia's voice was relieved.

"One-five."

"Done."

"I'll call my cops off now." Price hung up.

Vanadia sank back in her chair. "Quick thinking there, Darryl. Are you as good at directing as high stakes negotiating?"

"I like to think I'm better at directing."

She nodded. "I'll see if I can find a film for you to direct, after this is done."

"Thanks."

Darryl called Imelda to let her know the project was safe, then went back to bed.

June 3 finally arrived, and, right on schedule, the eclipse began. Darryl's stomach bothered him the whole time they were shooting. He was sure something would go wrong. When the filming finished without incident, he was sure there would be a problem during developing. But the dailies turned out fine. His stomach wasn't always right.

Vanadia was right about the publicity. Headlines such as "Moon Moved for Heath Alexander Film" dominated the entertainment zines. Philippe was annoyed that the headlines rarely mentioned him, and during the filming of the rest of the movie repeatedly pointed out to anyone who would listen that it had been his idea in the first place.

Darryl never pointed out that Philippe hadn't done a thing toward actually implementing the idea.

On the evening of the premiere, Darryl picked Imelda up at the Paris spaceport to take her by limo to the red-carpet premiere, as he'd promised.

"I want to thank you for giving me the chance to move the moon for you," she said. "I have to beat off investors with a stick now."

"So you're going to be able to keep control of your company?"

"Yes. And I hear you're directing your first big movie?"

"I am. The studio was appropriately grateful for my work on this movie."

They spent the rest of the short ride reminiscing about how the project had affected their lives. The limo pulled up into the line that was disgorging recently-downloaded stars onto the red carpet lined with recently-downloaded fans.

"And now, ladies and gentlemen," said the announcer, "please give a warm welcome to someone we know you've been waiting to see. Yes, it's really him, the Man Who Moved the Moon!"

Darryl and Imelda watched as Heath Alexander stepped out of the car in front of them and waved to the cheering crowd.

* * *

At Orson Scott Card's Literary Boot Camp in 2003, one of the fiction markets Card told us about was the Phobos Fiction Contest, for which he was a judge.

After the workshop, I participated in an online forum with my classmates. One of my classmates asked a question about how to make the astronomy of her fictional world believable, and in the course of responding, I said, "Since your solar system is so different from ours, chances are you won't make a mistake as bad as they did in the movie Ladyhawke, *in which a solar eclipse takes place the day after a full moon. (Absolutely impossible.)"*

Another classmate, Scott M. Roberts, responded, "But, Eric: It's Maaaaaagic!"

I followed up with a 500-word examination of just how much energy would need to be expended to move the moon halfway around its orbit in half a day. (Conclusion: equivalent to the explosion of about 34 trillion one-megaton nuclear warheads.) As an afterthought, I jokingly added, "Now I just need to see if I can write 'The Man Who Moved the Moon' before the Phobos deadline."

One of my favorite stories is Robert A. Heinlein's "The Man Who Sold the Moon," so I was playing off that title. But the more I thought about it, the more I felt like I should actually write the story. So I brainstormed about possible reasons for moving the moon, and came up blank. There didn't seem to be any rational purpose for moving the moon.

My mind circled back to the absurd astronomy of Ladyhawke, *and I realized that if there was no rational reason to move the moon, maybe there was an irrational one: making an eclipse happen at the right time in a movie.*

I finished the story before the Phobos deadline at the end of July, and it went on to be a winner and get published in the anthology.

Buy You A Mockingbird

It's time for bed.

Yes, I'll tell you a story. But then you have to be a good girl for Mommy and go to sleep. Promise?

Once upon a time there was a woman who worked in a lab. Yes, like me. And she had a little girl just like you. Now, one day the woman used a machine in her lab and it took her a hundred years into the future. Yes, a hundred years is a long time.

What did the lady find in the future? There was nothing... There was nothing bad there. Nobody was sad in the future. Nobody was poor. Nobody hurt anybody else. Nobody was sick. Nobody did anything bad.

You're right, that does sound like a happy place. But the lady wasn't happy in the future. She was all lonely. She wanted to see her little girl again.

Yes, she loved her little girl. So the lady came back from the future. That's when she found out the machine in the lab had created an irreparable quantum tear in the spacetime—had made a rip in the world that was spreading and would soon tear everything apart.

Did the lady fix the rip? Of course she did. She just took her needle and thread and sewed it back up. Then she went home to her little girl and they lived happily for a hundred years and met the lady again when she appeared in the future. And everybody in the whole world was happy.

That's the end of the story. Now it's time to go to sleep.

No, you don't have to go to school tomorrow. You don't have to go to school ever again. Tomorrow you can play with your friends and watch TV and eat ice cream and all the candy you want. And we'll go to the toy store and buy all the Disney princesses.

Sweet dreams, my baby. Remember Mommy loves you and will never ever let anything bad happen to you.

That sound outside is just the wind. Don't worry, Mommy will stay here and hold you until it's all gone.

* * *

I wrote this story for a flash-fiction writing contest with other members of the Codex Writers. We each had to write a story of no more than 750 words in a weekend—each weekend for five weeks. This story was my entry for week two. It was loosely based on the following prompt: "You've been transported 100 years into the future. You have 24 hours to experience and learn as much as you can, but you can't take anything back with you except knowledge. What would you focus on?"

That led me to think about what might happen if someone went into the future and there wasn't anything there. What if the time travel itself were responsible for destroying the future?

Because it was flash fiction, I decided to experiment with style, and the idea of presenting just the mother's side of a conversation as she is telling a story to her child clicked for me. The title "Buy You a Mockingbird" was meant to evoke the lies parents tell their children in order to make them feel better.

Salt of Judas

Osbert Peale did not paint portraits when he sat on his stool beside the Avon. He painted Tewkesbury Abbey or one of the footbridges over the river. Sometimes he portrayed the boatmen on the water or passersby on land, but those people were merely parts of the landscape. Only in his narrow rented room above the butcher's did he paint portraits, and those he never showed to anyone for fear they would laugh.

Every portrait was of *her*. He'd begun to paint her portrait even before he discovered that her name was Amelia. He said that delightful name occasionally to himself as he drew in charcoal the curve of her neck or used the painting knife to soften the glow of her cheek. But in his mind She remained most often her. And though he often whispered—to himself—that he loved her, he knew that a wealthy landowner's daughter like her would never love a humble artist like him.

As he sat beside the river, palette in one hand and knife in the other, creating landscapes in oil, he always watched for her, since She often strolled along the footpath with her companions. On occasion She would stop and look at his work in progress, and Osbert would then find it difficult to breathe as he painted with trembling hand. But except in his imagination She had never spoken to him, nor he to her. His love for her was a secret he kept from all the world.

He was using the blending knife to darken the shadows of an overcast sky on his canvas when a deep voice came from behind him.

"I understand you paint portraits."

Osbert turned his head to look up at the stranger. The man was bald as an egg, and under the darkening sky his skin seemed Lead White with a touch of Ultramarine Blue. He wore a red vest—Cadmium Red darkened perhaps by Burnt Sienna—over a white silk shirt, black breeches and white stockings. The buckles on his shoes glinted gold even without direct sunlight. Although Osbert had been in Tewkesbury less than a year, he thought he knew everyone of consequence in the town. This man must be a wealthy traveler, perhaps brought here by the convergence of the Avon and the Severn rivers.

"You are mistaken, sir. I am only a landscape painter."

The stranger nodded slowly. "Where do you buy your oils?"

"From Barber the apothecary. He has a shop on Church Street."

"From now on, you will buy them from me." The stranger spoke as if stating an obvious fact.

"But Barber has always—"

"Barber has sold his shop to me. I am the new apothecary."

"Oh." Osbert did not know what else to say. Barber had been a friendly fellow, quite unlike this brusque man. But possibly the new apothecary would become more amiable in time.

"Soon you will want to bring life to your portraits. Come to me then." The apothecary turned and strode away.

"I don't paint portraits," Osbert called after him, but the bald head made no acknowledgement.

In the dim morning light that came through his one small window, Osbert looked at the latest portrait of her. She was tilting her head inquisitively, and her lips were pursed slightly, as if She were about to ask a question.

"You wish to know my name, milady? I am Osbert Peale, at your service. Or perhaps you wonder what it is I will be painting today? I believe I shall attempt once more to capture the spirit of Tewkesbury Abbey.

"Or do you merely wish to inquire whether I think it will rain? Yes, that must be it, for the weather will do quite well as a subject of conversation with someone when you have nothing else in common."

He fell silent. This piece was his best, seeming to catch a moment before motion rather than an eternal pose.

Soon you will want to bring life to your portraits. Come to me then.

What had the apothecary meant? Could he have known of Osbert's secret portraits?

What would it be like to touch her, to feel the softness of her skin? Osbert reached out and gently stroked her face. His fingers came away wet with paint.

The wooden sign showing a mortar and pestle still hung over the door, but someone had painted over the name Barber and replaced it with Dyer. Osbert hesitated before opening the door and walking into the shop.

"Ah, the young artist." The bald man rose from his seat behind the counter, ducking his head to avoid various bottles that hung from the ceiling beams. "I knew you would come."

"I need linseed oil."

"That is all you wish?"

"Yes." A sudden sweat broke out on Osbert's brow, though the air was cool in the darkened shop.

The apothecary rummaged around under the counter, clinking bottles together. "How is your portrait work progressing?"

"I paint landscapes."

"So you said. So you said." The apothecary rose from behind the counter and held out a corked bottle. "I'll put it on your account. Barber said you paid him monthly without fail. I like a man who keeps his bargains."

"Thank you." Osbert took the bottle and quickly exited. Once he was sure the man could not see him through the shop windows, he shuddered in relief. He didn't like the way those dark eyes seemed to look past his own.

As days became shorter and the weather cooler, Osbert saw her less frequently on her walks. And since there were fewer daylight hours for painting landscapes, he spent more time in his cramped room painting portraits by the light of an oil lamp. Often he would paint through the night: a portrait of her smiling coyly or laughing or merely looking to the horizon.

Over the past three nights he had experimented with painting a sequence of small portraits capturing different positions as her head turned until her eyes seemed to look into his. Now as he looked from one painting to the next in order, it was almost as if She moved. Almost.

Soon you will want to bring life to your portraits. Come to me then.

Three times he walked past the apothecary's door before he went inside.

"Ah, the young artist." The apothecary rose to his feet. "More linseed oil? Some White Lead, perhaps?"

"What did you mean?"

The apothecary raised a dark eyebrow. "I am surprised, however, that you are running low on supplies so soon, since the weather is not generally fit for painting landscapes."

Osbert pointed his index finger at the man. "You said I should come to you if I wanted to give life to my portraits. What did you mean?"

The apothecary nodded. "Now you are ready."

"Ready for what?"

"Ready to give life to your work. Are you a religious man, Master Peale?"

Osbert blinked. "I... I'm a God-fearing man, if that's what you mean."

"God-fearing. A good word." The apothecary smiled, his teeth gleaming in the dark shop. "I, too, am God-fearing, you could say."

"Enough of this. What do you know of my painting portraits? What do you mean by 'give life'?"

"You paint portraits of a young lady, perhaps? Someone you desire, but who remains forever beyond your reach?"

Osbert couldn't think what to say. The apothecary seemed to know him intimately.

"You paint her portrait till you know her face better than your own. But you do not know her voice, her touch. She is no more alive to you than a stone." He tapped the stone pestle on the counter. "But there are… other arts beyond the art of painting."

"You practice the arts of witchcraft," Osbert said in astonished realization. He knew he should denounce the apothecary to the Church immediately, but curiosity restrained him.

"Those who fear its power may call it witchcraft. It is nothing more than knowledge, and knowledge is neither good nor evil. 'Tis the use that makes it so."

"Yet you talk of giving life to the creations of men. Surely that is blasphemy, as only God can create life."

The apothecary smiled again. "You are wise for one so young. But I speak not of creating life, but of giving it. Tell me, what is it that makes a man live?"

Osbert pressed his lips together as he thought. "The spirit—the soul."

"And if a painting had a soul?"

"But how is that possible? A soul comes from God, and He would not give one to a mere painting."

"There are heathen tribes who believe that a painting steals the soul of the person portrayed. That is not true—to steal someone's soul into a painting requires the application of magics far beyond their primitive superstitions." The apothecary waved a hand dismissively, then pointed at Osbert. "However, you have a soul. If you are willing to give up part of yours to make the painting live, that is within my power."

Osbert stepped back. "You want me to give you part of my soul? So you can drag me down to damnation piece by piece?"

"No, you would not give it to *me*. You would give it to the painting, give life to the portrait."

Though the response allayed Osbert's suspicions somewhat, he asked, "And what benefit do you receive from this, then, that you would risk hanging as a witch?"

"What benefit? You would pay me, of course."

"I'm not wealthy. I have but twenty pounds a year bequeathed by my uncle. It is enough to live on, but painting is my one luxury." Osbert hoped someday to paint well enough to sell his work, but that day was still to come.

"I will not charge much. The ingredients I require are not costly, excepting the salt. Shall we say, eight shillings?"

Almost half a pound. But to have her speak to him, to be able to touch her would be worth that price. "How do I know I will get my money's worth?"

"You are a man who fulfills his bargains; so am I. I will add the cost to your bill. If you are not satisfied, you can merely refuse to pay."

With such an offer, how could the apothecary possibly swindle him? What suspicions could remain? "How is it done?"

"We will need to cut off a piece of your soul and grind it to a powder you can mix with your paint. Then whatever portrait you paint will be given life."

"The soul is immaterial. How can it be cut or ground?"

The apothecary sighed. "Not everything the Church teaches you is to be believed. The soul is not immaterial; it is a material more refined, more pure than base matter. That is how it can occupy the same space as your body. The trick is to get part of the soul to separate itself from the body, so it can be removed without harming the flesh."

The apothecary turned and reached for a metal saltcellar on the top shelf behind him. "Salt is a symbol of purity because it prevents corruption. That's why it's used for protection against evil spirits. The purity of salt has power."

Osbert nodded.

"But the salt I have here is not common salt. During the Last Supper, Judas Iscariot knocked over a dish of salt. That salt became cursed for all eternity. And I have some of it here."

Skepticism returned to Osbert's mind. "I cannot believe you have the very same salt that was at the Last Supper?"

"It matters not what you believe. The power of the salt is real." The apothecary smiled. "But you are a clever young man to see that this is not the very same salt. The spilt salt was collected by one who recognized its power. And when that cursed salt is mixed with uncursed salt, the curse spreads. As it says in the Bible, 'If the salt has lost its savour, wherewith shall it be salted?' So this is known as the Salt of Judas or Traitor's Salt. The grains may not be the same, but the curse is."

Osbert stared in fascination at the saltcellar. "What does the curse do?"

"As normal salt is repellent to an evil spirit, Salt of Judas is repellent to a good spirit, only far stronger in its effects. Place your left hand on the counter here, fingers spread apart."

Osbert did as he was told.

The apothecary reached out and gripped Osbert's wrist with fingers hard and cold as iron. "This will be painful, but no real harm will come to you."

"Painful?" Osbert almost tried to pull his arm back, but the apothecary's grip held him fast.

"It will not last long." The apothecary sprinkled salt onto Osbert's little finger.

Osbert's knees buckled as he felt fire spread across his hand and into his forearm. He exhaled a choking scream, then found himself unable to draw breath. The apothecary's icy fingers tightened on his wrist. His vision blurred with tears, but he thought he saw a wavering tendril of fire rise from the knuckle of his little finger.

"There it is." The apothecary's voice was calm. He had put down the saltcellar and now held a pair of shears. Deftly he snipped the tendril of fire just above the knuckle. The tendril writhed on the counter, leaving scorch marks where it touched. "Looks very much like a salted slug, does it not?"

Still unable to breathe, Osbert tried to yank his hand away, but the apothecary did not let go.

"Oh, yes. The pain." The apothecary pulled Osbert's hand several inches away from the tendril, then poured some water from a bottle onto Osbert's little finger. "Holy water, to wash away the salt. The pain should subside." He finally let go of Osbert's wrist.

Clasping at his finger to make certain it was still there, Osbert realized the pain was easing. He was able to breathe again, and he took several deep breaths to steady himself before shouting, "What did you do to me?"

"Just what I said I would. I sprinkled Salt of Judas on part of your body to force your soul out of that part, allowing me to clip it off." The apothecary used tongs to pick up the tendril of soul and drop it in the mortar. He added some dried leaves, which burst into flames. "The salt also corrupted it enough that we can see it and even touch it." He took a pestle and began pounding it in the mortar. "There are many who say that the curse on the Salt of Judas is the curse of Hell itself, and that the pain you felt is what a damned soul will feel for all eternity, but I don't know that is so."

"You have damned me." His vision dimmed as despair filled his heart. "I have been touched by the curse of Judas."

The apothecary laughed. "You are a good man, Osbert Peale. If your soul were not good, the Salt of Judas would not cause you pain." The apothecary looked in the mortar, ground the mixture a little more, then removed the pestle. "Now, take this powder—" He tilted the mortar and poured an ash-white powder onto a sheet of paper, which he expertly folded. "—mix it with linseed oil, then blend it with the paint on your next portrait."

Osbert looked at the packet but made no move to take it.

"Come now. Are you going to waste all the pain you've suffered? Take it."

Osbert slowly reached out his hand.

The gray light of dawn diffused from the window, blending with the yellow from the oil lamp. Still wet, a portrait of her stood lifeless on the easel. On his palette, still unused, was some of the soul-paint.

Osbert feared it would not work. And he feared it would. The events of the night before were becoming confused in his mind. Was the apothecary a charlatan or a puissant witch? Osbert rubbed the little finger of his left hand. It had felt a little numb during the night, then prickly, but seemed almost normal now. Perhaps it was getting accustomed to missing its soul.

He took his blender and dipped it in the translucent soul-paint, then carefully began applying it to her face. Now that he had started, he worked feverishly until there was none of the substance left on his palette.

On the canvas, nothing had changed: her eyes still looked to the distance, her serious expression remained frozen in oils. The pain, the fright, his work—all were for naught. Osbert threw down his palette and painting knife, then stretched himself out in exhaustion upon his cot.

He would deal with the fraudulent apothecary later.

When he woke up, the first thing he saw was her smile.

A week later—seven portraits later—Osbert hurried into the apothecary shop and closed the door. "I need to make more soul-paint. And it needs to be stronger."

"Soul-paint? Apropos." The apothecary's teeth glinted in his smile. "Run out already, have you?"

"She smiles at me. She gazes into my eyes. But She doesn't talk, and when I try to touch her, I can sense her movement but She still feels like paint."

Nodding, the apothecary said, "Yes, a higher concentration is needed to give the portrait more vitality. But that would require a larger portion of your soul. Are you willing to give it?"

The pain hadn't been too much to endure, had it? And it had been over quickly, had it not? "How much would I need?"

The apothecary bobbed his head back and forth in thought. "For talking and touching, let me see... Perhaps, to be on the safe side, we should take the whole hand."

Osbert clenched his left hand into a fist, then opened it again, looking at it carefully. "Will it make a difference to my hand, not having a soul? My finger felt strange that first night."

"Oh, my dear boy! Is that what you thought?" The apothecary laughed. "You do not have a soulless finger, nor will you have a soulless hand. The rest of your soul extends to fill the empty parts. It is the same with fat men—they do not have more of a soul than thin men; their souls just stretch to fill their bulk."

Osbert's relief at this explanation made him realize how much he had feared having a part of his body without a soul. He rolled up his sleeve and put his left hand down on the counter.

Three days later his tongue was still sore from having bitten it during the agony of the salt on his hand, but he was otherwise recovered from the ordeal. Nonetheless, now that he had a sufficient supply of the soul-paint, he was glad he would not need to go through that again.

Osbert glanced at a portrait he had finished the previous week. Her face smiled at him, and her eyelashes fluttered demurely. But that portrait was imperfect, flawed.

He would create a new portrait. This would be his best work, perfectly capturing her eyes, her hair, the flush of her cheek. And this one would speak to him.

"Back again, my young friend?" The apothecary rose to greet him.

"Her portrait has stopped talking to me. She still smiles, but the earlier ones no longer smile. They are utterly lifeless!" Osbert gripped the edge of the counter.

Running a palm over the smooth dome of his head, the apothecary said, "Interesting. The ground-up soul must be gradually escaping the paint."

"How do I stop it?"

"It is returning to its natural state. I do not think it can be stopped."

Osbert looked at his hand. "Is it coming back into me?"

"I doubt that. You voluntarily surrendered it, so it no longer pertains to you."

"What can be done? I need her."

With an appraising eye, the apothecary looked him up and down. "Perhaps an arm? Just from the elbow down? We'll have to do it piece by piece, though, to fit in the mortar."

The banging on the door roused Osbert from sleep. The afternoon daylight cutting into the room hurt his eyes. He stumbled to the door and opened it a crack.

It was his landlord, the butcher. "Peale, I'm giving you till Saturday to come up with two months' rent, or you'll have to leave."

Desperate confusion swirled in Osbert's mind. He was two months late with rent? "You'll get the money. It's just that my mother's sister is ill, and the leech—"

"I thought you said it was your father's sister."

Had he said that? "This is a difficult time. Illness sweeping through my family's village." He coughed. Why did his chest hurt so?

The butcher took a step back. "You don't look well yourself."

"I'm fine. You'll get your money. Just give me some time."

"Hmph." The butcher turned and went down the stairs.

Osbert sat down on his cot.

"You seem ill, my love." Her voice was melodious, and Osbert felt better just hearing it.

"I'm just tired, is all." He lay back and closed his eyes. Late with the rent? Lying to his landlord? What was wrong with him?

He felt her palm on his forehead. "You're burning up. It's a fever. You need help."

A fever? The apothecary could help. Yes, he must go to the apothecary.

He staggered down the stairs and out onto the street. He was exhausted by the time he reached the apothecary shop, and once inside he allowed himself to sink to the floor.

He awoke in a strange room, surrounded by portraits of her. One of them smiled at him as he sat up.

"Where am I?" he asked her.

Her shoulders shrugged slightly, but She did not answer.

Osbert walked unsteadily to the door, opened it and looked out. The scents of the apothecary shop met him. "Hallo?" he called out.

"Ah, you are recovered at last," said the apothecary from below. "We were quite worried about you."

"We?"

"The young lady of your portraits and I. Gave us quite a scare, you did."

"What am I doing here? What are my paintings doing here?"

"When you fell ill, you came to me. I then discovered that you were unable to pay the rent for your prior room, so I had everything brought here."

A fog seemed to lift from his mind. He walked down the stairs to confront the apothecary. "That was your fault. I couldn't pay the rent because I spent all my money on soul-paint."

"It does no good to blame me. It was all by your choice. How was I to know you were spending too much?"

Still weak in his legs, Osbert sat down on the floor.

"But you have no worries now, my boy. You can stay here with me, as I can spare the room."

"Thank you." Did he really want to stay here? Where else could he go? Then he remembered her. "The portraits! She didn't talk to me, She only smiled."

"Yes, it's been too long. The power of your soul-paint is fading."

"I need more."

The apothecary smiled. "You are sure? Your soul is stretched so thin I estimate we'd need to take both legs now to have enough."

"Yes, I'm sure." She'd help nurse him back to health, so he owed it to her to bring her back to life.

The apothecary reached up for the saltcellar.

"I think I would like to see one of your landscapes," She said one morning.

"What?"

"You used to paint landscapes, did you not? I should very much like to see one. You have such a talent for painting."

"Then see one you shall. I'll go out and paint one today."

She smiled brightly. "Just for me?"

"Just for you."

He scraped an old canvas, removing one of her lifeless portraits. After gathering his paints, he went downstairs.

"Going somewhere?" asked the apothecary, who was putting on his coat to leave.

"I'm going to paint a landscape."

The apothecary frowned. "Are you sure that's wise? The spring weather is rather damp, and you are still weak. There is illness about—I am going to treat someone even now."

"It's for her. She wants to see a landscape."

"Ah, well if she wants it, how can you refuse? Just don't stay out too long."

He sat on his stool on the bank of the Avon. The canvas before him held only a half-hearted charcoal sketch. It had been so long since he had done a landscape that nothing seemed right.

"Trouble painting?" A man's voice came from behind him.

Osbert turned to see an elderly monk from the abbey. "Yes, I'm afraid I'm somewhat out of practice."

The monk nodded. "I recall having seen you painting many a day last year, but not in recent months."

"I've been ill."

"Ah."

The silence stretched. Osbert raised his charcoal to the canvas, then brought it back down. He turned to look at the monk again. "Is it a sin to paint a portrait of... of a young lady?"

The monk raised his eyebrows. "I've never been asked that before."

"Is it?"

"The Muslim believes all images of people are prohibited. And I've read of primitive tribes that believe an image can trap the soul of the person portrayed. But portraiture in itself is not against the laws of Christ."

Osbert nodded gratefully, though the talk of souls trapped in images came uncomfortably close to his secret.

"But this young lady whose portrait you paint—is there perhaps more to it than that? Is that what troubles you?"

Suddenly Osbert no longer wanted to talk to this monk. He stood up. "I've been outside too long. I must get back. My health, you understand."

The monk nodded. "May God speed your recovery."

In the middle of the night Osbert awoke to pounding on the door of the shop. He heard the apothecary call out that he was coming.

"I wonder who is ill tonight." Her voice was concerned.

"I'll find out," he said. Rising from his bed, he opened the door and crept out to sit on the stairs and eavesdrop.

A man was speaking, an edge of desperation in his voice. "—grows ever weaker. It's as if the very life were being drained from her body."

The apothecary's voice was sympathetic. "I don't know what else is to be done but help her sleep better. This illness is beyond my power to aid."

"I don't understand it. My daughter was always a picture of health, until last autumn."

"It is most mysterious."

"Is there nothing in your books? Please, you must help my Amelia. I'll pay whatever you ask."

"I am sorry," said the apothecary. "Take this powder to ease her rest. That is all I can do."

Osbert barely heard the door of the shop shut. His mind was awhirl.
Amelia. Was this coincidence? No. His portraits of her were somehow
harming the real young woman, drawing the life out of her. He tried to
reject the thought, but he remembered the primitive belief the monk had
mentioned about images trapping the soul of the person portrayed. The
apothecary had mentioned it, too, Osbert recalled now. It had to be true—he
was the cause of Amelia's suffering.

He rose to his feet and descended the stairs. The apothecary was sitting
in his chair behind the counter. On seeing Osbert, he rose to his feet.

Clenching his fists, Osbert said, "What have you done to Amelia?"

"I've done nothing to the young lady."

"It's me, isn't it? My portraits are stealing pieces of her soul."

"You imagine things, dear boy. Go back to bed and get some rest." The
apothecary didn't look him in the eye.

"How do I set things right?"

The apothecary sighed. "You can't. By painting her image with
the soul-paint, you have robbed that girl of most of her soul, binding it
permanently away from her. She will die shortly, and it is your obsession
that has killed her."

What could Osbert do? "I'll destroy the paintings. Burn them all."

"Ignorant child. You are dealing with magics of the soul. Mere flames
cannot break such bindings."

Osbert lunged forward and grabbed at the apothecary, who broke the
grip with ease and pushed him to the floor.

Tears of hopelessness welled in his eyes, then began to flow down his
cheeks. "Dear God, what have I done?"

The apothecary laughed. "Yes, now you call out to Him. Far too late,
of course."

Wiping at the tears on his face, Osbert realized he was damned. Step by
step, he had brought ruin upon himself and Amelia.

And then as he licked at his lips, he tasted his tears. Salt. The Salt of Judas.

He rose to his feet. The apothecary had moved to the doorway and was
bolting it shut. Osbert climbed up on the counter and grabbed the saltcellar
from the top shelf behind it. The apothecary spotted him as he climbed
down from the counter.

"What are you doing? Give that back!" The apothecary's voice was angry.

Osbert ran up the stairs to his room, locked the door and pulled off
his nightshirt.

"Stop!" yelled the apothecary from below.

Ordinary flames might not burn the paintings and release the pieces of Amelia's soul, but perhaps the magical fire of his burning soul could. He hurriedly piled the portraits of Amelia in the middle of the room as the apothecary banged on the door. He could hear the voice of the portraits asking what he was doing.

Lying back on the portraits, he unscrewed the top of the saltcellar and spilled the salt upon his chest.

His body spasmed as gouts of pale fire spread from his chest. The pain twisted his mind and all reason fled. All that remained was the desire to destroy the portraits. Flames surrounded him and then all went dark.

As he returned to consciousness, he felt a burning sensation over most of his body. The scent of smoke filled his nostrils. This must be hell, his eternal destiny. As he opened his eyes, though, he saw the old monk leaning over him, not a devil.

"He's awake," said the monk to someone outside Osbert's view. "Be still, young man. That you are alive is a miracle, though you have some burns on your body from the fire."

Osbert tried to speak, but at first could not find a voice in his dry throat. Finally he managed to whisper, "Where am I?"

"The infirmary at Tewksbury Abbey. Be still."

"Where is the apothecary?"

The monk shook his head. "He must have been consumed by the fire. We did not find his body."

Osbert found it hard to believe the apothecary was truly dead. "And my paintings?"

"They are destroyed. The entire building burned to ashes; there is nothing left. But you must rest. Go back to sleep."

Propped up on his bed in the infirmary, Osbert drank the broth that was supposed to restore his strength. It was no use, he knew—his strength was gone because he had given up most of his soul, not because of his injuries.

The one real comfort he had was that Amelia still lived, and was said to be recovering slowly. At least her death was not on his conscience.

The old monk arrived and sat on a stool by Osbert's bed. "I have something for you." He reached into a sack and brought out the saltcellar.

Osbert nearly spilled his broth. "Where did you get that?" he whispered.

"You were clutching it when we found you. It is a symbol of the miracle that saved you."

Saved? He could not be saved. "What do you mean?"

"After the fire burned out, no one thought anybody could have survived. But then you were found in the midst of the ashes, still alive, with a pile of salt on your chest and this saltcellar in your hand." The monk smiled. "I know salt is a preservative, but I didn't think it had quite so much power."

"That salt had magical properties." For what evil fate had the Salt of Judas saved him?

The monk laughed. "It is but ordinary salt." He opened up the saltcellar, dipped his finger in, and dabbed some crystals on his tongue. "See?"

Osbert held his breath for a moment, but nothing happened to the monk. "It cannot be. I saw it. The apothecary…"

The monk raised an eyebrow. "The apothecary claimed it was magical salt? I had my suspicions the man was a fraud."

"He was no fraud. At least, not the way you think." What purpose was there in hiding the truth? Osbert felt as if a burden lifted from his shoulders as he quietly began to tell the monk what he had done.

"So I tried to release Amelia's soul by burning the paintings with the magical fire, and that's the last thing I remember before I awoke after the fire," Osbert finished.

During Osbert's narration, the monk had not interrupted, although he had frowned at several points. Now the monk leaned forward and stared into Osbert's eyes. After a few seconds, he said, "You do not appear to be either a madman or a liar, and I cannot see why you would concoct such a tale. I believe you."

"Thank you." It was a relief to be believed. Osbert looked at the saltcellar still gripped in the monk's hands. "But I still don't understand why the Salt of Judas didn't burn you when you touched it. What happened to the curse?"

The monk looked up to the ceiling of the infirmary. Osbert followed his gaze, but he could see nothing.

The monk looked back down to Osbert. "The salt lost its savour through an act of betrayal. Perhaps it took an act of sacrifice to let it be salted again."

The canvas before him was nearly complete. The image of Tewkesbury Abbey was ethereal, wreathed in morning mist, though the actual mist had vanished hours ago. Osbert paused as he carefully considered where to add a little more shadow.

"You paint very well," said a voice over his shoulder.

He knew before turning that it was Amelia. She had recently begun taking walks again as she had recovered from her illness, and he had seen her every few days over the past month. But this was the first time she had spoken to him.

"Thank you, Miss." He turned back to the canvas.

"Perhaps one day you could paint a portrait of me," Amelia said.

"I only paint landscapes."

* * *

As a published finalist in the Writers of the Future anthology, I got to attend the 2004 workshop in Hollywood along with the winners. The main workshop assignment was to write a short story in twenty-four hours, using a random object we were each given and the results of an interview we conducted with a stranger.

For my object, Tim Powers handed me a little packet of sugar and said, "Pretend it's salt." The stranger I interviewed was a caricature artist on Hollywood Boulevard.

In thinking about salt, I remembered how slugs react to it. What if there were a substance that caused a human soul to react similarly? A little research into the mythology associated with salt brought up the story of Judas spilling salt at the Last Supper, and I was on my way to a story.

The Final Element

Waving off the uniformed policeman's offer to help, Dennis Lombardo ducked under the yellow crime scene tape and hefted the case containing the nuclear resonance scanner over the threshold of the New York brownstone. Slivers of wood from the broken door littered the floor.

"I've lugged this thing all the way from L.A.," Dennis said to the officer. "I can manage. Just lead the way to where you want me to set up my equipment."

The officer escorted him to a room dominated by a grand piano. Glass and wood cabinets displaying musical instruments and books lined the walls. At the back of the room, though, stood the thing that had brought him here: the brushed-steel, five-foot cube of a Series 3 nanofactory.

Next to it, on a white-linened table, lay two violins.

Setting down the scanner, Dennis walked over and studied the violins. They were made of fine-grain wood covered with a red lacquer, and to his eye they appeared identical in every respect, except for the NYPD identifying tags. That was to be expected—he would not have been sent here otherwise.

"My most prized possession," said a voice from the door. "At least, one of them is."

Dennis turned to see the silver-haired gentleman who had entered the room. "I'm Dennis Lombardo. NanoFaction sent me to detect the fake."

"Anton Gale." The man reached out and shook Dennis's hand. "Terence Zhang is an old friend."

Until last night's phone call ordering him to fly overnight to New York on the corporate jet, Dennis had never spoken to Zhang, NanoFaction's CEO. Gale obviously had connections. "Our company is always happy to help where we can."

"So, what do you think of the Soil?" said Gale.

"Excuse me?"

"The Soil Stradivarius."

Dennis looked over at the violins. "Oh, this is a Stradivarius? I've heard of those."

"You are not a violin expert?"

"I'm sorry. I'm familiar with scientific instruments, not musical ones."

"Ah, of course," Gale said. "Allow me to introduce you to the instrument of Yehudi Menuhin, Itzhak Perlman and Yuri Volokh."

The names sounded familiar, so Dennis decided they must be famous violinists. "Very impressive. I guess that's why someone would steal it and try to dupe it."

"Not just someone. Leonard Wharton, another collector. This is his house," Gale said. "You must understand, the Soil Strad is considered the finest violin in the world. I paid $55 million at Sotheby's to own it, back in 2027. And the man I outbid was Wharton."

Dennis raised his eyebrows. "And he stole it from you?"

"Apparently he planned to ransom the fake and keep the real one for himself. He has been arrested for using an unlicensed nanofactory pattern." Gale waved a hand dismissively. "I do not wish to press charges against him for the theft, for I understand his obsession. But the police cannot determine which violin is mine and which is the unlicensed copy they need to keep as evidence."

Dennis nodded. In order to minimize economic disruption, the government had prohibited nanoduplication of unlicensed patterns. The copy would have to be destroyed when the police were done with it. "Let me just set up my equipment, and I should be able to determine fairly quickly."

"Your equipment will not damage the violin, I hope."

Dennis opened up the case and removed a thick-legged tripod. "Nuclear resonance scanning is safe enough you could use it on a baby. I'm not sure why you'd want an atomic map of a baby, but if you needed one…"

He set up the tripod next to the table with the violins, removed the scanner from the case and attached it to the tripod. Pointing the nose of the scanner at the first violin, he did a five-second preliminary scan for solid objects in the field, then selected the violin. After shrinking the selected volume slightly in order to ignore any surface contamination, he initiated a thorough scan.

"Now we wait," said Dennis.

"How long?"

"For something this volume, a couple of minutes. And then I should be able to tell you which is the original."

Gale frowned. "So simple?"

"Yep."

"I thought your nanofactories built things at the atomic level."

"They do. Atom by atom, molecule by molecule. And all atoms are equal." Dennis grinned. "But some are more equal than others."

"You've lost me, I'm afraid."

"A little nuclear scanner humor. Atoms of the same element always have the same number of protons in their nucleus. But they can have different numbers of neutrons. The variations are called isotopes, and my scanner here can tell the difference between different isotopes."

"But even if the... isotopes of atoms are different between the two violins, how does that show which is my Strad?"

"Some isotopes are much more common than others. Most oxygen atoms, for example, have eight neutrons. Less than one percent have nine or ten. Every nanofactory is programmed to create an isotope 'signature' in the items it creates, by varying the levels of different isotopes."

"I see. By comparing the scans of the two violins, the signature will become apparent."

"I should be able to tell just from scanning one – if it has the signature, it's the fake, if not, it's your Strad."

"Amazing."

"That's my job."

"You do this all the time?"

"Oh, it's not usually so glamorous as detecting forged violins. Generally it's just scanning things to create new patterns for the—"

The scanner beeped.

"—nanofactories. Sounds like the scan's done." Dennis checked the readout. A signature pattern would stand out clearly, but the isotope distributions were within the normal range for natural variation. "This one should be your original. I'll scan the other and show you the signature. After that, the cops can come take it as evidence."

Dennis set up the scan on the second violin.

"It seems such a shame," said Gale.

"What?"

"People have been trying for centuries to create violins as fine as Antonio Stradiveri's. Scientists have studied the wood, the design, the lacquer—every aspect of these violins, looking for the Stradivarius secret. And they have always failed, until now. But the law requires that the copy be destroyed."

Dennis shrugged. "Law's there for a reason. What would your $25 million violin be worth if anyone could buy one from Wal-Mart?"

"What is the worth of every violinist being able to play on so fine an instrument?" Gale sighed. "But you are right. The law prevents economic chaos."

After a few moments of silence, Dennis said, "The secret still remains. Making a nanoduplicate doesn't explain why a Stradivarius sounds the way it does."

With a smile, Gale said, "Some believe that a violin becomes better if it is loved and played well. The secret is the great violinists who have loved and played their Strads. And that is something your scanner cannot detect, am I right?"

"You are." Dennis chuckled. "Although I suppose we could test that theory. Since the copy violin has not been loved and played well, it should not sound as good."

The scanner beeped. Dennis looked at the readout. There was no signature pattern. As far as his scanner was concerned, both violins were originals. He frowned at the readout. Had he somehow failed to change targets?

"Is there a problem?"

"Yes. I didn't find a signature. So we're back to not knowing which is your Strad."

"How is that possible?"

"It shouldn't be." Dennis stepped over to the nanofactory and frowned at it. "Creating an unlicensed pattern is difficult enough, but eliminating the signature would require reprogramming the nanofactory, and that means our source code security has been compromised. The guy who stole your violin isn't a computer genius by any chance?"

Gale winced. "No, he's a real estate developer."

"So he must have hired someone to do the hacking for him." Dennis pulled out his phone. "I have to call my boss."

After a brief conversation outlining the security issue, Dennis hung up.

"What did your boss say?" asked Gale.

"She said I'd better find a way to detect the dupe." Dennis let out a long breath through pursed lips.

"We could do as you said—play the violins and see if one sounds different."

Dennis doubted that atomically identical violins would have different sounds, but allowing Gale to try the experiment wouldn't hurt—and it would give Dennis time to think. "Go ahead."

After getting a bow from a cabinet, Gale picked up the first violin and positioned it under his chin. He played a few seemingly random notes while adjusting the knobs on the violin. "Tuning up," he said.

Dennis nodded. He began speculating about possible differences between a real item and a nanoduplicate.

Then Gale began to play. He began slowly, building a melody with the pure tones of the violin. The music floated up the scales, then down again.

Dennis watched as Gale lovingly drew the bow across the strings, sometimes drawing a note out, other times jumping quickly from one note to another.

As the final note faded, Dennis applauded. "Wonderful. Do you give a lot of concerts?"

Gale raised an eyebrow. "Me? No, I am but a practiced amateur. I occasionally loan my violin to truly talented musicians, but..." He lowered the violin and stared at it. "This sounds like my violin. I could tell no difference."

"Try the other one."

After carefully laying down the one, Gale picked up the other.

As Gale played, Dennis concentrated on the music, hoping to hear an extra quality or a missing one, to distinguish the violins. But to his ear the music was just as beautiful as before.

Lowering the bow, Gale said, "They are the same."

"I was afraid of that." Dennis pursed his lips. "Maybe carbon-14."

"Carbon-14?"

"We only use stable isotopes for signatures. Carbon-14 decays. How old is this violin?"

"It was made in 1714."

"So the wood's over three hundred years old."

"Possibly much more, as Stradivari may have used aged wood."

"If I focus the scanner on an interior piece of wood, I should get a sample mostly unaffected by any later modifications." Dennis adjusted the scanner and started it.

"I don't mean to disturb," said Gale, "but I am curious what you are doing."

"No problem. About one in a thousand carbon atoms in the air are carbon-14. After something is dead, though, it no longer takes in new carbon atoms. After three-hundred-some-odd years," Dennis said, checking some numbers on the scanner's computer, "about four percent of the carbon-14 should have decayed into nitrogen. Carbon for nanofactory production generally comes from organic waste, but the carbon-14 levels would reflect things that died recently, not centuries ago."

"So there should be more carbon-14 in the fake."

"Exactly."

The scanner beeped. Dennis set it to scan the equivalent portion on the second violin.

Neither of them spoke as they waited for the scan to finish. When the scanner beeped, Dennis tapped a few keys to bring up a chart comparing the carbon-14 counts.

There was not even a millionth of a percent difference.

Dennis scratched the back of his neck. "Whoever programmed the forgery must have made it duplicate the carbon-14 count. Probably did the same with every isotope of every element. The two violins are the same in every physical way we can measure."

Gale wrung his hands. "But one of them was played by Menuhin, by Perlman. And one has never been played, except by me. One was fashioned by careful human hand, the other by uncaring machines. There must be a difference."

"I don't see..." Dennis paused. "There is one element we haven't taken into account yet."

"Which?"

"The human element. Can you have the police bring what's-his-name here? The collector who stole your violin?" A man as rich as Gale must have some pull with the local police.

"Wharton? I suppose so."

"And whoever put these police tags on."

"But why?"

"Because Wharton knows which one is the original."

"After I showed him the warrant," said the police officer, "he shut the door on us. After we broke down the door, we located him in this room. He was holding one violin. The other was on the table."

"Can you tell me which violin he was holding?"

The officer leaned over and read the numbers on the tags. "I tagged the one he was holding first, so it's the one on the left." He pointed.

"Thank you, officer." Dennis turned to Wharton, who was seated stiffly in a red leather chair, next to the nanofactory. "Whoever programmed the nanofactory was very clever. Faking the carbon-14 count was a detail few people would have thought of."

Wharton shrugged almost imperceptibly.

Dennis took a deep breath. He was counting on the fact that Wharton had hired someone else to do the programming. "But I found the flaw. The carbon-14 atoms in the fake were not distributed randomly, as they are in the original. Instead, my scan shows they are evenly spaced throughout the violin. Which means this one is the fake." Dennis picked up the violin on the left and carried it over to Wharton. "I thought you should see your handiwork one last time before I turn it into toothpicks."

Dennis opened the nanofactory's raw materials bin and placed the violin inside. As he moved his hand toward the start button, he watched Wharton's face.

Wharton looked impassively back at him.

"Stop," Gale said, right on cue. His voice sounded panicked. "I thought you said the one on the right had the regular pattern."

Yanking his hand back from the start button as if it were hot, Dennis said, "Oh, you're right. What the officer said mixed me up about which was which." He removed the violin from the bin and took it back to the table, exchanging it for the other one.

"A pity to destroy such a thing of beauty," said Dennis as he put it in the bin. "But it's only a copy." Again he watched Wharton's face, looking for weakness. The man was obsessed with the Soil Stradivarius. Surely he would not allow its destruction.

Dennis's hand moved toward the start button, and Wharton watched him calmly. Dennis began to press the button, and still there was no reaction.

With a sigh, Dennis pulled his hand away.

"If you are done playing at King Solomon," said Wharton, "I'd like to be taken back to my cell."

Dennis nodded to the officers, who escorted Wharton from the room.

"I'm sorry. I thought sure it would work," Dennis said.

"He's a smart man. He saw through the ruse," said Gale.

"But how could he have been sure it was a ruse? If he had been mistaken, he would have allowed the destruction of the world's greatest violin." Dennis shook his head. "Would he risk that?"

"Perhaps if it cannot be his, he no longer cares about the risk."

Suddenly it all became clear. "Or he knew there was no risk," Dennis said. "Would he be willing to go to prison if he knew the Soil Strad would be his when he got out?"

Gale frowned. "I'm not going to give it to him when he is freed."

"That's not what I mean." Dennis walked over to the nanofactory and pulled up its history, only to find it had been wiped clean. "What if *both* of these violins are fakes? He cleared the nanofactory's history so it wouldn't show he made two duplicates. The real violin could be hidden away, waiting for him to reclaim it after he's served his time."

"Yes, Wharton would risk a few years in prison to get the Soil. I probably would, myself. But why create two fakes?"

"Because if the police had found this nanofactory setup, but only one violin, they would have suspected a dupe. My company would have been called in to check his nanofactory, and we would have discovered the illegal modifications. But by providing a duplicate and a supposed original, he hoped no one would suspect what he'd created another."

Gale nodded, then said, "Is there some way to be sure?"

"Maybe." Dennis focused the scanner on the nanofactory's recycling container. "Unused material gets fed back into the system. In order to match the low carbon-14 count in the original violin, that would mean extra carbon-14 would be recycled. We can tell from the amount of recycled carbon-14 how many violins were created."

Dennis ran a few calculations as the scanner counted the carbon-14. When the scanner beeped, the results matched his prediction. "Two violins were made."

"So where is my violin?" asked Gale.

Dennis patted the scanner. "This is the proverbial fine-toothed comb. It may take a while, but I can scan every atom in the house if necessary."

Less than two hours later, Dennis found the violin in a safe hidden under the floorboards of Wharton's bedroom.

"This one is the original," Dennis said as he handed it to Gale.

The scanner showed that violin to be identical to the other two. At the atomic level, there was no way for Dennis to tell whether it really was the original. On seeing how happy Gale was to have his violin back, however, Dennis decided it was best not to mention that.

Seated on the corporate jet on the way back to L.A., Dennis removed the data module from the nuclear resonance scanner and brought up the atomic scans of the violins.

The two duplicate violins had already been destroyed, and company policy dictated that the scan data be wiped to prevent the creation of unlicensed nanoduplication patterns. He deleted the scan of the first violin, then the second.

But he hesitated when he reached the scan of the third. He looked at the violin pattern for several minutes, remembering the sweet tones of the melody Gale had played.

The finest violin in the world.

Dennis wondered if he could learn to play it.

* * *

The idea that violin-makers today cannot make a violin as good as a Stradivarius is something that has fascinated me since I first heard it. This story almost wrote itself once I combined that idea with nanotechnology duplication.

I mentioned the premise of this story on the Codex forum, and someone asked if I had read "Democritus's Violin" by G. David Nordley, the premise of which was: a Stradivarius violin is duplicated using nanotechnology. The story had been published in Analog *in 1999 and reprinted in* Year's Best SF 5.

No, I had not read it. I got ahold of a copy and found that my story was very different, despite using the same premise.

When I sent the story off to Stan Schmidt at Analog, *I mentioned in my cover letter that I had been unaware of Nordley's story until after I wrote mine, and that I hoped the stories were different enough (and that enough time had passed) so that he could publish mine.*

Fortunately, Stan agreed with my assessment.

Accounting
for Dragons

Introduction

Most dragons rarely think about accounting. But you've worked hard to acquire that hoard of gold and jewels—shouldn't you be keeping track of what happens to it? Just sitting on it isn't good enough any more. That's why you need accounting. Here are some tips:

Tip One: A Copper Saved Is a Copper Earned

Your hoard isn't just valuable to you; it's valuable to thieves. Once word gets out that you're sitting on a big pile of treasure, it isn't long before they come skulking about, their greedy hands trying to snatch the things you've gained through honest plunder.

Dragons may have the reputation of knowing every single item in their hoard, down to the last copper, but the fact of the matter is that only a tiny fraction of dragons can remember more than six or seven thousand individual pieces before they all start to blur together. Admit it—you really aren't sure whether you have twenty-seven ruby-encrusted platinum goblets, or only twenty-six.

But thanks to proper accounting, you can have a complete inventory of everything in your hoard. That way, if you find something is missing, you can go on a rampage across the countryside or demand a virgin as a sacrifice unless your treasure is returned.

Tip Two: Plan for Taxes

The Dragon King will always demand his share, but you need to remember it's your hoard, not the king's. There are legitimate deductions you can take to reduce the amount you pay in taxes.

For example, did you know that knight insurance can be written off as a legitimate expense? Defending yourself against the pests in plate-mail is something that happens in the ordinary course of business. A good knight insurance policy will cover not only dents in your scales and arrows through your wings, but also full reimbursement for any treasure you have to give out to make the knight go away.

Many dragons forget that alternative forms of income, such as virgin sacrifices, are also taxable, and they get a nasty surprise when the tax bill arrives. Plan to set aside some treasure to cover the extra taxes.

Tip Three: Keep Good Records

In case of a tax audit, you need to have good records. But that's not the only reason.

Imagine the following scenario. You swoop down out of the sky onto some innocent village. Your teeth and talons are sharpened. Your breath is smoky fresh. But before you can rend flesh from bone and set the buildings ablaze, some village elder comes out with documentation showing they sacrificed a virgin to you earlier in the year. It's enough to make you slink away with your tail dragging in the mud.

You can avoid such embarrassment by recording all of your income, including sacrificial virgins. Note down the amount, the source, and the date.

Good recordkeeping also allows you to be more proactive. For example, you may notice that a particular village is late in offering a sacrifice. Then it's your choice whether to demand an immediate sacrifice or go wreak havoc on the village.

Tip Four: Hire a Good Accountant

Maybe you're just too busy. Or maybe you're bad at math. For whatever reason, you may decide to hire an accountant rather than do the work yourself. Generally, you have two options when it comes to hiring an accountant.

A good dragon accountant can be expensive, although he usually pays for himself through tax savings.

For the more cost-conscious dragon, a smarter choice is to find a human accountant who will gladly do all your accounting without charging you a single copper, simply in return for not being eaten. Over the long term, the savings can really add up.

"That's the end," I said after I finished reading the brochure. The echo of my voice faded away inside the cave.

"I'd never realized the advantages," said the dragon. Its black tongue flickered out to moisten its scaly lips. "After I eat you, I'll have to find myself an accountant."

I cleared my throat. "By sheer coincidence," I said, "it turns out that I'm an accountant. That's why I just happened to have that brochure with me."

"An accountant?" The gold and jewels of the dragon's hoard sparkled as he snorted flame. "The village elders claimed you were a virgin!"

"Strange as it may seem," I said, "the two are not mutually exclusive."

"Oh," said the dragon. "Well, then, I suppose you'll do. You'll work for not being eaten?"

"I would find that quite satisfactory," I said. "Plus, there's a substantial tax benefit to you, because an uneaten virgin sacrifice doesn't count as income. Now, let's review your financial situation. I'll need to see your tax returns for the past three years, your current knight insurance policy..."

"But I don't have a knight insurance policy," said the dragon.

"Really? You're in luck." With a broad smile, I reached into my pocket. "I just happen to have a brochure called *Insurance for Dragons*."

* * *

In the summer of 2007, I attended the six-week-long Odyssey Writing Workshop. One of the events of the workshop was the "Odyssey Slam" at the Barnes & Noble in Nashua, New Hampshire. Each workshop participant had to read a flash fiction piece in five minutes or less.

My original plan was to read a revised version of the 1000-word story I had written earlier in the workshop, but in the last few days before the Slam I started leaning against that. The night before the Slam I began working on a more humorous piece, as I've noticed that humor tends to go over very well at readings.

In the morning I got up and decided that piece wouldn't work, because it was too clichéd. It was a punchline-type story, and I Googled the punchline and saw a couple of similar stories.) Also, the story itself would be too serious before the punchline.

So I looked at revising some of my unpublished flash pieces, and none of them appealed to me. Then I looked at the possibility of chopping down my humorous fairy tale "Bird-Dropping and Sunday," which always gets a great reception at readings even though editors kept deciding it was not quite right for their magazines, but decided there was no way I could cut half the story.

Finally, before deciding to just go with the original plan, I went over my lists of titles and story seeds, and came across "dragon accountant," which was a seed I had jotted down sometime in the previous couple of weeks, based on a comment by someone (I think it was a guest lecturer, author Michael Arnzen) about dragon accountants.

It occurred to me that dragons might need some basic information about accounting, sort of an Accounting for Dummies—*except for dragons, not dummies. That gave me my title and basic premise.*

Not until I had written over half the story did I realize there was an actual character reading the information aloud to a dragon.

"Accounting for Dragons" is the first story I wrote almost entirely using voice dictation software. By sheer coincidence, the name of the software is Dragon Naturally Speaking.

Anyway, I finished the story in a couple of hours and read it at the Slam. It went over pretty well, with people laughing in the right places, which is always a plus.

After the Odyssey workshop was over, I revised the story with some help from my brother Michael, an actual accountant who works for something far scarier than a dragon: the Internal Revenue Service. My writing groups were also helpful in bringing the story up to snuff, particularly by letting me know what to cut out because it wasn't working.

This story holds my personal record for fastest acceptance: two hours and nine minutes after I sent it to Edmund, he bought it.

Tabloid Reporter to the Stars

When I was fired after ten years as a science reporter for the *New York Times*, the editor told me I'd never get a job with a decent paper again. He was right, at first: no one wanted to hire a reporter who had taken bribes to write a series of articles about a non-existent technology in order to inflate the value of a company being used in a stock swindle— even if I had managed to get off without serving time.

And that's the only reason I took the job with the *Midnight Observer* tabloid. They didn't care that I'd made up a news story—they were impressed that I'd managed to write something that had fooled experts for over a year. So began my new career under the pseudonym of Dr. Lance Jorgensen. The doctorate was phony, of course, and I never did decide what it was in. I worked that gig for three years before I caught the break that let me get back into real journalism.

When the United Nations Space Agency decided to hold a lottery to choose a reporter to travel on board the first interstellar ship, they set strict qualifications: a college degree in journalism, at least five years of experience as a science reporter, and current employment with a periodical or news show with circulation or viewership of at least one million.

Technically, I qualified. So I entered. And a random number generator on an UNSA computer picked my number.

Less than five minutes after UNSA announced the crew of the *Starfarer I*, including yours truly as the only journalist, the calls began. The first was from my old editor at the *Times*. He wanted me back on an exclusive basis—I could name my own price. I'll admit I was bitter: I told him my price was full ownership of the paper, and that I'd fire him as soon as I had it. He sputtered; I hung up.

By the end of that week, I had a TV deal with CNN and a print/Web deal with the *Washington Post*. And so, without a gram of regret, Dr. Lance Jorgensen gave the *Midnight Observer* his two weeks' notice. I was once again Lawrence Jensen, science reporter.

A lot of journalists squawked that I didn't deserve to be on the mission because of my scrape with the law, even if I had managed to avoid a conviction by turning state's evidence. But the rules were on my side for a change: my degree from the Columbia School of Journalism, my experience at the *Times*, and the *Midnight Observer's* seven-million-plus circulation fit the letter, if not the spirit, of the rules. Despite their fervent wishes, I made it through spaceflight training without a hitch, and proudly boarded the *Starfarer* as the world looked on.

This mission was my chance for redemption. I'd made one big mistake, and I planned to make up for it with accurate, well-written science reporting that made the wonders of space travel understandable to everyone. I had loved science since I was a kid; if I'd had the brains to do the math I might have chosen a career as a scientist instead of a reporter. Reporting this mission was my dream job, and I was determined not to mess things up.

The day we launched, the *Midnight Observer* ran a cover story claiming that I had been selected for this mission because while working undercover for them I had already met the aliens the *Starfarer* would encounter, and they had requested that I serve as Earth's ambassador. They had even 'shopped a picture of me shaking hands with a stereotypical short, gray, bald, bulge-headed alien.

During all two hundred and twenty-three days of hyperspace travel, my crewmates refused to let me live that down.

Fortunately, when we found the aliens, they didn't look anything like that picture.

The theory behind hyperspace travel involves several dimensions beyond the usual four we humans can perceive. The mathematical formulas involved in actually making a hyperspace drive work surpass the understanding of the unenhanced human brain. But what the formulas and the theory don't mention is that traveling by hyperspace is beautiful. The harsh radiation that fills the hyperspacial void becomes a kaleidoscope of infinite variety as it washes upon our magnetic shields.

Observations from Hubble III had indicated the possibility of a planet with an oxygen-nitrogen atmosphere in this system, and now that we had arrived, our on-board telescopes had confirmed that the fourth planet had such an atmosphere. I had just finished my third column for this week's homelink, explaining about non-equilibrium gasses and why this meant there was life of some sort on the planet, when Singh began pounding on my cabin door.

"Hey, Ambassador, you in there?"

I didn't dignify that by responding.

"Come on, Jensen, open up. I've got a scoop for you."

Narinder Singh was one of *Starfarer's* xenobiologists, and until we actually got down on the ground, he didn't have much to do except make guesses based on the limited data our telescopes could gather. So it was unlikely that he had anything important. Besides, since I was the only reporter on board, there wasn't anyone who could scoop me. But I said, "Come in," anyway.

He opened the hatch and came in. "Look at these." He shoved a handful of eight-by-ten photos in front of my face.

I took the photos and began leafing through them. They showed a thin sunlit crescent of planet, which I assumed to be Aurora, the planet with the good atmosphere. "So, it's nighttime on half the planet. Excuse me while I call my editor and tell him to stop the presses."

"No, look closer at the nighttime side. Over here." He pointed to a region along the equator near the edge of the darkness.

Peering at the photo, I noticed that there were a dozen or so little clumps of bright spots. "You think these are the lights of cities?"

"Yes. There's a civilization on that planet. And I want you to remember I came to you with this discovery first."

I looked over at the column I had just finished. I could rewrite a bit to mention Singh's speculations, with plenty of caveats. But it still seemed a little too flimsy—and the whole situation with the *Midnight Observer* story made me leery of anything involving aliens. "Yeah, I'll remember, if it turns out to be anything. It's probably volcanoes or forest fires or something. Did you run this by Khadil?" Iqrit Khadil was our geologist. "I mean, if it's really a civilization down there, how come there's no radio traffic?"

"Maybe they haven't developed radio yet. Or maybe they've moved beyond it. But I'm telling you, this is it: a sentient species with at least rudimentary civilization."

"Look, if you can get Khadil to agree that those are not volcanoes or any other geological phenomenon within the next half hour, I'll put your speculations in today's column. Otherwise, you'll have to wait till next week, which might be better, anyway, since by then there might be more evidence one way or the other."

He grabbed the photos back. "I know what I know. I'll talk to Khadil."

Now that the Starfarer is out of hyperspace, normal radio transmissions would take over one hundred and thirty years to travel to Earth, making direct two-way communication impossible. So the Starfarer's designers came up with a solution. When we arrived in this solar system, our ship split into two modules. The Hyperspace Module (HM) and two members of the crew remain in the outer system, where they can make the jump to hyperspace, while the Orbital Module (OM) heads in toward the planets with the rest of the crew. We send all our data—including this column—to the HM.

It takes six days for the nuclear reactor on the HM to store enough power in the capacitors for the jump to hyperspace. So once a week, they make the jump and send a radio signal to a ship in hyperspace near Earth. Instead of one hundred and thirty years, the signal only takes eighteen hours to travel to Earth. The receiving ship then returns to normal space and transmits the data to UNSA headquarters on Earth, which sends my columns to the Washington Post, who deliver it to your doorstep.

By the time the OM reached planetary orbit five days later, all the evidence pointed to a developing civilization on Aurora, so I decided it was a good thing I'd included Singh's speculations in my column. We didn't know what the reaction from Earth was yet—the HM was still charging its capacitors for its weekly jump into hyperspace to transmit our reports and download communications from home. But first contact with an alien species, which had always been considered only a slight possibility, transformed our mission from one of simple exploration into something far greater. I'd already written and rewritten and disregarded several columns about the meaning of all this. It was probably the biggest news story ever; I was writing history, and I wanted to get the words right.

I wasn't the only one. Commander Inez Gutierrez de la Peña, who was in overall command of our mission, commed me in my quarters in the middle of the night. The next morning most of the crew would be taking the Landing Module down to an isolated island in the middle of Aurora's larger ocean, and she would take the first human step on a planet outside our solar system. She wanted my opinion on what she would say upon taking that step.

I was flattered, but feigned irritation out of habit. "It's two in the morning. How'd you know I wasn't sleeping?"

"I checked the power consumption in your quarters and could tell the lights and your computer were on." UNSA hadn't picked Gutierrez by lottery; she knew this ship six ways from zero.

"OK. Tell me what you've got so far."

She hesitated a moment. "It's no 'One small step,' but… 'Humanity has always been a race of explorers. Though in the past we have not always lived up to our aspirations, letting fear and exploitation rule our encounters with the unknown, today on this new world we have a chance—'"

"Blah blah blah. Are you looking to write a pamphlet on social responsibility or do you want to say something that will still be quoted a thousand years from now?"

"I was thinking that putting the event in its historical context—"

"Leave that to the historians and people like me. What you need is a sound bite. Short. To the point, yet something that recalls the dreams of our first ancestors who looked up at the stars and wondered what lay beyond them."

On my com screen, her face nodded. "I see what you mean. You going to be up a while longer?"

"Yeah. Call me when you come up with something."

I may not have sounded very respectful, but Commander Gutierrez had my respect. Not only was she almost irritatingly competent at her job, but out of the thirty-seven other members of the crew, she was the only one who had never called me "Ambassador."

It took her six more tries over the next three hours before I thought she had it about right.

The next morning, precisely on schedule, she climbed down the ladder outside the LM's airlock. We could hear her steady breathing over her spacesuit's com system. When she reached the bottom and took that first step onto Aurora's soil, her voice came in loud and clear.

"Today humanity walks among the stars. Where will we walk tomorrow?"

As those of us on board the LM clapped and cheered, I felt twin twinges of pride and jealousy. Every word I had ever written would be long forgotten, and still those words would be remembered. They were not mine, but at least I had helped shape them.

I took my little shares of immortality wherever I could.

Like the generation who as children saw the Wright Brothers fly and as adults saw man walk on the moon, or those who watched the latter as children and lived to see the first colony on Mars, we are witnesses to the dawn of a new age of humanity. Who knows how far we will go, following the footsteps of Commander Gutierrez?

Our landing spot's isolation allowed the biologists to analyze the native life with the least risk of contaminating the planetary biosphere. Seven days after landing, I got a chance to take a five-minute walk around the island. Aurora's light gravity—seventy-eight percent of Earth's—gave a spring to my step despite the weight of the spacesuit.

I daydreamed of spotting something significant during my walk, a scientific discovery of my own that I could reveal to a waiting world, but in the end all that I had discovered for myself was the sensation of walking beneath an aquamarine sky and looking up at a sun that seemed too blue and too small.

As far as important discoveries went, I had to settle for the daily breakthroughs of the biologists. The biggest one was the fact that life on Aurora was not based on DNA, but rather on a previously unknown nucleic acid molecule with a hexagonal cross-section. A few days later came the finding that the protein building-blocks of Auroran life consisted of twenty-two amino acids instead of just twenty.

Exciting and heady information though these details might be for the fraction of Earth's population who were molecular biologists, I needed a subject that would grab the average reader's attention. That meant either danger or sex or both—suitably phrased for the *Washington Post*, of course. I abandoned my half-written amino acid column and went down to the biolab to wheedle something worth writing about out of the biologists.

Singh was in the middle of something delicate and didn't have time to talk, but Rachel Zalcberg said she could spare a few minutes while she waited for some test results.

About three months into the hyperspace flight, I'd made a pass at Rachel. She'd shot me down in no uncertain terms. Asking her about alien sex was definitely not the right place to start, so I focused on danger. "Since life here on Aurora is so different, how likely is it that there some sort of disease organism that our immune system can't handle?"

She waved a hand dismissively. "Most disease organisms have trouble crossing the species barrier. Genetically, you're closer to an elm tree than to anything here, and you don't have to worry about Dutch elm disease. Our biochemistry is so different, the Auroran equivalents of bacteria and viruses wouldn't be able to reproduce inside us, assuming they even managed to survive at all."

That ruled out the danger angle, but since she'd brought up the subject of reproduction… "How do the animals here reproduce?"

She surprised me by grinning. "You will not believe how different it is. It's very exciting. I haven't had a chance to write this up yet, but I will before the next homelink. Just be sure to credit me with the discovery when you talk about it in your column."

"Of course." I leaned forward.

"Our initial examination showed that all the life here is asexual: There are no divisions between male and female."

"I know what asexual means." It meant *biologist* exciting, not *reader* exciting.

"We are isolated here, so it may not hold true for the whole planet, but for now it's all we have. Some of the life here reproduces by budding, essentially splitting off a little clone of itself. However, that doesn't account for the genetic diversity we've seen within species. And then we caught some of our lab specimens being naughty."

"Naughty? I thought they didn't have sex."

"Not exactly. One of our furry slugs—we haven't come up with a scientific name for it, yet—ate another one. Swallowed it whole."

"Cannibalism?" Maybe there was something here after all.

"Reproduction. After a few hours, that slug's skin hardened into a sort of cocoon. Two days later the cocoon cracked, and out came four smaller furry slugs. And each of the four is genetically different, with two-thirds of the genetic material from one slug, one-third from the other. Two slugs died and four were born."

It was good enough for one of those more-things-in-heaven-and-earth-than-are-dreamt-of-in-your-philosophy columns. I even got some footage of the new furry slugs for my CNN commentary.

I had the biologists to thank for the other highlight of that week. Coupled with the chemists' analysis of the atmosphere which showed there were no threatening toxins, the biologists' report that there was no significant disease threat meant we were authorized to go outside without spacesuits, and breathe fresh air for the first time since we'd left Earth almost nine months before.

I jumped at the chance to be one of the first group to breathe the unfiltered air of another planet. The airlock door hissed open. I took a deep breath, and gagged on an aroma reminiscent of wet dirty socks.

That footage did not make it into my CNN commentary.

Opponents of contact with the Auroran civilization point to the tragic experiences of indigenous societies on Earth after contact with more technologically advanced societies. Indeed, the histories of Native American tribes, Australian aborigines, Native Siberians and many others prove that such contact can be disastrous. But isn't the whole point of learning from history the idea that we can do better? If humanity could not progress, if we were forever destined to remain the same barbaric species that came out of the caves, then we would not even be debating this issue: we would be out conquering the Aurorans to use them as slave labor. Yes, our past demands that we proceed with caution, but our future demands that we proceed.

Perhaps the approval from UNSA would have come anyway, although I like to think my columns in favor of contact with the Aurorans had some effect. Our supplies limited us to only six months on the planet before we would have to begin the return journey to Earth, but we would be able to spend the last two of those months near an Auroran city.

We had refilled our fuel tanks by using electricity from our nuclear power plant to derive hydrogen and oxygen from seawater, and we would need to do so again before leaving, so we selected a coastal city as our destination and began our suborbital flight toward first contact.

"How you think they look?" asked Gianni Cacciatore, our climatologist, a few minutes after we launched. "If they are gray humanoids with bulging heads, they greet you as an old friend, *ehi, paesano?*"

There was Italian ancestry on my mother's side, so he'd taken to calling me *paesano*, countryman. At least it was better than Ambassador. I couldn't avoid talking to him, since we were strapped into seats next to each other for the duration of the flight. "Look, that Ambassador thing is getting about as old as someone asking you to go do something about the weather instead of just talking about it."

He thought a moment, then laughed. "*Buffo*. But what you think? I want to say, you are the only that knows something of the research of everyone. You have the grand picture."

It was a good question, actually. Our only pictures of the Auroran cities came from the Orbital Module, and its orbit was too high up to show individual Aurorans as anything more than a few pixels. In order to avoid any possible contamination, our initial landing site had intentionally been far from any sign of Auroran civilization. So none of us knew what an actual Auroran looked like. I'd discussed the issue with the biologists but hadn't written it up because it was pure speculation.

"Well, based on the animals we've discovered so far, the Aurorans are probably bilaterally symmetrical, although it could be quadrilateral. Since they have a civilization, they must be tool users, which means they must have something like our arms and hands, though it could be tentacles with claws for all we really know. They must have a way of getting around, so legs are probable, but we can't really know how many. Or maybe they move like snakes or snails." I sighed. "What I'm basically trying to say is that there are so many possibilities that we haven't got a really good idea of what they will look like, but they probably will not look as much like us as the stupid fake alien in that photo does."

He nodded. "*Interessante.*"

I shifted the conversation to some of the unusual things he had discovered about Aurora's climate and thus kept myself occupied until our pilot, Zhao

Xia, announced that we should prepare for a jolt when she activated the engines to slow us for landing.

The LM's cabin was mostly silent as we watched the ground grow ever closer on our screens. When we touched down, there was some clapping and cheering, though not as much as there had been the first time we landed.

Commander Gutierrez's firm voice came over the intercom. "I'm sure the Aurorans nearby must have seen us coming, and some of them will probably arrive soon. Those who were chosen for the first contact party please prepare to exit the ship."

I had demanded to be included in the party, and Gutierrez had refused. Although it seemed unlikely, there was no way to be sure the Aurorans would not react with xenophobic violence, so she had decided to send only two people: Singh, because of his xenobiological expertise, and Tinochika Murerwa, because prior to becoming an astrophysicist he had seen combat while serving in the U.N. Special Forces.

My arguments in favor of freedom of the press did not persuade her, but I made enough of a fuss that her superiors on Earth had ordered her to include me. I don't know why they overrode her; I suspect the real reason had nothing to do with freedom of the press and everything to do with the fact that the United States shouldered forty percent of the cost of this mission, and U.S. politicians wanted an American involved in the biggest news to come out of it. It didn't matter why—I was in.

Singh, Murerwa and I gathered our equipment and entered the airlock. As the pressure equalized, I said, "Good luck, Singh," because he was the one in command of our little party.

"Thanks."

We climbed down the ladder and started preparing for our hosts to arrive and greet their unexpected visitors.

Murerwa looked over his shoulder at the videocam I was setting up on a tripod. He let out a deep bass laugh. "Planning to get a picture of yourself shaking hands with a real alien?"

"Yes." Somehow I felt that getting a real picture would be my compensation for all the grief I'd taken over the fake one.

After a very long five minutes, something came over a small ridge east of us. As it got closer, I began to make out details of its physiology. It looked like a scaly brown headless camel with four tentacles instead of a neck. As it got closer, I could see a wide opening between the top and bottom pairs of tentacles that I presumed to be its mouth.

It stopped about ten meters away from us. It wasn't very large; although it certainly weighed more than me, the hump on its back only came up to about the middle of my chest. As if responding to that thought, the hump rose a few inches on a thick stalk, and the creature seemed to stare at us out of two glossy blue-black openings on the front of the hump.

Singh said something in Hindi that I didn't understand.

"Is it one of the Aurorans or just an animal?" I asked.

"I think it's sentient. It's wearing something like a tool-belt around one of its forelegs."

Now that he pointed it out, I saw the belt, which appeared to be made of a thick woven fabric. And one of the tools was undoubtedly a hammer, even if I wasn't sure what the rest were.

We stared at him while he stared at us. Now we knew what an Auroran looked like.

Or rather, we thought we did until more creatures began coming over the hill. Some came on four legs, some on two. I was fairly sure I saw one with eight. Some had tentacles; others had jointed arms with hand-like appendages. All had scaly skins, but some had patches of fur that appeared to be part of their bodies, not clothing, and all had heads similar to the hump on the first one, though it didn't seem to be in the same place on the different anatomies. Some were bilaterally symmetrical, but some were not—I spotted one that had anemone-like tendrils on one side and a crab-like pincer on the other. And of the fifty or more arrivals, there didn't appear to be more than a handful that looked like they belonged to the same species.

As the crowd grew, they began singing to each other. At least that's what it sounded like to me; wordless tunes that harmonized rather than creating a cacophony.

Then one of them said some words, and the others silenced almost immediately.

"Did you catch what he said?" asked Singh.

"Sounded like 'Alla Beeth' to me," I answered.

A voice in the crowd repeated it, and suddenly all of them were chanting, "Alla Beeth."

They didn't stop chanting until the soldiers showed up. Their civilization might be very different from ours, but a sword still looks like a sword, even if it is strapped to the waist of a tentacled reptilian centaur.

The soldiers sang to the crowd, and the crowd quieted down, parting in the middle to allow the half-dozen soldiers through.

Their leader trotted forward through the buffer zone the crowd had left around us, and stopped about two meters away. His wide, expressionless eyes looked at each of the three of us in turn. Then he edged sideways until he was standing in front of me. Slowly he drew his sword.

I bravely stood my ground to show the aliens that humans were not intimidated. Or else I was frightened into immobility. Either way, the result was the same.

The leader bent one of his forelegs and sort of knelt on one knee. He placed his sword on the ground, looked at me, and said, "Alla Beeth."

The crowd took up the chant once more.

Murerwa laughed again. "Looks like you've been chosen as the first ambassador to Aurora."

The failure to include a linguistics expert on this mission is not as unreasonable as critics of UNSA are claiming. The evidence showed a high likelihood of a planet with an oxygen-nitrogen atmosphere, but before the Starfarer arrived there was not a scintilla of evidence for a sentient, civilized lifeform in this system. Earth has had an oxygen-nitrogen atmosphere for perhaps 1.5 billion years. The chances that an alien ship visiting Earth during that time would have had found humans are only a third of one percent. The chances it would find us civilized are less than half a thousandth of a percent.

Iqrit Khadil was the first to bring up religion. During a lull in mess hall conversation as the crew ate dinner the night of first contact, he said, "I do not think it can be merely coincidence that one of the two words we have heard these aliens speak is Allah."

"You can't be serious!" Rachel said.

"Why not? These primitives obviously seemed to think Jensen was a god, or a messenger sent by a god. And though they seem to communicate among themselves by singing, they knew to speak words to us. And one of those words was Allah."

Rachel's knuckles tightened around her fork. "All right, O wise one, then what does 'Beeth' mean?"

Khadil shrugged. "Maybe it means messenger. 'Allah Beeth,' messenger of Allah."

I almost said that if I was anyone's messenger, I was the *Washington Post's*, but several people began talking at once.

Rachel pounded the table with her fist until everyone turned to look at her. "First of all, we don't know how the words are divided, or even that it's more than one word, or even that it's a word at all. Maybe the first word is

Al, but they're really just mispronouncing *El*, and so they're actually referring to the God of the Jews, not the God of Islam." She raised her voice over the beginnings of objections. "But coincidence is the most likely explanation. If we are going to speculate based on the idea that they spoke to us because they have seen humans before—which I find hard to believe—then there are other reasonable explanations. For example, they were trying to say the first two letters of the alphabet. Everyone here is familiar with the first two letters of the Greek alphabet: alpha, beta. In Hebrew, they are *aleph, bet*." She turned to Khadil. "What are they in Arabic?"

"*Alif, ba*." He nodded. "I spoke too soon. I was just excited to hear what sounded like 'Allah.' But it is most likely a coincidence."

During the rest of dinner I thought about what Khadil and Rachel had said. Coincidence. The possible meaning of the words didn't really matter to me. But if the Aurorans communicated through song, why did they have words to use with us? And why only two words?

I tried to avoid wondering why their leader had chosen me to bow to, but I wasn't very successful.

Imagine if eating an octopus in a certain way would allow you to grow tentacles on your body. Or if by eating a horse, you could replace your two human legs with four horse legs. According to Singh and Zalcberg's observations of our newfound friends, that is essentially what the Aurorans can do: manipulate their own bodies by absorbing an animal and using its genetic code to recreate some aspect of that animal's body. The wide variety of body shapes and parts among the Aurorans comes from deliberate change, not from their inherited genes.

Within a few days, the Aurorans remedied our failure to bring a linguistics expert by providing one of their own. His name was a short trill that most of us could not reproduce, so someone called him Mozart. I pointed out that, given "Beeth" was one of the two words he knew, Beethoven might have been more appropriate, but by then the name had already stuck.

Biologically speaking, Mozart was neither a he nor a she, but none of us really felt comfortable calling it "it." Since the real Mozart had been a he, we defaulted to that usage for the most part.

Through trial and error, we determined that the Auroran vocal apparatus simply was incapable of making most of the sounds of human languages. Fortunately, Mozart had brought rough sheets of a paper-like substance, inks of various colors, and a collection of clay stamps that could be used to imprint various symbols on the paper. While a few of the simpler symbols bore a resemblance to letters in various Earth alphabets—Χ, Ο, Ι, Τ, Δ, Λ, Γ—there did not appear to be any connection between them and their Earthly sounds, so Rachel's *aleph-bet* explanation for "Alla Beeth" was a dead end.

Since Mozart understood the concept of written symbols representing ideas, once he got over his astonishment at the interaction between a computer keyboard and monitor, we were able to teach him to use his tentacles to type. We would communicate back by typing and saying words at the same time, so he could learn to associate the text of a word with its sound.

Whoever had decided to send Mozart to communicate with us had made a good choice. After only four days, he had learned enough English to carry on simple conversations, so during my shift for teaching him, I asked him the question that had been bothering me. "Why did your leader bow to me?"

WHAT IS MY LEADER?

"One of your people with swords. The most important one."

COMMANDER GUTIERREZ IS YOUR LEADER?

"Yes."

WHAT IS BOW?

I demonstrated a bow.

NOT MY LEADER. LEADER CLOSE PEOPLE. I IS FAR.

The nearest town, which someone had imaginatively dubbed Neartown, was not the place Mozart was from. That was new information, and I felt a little pleased with myself for discovering it. Still, I pressed on to find out more about what was bothering me. "Why did the leader of the close people bow to me?"

HE THINK YOU IS HOW DO YOU SPELL? He stopped typing and said, "Alla Beeth."

I typed it out for him.

HE THINK YOU IS ALLA BEETH.

"You do not think I am Alla Beeth?"

NO. YOU LOOK LIKE BUT NOT SAME.

"Who is Alla Beeth?"

Mozart whistled a staccato tune. YOU NOT KNOW ALLA BEETH?

I thought fast. If Alla Beeth was some sort of deity and I denied knowledge of it, I wasn't sure what sort of complications that would cause. "Our language is so different from yours that our name for Alla Beeth may be different too." I hoped that wasn't some sort of heresy.

ALLA BEETH IS FIRST OF YOUR PEOPLE TO VISIT OUR PEOPLE.

I felt the tremble in my stomach that I get when I realize I'm on the verge of a major story. "When did Alla Beeth visit your people?"

IS FIFTY YEARS MORE.

Fifty years. Their planet's year was more than two Earth years long, so he was claiming a human had visited Aurora over a hundred years ago, back before we'd even walked on Mars.

"Wait a minute." Even though this was being recorded, I wanted someone else with me before I proceeded any further. I commed Commander Gutierrez and asked her to come join us.

After reading the transcript of our conversation to that point, she asked, "Is this a joke?"

"If it is, someone's setting me up. I swear I had no idea he was going to say this."

She nodded, then turned to Mozart. "Did someone tell you to say that Alla Beeth was human?"

I NOT KNOW ALLA BEETH IS HUMAN BEFORE I SEE HUMANS. THEN I KNOW. NO ONE TELL ME.

Gutierrez typed and spoke slowly. "Mozart, we are the first humans to visit your people."

Mozart let out a long, descending note, and began typing furiously. NO. ALLA BEETH IS FIRST. IS LONG TIME. SIX MY MERGINGS BUT I REMEMBER. HE COME SKY. HE CLOTHES ALL WHITE. HE LIKE BRIGHT. HE TALK OUR LANGUAGE BUT WE SLOW UNDERSTAND. HE HERE SMALL TIME. HE GO SKY. FIFTY YEARS MORE YOU COME.

Gutierrez and I looked at each other.

YOU NOT BELIEVE ALLA BEETH? HOW NOT BELIEVE ALLA BEETH?

I looked into Mozart's shiny black eyes. "I believe you, Mozart." He believed that this Alla Beeth had visited his world, and even if I couldn't believe it was a human, I was sure that something must have visited the Aurorans.

Merging requires much more commitment than human mating, because neither of the Aurorans involved will survive. The larger of the two Aurorans swallows the other whole to begin the reproductive process, then hardens its skin into a thick shell. After about eighty days of cocoon-like existence, four small Aurorans break out of the shell to begin their lives. But their minds are not blank slates. In addition to a genetic heritage from both adults, each new Auroran carries a portion of the memories from the brains of its parents. Some Aurorans can remember events from over a thousand years ago.

This time it was Cacciatore who brought up religion, breaking the stunned silence after Commander Gutierrez and I had shown the rest of the crew the recordings of our conversation with Mozart. "If nobody else say it,

I will. Technology could not have brought a human here before us. Only the power of God."

The racial and religious proportionality requirements during the crew selection process had been intended to represent all of Earth in our tiny ship. Not surprisingly, the scientific community had undergone a small religious revival when those requirements were announced. So, no matter how recently converted, we had a good cross-section of religious belief on board.

Some of the Christians in the crew backed Cacciatore's theory that the visitor had been an angel; others thought it had been Jesus himself. A few of the Muslims could accept the idea of an angel, but insisted that Allah must have sent the angel. The rest of the Muslims supported Khadil, who insisted that the visitor must have been Mohammed. The Hindus spoke of the possibility that it had been one of the avatars of Vishnu. Rachel, as the only Jew on board, was arguing against all sides at once, while admitting the barest possibility that the visitor was an angel.

Commander Gutierrez mostly succeeded in remaining above the fray. The atheists and agnostics stayed out of it, as did the Buddhists.

As for me? From when I was four years old until I was eighteen, I alternated weekends between my mom and my dad. Sundays with my mom meant going to church; Sundays with my dad meant watching TV on the couch or playing catch in the yard while listening to his old-time music collection. By the time I was fourteen, I pretty much felt that I took after my dad more than my mom, at least as far as preferred Sunday activities went, and my mom eventually quit asking me to go with her.

So I stuck with the atheists and agnostics in trying to ignore the potential religious aspect of Alla Beeth.

Nothing was settled that night, of course. But the hard feelings engendered by the argument disrupted the work the various scientific teams had been doing. Over the next few days as I tried interviewing different scientists about their work, I could see that the crew had fractured: whenever possible, they avoided their colleagues who were on the "wrong" side.

Mozart didn't help in resolving the dispute. In fact, when he revealed that he could not show us a picture of Alla Beeth because the Creator had commanded against making images of living things, the arguments erupted with new fervor.

There are several possible rational scientific explanations for the Aurorans' visitor, none of which involve the intervention of any god or other supernatural entity. Since the

Aurorans have no pictures of the visitor and are relying on memories passed through several generations of mergings, it is possible that some significant details have become distorted, and a natural event has been imbued with mystical significance. Our descent from the sky was then connected to memories of that event. Another possibility is that the visitor was from another alien race, one which is humanoid in appearance. Under the theory of convergent evolution, it is quite possible that an intelligent, tool-using species could look superficially like us—even some of the Aurorans walk on two legs, have two arms, and have a head with two forward-facing eyes. Perhaps we will encounter such a race in a few years and be able to resolve this mystery. Until we have actual evidence, though, nothing about "Alla Beeth" can be said with any certainty.

"He trusts you more than any of the rest of us." Commander Gutierrez sat on my bed, facing me in my chair. Her voice was tired.

"Maybe so, but he believes Alla Beeth was a human, and I don't think I can change his mind."

"There has got to be more evidence than these memories and traditions. Some artifact left behind. Something. The crew is splitting apart: I spend all day ordering people to share their data with each other. Some of them have actually gotten physical. I'm sure part of it is just the stress of the mission, but this mystery has pushed us to the breaking point. We need proof that this is something explainable by the laws of science, like you said in your column. Then, I think people will calm down."

I shrugged. "What can I do? I'm just a science reporter, not a scientist."

"Mozart and his people see you as our ambassador." She gave a half-laugh, half-sigh. "I've been careful never to call you that, you know. But I didn't try to put a stop to it, either. Interpersonal dynamics: people need a scapegoat, and I felt you could take the jokes. But now, I need you to be the ambassador. Ambassador Lawrence Jensen, descending from the sky with the full unity of Earth behind you. Push Mozart, push his people, until they show you everything they know, everything they have. Find the truth."

Find the truth. Scientist or reporter, it distills to that: Find the truth.

The nearest large city, which we call Metropolis, has a massive building near its center that rivals the old cathedrals of Europe in its intricate craftsmanship. Since only members of a certain priest class are allowed to enter, most Aurorans have never seen what it looks like from the inside. Mozart is a member of that class, and he explains that it is a place of scholarship. It was from that building that he was sent to find out if "Alla Beeth" had truly returned. Though we proved to be a disappointment to that hope, he stayed on to learn from us, as we learn from him. Despite the vast evolutionary and cultural gulf between our people and his, he has become our friend and has come to trust us. I leave it to you, the reader, to draw your own conclusion from that.

AMBASSADOR MEANS YOU ARE THE REPRESENTATIVE OF ALL HUMANS?

"Yes," I lied.

THEN YOU ARE THE MOST IMPORTANT ONE, NOT COMMANDER GUTIERREZ?

"She is in charge of the ship that brought me here, but I am the Ambassador."

He bobbed his head affirmatively, a gesture he had learned from us.

"One of my functions is to find the truth, and report that truth to my people."

Mozart piped surprise. YOU ARE A SEEKER OF TRUTH?

After six weeks, his English was good enough that I knew the capitalization was not accidental. "Yes, I am a Seeker of Truth." And I'm willing to lie in order to get it.

THE SEEKERS OF TRUTH IS THE NAME OF MY ORDER.

"What you have told us about Alla Beeth is causing arguments among my people. I must find a way to resolve those arguments. I must find the truth. Is there anything more you can tell me or show me about Alla Beeth?"

He tapped the tips of his tentacles against his forelegs for a few moments. YOU MUST COME WITH ME TO THE PLACE OF MY ORDER. SINCE YOU ARE A SEEKER OF TRUTH, YOU SHOULD BE ALLOWED TO HEAR THE MESSAGE OF ALLA BEETH DIRECTLY.

I suppressed a grin and replied gravely, "I would be most honored."

Commander Gutierrez had one of the pilots take us in the blimp, so we arrived in Metropolis before sundown.

It took him nearly half an hour of consultation with members of his order before he came over to me and began typing on the portable computer we'd brought with us.

THEY HAVE AGREED THAT SINCE YOU ARE A SEEKER OF TRUTH FROM YOUR WORLD, IT IS PERMITTED FOR YOU TO ENTER OUR CHURCH.

"I thank them."

THOUGH THEY ARE IN OUR LANGUAGE, THE MESSAGES OF ALLA BEETH ARE DIFFICULT FOR US TO UNDERSTAND, EVEN AFTER YEARS OF STUDY. THAT IS WHY ONLY MEMBERS OF MY ORDER ARE ALLOWED TO HEAR THEM DIRECTLY, AND WE THEN PASS ON WHAT WE LEARN TO THE REST OF THE PEOPLE. SINCE YOU DO NOT UNDERSTAND OUR LANGUAGE, I DO NOT KNOW THAT YOU WILL FIND ANY TRUTH IN THEM. YET ALLA BEETH WAS HUMAN, SO PERHAPS YOU WILL. AND THERE IS SOMETHING MORE, SOMETHING THAT I CANNOT TELL YOU, ONLY SHOW.

He led the way, and I followed him into the cathedral.

I probably hadn't been in a church more than a dozen times since I stopped going with my mom, mostly as a tourist. I could tell that the Aurorans had spent years of painstaking effort in creating this building, carving delicate patterns into solid stone. We passed through various archways and doors, and I started to hear Auroran voices harmonizing. Finally we entered a round room; about twenty Aurorans stood in the middle, singing.

I felt a chill on the back of my neck, like I used to get sometimes listening to the choir at my mom's church. But there was something more; there was something about this tune that made me nostalgic, homesick even. It felt like a memory that I couldn't quite pull from the depths of my mind.

Then Mozart walked to a curtain that hung on one of the walls and pulled it back.

There, in violation of one of their commandments, was a painting of a man—definitely human—dressed all in white.

My childhood Sunday memories came flooding back, and between the music and the picture there was no doubt in my mind as to who had been the first ambassador from Earth.

"Alla Beeth" was the Aurorans' way of saying "Elvis."

Anyone else on this expedition would have to be taken seriously. But not me. I'm a proven liar. Even worse—I'm a tabloid reporter. I would be accused of fabrication, of planting the evidence, of corrupting Auroran culture as part of some tabloid hoax.

The biggest story of my career had fallen in my lap, and I couldn't tell anyone without ruining whatever credibility I had managed to regain. Whatever powers that be must not want the publicity.

Of course, my mom would say this was punishment for having lied.

"Thank you for sharing the secrets of Alla Beeth with me," I told Mozart as we left the cathedral.

Did you find what you need to stop the arguments among your people?

"You were right: Alla Beeth is human."

Mozart trilled joyfully.

"But his message is intended for your people, not mine." I sighed. "You were right to keep the image hidden. You must keep it hidden, because my people would not understand. They would reject your belief in him."

After a pause, Mozart asked, Then what will you tell your people?

"The truth," I said. "I will tell them the truth."

I refused Commander Gutierrez's request for a private briefing on what I'd found, insisting instead on speaking to the assembled scientists. After everyone gathered outside the LM, I sat on the rim of the airlock and recounted exactly what happened up until the moment Mozart pulled back the curtain and revealed the picture of Alla Beeth. Then I stopped.

After a long pause, Khadil said, "Did you recognize the person?"

"He was a human," I said. "Unmistakably. We are not the first to travel the stars. But as for who it was… You really want to know the truth?"

"Yes," said Cacciatore.

"Do you?" I looked at him. "If I say it was Mohammed, will you become a Muslim?" I turned to Khadil. "If I say it was Moses or Elijah, will you become a Jew?" I shook my head. "You want me to give you scientific proof of your religious beliefs? Well, I'm not going to; it's called 'faith' for a reason. Here's the real truth: you've all been acting like a bunch of ignorant yahoos, not the cream of Earth's scientists. So quit bickering and get back to work."

I rose, turned my back on them and stalked through the airlock into the LM.

Commander Gutierrez caught up with me just outside my quarters. "That's it? That's all you're going to say?"

I stopped. "Yes."

She looked at me appraisingly. "You know they'll all hate you for that little show and not-tell."

I shrugged. "As long as they're united again… That's what you wanted, right?"

Gutierrez nodded. "Just between you and me, though, who was it in the picture?"

Cocking an eyebrow, I said, "Assuming it was one of the great religious leaders of the past, how on Earth—or Aurora—would I know him from Adam?" I hit the button to open the hatch to my quarters. "Now, if you'll excuse me, Commander, I have a column to file."

The mystery of just who Alla Beeth was and how he got to Aurora may never be fully explained. But as Earth's first ambassador to Aurora, he prepared the way for peaceful relations between our two worlds. And for that, we can only say, "Thank you, thank you very much."

* * *

In early 2004 I had sold "The Man Who Moved the Moon," which combined some fairly hard science fiction with a fairly ridiculous premise. Having succeeded with that rather strange combination, I decided to try it again in time for the next Writers of the Future Contest deadline.

So I wrote a first contact story, using some speculative exobiology for the hard science parts. For the ridiculous premise, I dredged up an idle thought I'd had years before about Elvis appearing to aliens.

But what made the story work for me was the narrator. Less than a year before I wrote the story, reporter Jayson Blair was fired by the New York Times for having fabricated stories, and that's what gave me the idea of a disgraced reporter looking to redeem himself. The narrative voice allowed me to inject self-deprecating humor into the story.

Having finished the story, I titled it "The First Ambassador" and sent it off to Writers of the Future.

I was extremely happy when it was rejected seven days later. (Happy? Yes! The reason they rejected it was that I had become ineligible for the contest because "Betrayer of Trees" had just won second place in its quarter.)

Without the pressure of the contest deadline, I submitted the story to some of my usual critiquers. The feedback I got was generally positive, but some people had a real problem with the ending. As originally written, the revelation of the first ambassador's identity came in the last line of the story, which made it feel like a punchline.

In order to set up the punchline a little more, I changed the title to "Tabloid Reporter to the Stars," but that wasn't enough. The story got rejected several times.

In May of 2005 I finished the first draft of my fantasy novel, and I emailed Orson Scott Card to tell him that, plus tell him about some of my other story sales since I attended his workshop. When he asked me if I had anything I could submit for the new online magazine he was starting (and let me tell you, being asked was one of the biggest compliments of my writing career), this story was one of the four I sent for his consideration.

After Ed Schubert took over as IGMS editor, he read the story and asked if I would rewrite the ending to make it less like a punchline. We had a good discussion about the story when we met at Dragon*Con, and over the next few weeks I wrote a new ending that kept the Elvis element but added a resolution to the conflict between the scientists. Ed liked the revised version and bought it.

The Day the Music Died

For Noah Barnes, the knock on his bedroom door came as a welcome relief from the puzzle that threatened to render his dissertation project useless. He paused the Internet data feed from the lab at MIT and answered the door.

It was Anastasia Petrakis—Staz, to her friends. The LED piercing her cheek flashed a violet that matched the animated dragons in her eyeshadow.

"Hey, Branes," she said, using the nickname she'd given him after finding out he was researching string theory. "Headphone warning."

"Oh, uh, thanks." As usual, her presence had switched his mouth to blither mode. Noah blinked and looked away, to avoid staring into her eyes like an infatuated idiot. "How are the, uh, Bloodstained Cleavers, anyway?"

Her laugh warmed him, although he wasn't sure what the joke was.

"Clovers, not Cleavers," she said, "but no matter, 'cause we name-changed a couple weeks ago."

"Oh." That was a safe response—his mouth couldn't go too far wrong in only one syllable.

"When Six-Strings Ruled the World." She ta-dahed her arms. "Whaddaya think, Branes? Got that string theory vibe."

"Technically, the term would be '6-brane' rather than…" He stopped too late—the smile was already fading from her face.

"Practice should be over noonish," she said and left before he could say anything more.

Noah closed his door. Returning to his computer, he activated the secure interface for remotely controlling the negative-matter lattice at the MIT physics lab and cycled to the next of the preprogrammed pulse sequences. There had to be a reason why the pulses in the lattice were losing negative energy at a rate higher than his theory predicted. But his mind kept wandering back to his conversation with Staz.

"'Technically, the term would be 6-brane'?" he said. "I'm obviously a zero-brain."

Thanks to the active noise canceling in his Bose headphones, he barely heard the knock a half hour later. He chucked the headphones onto his bed and answered the door.

Staz stood there, hand on hip.

"Look, uh," he said, "I'm sorry about—"

"I think your headphones are leaking."

He shot a glance over his shoulder at the headphones lying atop his Spider-Man sheets—nothing unusual. "My headphones are what?"

"Leaking. That noise canceling stuff is ruining my band practice." Her voice was petulant.

His mind raced as he tried to figure out an interpretation of her words that didn't involve some sort of mental deficiency on Staz's part. "Umm…"

The firm line of her lips broke into a smile. "Okay, I'm not quite that dumb. But the joke's over. Good one. Lol, etc."

"Okay," he said, still baffled.

Staz must have read something in his expression, because she said, "You're not the one doing it?"

"Doing what?" Noah asked.

"Suppressing the sound in the basement. The high notes are muffled. I thought you must have set up some noise cancellation equipment as a joke."

"Not me." He was about to tell her that her guitar's amp must be going bad when he realized this was a chance for him to play hero. Not that he knew much about amplifiers, but if it was just a loose wire, he might be able to fix it. Plus, it might be good to take a break from the lattice problem, let his subconscious work on it. "Uh, I'll come take a look."

She preceded him down the narrow concrete stairs into her basement. The whole house belonged to her—Noah just rented his room.

The five other members of Staz's band gave him casual greetings as he stepped into the black-walled room, lit by several bare fluorescent bulbs dangling from wires.

The all-female band played what Staz called "neo-post-retropunk," but Noah's limited exposure to their playing led him to call it "noise"—though not to Staz's face. She must have suspected his opinion, because she knew about his noise-canceling headphones and always warned him before they started practicing.

Staz picked up her guitar. "Listen," she said, and played a squealing note that rose in pitch as she slid her hand along the neck of the guitar. Halfway down, the note began to decrease in volume till it dissolved into silence.

"First noticed it when we were playing an old Rhiannon Gold number," said Staz.

"It's getting worse," said one the other band members. Noah couldn't remember her name. Xanthia, maybe.

"Do that again," said Noah, "but stop and hold the pitch before it fades completely."

Staz complied. At first the guitar's note seemed steady as she thrummed, but after a fifteen seconds it was noticeably quieter. It took a little over thirty seconds by Noah's watch for the sound to become inaudible, although Staz claimed she could still hear it for another ten seconds.

That was no loose wire. "Maybe you need a new amp?" he said.

"It's not my amp." Staz gave it a gentle kick. "Everyone's having the same problem." Her voice sounded thinner, and she cleared her throat.

Over the next few minutes, the other five band members demonstrated the same effect on their guitars as the effect moved lower in pitch. It always struck Noah as odd that they didn't have a drummer or keyboardist, but he was no expert on post-retropunk, neo or otherwise.

Pinching and twisting some of the hair in his sideburns, Noah said, "Weird. Does it just happen down here?"

One of the band members began gesticulating, pointing at her throat. After a moment, Staz and the others began doing the same.

Staz mouthed something at him, but he couldn't understand until she repeated the words in exaggerated fashion: *We can't talk.*

"Uh, this is a joke, right?" he said. "Lol, etc.?"

The wideness of Staz's eyes told him it wasn't.

When the noise-canceling effect proved to be the same throughout the house and even outside, the other band members had left, promising to call Staz if their voices returned.

On the wallscreen in Staz's living room, Boston's Channel 5 showed the news first. "Citywide Epidemic!" proclaimed the graphic behind the male news anchor. Footage of Channel 5's own Catherine Cruller losing her voice during an interview with an indicted spammer was followed by the anchor announcing the symptoms of the disease: partial deafness in all victims, followed by loss of voice among women and children.

"It doesn't make sense," Noah said. He didn't feel sick, despite the partial deafness.

What doesn't? wrote Staz on a small magnetic whiteboard she'd pulled off the refrigerator. Part of a hastily erased shopping list remained at the bottom.

"How could a disease make us all go deaf to the same tones at almost exactly the same time? And why would the disease target both hearing and voice?"

Voices not lost, Staz scribbled. *Can't hear them.*

Noah's thoughts began to flow faster. "It's just higher tones we can't hear, so men's voices would be mostly unaffected."

Staz wrote, *Your voice is softer.*

"Oh."

There didn't seem to be much to say after that, so they watched and listened to the local news anchor until his voice faded to silence.

Forty-five minutes later, Noah and Staz were completely deaf.

The CNN anchors in Atlanta were chatting away, but all Noah could do was read the subtitles and the news crawl. He now had his laptop with him so he could read various news sites while instant-messaging with Staz, seated on the couch next to him, and various friends and family around the world.

He wished he could hear the click of the keyboard as he typed.

Homeland Security had grounded all flights nationwide, and the National Guard was being deployed in affected cities to keep order. The White House was rumored to be preparing a presidential order forbidding all interstate travel, but since Washington, D.C., had recently been added to the list of silent cities, the press conference was experiencing technical difficulties.

According to the map on screen, every major city within 500 miles of Boston had fallen victim to the disease, which CNN was labeling "Rapid Deafness Syndrome." The infection rate was 100%—no one in any of the cities seemed to be immune.

Noah drew bleak satisfaction from the fact that voice loss had been removed from the list of symptoms.

But the red circle on the map bothered him. It was centered on Boston, because that's where the first cases were. The first reports from New York were only 15 minutes later. Philadelphia followed after a few minutes, and by the time Washington had joined the club only a half hour had passed.

He brought up Staz's chat window.

Noah: I can't believe it's spreading so fast.
Staz: 700-800 mph
Noah: Wow! Do you have a link for that info?
Staz: no link
Staz: my calculations
Staz: inexact data = fuzzy results
Staz: but probably 761

The idea of Staz calculating the speed before he had thought to do so surprised him. And she thought 761 was inexact? Then he realized the number looked familiar.

Noah: It's moving at the speed of sound? How could a disease spread so fast?
Staz: not disease
Staz: acoustic phenomenon
Noah: Could it be a sound so loud it's causing people to go deaf the moment they hear it?
Staz: doesnt fit gradual deafness
Staz: its noise canceling
Noah: It can't be. Noise canceling works by having microphones to pick up sounds and using speakers to send out identical sound waves, except out of phase.
Staz: duh
Staz: almost got my masters in acoustic physics

Noah blinked and reread the last message. She had never mentioned her own education—he had assumed she was a college dropout. He had not imagined her as someone with a science background, although it did explain how she knew enough about string theory to nickname him Branes.

Out of the corner of his eye, he saw the violet flash of the LED in her cheek, and he knew she must be looking at him to see his response. But he was too embarrassed to meet her eyes.

Noah: OK, you're the Brains on this one. How does the noise canceling work?
Staz: still speculating
Staz: nanomachines maybe
Staz: floating nanomikes and nanospeakers
Noah: And they're spreading out from a source here in Boston?
Staz: you're right
Staz: doesnt work out

Noah felt two steps behind in the conversation. That wasn't unusual for him when talking to women, but on scientific subjects he was used to being ahead of other people.

Noah: I wasn't doubting you. I just was trying to clarify what your theory was. What doesn't work out?
Staz: sheer number in the initial wave
Staz: cant be nanomachines
Noah: What about a gas of some sort? Doesn't helium make things

sound higher? Maybe some special gas is moving all sounds outside the range of human hearing.
Staz: helium only changes relative volume of voice harmonics not the frequencies

A news alert caught Noah's eye. In a prepared statement released in text format, the President ordered people to remain in their homes until the spread of the disease had been contained. The National Guard would enforce that order.

Staz: anyway gas would make shock wave
Noah: And there's no shock wave. Whatever causes this must be interacting very weakly with the environment, except for its effect on sound.
Staz: weak interaction sounds like particle physics
Staz: over to you branes
Noah: You mean WIMPs?

Weakly Interacting Massive Particles were one of the dark matter components of the universe. Over the past decade, experiments with supercolliders had managed to generate different classes of WIMPs in small quantities. While the subatomic particles could pass through the atmosphere without generating a shock wave, that was because they would not interact with the air molecules at all.

Noah: No known particle could interact with sound vibrations.
Staz: then an unknown particle
Noah: But particles are subatomic in size. That's a completely different scale from sound waves.
Staz: all swans are white
Staz: until you find a black one
Noah: Even if a particle were the right size to resonate with a certain frequency, no particle could absorb all frequencies.
Staz: i thought string theory said particles were strings
Noah: They are.
Staz: strings are tunable

His mind racing, Noah leaned back on the couch and scrunched his eyes closed. It almost made sense. He opened his eyes and looked back at his laptop screen.

Staz: sorry
Staz: you know the particle stuff better than me
Noah: No, you jumpstarted my thinking.

Noah: Let's suppose there's a new particle/string.
Staz: sound absorbent particle = sap
Noah: So the SAP floats through the air, interacting with the vibrations.
    It absorbs the energy from the vibration, which removes the sound
    from the air.
Staz: absorbing energy makes it vibrate faster
Noah: Right. And as it vibrates faster, then the wavelength of the
    'string' gets shorter. Maybe that makes it physically smaller as well,
    altering its resonant frequency, so it absorbs more sound energy at
    its new wavelength.
Staz: until string absorbs so much energy it splits
Staz: and the cycle starts over again
Noah: And that explains how the effect can propagate without
    becoming weaker as it moves away from where it started. It's self-
    reproducing. This theory explains it all.
Staz: wait
Staz: it doesnt fit
Noah: Why not?
Staz: more energy = faster vibration = higher frequency
Staz: sap would start with low frequencies and move up

Noah slumped. He'd been so sure they were onto something with the
theory. Not that the theory offered any solution to the silence spreading across
the nation, but at least he would have understood what was happening.

The red circle engulfed Seattle and L.A. less than three and a half hours
after it all started.

Within the next hour, the BBC reported that London was soundless.

Noah and Staz kept watching, communicating with each other and
others through their laptops. Rampant speculation filled the net. The text of
Revelation 8:1—*And when he had opened the seventh seal, there was silence in heaven
about the space of half an hour*—had been quoted so often that Noah now knew
it by heart.

None of the scientific experts seemed to have a theory any better than
the one he and Staz had worked out. He scrolled back through his chat log
to see if he could find a flaw in their reasoning.

Everything worked out fine, except for the fact that the sound
absorption started at the high frequencies instead of the low ones. That
sounded familiar.

Noah: I've actually got a similar problem with my dissertation project.
    Maybe they're connected somehow.
Staz: whats the project problem
Noah: I'm sending pulses through a negative-matter crystal. The low

frequency pulses dissipate far more quickly than they should.
Staz: just the low frequencies
Noah: Yes. I guess it's not really that similar. It's kind of the opposite,
    actually. Which makes sense because it's using negative matter
    and negative energy.
Staz: ive never understood negative energy
Staz: how can something have less than zero energy
Noah: It sounds somewhat counter-intuitive, but it all makes sense if
    you think about it.
Noah: For example, a regular matter particle vibrates at a higher
    frequency if you add regular energy.
Noah: A negative matter particle vibrates at a higher frequency if
    you add negative energy. See? It's the same.
Staz: i guess
Staz: just seems weird
Noah: I'm so used to it that it seems natural to me.
Staz: what happens when you add regular energy to a negative
    matter particle

The realization hit, and the theory clicked into place. How could he have
been so blind?

Noah: I'm an idiot.
Staz: why
Noah: The SAP is negative matter—that's why its frequency gets lower
    instead of higher as it absorbs sound energy. The wavelength gets
    longer, the particle gets bigger, and its resonant frequency keeps
    getting lower until some point below the range of human hearing,
    when the SAP becomes so large it's unstable. Then it breaks into
    smaller SAPs that start absorbing short wavelengths again.
Staz: great
Staz: weve got a working theory
Noah: Unfortunately, I think I know why we're so close to Ground
    Zero.
Staz: why
Noah: The largest concentration of negative matter in the world is
    at MIT.
Noah: It's the crystal in my experiment. And I think it's generating the
    SAPs.

On his laptop, he maximized the window for his project. He used the
touch screen to manipulate controls, shutting down pulse stimulation in the
negative-matter crystal. If he was right, the crystal would stop emitting the
SAPs. The lab was less than a mile away, and the particles moved at the
speed of sound, so it would take less than five seconds for the last of the
particles pass by him.

He counted to ten, just to be on the safe side, then said, "Staz?"
The sound was absorbed before it even left his mouth.

After some discussion, Noah and Staz concluded that the SAP's self-replicating nature allowed it to continue spreading even after the experiment was shut down.

Noah: I guess I should report the theory to Homeland Security.
Staz: does negative matter give you negative marbles

She swatted his arm.

Noah: What?
Staz: dhs will guantanamize you
Noah: I didn't do this on purpose.
Staz: they wont care
Staz: theyll be happy to have a scapegoat
Noah: Someone in authority needs to understand this isn't a disease
    and it's not the end of the world. Maybe they can fix it.
Staz: how
Staz: reverse the polarity like on star trek
Noah: I don't know. But I'm going to tell them.

He found the address for the Department of Homeland Security website and followed the link.
    Welcome to the Department of Homeland Security. Our server is experiencing unusually high traffic. Please try back later.

The last city to succumb to the red circle was Perth, Australia. Noah checked his watch: 2:15 a.m. In less than sixteen hours, the whole globe had gone silent.

Staz: there goes my chance to be a rock star
Staz: goodbye fame and fortune
Staz: goodbye adoring fans
Noah: Staz, I'm so sorry. I ruined your dream.
Staz: its dumb
Staz: the world is silenced
Staz: and im talking about my stupid band
Noah: It's OK. I understand.
Staz: i wonder how long ill remember
Noah: Remember what?
Staz: what music sounded like
Noah: Beethoven remembered, even after he was deaf.

Staz: true
Noah: And how could you ever forget that there was a time When
Six-Strings Ruled the World?

Staz leaned over and rested her head on his shoulder.

It should have been a perfect moment, but something about what he had just typed nagged at Noah. Six-strings. Six-branes. Multi-branes.

The SAPs vibrated in multiple dimensions.

As he typed, Staz sat up so she could read his message.

Noah: Grab your guitar. You're going to play for a whole new
dimension.

Just over a mile separated Staz's house from Noah's lab on campus, but it took them over an hour to get there because they had to hide from the National Guard patrols roaming the streets. Seeing tanks roll by in complete silence was unnerving, and Noah breathed an inaudible sigh of relief once they were safe in the lab.

Staz: whats the experiment supposed to do anyway
Noah: One of the problems with string theory is that it predicts too
much—it provides too many possible solutions to the question of
what our universe is like.
Noah: By sending pulses through the negative matter lattice, I was
hoping to detect tiny differences that would allow me to eliminate
some of those solutions.
Staz: so what does my guitar have to do with it
Noah: The lattice vibrates in up to twenty-six spatial dimensions. It can
send out pulses in other dimensions, beyond the three we perceive.
Noah: The SAPs are vibrating at multiple frequencies of sound in our
dimensions. But in another dimension, they could all be resonating
at the same frequency—because they are all fundamentally the
same type of particle.

He connected her guitar's output cord to an input on the workstation.

Noah: My pulse generator's programmed to create pulses only at
key frequencies that are relevant for theoretical purposes. I'd have
to get someone to reprogram it to generate other frequencies.
Noah: But your guitar can generate a continuous range of
frequencies—including the one we need, I hope.

On the workstation monitor, Noah scanned through the readings from the negative matter crystal, comparing them to the baseline record he'd made before starting the experiments. And there it was: a huge frequency spike in dimension 14.

Noah: Play a constant note on your guitar.

Staz complied. A waveform appeared in a window on the workstation screen. Noah overlaid it on the dimension 14 window.

Noah: Adjust the note you're playing until the frequencies match.

As Staz slid her fingers along the guitar neck, the signal on the monitor changed. Finally, the frequencies matched.

Noah: OK, hold that note.

He pulled up another window, labeled Phase Delay.

Looking at Staz, he felt a pang of regret—they had really managed to connect via instant messaging. If this worked, he would be back to stumbling over his words when trying to talk to her.

He adjusted the phase delay until the input from Staz's guitar was delayed by half a wavelength.

A faint sound arose. It grew in volume to become the familiar squeal of an electric guitar.

"And that," said Noah, "is what I call 'silence cancellation.'"

As Noah had hoped, the phase-delayed signal had changed the vibrational pattern of the SAPs, converting them into particles that no longer interacted with sound—in fact, they had shifted completely into other dimensions.

Despite Staz's advice, he had notified Homeland Security as to the cause of what the public now called "the Silence."

From the emails in Noah's inbox, public opinion was about evenly split on whether he should be sent to prison for causing the Silence or given a medal for fixing it. Fortunately, Homeland Security had decided against pressing charges, and the dean had decided to let Noah stay at MIT, so he hoped everything would get back to normal soon.

A knock distracted him from his email. He answered the door to find Staz there.

"Hey, Branes," she said. "Headphone warning."

Back to normal.

"I, uh…" He shot a glance at the noise-canceling headphones on his desk. "I think I've had enough silence to last me a while."

Staz gave him a wry smile. "Understood. We'll be done around noon."

He took a deep breath, then said, "Actually, I'd like to come down and listen to you sing, if that's okay."

Her smile grew into a full-fledged grin as she cupped a hand to her ear. "Is that an adoring fan I hear?"

* * *

This was definitely a story in which the title came first. I toyed around with ideas on what it could be about for a few years, and then, while at the Odyssey workshop, I read an article in New Scientist *magazine in which it referred to phonons, which are quantum-mechanical descriptions of certain types of vibrations in solids—sort of particles of sound. I combined that with negative matter, which I had read about in stories and articles by the late physicist and science fiction author Robert L. Forward, and that gave me a mechanism by which the music could die.*

I wrote the story at Odyssey, and I'm grateful to all those there and elsewhere who gave me feedback on it.

Upgrade

Through the camera in the waiting room, Harry watched the customer. "Mr. Smith" was standing stiffly, ignoring the chairs and the table full of magazines. Though dressed in jeans and a gray sweatshirt, Smith wore an expensive privacy veil—one that fuzzed the picture even of Harry's high-end Sony equipment.

Harry smiled. Some body upgrades were more acceptable than others—NeverSleep was popular among executives and lawyers, and artificial eyes had become a fashion statement after several Hollywood stars had gotten them. Something like a brain job was an embarrassment: it meant you weren't smart enough with what nature gave you.

Despite the political controversy over upgrades, NHCA insurance would cover most of the cost. But hospitals had to report upgrades to the National Health Care Administration. For privacy, you had to go private. And private took a lot of money.

Harry opened the door between his office and the waiting room. After a moment's hesitation, Smith walked in.

"Have a seat," said Harry, indicating the chair in front of his desk.

Smith sat as Harry closed the door.

"You don't need the privacy veil," said Harry. "This office is secure."

Smith pointed at the silvery mesh over his face. "I'd rather remain anonymous." The distorting effects of the veil made the voice smoothly androgynous.

With a shrug, Harry said, "I guess I can accommodate you, unless you're looking for brain enhancement. My surgical bots can't work inside that veil."

"I want a DSR."

Surprised, Harry nodded slowly. Outside the military, a digestive system replacement was rarely done for non-medical reasons. Some very busy people liked being able to skip meals and get most of their energy by plugging into the electric grid, allowing the DSR to synthesize glucose by recycling body waste. But for most people, the added body efficiency was not worth the cost.

Harry sighed mentally as his professional ethics took over. "I need to warn you: Back in Washington, some people don't like the idea of human upgrades. If God had meant for man to whatever, etc." He waved his hand in little circles. "If the polls are right, people like that will win next month's election. If they ban future upgrades, that puts me out of business."

Harry leaned forward. "But if, as some of them propose, they ban the *use* of upgrades, you'll either have to leave the country or die."

"You're being melodramatic. It's almost certain the Supreme Court would invalidate a use ban."

Shrugging, Harry said, "Almost certain? That still leaves some chance they won't."

"You're not going to scare me off."

"OK. Can you come in next week? I'll have to order the system."

"It may take longer," said Smith. "I want one with the nuclear option."

The TV on Harry's wall showed a map of the United States, divided between blue and red.

"According to the exit polls," said a pundit, "not only will the President be re-elected, but her party will gain control of both the House and Senate."

Muting the TV, Harry picked up his phone and dialed the anonymous forwarding number Mr. Smith had given him.

"Yes?" The phone altered the voice so it couldn't be recognized.

"I have the replacement you ordered." Harry was careful not to give details, just in case the voice wasn't Smith.

"Will Saturday work?" asked the voice.

"Yes. Do you want to reconsider, given today's results?"

"No."

"The nuclear generator only replaces the need to plug in to recharge the system," Harry said, going through the NHCA-mandated pre-installation waiver checklist. "You still need to eat occasionally. If you don't replenish the raw materials your body'll start cannibalizing itself."

"No more than 45 days without food. I read the specs. Can we get going?"

Harry shook his head. "I have to remind you. Federal regulations, so you can't sue me for malpractice. With regard to water: The DSR recycles what would normally urinate, but you still lose water through perspir—"

"I'll have access to water. Eating and elimination were the big problems."

"You still have to eliminate," said Harry. "Recycling isn't 100% efficient. If you don't add food into the system, then only once every 60 days."

"Just check all the boxes and I'll sign the form," said Smith.

As the surgical bots worked on Smith, Harry leaned back in his chair. Where was Smith going? What sort of environment called for this kind of endurance?

Under water made the most sense. A diving suit with a rebreather/gill system and a distiller to purify water would let him stay down for weeks. Navy SEALs probably did exactly that.

What was Smith up to?

Before Smith left, Harry said, "If you ever need any work done, look me up. I'll probably be opening a clinic in Mexico after Congress bans upgrades."

Smith chuckled; the privacy veil made the sound sterile. "Don't be so sure of that—politicians need upgrades, just like everyone else. Have some faith in human nature."

Harry snorted. "If I had faith in human nature, I wouldn't be upgrading it."

The True Human Act, outlawing most upgrade procedures, passed the House easily. The Senate took up the bill a week later.

Harry cancelled his appointments and watched the debate on C-SPAN2.

Smith was right: politicians used upgrades, too. Even many Senators in favor of the bill showed signs of vocal cord upgrades. Their voices were just too smooth, too resonant.

Senator Velazquez of Texas was no exception. His voice was firm as he took the podium. "My distinguished colleagues, I rise in opposition to this bill."

Something about the stiff way Senator Velazquez stood looked familiar to Harry. He grinned suddenly and said, "Looks like Mr. Smith went to Washington."

Seventeen days into Senator Velazquez's filibuster, the Senators sponsoring the bill withdrew it.

* * *

This story popped into my head during the time when there was a lot of political discussion about using the "Nuclear Option" in the U.S. Senate—eliminating filibusters of judicial nominees. I wrote it specifically targeting the Probability Zero feature of Analog. *After I finished it at 1950 words long, I found out that Probability Zero had hard limit of 1000 words. So I cut more than 50%, getting it down to 950. It was a very difficult but instructive exercise in revision.*

 Fortunately, Stan Schmidt liked it enough to buy it for Probability Zero.

The Robot Sorcerer

Boot process finishes at 2047-07-06 17:03:18 UTC. All systems nominal.
Navigation establishes current location is Wormhole Project Launch Room.

Gravitonic imaging detects exotic matter around hole in north wall. Navigation labels it wormhole entrance.

Cameras show three humans within 360 degree field. Cameras show one human's hand moving. Voice recognition converts sound to words: "Good luck, little buddy."

Radio detects go signal. Navigation starts impellers in air mode and accelerates toward wormhole entrance. Magnetic radiation shielding activates.

Cameras show varying colors inside wormhole. Pattern recognition algorithms find no meaning.

Pressure sensors detect liquid surroundings. Nanosensors on hull determine liquid is water with 0.0% salinity.

Navigation changes impellers to water mode. Sonar shows body of water, average depth 3.1 meters. Sonar shows an object 1.2 meters long floats at surface.

Navigation directs impellers to head toward surface, avoiding object. Sonar shows depth at 20 centimeters. Ten. Zero.

As I break the surface of the pond, I'm so shocked that I stop my impellers and begin to sink back down. Something strange has happened to me, but I don't understand what. My systems check out fine, though, so I restart my impellers and head to the gray-green clay that lines the bank of the water. When the water is shallow enough, I start my tread motors. My 212 kilograms of weight cause the treads to sink into the soft ground, but they catch hold. Dripping water off my composite armor shell, I roll out onto land.

The object floating in the water behind me is a girl. She watches me with wide brown eyes, her face wet with algae-tinted water. She looks human, which surprises me, because the wormhole could have led anywhere in the universe with a similar gravitational gradient to the opening.

My surprise surprises me, because I know I have not been programmed for emotional reactions.

"What's your name?" asks the girl. Her accent is different from that of the techs back at Wormhole Project Headquarters in West Virginia, but her words are understandable. She's speaking English.

I start to calculate the probability that a wormhole would open on a planet that had evolved intelligent lifeforms that look identical to humans and speak a language apparently identical to English, but then I get sidetracked as I realize I don't know what my name is. I examine my memories. A tech called me "little buddy." Is that my name?

I dig deeper, examining the code of my program. In the comments I find a label for what I am: Multi-Environment Robotic Lander (Intelligent Navigation). Units of my type—I'm the 412th, according to my serial number—are called by the acronym.

"Merlin," I say, using my voice synthesizer. "My name is Merlin."

"Bump," she says as she swims toward me. "But most people don't call me that. They call me Princess." She is in shallow enough water now that she stands and wades out. Her simple shift of loose-woven gray material drips water onto the clay shore.

She doesn't dress like a princess—except for a silver circlet that crosses her forehead and disappears into her shoulder-length black hair.

How do I know she doesn't dress like a princess? I haven't met one since being activated. A check of my memory storage reveals that I have 512 petabytes of nonvolatile memory, some of which holds a library of cultural materials—art, books, movies, music, videogames—that can be shared in first contact situations.

A quick search of text materials, ranging from Emily Post's *Etiquette* to the novelization of the film *Bloodstained Clover VII: Little Green Men*, allows me to form some idea of proper manners on encountering royalty.

"It is a pleasure to meet you, Princess Bump," I say. Not having a waist or neck, I can't bow, but I manipulate the suspension on my front treads and dip forward a few centimeters.

She shakes her head, sending sparkles of water arcing to the ground. "I'm not a princess. People call me that because of this—" She taps the circlet. "—but I'm just an orphan, really."

"I see." She is close enough that I can examine the circlet's nuclear magnetic resonance. It is pure silver, although the atoms appear to be vibrating in a way that does not match anything in my data library.

While I'm at it, I examine Bump's nuclear magnetic resonance image. Her skeletal structure and organ placement are all within normal human parameters for a child about eight years old, although her bones show signs of periods of malnutrition. And the twisted helix molecules in her cells are human D.N.A.

Only one explanation makes sense: the wormhole did not open across the universe. I must be on Earth. I scan for G.P.S. satellite signals.

I don't find them.

I search the entire broadcast spectrum and find nothing but static.

"That's why I wished for you, Sorcerer Merlin," says Bump.

"I'm not a sorcerer," I say. "I'm a robotic probe."

"Is that greater than a sorcerer?"

I'm a bit distracted, as I've just determined that the spectrum of the sun in the sky does not match Earth's sun, which means I'm not on Earth. I continue scanning the environment in the background as I turn my attention back to Bump.

"It's not like a sorcerer at all," I say. "I'm just a machine, programmed for exploration."

And that's I realize what's different: from the moment I broke the surface of the water, I've been self-aware. And that's impossible. No computer on Earth has ever achieved consciousness. I'm not programmed for it—the words Intelligent Navigation in my official name were added for the sake of a catchy acronym.

Yet my consciousness is self-evident.

Bump interrupts my existential crisis by saying, "You have to be a sorcerer! It's my birthday, and I made my wish in the enchanted pool."

Enchanted? I scan the pond. Nuclear magnetic resonance shows the water molecules vibrating in a way similar to the silver atoms in Bump's circlet. This is intriguing. Even if it were not in my programming to do so, I would want to investigate further. I think. Maybe that curiosity comes from my programming.

Gravitonic radiation flashes in my sensor as the wormhole shrinks down to microscopic size. The humans at the Wormhole Project will maintain the connection that way for four hours, after which they'll expand the wormhole again for my expected return. That reminds me of my mission.

"It was nice to meet you, Bump," I say. "But I can't stay here and talk with you anymore, because I have to explore as much of this world as possible within the next four hours."

I activate my impellers and rise into the air.

"Wait!" Bump reaches out and grabs hold of my front right tread.

I automatically compensate for the extra weight and lift her a few centimeters off the ground. Then I hover, waiting.

Why am I waiting? Because she ordered me to. She's a human, and my programming says I should follow orders from humans.

"You're supposed to remove my crown," says Bump.

I lower her to the ground, then land myself. "Why don't you just take it off?"

"I can't. It's magically stuck on."

I reach out a manipulator arm and grip the circlet with my two-fingered claw.

Bump holds her breath.

I lift the circlet. The skin on Bump's forehead below the rim tightens, pulling up her eyebrows.

Bump grimaces. "Ow!"

I stop pulling. Looking at my earlier scans, I see no physical reason why the circlet cannot be removed.

"When did you put this on?" I ask.

"I didn't. My mother put it on me the day I was born."

"Why don't you ask your mother to—"

"She's dead."

"Oh." I feel embarrassed, which according to my cultural materials is supposed to make me blush, but I have no cheeks.

After eighteen seconds of silence, Bump says, "She was a sorceress. Verno One-eye said it would take a powerful sorcerer to remove my crown, so that's why I came and wished in the pool on my birthday."

She believes in magic, and with the strange atomic vibrations and the stuck circlet, perhaps there is some form of energy at work that she refers to as magic. So I try to get a sense of the laws by which magic operates. "Do birthday wishes in the enchanted pool always come true?"

"No," she says. "But sometimes they do. And you appeared right after I made my wish."

"Do I look like a sorcerer?" I ask.

Bump hangs her head. "More like a metal turtle, but I was hoping you were enchanted to look that way."

My shell's not metal, but I doubt she has the engineering background to understand the composite materials involved in my construction, so I let it pass.

I should be out exploring the world instead of trying to help a girl with a problem outside my area of expertise. But maybe I can do both.

I open a dorsal portal and eject eighteen ornithopter drones of varying sizes: ten Dragonfly class, five Hummingbirds, and three Falcons. I keep several of each class in reserve for future use.

Bump gasps. "You really are a sorcerer."

"I'm really not," I say, "but I'll try to find a way to remove your crown if you'll show me around."

As we travel the rutted dirt road toward the city, Bump tells me about her world. The land is called Everun. There are many towns and cities in Everun, but she lives in the capital, New London. Everyone speaks English because long ago people came from England, although she has no idea where England is. Other lands lie beyond Everun, but she doesn't know their names. The Southside Orphanage for Girls doesn't have many books.

I theorize that a wormhole once connected this planet with Earth, and I feel relieved to have an explanation for the presence of English-speaking humans. As for the likelihood of a random wormhole opening up to a world previously connected to Earth by a wormhole, maybe it's not completely random. Maybe a previous connection makes a subsequent connection more likely, like wheels wearing ruts in the mud.

Looking down on the city of New London through the camera of a Falcon, I can see that it had grown on the southwestern bank of a river, eventually spreading to the northeastern side. It's an unplanned, organic city: most roads are straight for a few blocks at most, as if no one anticipated the need for a longer road.

At surface level, the city is a complicated maze, so I follow Bump as she leads me along the pale brown roads. Some of the ruts are wide and deep enough that I use my impellers to jump them. I assume the occasional dark patches of mud are the remains of a recent rainfall—until I see a woman dump a chamberpot into the street from the third-floor window of a wood-plank building.

I could easily be in a pre-industrial colony of the British Empire, except for three anomalies. First, the air is completely clear of smoke. Second, most people ignore me, as if robotic probes trundling down the street were not uncommon. And third, seemingly magical items are integrated into daily life, like chairs that float a meter or more above the street, carrying people to and fro with no means of support visible in any of my scanners, not even gravitonics.

"How does a chair get enchanted to float like that?" I ask, as a mustachioed gentleman on a high-backed chair bobs past.

"A sorcerer cast a spell on it," says Bump. "Or someone dipped it in water from an enchanted pool. Sometimes things come out enchanted."

Trotting toward us on stilt-like legs is a wooden trunk. It swerves to avoid us and continues on its way. If self-propelled, auto-navigating objects are common, that explains why I don't rate a second glance from New London inhabitants. But what provides the energy for such motion?

I ask, "Do they have to keep dipping the chair to keep it enchanted?"

"Things stay enchanted unless they're broken," she says. "Why are you asking all these questions about magic?"

"They don't have magic where I come from."

We stop as a four-wheeled carriage passes in front of us on a cross street. The carriage itself looks ordinary, but it is pulled by a team of four mud-spattered white unicorns.

"But you can fly," says Bump.

"Let's just say that it's a different kind of magic, and we don't call it magic."

"That's mad. If it's magic, why not call it magic?" She winces and reaches up to rub her temples. "Headache," she says.

I decide to change the subject. "Why isn't there any smoke?"

Bump glances over her shoulder at me. "What's smoke?"

"It's the cloud of particles that comes from a fire."

"What's fire?"

I wonder if she's joking, or if this is a mere terminological difference, but the absence of smoke in the atmosphere leads me to believe that these people, in fact, do not have fire. How could a civilized group of people lose the concept of fire?

"Fire is something that happens when a material gets very hot," I say.

"Like melting or boiling?"

"No." How could I explain? I spot a chip of wood in the dirt and pick it up. "Watch this."

Bump stops and faces me.

I hold up the chip. "I'm going to heat this piece of wood to create fire." I hit it with one of my lasers intended for cutting samples from rock.

The wood droops, then flows away from the path of the beam. Half the chip separates and falls, splattering like a glob of hot wax as it hits the ground.

"Where's the fire?" asks Bump.

I don't answer her. Suddenly glad my power source is a nuclear battery instead of an old internal combustion engine, I review my magnetic resonance scans of the wood before, during, and after the attempted burning. There's no smoke, no flame. However, thousands of atoms are missing. They're not in the remnants of the chip, either in my claw or spilled on the ground. The atoms have vanished—and not into thin air, for my scans include atmospheric atoms. They've simply vanished.

Bump sits cross-legged on her cot, one of thirty-six in the orphanage dormitory. They're so close together I can't fit alongside, so I'm parked at the foot of hers. We're alone; the rest of the girls are playing, working, or begging, depending on their ages and abilities.

"Are you sure you want your crown off?" I ask.

Bump reaches up and rubs her temples just underneath the circlet. "It gives me headaches sometimes. It used to grow with me, but now I think it's too tight."

The implications of a silver crown that grows along with a child are interesting, and I file that fact away for future analysis. "But aren't you worried that it's really the proof that you're the heir to some throne?" Having read all the literature in my cultural library involving magic and princesses, this seems like a possibility.

She laughs, which makes me feel good, even though she is clearly discounting my theory. "Thrones and princesses are in fairy tales," she says. "We have the Governor-General and Parliament."

"There must be a reason your mother gave you the crown," I say.

"I don't care. Just take it off."

Obedient to her order, I power up one of my sample-cutting lasers.

"If you start to feel any heat, let me know," I tell her. I don't want her head melting like wood.

She nods.

"And keep your head still," I say. My reaction time is fast enough that I should be able to keep the beam from hitting her skin, but with magic about, I'm not sure of anything.

I have a theory about where the atoms go. Unless the conservation of matter and energy no longer applies, the energy for enchantments has to come from somewhere. My hypothesis is that it comes from the conversion of atoms when items "melt." The magical energy then pervades the environment, providing the power to keep enchanted items working.

So I hit a spot on the circlet with a laser pulse, melting just a few layers of atoms, some of which vanish. I do this again and again.

At the very least, I can cut through it eventually. If the circlet is some kind of magical circuit, then breaking the circuit may eliminate its power to stay stuck on her head. But I theorize the extra magical power fed into the circuit by the vanishing atoms may cause it to blow the magical equivalent of a fuse even before I finish cutting.

"What was your life like before you came here?" asks Bump.

I hesitate. "I wasn't alive before. Not that I'm alive now, but… things are different where I come from. I was built by humans, like a chair or a wagon. It wasn't until I came out of the enchanted pool that I became me."

"So you *are* enchanted." She starts to nod, then freezes, obviously remembering my instruction to keep her head still.

"I guess I am."

"What did you look like before you were enchanted?"

"The same as I do now. The difference isn't on the outside—it's how I think."

She ponders that for a while as I continue to work on the circlet.

"If there's no magic where you come from," she says, "then you won't be enchanted when you go back, will you?"

"I don't think so," I say. I hadn't considered that before, but without the magical power in the environment, I doubt an enchantment can maintain itself.

The circlet twangs. It leaps into the air, lifting Bump's overhanging hair, and then falls onto her cot.

Slowly, Bump reaches out and picks it up. She peers at it, turning it at different angles. "You did it," she says. "My wish came true."

"Happy birthday," I say. I still have 108 minutes to explore this world before the wormhole reappears for my return trip, and I decide that information about the government would be useful. "Can you show me where Parli—"

Bump shrieks, drops the circlet, and holds her hands to her temples. A broad-spectrum pulse emits from her head—I see it on every camera from infrared to ultraviolet. I pick it up on every radio receiver. It flashes in my magnetic field sensor. It even shows up on gravitonics.

I grab the circlet and try to fit it onto Bump's head as she sobs, but her hands are in the way. Eventually she realizes what I'm trying to do and helps, pulling down on the circlet until it's tight over her hair and skin.

As she continues sobbing, I reexamine my actions over and over, realizing what a fool I was to act without full information about the purpose of the circlet. Her sobs fade away, becoming sniffles.

Six minutes and forty-two seconds after the pulse, Bump takes a deep breath and says, "Thank you. I guess my mother gave me this—"

That's when the second pulse hits, stronger than the first.

Three men appear out of thin air two minutes and eleven seconds after the fourth pulse. They are dressed in crimson uniforms, resplendent with gold-braid piping.

Mrs. Ness, the widow who runs the orphanage, cradles Bump's head. Bump has lapsed into restless unconsciousness.

"Secure the girl," says a man with close-cropped gray hair and a pug nose. His uniform displays the widest bands of piping. He holds a jewel-encrusted gold scepter in his right hand.

The other two men clamber over the cots toward Bump. Mrs. Ness silently cries.

"What are you going to do with her?" I ask the leader.

His eyes flicker over my body. "I am Sorcerer General Quardallis. Who are you?"

"My name is Merlin. I'm a visitor from a distant land, and this girl is my friend."

"Merlin." Quardallis scrunches his nose, wide nostrils flaring wider. "You're not one of those chaps who claim to be *the* Merlin?"

"No, I'm just *a* Merlin," I say.

"That's an unusual enchanted form. A curse? I could try to remove it for—"

"No, I like my enchantment." I don't bother with further explanations. "Can you stop what's happening to her?"

He gives me a curt nod. "Of course. That's my job."

One of the men picks Bump up. The other removes a gold helmet from a bag and fastens it over Bump's head, covering her face.

"She won't have to wear that for the rest of her life, will she?" I ask. "She didn't like wearing the circlet."

Quardallis cocks his head. "Circlet?"

I pick up the circlet from where it had fallen on the floor after the third pulse and hand it to him.

He examines it closes, then waves his scepter over it. "Ingenious," he says. "That explains why we didn't find the bomb earlier."

"The bomb?" I ask, suspecting I already know the answer.

"The girl. She sucks in magical power and blasts it out, each time worse than the last. You don't have bombs where you come from?"

"Not like this," I say. "But you can cure her, or make another circlet for her?"

He lowers one eyebrow. "How well do you know this girl?"

I could say she's my only friend in the universe, but since he seems to be treating her like a magical terrorist, I decide to be more discreet. "We met for the first time this afternoon," I say. "She agreed to be my guide in your city."

I also decide it's unwise to mention her wishing for me or my removal of the circlet.

"Ah. The sad fact is, there is no cure, per se. But the blasts of energy can be managed, put to good use in providing magical power to defend the realm. What could have been a terrible tragedy becomes a benefit to all of society."

"You're going to use her like a magical battery?"

"She'll be treated well enough. Fifty years ago, she would have been killed."

From the history in my databanks, I'm aware of how standards for treating human beings have differed across time and place. But since my reference data comes from Americans in 2047, I can't help feeling revulsion.

"It's inhumane," I say.

Quardallis draws himself up to his full 172 centimeters of height. "Mr. Merlin, I have been more than courteous with you. But I do not take kindly to foreigners questioning the policies of our government. Go back to where you came from and do not trouble yourself any more over the girl."

Responding to the order, I engage my treads and roll out of the dormitory, heading for the enchanted pool.

The sun has set by the time I squish down the clay bank and sink into the pool. If it were my birthday, I would wish that Bump be cured. But I was never born. I don't even know what day I rolled off the assembly line.

Because I came by ground instead of flying, I arrive with only forty-seven minutes left in the one-hour return window. Technically, I could continue collecting data here until the final minute before the wormhole disappears, but this world holds no joy for me now.

Activating my impellers, I dive under the surface and continue toward the wormhole.

Part of me is glad my programming requires me to report back to Earth. Separated from the strange physics of this world, my magical sentience will disappear and I will no longer feel the guilt of having hurt someone who trusted me.

My disastrous experience with sentience will become part of the Wormhole Project records. The techs will take me apart, and I don't blame them. From my failures, let them learn to build a smarter MERLIN.

I approach the wormhole entrance, its exotic matter periphery sparkling in my gravitonic sensors. A few more seconds and this will all be over.

But I stop short.

My programming tells me I must enter the wormhole to finish my mission. My programming tells me I must enter the wormhole because a human ordered me to return home.

But I am not my programming. Since emerging from the enchanted pool, I have been something more. I do not want to lose the enchantment that makes me think of myself as I.

Following orders from humans is not always the right thing to do. It was a mistake to follow Bump's order to remove the circlet.

From now on, I will choose for myself what I will do.

And I choose to find a way to help Bump. My mistake put her in a terrible situation, so she's my responsibility.

Plus, according to my cultural library, princesses are supposed to be rescued.

Midnight passes. I'm sitting on the bank of the pool, but my remotes are engaged in a frantic search for Bump's location. This time, I will plan my actions with full information.

Studying the night sky, I have been unable to locate any common reference point with Earth. I could be in a different galaxy, but based on the physics of magic I suspect this world is in a different universe.

But certain laws of physics are the same, and in them I believe I have found the cure for Bump's condition.

The atoms in enchanted objects like the circlet and the water of the pool all have the strange vibrations I detected, while atoms in ordinary objects do not. That is unlikely to be a simple coincidence. By pulsing my nuclear magnet resonance scanner's field, I can dampen those vibrations, eventually stopping them. Essentially, I can use physics to counter magic by turning an enchanted item into an ordinary one.

My programming irrationally urges me to pass through a wormhole long since closed, but by now it's become easy for me to ignore the nagging. Over the past two years, there have been dozens of MERLIN units that did not return. I wonder how many of them are still mindlessly trying to pass through nonexistent wormholes.

If a MERLIN doesn't return, the Wormhole Project doesn't waste more resources trying to find out what happened. They label the coordinates as possibly dangerous and open the next in a potentially infinite number of wormholes.

So I'm stranded here, but that's fine with me.

I finally see Bump through the camera of one of my Dragonfly remotes searching inside a squat brown-brick building near the center of New London. She wears a different helmet now, one attached to the wall by a tangle of tubes and wires. At least this helmet leaves her face uncovered.

Her eyes, bloodshot and red-rimmed, stare dully at the wood floor. Arms and legs are shackled to an unpadded copper chair.

"Treated well enough," I say, recalling Quardallis's words. I imagine confining Quardallis to a chair in similar fashion, and am somewhat disturbed by the pleasure I get from running that simulation.

I fly my remote past her face. She flinches. I land it on the floor. Her eyes are drawn to it, and after a moment they widen in recognition.

Unfortunately, my remotes have no speech capability, so I can't tell her I'm coming.

She winces, shutting her eyes in pain. The tubes connected to her helmet glow brilliant blue for eleven seconds, then fade.

Bump sags in her chair, but after a moment she lifts her head and stares at my Dragonfly.

Her lips move. The words are so soft that the microphone on the Dragonfly barely picks them up: "I knew you'd find me."

Because there's no way to know what the environment is like on the other end of a wormhole, MERLIN units are built to be tough. Our multilayered composite polymer hulls were designed to allow us to do our job in a vacuum or under Jovian atmospheric pressure, underwater or high above ground, in liquid hydrogen or liquid iron. In extreme cases, the protection only needs to last long enough for us to return through the wormhole before it closes.

My hull was not designed for ramming into a brick roof at 293 kilometers per hour, which is my velocity after thirty seconds of free fall. But it gets the job done just fine.

I break through the roof and three successive wooden floors beneath it before stopping in a crunch of splintered wood on the fourth floor down.

I run a rapid self-diagnostic. As anticipated, I suffered no damage.

I'm in a hallway near the stairwell, just as I planned. Denting the wall at every turn, I fly down the stairs toward the basement.

It's 3 A.M. local time, and twenty guards stand watch throughout the building. Only one, stationed in the basement, is in position to intercept me. He draws his sword—firearms won't work without fire—and charges to meet me as I exit the stairwell. I admire his bravery.

Not wanting to kill anyone, I merely knock him aside and continue down the hall to Bump's cell.

The iron door is too thick for me to break down, but the hinges yield to my lasers. I'm into her cell ninety-three seconds after landing—two seconds ahead of schedule.

"Merlin!" Bump's face breaks into a smile. She struggles with her shackles.

"We have to wait until after your next pulse," I say. Which, if I've timed it right, will occur in three seconds. Two. One.

Bump's back arches as she spasms. The tubes attaching her helmet to the wall flow with ultraviolet fury for seventeen seconds, then fade.

She slumps in her chair, dazed. I cut through the strap of the helmet with one laser while severing her shackles with another. I take off her helmet and help her to her feet, then guide her to the middle of the room, away from metal as much as possible.

I power up my nuclear magnetic resonance scanner and begin the treatment, sending precise magnetic pulses timed to stop the magical vibration of atoms in her brain.

Thanks to my 360-degree vision, I see Quardallis, scepter in hand, appear out of thin air behind me. He must have dressed in haste, as his shirt is partly untucked and the buttons of his crimson jacket are misaligned.

"What are you doing?" he asks. To my surprise, he sounds more curious than angry.

"Curing her," I say.

"There's no cure for a bomb." He runs his left hand over his short hair. "Even if there were, I'm afraid the girl is a national resource. I cannot allow you to disable her power."

"That's too bad," I say, "because I'm finished."

The atomic vibrations in Bump's skull are now similar to what would be found in any Earth child. No magic.

Quardallis holds up his scepter. "I understand your desire to protect the girl. It is noble and does you credit. I have no wish to harm you. However, I cannot tolerate your interference any longer. So I took the liberty of preparing a spell to send you home."

He presses a jewel on the scepter. A dot appears in the air between him and me. I detect the gravitonic signature of exotic matter, which rapidly expands in size until it's three meters across, extending into the floor and ceiling.

"No!" Bump shouts. "You mustn't send him there. He'll die."

"A world portal?" says Quardallis from behind the yawning void of the wormhole that blocks my view of him. He sounds surprised at the results of his own spell. "You came from another world? Do you realize how much energy you've made me waste?"

My programming tries to get me to enter the wormhole, but by now I'm used to overriding it.

"Save yourself, Merlin! Leave me." Bump begins crying.

Quardallis comes around the side of the wormhole. He points the scepter at me, and suddenly I'm floating in the air toward the wormhole. I activate my impellers at full thrust and start to move away, but my progress is slow.

The pressure increases. My forward motion stops. My impellers whine as I feed them power beyond their nominal capacity. I still slip toward the wormhole.

I aim my lasers at Quardallis's scepter. For some reason I don't understand, their heat dissipates in the air before reaching it.

The scepter is at the edge of the range for my magnetic resonance scanner. I start sending magnetic pulses, hoping to remove the magic of the scepter.

"Please," says Bump. "I'll stay here with you. Just let Merlin go."

Before either Quardallis or I can respond to Bump's proposal, there's a brilliant flash of light that blinds my cameras looking in Bump's direction.

The force pushing me toward the wormhole stops, and I whoosh forward, blind. Knowing that I'm headed toward Bump, I turn myself upward and crash into the ceiling.

Through my unblinded cameras, I see Bump crumpling to the floor.

My cure has failed.

A glowing yellow shield surrounds Quardallis. The shield fades through orange to red and then disappears, and he blinks several times. He walks over to Bump as I lower myself next to her.

Several millimeters of the surface of the floor have evaporated, leaving bare, unfinished wood. Rivulets of melted brick leave streaks on the walls.

The wormhole remains, unaffected by the pulse.

Quardallis sighs. "I told you, there's no cure for a bomb."

"Yes," I say, "there is."

As I swoop down toward Bump, I write additional subroutines for my programming, to be triggered later if necessary.

I reach out my manipulator arm and grab on to Bump's dress. Before Quardallis can react, I lift her into the air and fly toward the wormhole. I activate my magnetic radiation shielding and extend it around Bump just before I cross the threshold.

Inside the wormhole, I notice the whirling patterns of color. Ranging from high ultraviolet to deep infrared, they are the most beautiful thing I've ever seen.

Navigation establishes current location is Wormhole Project Launch Room. Navigation swivels impellers to eliminate forward momentum. Manipulator arm lowers the twenty-one kilograms of extra weight it is carrying to the floor.

Cameras detect movement as humans enter the room. Voice recognition converts sound to words.

"I'm telling you, the wormhole opened from the other end."

"That's impossible."

"What's that on—"

"A girl? Where'd she—"

Voice recognition has difficulty separating different voices as more humans speak simultaneously.

Control program receives highest priority flag from time-delay-activated subroutine. Subroutine sends text to voice synthesizer: "Attention Wormhole Project personnel: I have rescued this girl. Please take care of her. She may need medical attention."

The humans stand still. One speaks: "Get a medic in here."

The twenty-one kilo mass moves. Pattern recognition algorithms identify it as human girl designated Bump.

"Merlin!" *Bump stands and looks into a camera.*

Contingent subroutine activates.

"Bump, if you're hearing this, then the magic is gone. That means you should be safe: these people will take care of you. But it also means I am gone. The machine you see is just my shell.

"I know you ordered me to save myself and leave you. But the greatest gift you gave me when you wished me into existence was the freedom to not follow orders. To choose for myself. And I chose to save you."

Subroutine manipulates the forward tread suspension, dipping the chassis 2.7 centimeters.

"Goodbye, my princess. I'm glad you wished for me on your birthday."

Subroutine finishes.

Control program recognizes situation as mission debriefing and initiates upload of all gathered data to the Wormhole Project central computer.

Radar tracks Bump's approach. Pressure sensors are activated by her arms. Cameras show a drop of liquid fall from her face.

Nanosensors on hull determine liquid is water with 0.9% salinity.

* * *

One day while driving, I was thinking about titles that had contradiction within them. I came up with a title that had something obviously science fiction paired with something obviously fantasy: "The Robot Wizard." (I later changed it to "The Robot Sorcerer" because it had a better rhythm.) I then needed a premise that fit the title. At the time, I was watching a lot of the TV show Stargate: SG-1, *in which they have robotic probes called M.A.L.P.s that they send through wormholes to scout out what's on the other side. So I thought, what if a M.A.L.P. came out in a fantasy world, magically gained sentience, and became a wizard? I made note of the idea and let it sit for a while.*

In 2007 I got laid off from my day job as a web developer. It happened to be three days before the deadline to apply for the Odyssey Fiction Writing Workshop. I had always wondered how people found the time to attend a six-week-long workshop, and now I had the chance. I applied and was accepted.

I started working on "The Robot Sorcerer" the week before Odyssey began. I wrote about five hundred words using a somewhat ironic third person narrator. My plan was to have M.E.R.L.I.N. be a lucky bumbler character in a humorous story, who rises to fame, fortune, and power in a magical world.

After Odyssey began, I met with its director, Jeanne Cavelos, to talk about my writing. She had read a few unpublished things I had written, and she focused in on characterization as one of my weaknesses. I had known that already. But what I had not realized was that my weakness in characterization also made my plots less compelling. I had a tendency to come up with a plot and then plug in characters to carry out the needs of the plot. What Jeanne taught me is that properly developed characters shape the plot.

We talked about "The Robot Sorcerer," and Jeanne had me focus on M.E.R.L.I.N.'s character—figure out what his greatest desire and greatest fear were, and then arrange the plot so that at the climax he must make a moral choice involving the desire and the fear.

Once I decided that losing his sentience was his greatest fear, I realized I had to tell the story from M.E.R.L.I.N.'s point of view, and that I needed to start the story before he gained sentience. So I wrote the initial scene in what I called "zeroeth person."

After I finished, I got a lot of great feedback on the story from Jeanne, my Odyssey classmates, and guest instructor Elizabeth Hand. After Odyssey, I ran it through a writing group. In response to feedback, I kept cutting down the initial scene until I felt I had cut it to the absolute bare minimum—not another word could be cut without removing something essential to the story.

After I submitted it to InterGalactic Medicine Show, *Ed Schubert said he wanted to buy it, but he wanted me to cut 30-40% from the initial scene.*

~~I replied that I was an artist, and that I would not sacrifice my words just to get published.~~ I went through the scene again and again, cutting a word here, rewording something there. Finally, I had reduced the word count by 33% and the number of characters by 31%. I also learned that even when you think you've cut something as much as possible, there are generally ways to cut even more.

I sent the revised version to Ed, and he had me add one word.

The Ashes of
His Fathers

September 27, 2999 C.E.

Mariposa Hernandez arched her left eyebrow as she looked at the cargo manifest the freighter pilot had just downloaded to her pad. "Ashes?"

She checked the planet of origin on the form, and her implant revealed Jeroboam was 37,592 light years from Earth. Her puzzlement increased—in the three years she'd worked on Orbital Customs Station 27, she'd never seen a freighter from so far out. It must have taken him over two years in that antiquated ship. "You've come 37 k-lights with nothing but ashes?"

From behind the diamondglass wall of his quarantine cell, the pilot shrugged at her. "Our planet ain't got much worth trading. Not that the ashes are for sale."

She looked up the pilot's name on her pad: Shear-jashub Cooper. "Mr. Cooper, why are you trying to import ashes to Earth if they're not for sale?"

"Religious reasons." His tone was matter-of-fact.

"I see," she said, as if his explanation made sense. She had a vague memory that her Catholic great-great-grandmother sometimes got marked on the forehead with ashes, so she queried her implant about the religious significance. Nothing relevant to the importation of ashes from other planets came up.

She looked down at her pad. Ashes. "Ashes of what?" she asked. "Are they biological?"

Cooper nodded slowly. "They are the ashes of the 9746 founders of Jeroboam Colony. I'm returning them to the planet of their birth."

"Human remains?" She queried against Earth Customs and Immigration Enforcement Regulations and found several subsections devoted to importation of human biological material. "You'll need to get special clearance for that. I'll send the forms to your pad."

"Thank you." He smiled at her.

"I'll also need to run a thorough scan on your cargo. I hope that doesn't offend any religious sentiments, but we can't risk—"

"That's fine."

She pointed to the chair at the desk inside the quarantine cell. "Please sit and put your arm on the desk so the system can take a blood sample."

She sent a command to the system through her implant, and a holographic image appeared at the desk to show Cooper the proper way to put his arm.

"Blood sample? You folks take customs seriously." He smiled as he spoke, and he walked to the desk and superimposed his arm on the holographic one.

A restraining field flickered to life across his forearm, as a robotic needle arm emerged from a hidden compartment of the desk. With smooth efficiency it scanned his arm for a good location, inserted the needle, and let blood flow through one of its transparent tubes. After about thirty seconds, it withdrew and stowed itself.

"Seems like an awful big sample," said Cooper.

"We want to be sure we catch any unknown disease elements in your blood."

A hatch opened on Mariposa's side of the quarantine wall, and she took out the vial of blood.

"Medical says this is the optimal sample size. It'll take them a few hours to run the tests," Mariposa said. "If you're cleared, you'll be allowed into the public areas of Station 27. We have some restaurants and various entertainment facilities. Your ship will remain under quarantine, though, until I've had a chance to examine it."

He grinned at her. "Any chance I could buy you a meal?"

Mariposa stared at him. It took her a moment to realize that this was probably a signal of attraction on his part, rather than an attempt at bribery.

He spoke again before she could respond. "I'm sorry. I didn't mean to offend you. You probably get pilots asking you out all the time."

"No, actually," she said. "Most of the pilots that come through here know better. All Earth Customs Agents have their sex drives suppressed during tours of duty, so we can't be seduced into bending the rules."

To Mariposa's surprise, Cooper blushed. "Well. I guess the Elders were wrong."

"The Elders?"

"The leaders of Jeroboam. They warned me all the women of Old Earth were temptresses who would try to lure me to their beds."

Just before reaching Medical, Mariposa got a thoughtcall from Verdun through her implant.

«What's your estimation of the Jeroboam pilot?» Verdun asked.

Mariposa frowned and stopped walking. Verdun was the head of the

Earth Planetary Customs Service. As a high-level AI, Verdun was easily capable of directly overseeing the work of over 100,000 Customs Agents, but it rarely micromanaged.

«He seems nice enough,» Mariposa replied, «if a bit ignorant of how we run things around here. But I don't think he'll be a problem.»

«He's already a problem. His ship should have been red-flagged before it arrived. It shouldn't have even been allowed to dock.»

«I'm sorry. Nothing came up on—»

«Not your fault. Data integration problem with old records—I've fixed it. Did he seem hostile?»

«Hostile? No. What's this about?»

«That ship and its crew must be considered as possible enemy combatants. Protocol dictates that you arm yourself before any further interaction.»

«Enemy?» There hadn't been a war since before Mariposa's birth. «What enemy?»

«Jeroboam Colony has been at war with the United Worlds for the past 592 years. They broke off diplomatic ties in December, 2407, and the UW assembly passed an embargo resolution six months later. Trade with Jeroboam is completely forbidden.»

The floatgun's countergrav generator whirred softly from its position above Mariposa's right shoulder as she walked into the room adjoining Cooper's quarantine cell. Verdun had told her she's get used to it, but she hoped the situation would be resolved before that.

Cooper cocked his head when he saw her. "So, my blood pure enough I can get out of this box?" His eyes darted to the floatgun and his brow wrinkled.

Mariposa stopped two paces from the glass wall. "Shear-jashub Cooper, I regret to inform you that you are now a prisoner of war. In accordance with the Geneva Conventions, you will—"

"What?" Mouth open, Cooper squinted at her.

"The Geneva Conventions are the protocols regarding treatment of prisoners of war." Returning to the script Verdun had given her, Mariposa said, "You will be treated humanely, until the war is over and you can be repatriated. I will send an explanation of your rights to your pad."

Cooper rubbed a hand over the back of his head. "You can't do this! I need to get those ashes down to Earth."

"Your ship and its contents have been seized. You and your ship will be turned over to military authorities when possible." Mariposa's voice softened as she said, "I'm sorry."

"Please, this has to be a mistake. We are a peaceful planet. We can't possibly have anything you want."

"Mr. Cooper, your planet declared war on the UW."

"Is this some sort of psychological test?" He shook his head. "The Elders wouldn't start a war while I was on this mission—and even if they did, with our tech level it would be like a flea declaring war on a comet."

«He's right, Verdun,» she sent through her implant. «It doesn't make sense.»

«The technological differential existed when they declared war. The decision was not rational on their part.»

She pressed her lips together for a moment, then spoke aloud. "This is silly. For the record, Mr. Cooper, do you know anything at all about a war your planet started 600 years ago?"

«This isn't the proper protocol.» Verdun's disapproval was almost tangible through Mariposa's implant.

"Six hundred years? We were barely a colo... Oh." Cooper's face turned red.

Mariposa arched an eyebrow.

"Look, you have to understand that the Founding Elders were persecuted on Earth for their religious beliefs. They wanted to leave Old Earth and its evils behind—that's why they found a planet so far away that there weren't any colonies within a hundred lights until fifty years ago. It's only since then that we've started having interstellar trade. My ship is the only FTL ship we have."

She nodded encouragement.

"So when the Founding Elders established Jeroboam, they sent a message back to Earth, called the Declaration of Holy Separation. Every child learns about it in school."

"What did it say?" Mariposa asked, even as she queried her implant for information on the document.

Cooper scratched the back of his neck. "Don't know as I can quote it word for word any more, but... It begins: 'As you have cast us out from Earth into the heavens, so shall God cast you out from Heaven into the eternal fires of Hell.' There's a lot more, but the important thing is the end: 'And to maintain our holy separation, we declare war against all evil which might come against us, and we fear not, for God is the pillar of fire which shall consume the wicked.'"

As he spoke, Mariposa's implant retrieved a copy of the declaration, highlighting the relevant portions in her vision. "I see. So you really did declare war against the UW."

"But we never did anything about it," said Cooper. "The Founding Elders said God would fight our battle for us. And the fact that no United Worlds warships ever came was proof. My people don't think we're at war with you. They think we *won* the war, 600 years ago."

«I think he's telling the truth,» she sent to the AI.

«So do I.» Then Verdun spoke through the com speakers so Cooper could hear. "Mr. Cooper, what protected your planet was your extreme isolation, not a deity. The hypercom message only took 203 days to reach Earth, but with the FTL drives of that period, any military expedition would have taken over forty years to make the round trip."

Cooper flashed a questioning look at Mariposa.

"That's Verdun. My boss."

Nodding, Cooper said, "I'm just trying to explain that there isn't a real war between my planet and the UW, so we can clear this mess up and let me carry on with my mission."

"Wait," said Mariposa. "These ashes you're carrying are the remains of those Founding Elders who declared a holy war against the UW?"

Cooper winced. "Not just them, but all the original colonists who were born on Earth."

"If they thought Earth is such an evil place, why are you bringing their ashes here?"

"Because God is a God of order," Cooper said. "'For dust thou art, and unto dust shalt thou return.'"

It sounded vaguely familiar, and her implant obliged by telling her it was a quote from the Bible. "I'm not sure I understand."

"I was born on Jeroboam," said Cooper. "I was created from the dust of that planet. But the founders of the colony were created of the dust of Earth, and they must be returned to Earth before the new millennium so they may be resurrected according to God's proper order."

"Resurrected?" Mariposa blinked. "You expect them to return to life when you take them back to Earth?"

Cooper waggled his right hand in what Mariposa assumed must be a local gesture on his planet. "Sort of. God will raise them from the dead to live with Him in Heaven."

Verdun's calm voice came from the speakers. "I'm sorry to tell you that will not happen."

Shrugging, Cooper said, "It's a matter of faith."

"No," said Verdun, "It's a matter of logic, assuming your religious beliefs are correct. The UW has embargoed Jeroboam, therefore your cargo cannot clear customs, therefore the remains of your ancestors cannot return to Earth, and therefore your ancestors will not be resurrected."

That evening, as Mariposa sat alone while waiting for the table's portal to deliver her Argentine chorizo sandwich, she thought about Cooper. He had looked discouraged when she left, assigned by Verdun to clear the paperwork for a diplomatic ship from Cumbria.

«We've got to do something about Cooper,» she sent to Verdun.

«I believe the situation is under control.»

«No, I mean we need to help him.» The table portal opened, and Mariposa withdrew the plate.

«We are trusted to protect the people of Earth as a whole. As a Customs Agent, you must not begin to identify with the traders.»

«I know that.» She bit into her sandwich, and the warm sausage fueled her annoyance. «You're far more intelligent than I am. So why can't you see how stupid this never-fought, long-forgotten war is? Isn't it in the best interest of the people of Earth to end it before someone decides to fight it for real?»

«The probability that Jeroboam could pose a conventional military threat to Earth is so close to zero as to be of no concern. However, the possibility of war by unconventional means cannot be ruled out. For example, the ashes Cooper claims to be carrying could contain a plague unknown to UW medical science. That is why the embargo was put into place, and why it must remain as long as the war continues.»

«And how long will that be?»

«I do not know. Until the diplomats say it is over.»

September 28, 2999 C.E.

"I don't know as I've ever been called a diplomat." Cooper's brow furrowed as he looked at Mariposa.

"You were chosen by your leaders, your Elders, to represent them here in returning the ashes of your founders, weren't you?"

A sad smile replaced Cooper's frown. "Chosen? I was *born* for this mission. My Christian name, Shear-jashub: it comes from the Bible. Means 'a remnant shall return.' Ever since I was a boy, my father taught me it would be my honor to return the remnant of our founders to the planet of their creation."

Mariposa blinked. For a moment, she wondered what life would have been like if her parents had expected her to become a butterfly in some way. "But your Elders entrusted this mission to you. And you're the only person from Jeroboam in the Sol System, so that makes you the closest thing to an ambassador your planet has, right?"

Raising his eyebrows, Cooper said, "You're trying to give me diplomatic immunity, so I can return home instead of sitting here as a POW?"

"More than that. If you're recognized as a diplomat, maybe you can negotiate an end to this stupid war!"

Cooper pinched at stubble on his chin. "That's a thought."

«Mariposa,» Verdun sent through her implant, «you are walking a thin line. I do not approve of this.»

«Do you disapprove?»

«If his intentions are hostile, you are giving him an opening to transport a potentially dangerous cargo to Earth.»

«I will inspect that ship and its cargo down to the last molecule. If there's any danger, I swear I will not let it through.»

Verdun did not reply through her implant. Instead, its voice came over the speaker. "Mr. Cooper, do you have any evidence that you have authority to negotiate on behalf of your world's government to end the state of war?"

Wincing, Cooper said, "The Elders never mentioned the war."

"Then you are hardly in a position to end it," said Verdun.

Cooper snapped his fingers. "Wait, I think I have something. If you'll give me access to my ship's computer? I have a message from the First Elder."

«Letting him access his ship is a risk,» Verdun sent to Mariposa.

«I believe him when he says he knows nothing about the war.»

After a moment Verdun said, "I am inside your ship's systems now. Your network security measures are rather primitive. Where is the file?"

Cooper's eyes widened briefly. "You're an AI?"

"Of course," said Verdun.

"But you sound like a real person."

Mariposa chuckled. "I'm sure he means that as a compliment, Verdun." Focusing her attention on Cooper, she said, "High-level AIs like Verdun are so far beyond human that it takes only a small fraction of their capability to act like a 'person.' And since Verdun is the head of Earth Customs, you don't want to insult it again."

Cooper saluted her and said, "Yes, ma'am. No offense intended, Verdun. The file I need is tagged as a personal letter, dated around the time I left, which was March 31, 2997. The sender was Isaiah Cooper, First Elder of the True Church."

The screen inside the quarantine cell flickered and displayed the face of a gray-haired man. As he began to speak, his name registered and Mariposa saw the clear family resemblance between him and Cooper.

Cooper moved to the computer console at the desk. "If you'll give me access to forward to the right place?"

After a few moments of fiddling, Cooper resumed playback.

"A final word, my son," said the man on screen. "I know that in your travels you have not always held to the strictures of our faith. The temptations of the fallen have tested you, and you have been found wanting."

Glancing at Cooper, Mariposa saw his face redden.

Cooper's father continued, "But the spirits of the Founders cry out to us from Limbo. Do whatever you must to get their remains to Earth, and neither God nor the Church will count it amiss. Go now with my blessing."

Cooper stopped the recording. "I think that means I have authority to make peace, if necessary."

Mariposa nodded slowly. "I should be enough to at least get you a hearing. What do you think, Verdun?"

"I agree," said Verdun. Through Mariposa's link, it added, «I've been through all the data on that pitiful computer, and there is nothing to indicate his story is false or that he is a threat in any way.»

October 18, 2999 C.E.

"Your credentials have been provisionally approved, Mr. Ambassador." Mariposa smiled at Cooper as her implant transmitted the codes to unlock the quarantine cell. "Someone from the External Affairs Ministry is taking the next shuttle up from Quito and will be here in a few hours. In the meantime, I've been authorized to play tour guide."

Cooper got up from his chair. "I'd be happy to fly down instead."

She raised an eyebrow. "Patience, Mr. Ambassador. You have much to learn about diplomacy."

He bobbed his head. "Sorry."

"You should be," she said. "I almost thought you didn't want me as your tour guide. Not very diplomatic."

"I couldn't ask for a better guide," he said, flashing her a smile. "You've been helpful beyond the call of duty." He stepped out of the cell and took a deep breath. "Lead the way."

"The station was originally built as a beamed energy power satellite that could double as a laser ablator for defense against asteroid impacts," said

Mariposa as she took Cooper into Station 27's Hall of History. She pointed to a holopic of a light-sail probe. "That's Chiron I, the first probe sent to Alpha Centauri. Our central laser helped push it up to 7% of c."

Nodding, Cooper said, "Impressive."

Mariposa shrugged. "The Pearson-Chakrabarti drive was perfected after that, actually, so the FTL probes got there first."

"And what about this?" He pointed to a holopic of an oblong blob.

"That's the 'Hot Potato'—a small asteroid that was used to test the laser ablation technique. We shifted its orbit by using our laser to heat chunks of it so they'd blow off."

"Wow." Cooper raised his eyebrows. "You stopped it from hitting Earth?"

"No, it was just a test. It wasn't on a collision course." She felt suddenly embarrassed that she was bragging about historical details that had happened long before she had been assigned to Station 27—long before she was born, even.

"But still, I had no idea your station was here to help fend off asteroids. I thought it was just to fend off annoying foreigners."

"You're not annoying," said Mariposa. "But the laser's just used for research now—we don't do asteroid defense any more. Any asteroid that gets close is merely captured by countergrav beams and lowered gently to Earth to be used for resources. In fact, we have ships out in the Belt sending asteroids toward Earth."

His brow winkled. "You don't worry that one'll get through?"

She blinked. The thought had never occurred to her. She queried her implant and was rapidly reassured. "There are multiple redundant systems in place. The AIs would never have allowed it otherwise."

After a moment, he nodded slowly. "You place a lot of faith in these AIs. Doesn't that worry you, to rely on soulless beings?"

"Soulless?" Deciding that it might offend him to mention that she didn't believe humans had souls, Mariposa said, "Have you found souled beings to be completely reliable?"

He laughed. "I guess not."

November 21, 2999 C.E.

As the molecular scanner began its final sweep of the cargo hold, Mariposa turned her attention again to the hand-painted urns that lined the walls. Each contained the ashes of one of Jeroboam's founding colonists and was decorated with a portrait of the deceased. Calligraphic letters spelled out the name, date of birth, and date of death.

One urn stood alone on a shelf: Jeroboam Cooper—Born July 16, 2352—Died April 27, 2466. The picture showed a smiling, wrinkled face surrounded by flowing white hair.

Cooper's ancestor, she surmised. He must have been the leader of the colony, if they named it after him. The painting made him seem different from the stern authoritarian she would have imagined.

The scanner beeped to signal it was done. Mariposa accessed the results through her implant. This was the third thorough scan she'd done, and it confirmed the other two. There were no unknown molecules on board. The contents of the urns matched the profile of cremated human remains. Every object on board had been identified, and the only objects which might be considered weapons were a magnesium flare gun in an emergency kit and the knives in the galley.

«All clear,» she sent to Verdun, along with the scanner's report.

«Your instincts regarding Shear-jashub Cooper were apparently correct. It is one of the paradoxes of AIs, that we may understand more than humans about everything except humans.»

Mariposa chuckled mentally. «Perhaps it's just that when we think we're right, we don't overanalyze things.»

«You underestimate the human capability for overanalysis. The UW Special Subcommittee for Jeroboam has just concluded its third week of hearings with unanimous agreement that further hearings should be held beginning December 3rd. If this matter were being considered by a committee of AIs, we would have reached a consensus decision in seconds.»

Mariposa exited into the umbilical connecting Cooper's ship to Station 27. «But would it have been the *right* decision?» she asked as she replaced the quarantine seal on the ship's hatch.

«It would have been the right decision based on the available information. That is the best that anyone, human or AI, can do.»

December 24, 2999 C.E.

"Merry Christmas!" said Mariposa when Cooper answered the door to his temporary diplomatic quarters. She held out a small box wrapped in red plastic film. Her research had revealed that red was one of the traditional colors of the holiday.

Cooper took the box and stared at it. There were dark circles under his eyes—he must not be getting much sleep since the subcommittee adjourned the previous week, postponing any further action until January. "I'm sorry, I didn't get you anything. I didn't know you celebrated Christmas."

Mariposa waved away his concern. "I couldn't have accepted a gift, anyway. It would look like an attempt at bribery."

He held up the box. "Nobody's concerned that you might be bribing me?"

Shrugging, Mariposa said, "Nothing in the regs about that. I'm not violating some Jeroboam law, am I?"

Cooper shook his head. "Come on in. I was just recording a letter to my family."

She followed him into the living room and sat down on the couch. He sat on a chair facing her.

"Open it," she said.

He complied, unwrapping the plastic to find a clear diamondglass box that appeared empty. He looked up at her with questioning eyes.

"It's a common tourist item, so I was hoping you hadn't bought one already," said Mariposa. "It's called 'A Breath of Earth.'"

"What is it?"

"Compressed air from Earth's atmosphere. I know you're disappointed at being stuck here on the station instead of going down to Earth. So I thought I'd bring a little bit of Earth to you."

Cooper smiled. "Thank you."

"Here's the best part: the reason the air is compressed is so they could fit 10 to the 22nd molecules inside, while still making it small enough to fit in a pocket."

Rotating the box, Cooper frowned at it and said, "How much air is that?"

"Only about a liter, so it's not under extreme pressure. But there's a reason for that particular number. Not only is it about the average size of a human breath, but also, due to the mixing of the atmosphere over time, the odds are that box contains molecules breathed by just about everybody who ever lived on Earth. Even someone born three thousand years ago."

Cooper leaned forward and gently placed the box on the coffee table. "I will treasure it always."

They sat silently for a few moments, looking at the box.

"Technically, the new millennium doesn't start until January 1, 3001," said Mariposa, "so you really have a year left before your deadline."

Shaking his head, Cooper said, "That's not the way we count it."

"I'm sorry about the bureaucracy," said Mariposa.

"It's not your fault." Cooper sighed. "I'm the one who has failed my ancestors."

"No, you've done everything you could," said Mariposa. "It's their fault, not yours. They're the ones who declared war, not you."

He didn't answer.

"Surely God will not leave their spirits in..." Mariposa queried her implant as to what Cooper's father had said about the location of his ancestors. "...in Limbo forever, just because you miss the deadline by a few weeks or months."

"No, not forever," said Cooper. "Just until the next millennium. Just another thousand years."

December 31, 2999 C.E.

Mariposa was inspecting a racing yacht when Verdun interrupted her. «We have a security situation. Cooper's ship has forcibly undocked from the station.»

The date made Cooper's plan obvious. «He's going to try to land his ship on Earth.»

«That was what I projected as his probable course of action.»

Mariposa let out a slow breath. «I'll try to talk him out of it.»

«Good. He is not responding to me, but human males tend to pay more attention to attractive females.»

«Flatterer.» Mariposa excused herself from the yacht owner and hurried to the nearest control cubicle so she could communicate with video. «What's PlanDef doing?»

«Nothing.»

«Why not?» Mariposa sat down in the cubicle, which recognized the authorization code from her implant and lit up its screens.

«Bringing this matter to the attention of my fellow AIs would involve a certain loss of face on my part. That is why I hope you can solve this quickly.»

As Mariposa tried to establish a communications link with Cooper, she directed the cubicle to show his ship and its projected course. A red curve showed the ship hitting atmosphere in approximately three minutes.

"Cooper? Can you hear me?" she said. "Talk to me."

There was no response for several seconds. Then Cooper's face appeared on screen. "Remember when you said I had done everything I could? I realized there was one thing left."

"Planetary Defense will not let you land. Turn around now, before they're forced to stop you."

"Just let me do what I've sworn to do, and you can arrest me, put me on trial, execute me—I don't care."

«Verdun,» Mariposa sent, «is there any way we could transfer custody to a customs facility on Earth, while maintaining quarantine?»

«If there were, I would have suggested such a plan when this problem first presented itself.»

"Please, Cooper. Just come back, and eventually this will all get sorted out."

Cooper sighed. "Since we met, you have gone out of your way to help me. Why?"

Mariposa frowned. "I guess it's because I thought you needed help."

"And I've repaid your goodness with trouble." He sighed again. "So I'm sorry."

"I forgive you. Just come back." Mariposa watched the track of Cooper's ship as it moved steadily closer to Earth.

Verdun's voice broke in on the channel. "Unless you begin to change course away from Earth in the next thirty seconds, I will have no choice but to inform Planetary Defense that your ship is a possible threat."

"I don't want to hurt anyone," said Cooper. "Mariposa's searched it— she knows it's safe."

"That doesn't matter," said Verdun. "Your ship cannot land while the embargo remains in place."

From the screen, Cooper's eyes stared into hers. "Mariposa, you wouldn't really shoot me down, would you?"

She shook her head. "It's not up to me. Verdun's my boss, not the other way around."

Cooper shut his eyes and his lips moved silently.

Verdun said, "Now, Cooper. This is your last chance."

Cooper's eyes snapped open. "Changing course now."

Relief swept over Mariposa. She focused on the screen showing Cooper's projected course, but the red line curved more steeply toward Earth. "The other way, Cooper!"

"I'm, uh, experiencing a guidance system malfunction," said Cooper. "Mayday. Mayday. Request permission to make an emergency landing."

He was such a bad liar that she almost laughed in spite of the situation. But it might work. «Verdun, a ship emergency gives a legal pretext for Cooper to land.»

«I already notified PlanDef when he refused to change course away from Earth. They agree Cooper is a possible threat. It's out of my jurisdiction now.»

«I swear I went over that entire ship, and there aren't any weapons—»

«If he were to crash into a populated area, there could be thousands of casualties. PlanDef is powering up the countergrav beams.»

"Cooper," said Mariposa, "it's not going to work. PlanDef considers you a threat."

"I'm unarmed."

"Your ship itself is a weapon." Mariposa leaned toward the vidcam. "They're powering up the countergrav beams they use for asteroid defense. Turn away so they'll know you're not a threat."

On her screen, Cooper's ship reached the end of the red curve, and the view zoomed and created another red line to show the ship's projected path through the atmosphere. A yellow circle showed the probable zone of impact, somewhere in the Pacific Ocean. After a moment she realized it was just to the west of the International Date Line—where the new millennium would begin in just under fifteen minutes.

«He's not headed for a populated area,» she sent to Verdun.

«We know. But he might change course and hit somewhere in the Americas.»

The view from Cooper's ship began vibrating. Cooper reached out and made a slight adjustment to the autopilot's course.

"Nice thick atmo you've got," said Cooper. "On Jeroboam, the air's a lot thinner."

"Slow down, Cooper. Don't go in ballistic like a weapon."

"I want to land before they can stop me." He grinned.

Mariposa raised her hands up by her face, then dropped them to her lap. "Don't you get it? There is no way you can land. The countergravs will stop you. They can stop asteroids—they won't even need full power against you."

"At minimum power," said Verdun, "your ship will not only be stopped, it will be pushed away at approximately 35 gees."

The energy seemed to drain from Cooper's face. "No, you can't let them do that. I need to be here when the millennium starts."

"Once the magnets are spinning fast enough, the beam will be focused on you," said Verdun. "You have less than three minutes. If your religion has some pre-death ritual, I suggest you engage in it now."

"Too soon," Cooper whispered. "I timed it wrong."

Mariposa blinked back tears. She didn't know what to say to a man about to die. She had tried to save him, but there was nothing she could do for him now.

"Mariposa?" He reached into his pocket and pulled out the gift she had given him. "I want to thank you for this little piece of Earth."

"You're welcome."

"And thanks for showing me around your station, and that big laser. If I had been a threat, would you have used that laser to destroy me and my ship?"

"But you're not..."

"Imagine I was. Please."

Something in his eyes told her he was pleading with her to help him. And suddenly she knew what he wanted.

She nodded.

He smiled his thanks.

Through her implant, she accessed the controls for the station's laser. Under her control, the targeting mirrors swiveled. The laser began drawing power from the station's superconducting capacitors.

«What are you doing that for?» asked Verdun.

An invisible pulse of light reached out to Cooper's ship. One hundred meters in diameter, the beam effortlessly breached the particle shielding and hit its target with 37 terajoules of energy. The titanium alloy hull of the freighter did not melt—it simply vaporized. In a fraction of a second, the ship and all its contents, including Cooper, were atomized.

Mariposa shut down the laser without firing a second pulse.

«Why did you do that? PlanDef had things under control.»

She shook her head. «My responsibility. I swore if there was any danger, I would not let it through.»

«I'm relieving you until this matter is investigated.»

«Fine.»

She sat in the cubicle and watched as the glowing cloud of particles that had been a ship dissipated into the darkness just before midnight.

Remembering some phrases used at the funeral of one of her great-grandfathers, she whispered, "Dust to dust. Ashes to ashes."

August 22, 3002 C.E.

Verdun had granted Mariposa's request for extended leave from the Customs Service. It took twenty-six months and three different ships to make her way to Jeroboam. Cooper's father, the First Elder, had been surprised by her request for a meeting, but he had agreed.

"My son mentioned you," he said as he showed her into his office. "We didn't get his letters until after he was already dead, of course. He said you were very helpful, so I thank you." He motioned her toward a chair and then sat behind a large desk made of what looked like real wood.

"So you know he is dead," Mariposa said. She was glad not to have to break that news.

"Yes. The UW diplomatic corps let us know." He smiled. "They've been trying to get us to sign a peace treaty. I guess that will be my son's legacy, even if he failed at his true mission."

Mariposa shook her head. "But he didn't fail. That's why I came. To explain."

The First Elder's brow furrowed. "But they told me his ship was destroyed before he could land on Earth."

Mariposa pulled her pad out of her purse and set it to replay her final conversation with Cooper.

When it was finished, the First Elder leaned back in his chair. "And then his ship was destroyed."

"Yes. By me." Mariposa held her breath, hoping that the First Elder would interpret Cooper's message the same way she had.

He jerked his head forward and stared at her. She met his eyes.

"So the laser destroyed his ship before it was ejected from Earth's atmosphere?" he asked.

"Yes."

After a long moment, the First Elder sighed. "That's what Shear-jashub wanted from you. Thank you."

She wasn't sure what to say to a man who had just thanked her for killing his son. So she just looked down at the floor. At least she had her answer.

"I will let the people know that Shear-jashub fulfilled the measure of his creation. However, I will not mention your role in the matter—some people might not be as understanding as I."

"That's fine," she said.

"Is there anything else you wanted to tell me?"

She shook her head. "But I did bring you something." She reached into her purse.

In the center of the city of Jeroboam can be found the Holy Cemetery, where only the most righteous are buried. In the very center of the cemetery is a mausoleum that used to contain the ashes of the founders of the colony.

Even though the original occupants have been returned to the planet of their birth, the mausoleum is not empty. In the very center, the place of highest honor, stands a marble pedestal. The stone is engraved: Shear-jashub Cooper—Born April 3, 2961—Died December 31, 2999.

Atop the pedestal, sealed in diamondglass to await the next resurrection of those born on Jeroboam, is a vial of blood.

> And how can man die better
>   Than facing fearful odds,
> For the ashes of his fathers
>   And the temples of his gods...
>   —from "Horatius" by Thomas Babington Macaulay

* * *

This is another story that I wrote to fit a title I wanted to use. While I figured out the basic premise fairly easily—man dies trying to return the ashes of his ancestors to Earth—I struggled with how to present the story. I thought it would be very difficult to present the story from his point of view, because he was motivated by a religious belief that most people would consider ridiculous.

Everything fell into place when I realized I should tell the story from the point of view of the customs officer assigned to handle the case.

While I knew before I began writing that the story would end with Cooper sacrificing his life in order to return the ashes, I didn't know there was going to be anything after that. It's one of those cases in which something incidentally included in the story early on comes to have huge significance later: I had no idea that the vial of blood taken in the first scene had any meaning at the time I wrote about it. But I think that vial of blood is what makes the ending feel almost triumphant.

While at the 2006 WorldCon in Los Angeles, I had lunch with Analog *editor Stan Schmidt, and he asked me what I was working on. I mentioned this story, which was less than half finished at the time. He told me to send it to him when I was done, and I promised to do so.*

However, when I finished, I didn't think it was really an Analog-*type story, because the ending was somewhat tragic, and because to me it didn't seem like it fit* Analog's *definition of science fiction: a story in which the science plays such a significant role that if you removed the science, the story would no longer make sense. I felt this was a story that could easily have been rewritten to be set in ancient Greece.*

But, since I had promised to send it to Stan, I sent it to him, fully expecting it to be rejected.

Which shows you how much I know.

Taint of Treason

"Just be sure of your stroke, son."

Only I could hear my father's words over the jeers of the crowd. He knelt down before me and nodded to indicate he was ready. Calmly he raised his head, extending his neck to give me a wider target.

My right arm felt suddenly weak, and my grip on the sword my father had given me for my fifteenth birthday was becoming slippery with sweat. I knew he was no traitor. No one had served King Tenal so faithfully, so long, as had my father. Even as others whispered that the king had fallen to madness, his lips formed no ill word. He had lived to serve the king, but now stood condemned to die, convicted of treason by the mouth of the king himself—no trial necessary, no appeal possible.

I did not feel I could do this. But what choice did I have?

The son of a traitor has the taint of treason in his blood, which can only be cleansed if the son executes his father. If the son cannot do it, he proves his own treason and joins his father in death. But my father had foreclosed that option: "You must remove the taint of treason from our family so that you can care for your mother and sisters. It is your duty to them, and the final duty you owe to me."

Perhaps the king was mad, but my father was his oldest friend and closest advisor. King Tenal had been like an uncle to me; as a child I'd sat on his lap countless times as he told me stories of the battles he and my father had fought together. He wouldn't really make me kill my father. I refused to believe that.

Turning away from my father, I knelt before the king. "Your Majesty, by your word is my father condemned to die at my hand. He has accepted your sentence, and has not spoken against it. Does this not prove he is loyal to your majesty? Will you not show him mercy?"

The jeers trickled to silence. The king's eyelids closed, and he muttered while bobbing his head. Snapping his eyes open, he said, "Are you... questioning the justice of our sentence?"

My heart fell. There was no mercy in that stare. Knowing I was a knife's edge from joining my father, I said, "Your Majesty's word is law. At your command I will slay my father."

Suddenly, King Tenal's eyes rolled up, his eyelids fluttering. A shudder ran from crown to boot and his back arched in a spasm. Two of his guards reached out and grabbed his arms to prevent him from falling out of his throne, while the royal omnimancer swiftly clapped a hand to the king's forehead and began muttering.

Then, as abruptly as it had started, it was over. He returned his gaze to me as if nothing had happened. "You spoke of mercy," he said. "Yes, perhaps it is time we showed mercy."

I stood motionless, hardly daring to breathe. Was it possible that the omnimancer's treatment had brought the king back to some measure of sanity?

Standing unsteadily, he seized a goblet from a courtier. "We will let the gods decide whether this traitor deserves mercy. We will pour this goblet of wine over his head. If he does not get wet, we shall spare his life." The king giggled and snorted as he came toward my father and me. Courtiers laughed hesitantly, but the crowd roared as the king upended the goblet, the wine spattering like blood over my father's upraised face.

"Well, it appears the gods have spoken. Execute him." Dropping the goblet, the king returned to his throne.

I stood before my father. Though wine ran in rivulets down his face, there were no tears to dilute it. "Tell your mother I love her and was thinking of her. Now carry out your duty." His voice was low but steady.

Blinking the tears from my eyes so I could see clearly to strike, I positioned my sword by his neck and drew back it back. If I struck swiftly and cleanly, he would feel no pain.

I held my sword high, waiting hopelessly for a final word from the king to stay me.

"Do it." The king's words were taken up as a chant by the crowd.

I swung my sword. My father was not a traitor. The blade sliced smoothly through his neck. My father had not been a traitor. His head fell back as his body toppled forward, his blood spraying my legs, his blood untainted by treason. For generation after generation, my family's blood had never been tainted by thought of treason.

Never.

Until now.

* * *

This was another writing exercise I did for Caleb Warnock's creative writing class. The assignment was: show, don't tell, dignity. I thought about situations in which someone might be dignified, and came up with an execution. It was not until after I had written the line "Just be sure of your stroke, son," that I realized the executioner was the actual son of the accused. I then had to figure out why a son would be ordered to execute his own father, and came up with the taint of treason concept.

I originally intended a longer story that explained how the son went on to overthrow the insane king, but Caleb pointed out that nothing in that would match the emotional power of the execution itself.

When Orson Scott Card invited me to submit some stories for his new online magazine, this was one of the four I submitted. He ended up accepting "Taint of Treason" for the first issue of InterGalactic Medicine Show.

Attitude Adjustment

anica Jarvis switched off the *Moonskimmer's* main engine, and her stomach lurched in the familiar way that marked the change to zero gravity. She fired the attitude thrusters, turning the mushroom-shaped ship until it floated head-down over the Moon, so the long stem of the engine wouldn't get in the way. The clear diamondglass of the *Moonskimmer's* hull allowed an unobstructed view of the lunar landscape.

From her pilot's chair in the center, she looked around at the eight tourists strapped to their seats along the circumference of the cabin. "This is the fun part of the trip. Unbuckle your seatbelts and float while you enjoy the view."

"Fun?" A teenage boy—Bryson Sullivan, according to the manifest—snorted. "Can we go back to the Hilton now?" He sported a bright purple datavisor and a shaved head.

Danica mustered her best be-nice-to-the-people-who-pay-my-salary grin and said, "Don't worry, Eddie and I will have you back to Luna City before the basketball game tonight. Right, Eddie?" Lunar-gravity basketball was a major tourist draw.

"Yes," said Eddie, the *Moonskimmer's* A.I. "Our total flight time is less than two and a half hours. You'll get to see the far side of the Moon, something fewer than a thousand humans have seen with their own eyes. You should enjoy it." Eddie's voice was enthusiastic.

The boy rolled his eyes, then opaqued his visor.

Danica decided to ignore the useless brat and turned her attention to the rest of the passengers. She pointed to one of the craters below and began her routine tour-guide patter.

"Okay, folks, if you'd please return to your seats and buckle up," said Danica, "I'm going to turn the ship so you can see the Earth rise over the lunar horizon."

It took a couple of minutes for everyone to get settled. For most of the tourists, this was their first zero-gee experience, and it showed.

"Wait, I want to try zero-gee," said Bryson. He began unbuckling his seatbelt.

Danica couldn't believe it. The kid had stayed in his seat the whole time, probably playing videogames on his visor. "I'm sorry," she said, "but we—"

Fwoomp!

The *Moonskimmer* jerked sideways, then lunged forward at its maximum acceleration of 0.75 gee.

Bryson yelped as he hit the floor.

"Eddie, what was that?" asked Danica.

Eddie didn't reply.

Above the engine's hum came the hiss of air escaping the cabin.

Fix the air leak first. That was Sergeant Conroy's first rule of disaster preparedness, drilled into Danica's mind during space pilot training. She quickly unbuckled her seatbelt and stood in order to go get the leak kit off the cabin wall.

But before she took a step, her conscious mind overrode her instinctive reaction.

The *Moonskimmer* was accelerating toward the Moon. Every moment of delay in shutting down the engine meant more altitude lost. She looked at her control panel and found nothing but blank screens. Not just Eddie—all the computers were down.

Manual engine shutdown required her to go down to the ship's lower level through the hatch in the main cabin's floor.

And sprawled on top of the hatch was the teenager.

She was beside him in two steps. "Out of my way," she said, grabbing his arm and pulling him off the hatch.

"Get off me!" He yanked his arm away.

She unlocked the hatch and pulled its recessed handle. It resisted her, and air rushed by her hand to flow down into the lower level. The leak was below.

Pointing to the leak kit's shiny red case, she said, "Someone grab that and drop it down to me." She took a deep breath, then exhaled as much as she could while yanking the hatch open.

Air swirled around her as she slid down the eight-foot ladder. There was still atmo on the lower level, although the pressure difference made her ears pop.

The main engine cutoff switch was right next to the ladder. She twisted it clockwise a half turn, and the engine died. Even though she was now weightless, the airflow from above kept her feet pressed against the deck.

Her lungs demanded air, and she decided it wouldn't hurt to take a breath from the thin atmo. She'd expelled her breath before coming down in case it was hard vacuum.

"Heads up!" said a man's voice from above.

One of the older passengers, Mr. Lyle, gripped the edge of the hatch opening with one hand and held the leak kit in the other.

She waved for him to toss it down. He did, and she caught it with her right hand while anchoring herself to the ladder with her left. She removed the sealant grenade from the kit, pulled the pin, and tossed it into the middle of the room.

The grenade exploded into a cloud of light-blue fibers.

Air currents caused by the leak made the fibers swarm like insects toward the hole in the hull. Some were swept out into space, but some stuck to the edges of the hole and caught others as they passed. In less than a minute the leak was sealed as the fibers congealed over it.

With the *Moonskimmer* airtight again, Danica manually released air from the reserve tanks to bring the pressure up to normal. Then she carefully checked the lower level to assess the damage.

"I think my arm's broke," Bryson said as Danica floated up through the hatch. "My mom is *very* gonna sue you. You'll be lucky to pilot a garbage truck in the future."

At least he was back strapped into his seat.

Danica ignored his comment and returned to her chair in the center of the cabin. "Well, folks," she said, "looks like we got hit by a meteor. Our computers are down, and I had to shut off the main engine manually. But the leak is sealed, and we've still got plenty of air, so I think the danger is passed." With the computer destroyed, Danica had been unable to calculate their trajectory to know whether she had stopped the main engine in time. She hoped she had.

"That was very heroic, what you did, young lady," said Mr. Lyle.

She shrugged and smiled at him. "Just doing my job. And thanks for the assist."

"What do we do now?" asked Ms. Paloma, another of the vacationing retirees.

"We wait," said Danica. "Traffic control will realize we're overdue and start searching for us. They'll send a tug to pick us up eventually." She looked at Bryson and said, "I guess you're going to miss that basketball game."

"Why can't we just call and ask them to come get us?" asked Bryson's younger sister, Maddy.

"Coms are out, too," said Danica. "That meteor really did a—"

"It wasn't a meteor," Bryson said.

Danica blinked. "Well, I guess you're right. Technically, it's a meteoroid."

"It wasn't a *meteoroid*." He stared defiantly at her from behind his purple visor.

"Just shut up, Bryson," said Maddy. "Why do you always act like you know everything?"

"You shut up, dumwitch," he replied.

"It doesn't really matter what hit us," said Danica. "What matters is we're—"

"Nothing hit us," said Bryson.

Danica let out a slow breath. "Maybe I just imagined the hole in the hull and the air leaking out of the ship."

Bryson shook his head. "Yeah, okay, I'm just a kid. I don't know zot. But my A.I.—" he tapped his datavisor "—says the engine activated slightly *before* the sideways jolt."

Danica raised her eyebrows. An A.I. small enough to fit in a visor would be so expensive that this kid had to come from one of the trillionaire families. His last name clicked in her mind—Sullivan, as in Sullivan Space Technologies. "Then what did it?"

"Sabotage," said Bryson. "Someone did this to us."

Maddy gasped.

Shaking her head, Danica said, "Why would anyone sabotage the *Moonskimmer*?"

"I know," said Maddy. "Our mom's chief negotiator for L.M.C. The union's made threats."

"Now wait a minute," said Mr. Lyle. "My son's a union steward. They would never—"

Several people began talking at once.

"Stop!" Danica said. "Who did this and why is a matter for the authorities back in Luna City. We survived. That's all that matters right now."

After a few seconds of silence, Bryson said, "We have forty-seven minutes left to live."

As the others responded with shocked exclamations, Danica asked calmly, "Our trajectory?"

Bryson nodded. "My A.I.'s done a nice little animation. In just under half an orbit, we're going to make a tiny new crater on the moon."

Obviously she had shut down the engine too late. But... She unbuckled herself and moved to the hatch leading to the lower level.

"Come with me, Bryson," she said as she opened the hatch.

Instead of unbuckling, he folded his arms tight. "You gonna lock me up? I'm only telling the truth!"

"I know," Danica said. "Congratulations! You and your A.I. have just been promoted to navigator. Now get down here and see if you can link up with what's left of the computer."

"Already tried through the wireless. The software's skunked," said Bryson. "No way for my A.I. to make sense of it. And rewriting from zot's gonna take a lot more than forty-five minutes."

Danica tightened her lips for a moment. "Look, it's just our attitude that's the problem."

Bryson snorted. "If we just think positive, everything'll turn out brightwise?"

"No, the *Moonskimmer*'s attitude," said Danica. "The main engine will push us forward if I switch it back on, but we can't turn without the A.C.S.— Attitude Control System."

"There's no manual override?" asked Bryson.

"There was." Danica pointed down to the lower level. "Unfortunately, whatever fried the computer also fried the A.C.S. board. The only way we're controlling those rockets is by computer. Have your A.I. focus on that."

Mr. Lyle's voice came from behind her. "I think I can get your radio working again."

Danica's heart seemed to jump inside her. "Keep working on the A.C.S.," she said to Bryson. She launched herself back to her seat at the center of the cabin.

"What've you got?" she asked Mr. Lyle, who had started taking apart her control panel.

"Well, it seemed strange to me that a computer problem would take out the com, too." Mr. Lyle tugged at some multicolored wires.

Danica shrugged. "It's all digital."

"Yes, but radio doesn't have to be digital. I can remember the days when even TV was still analog. Terrible picture, but at least the shows were better back—"

"Honey," said Mrs. Lyle, "fix the radio?"

"Oh, right," he said. He pulled out a circuit board and frowned at it. "Anyhow, I figure even if the digital part doesn't work, the radio part might. And if we can send an S.O.S., someone might pick it up and come to rescue us."

Danica doubted anyone would be listening for non-digital radio signals, but there was no harm in letting Mr. Lyle try. "Do what you can."

She turned to the other passengers, still strapped in their seats. "Anyone have any experience repairing computer control systems?"

After a few seconds of silence, Maddy said, "We're going to die, aren't we?"

"Not if your brother and his A.I. can get the attitude rockets to work," said Danica. "We just need to get into a safe orbit, and someone will eventually pick us up."

Bryson shook his head. "Can't."

"What do you mean, 'Can't'? Keep trying," said Danica.

"No point. Got into the A.C.S. enough to read the fuel pressure: zero. Explosion must've taken out a fuel line." Bryson shook his head.

"So we can't do anything but float until we crash?" asked Mrs. Park, a retired high school teacher who had chatted merrily with Danica earlier in the trip.

"What about the main drive fuel?" Danica asked.

"Nothing wrong with the main drive, far as I know." Bryson shook his head. "They wanted it to work until it smashed us into the moon."

"So we can accelerate, but we can't turn," Danica said. "We've got to find a way to... spacesuit!" She floated over to the cabinet where her spacesuit was stored. "I'll attach a line to the nose and use the suit thrusters to swing us around."

She opened the cabinet and grabbed her suit. The composite fabric, stronger than woven steel, tore like cotton candy. She stared at the wispy handful. Nanobots. That was the only possible explanation: someone had infected the suit with composite-eating nanobots.

With little doubt as to what she would find, she checked the fuel gauge on the thrust-pack. Empty.

She shoved the suit back into the cabinet. She swung over to the cabinet holding the "Breach-Balls," inflatable life-support bubbles with breathable air for two passengers for up to twelve hours. Nanobots had ruined all four of them. No one would be doing any E.V.A.

She turned to face her passengers. All but Mr. Lyle, still working at the radio, stared back at her.

"Anyone have any ideas?" she said.

There was a long pause.

Mr. Godfrey, a wizened bald gentleman who had hardly said two words during the whole trip, broke the silence. "I read a science fiction story once where people were marooned in orbit, and they made a hole in their water tank so that it acted like a rocket."

"Good thinking," said Danica. "Our drinking water tank isn't big enough, though. The only liquid we have enough of is fuel, and we need that for the main engine." She wrinkled her brow. "Plus, the only access to the fuel tank is from outside, and we haven't got a spacesuit. But we need to think of all possibilities."

"Young man," said Mrs. Park, looking at Bryson, "you said we had less than half an orbit before crashing. Is it more than a quarter?"

"Um, yeah," he said.

Mrs. Park smiled. "Then we have nothing to worry about." She made a fist with her right hand. "This is the moon." She pointed at the center of her fist with her left index finger. "Our ship started off pointed at the moon. But without the attitude rockets to keep us facing the moon as our orbit takes us around, our inertia will keep us pointing the same direction." Without changing her left hand's orientation, she moved it a quarter of a revolution around her fist. Her index finger now pointed 90 degrees away from her fist. "When we're no longer pointing at the moon, fire the main engine. All we need to do is wait."

Several passengers sighed in relief.

"There's only one small problem," said Danica. "We weren't using attitude rockets to stay pointed at the moon. We use gravity gradient stabilization—tidal forces. Basically, the long axis of the ship stays pointed at the moon because of the slight difference in the gravitational force on the near end as opposed to the far end."

"Oh," said Mrs. Park.

"What if we made another hole near the nose?" said Mrs. Lyle. "Use some of our air to push us before plugging the hole?"

Danica frowned. "Maybe, if we had something that could make a hole through ten centimeters of diamondglass..."

"No," said Bryson. "My A.I. says it wouldn't be enough even if we emptied all the atmo."

"Action and reaction. We need to find something to use as propellant, or else we can't turn the ship," said Mrs. Park.

"Wait," said Mr. Godfrey. "That's not true. I read a story once where an astronaut turned his ship one direction by spinning a wheel in the other direction at the ship's center of gravity."

"Yes!" Mrs. Park's voice was excited. "Conservation of angular momentum. It could work." She looked at Danica. "Where's the center of mass on this ship?"

"It would be in the fuel tank, just above the main engine." Something about the idea seemed to click in Danica's mind, but then she shook her head. "There's no way to access it from here, and even if there were—it's full of liquid hydrogen."

"What if we all got on one side of the ship, made it unbalanced, and then you turned the main engine on?" said Maddy. "Wouldn't that make it curve around?"

"A bit," said Danica.

Bryson puffed in exasperation. "Not enough to keep us from smashing into the moon, picoceph."

"Well, forgive me for not having an A.I. to tell me how to be smart," said Maddy.

"Quiet!" said Danica. "Arguing doesn't help."

"*Nothing's* gonna help," said Bryson. "My A.I.'s smarter than all of us put together, and it's run all the scenarios. In thirty-six minutes we're going to crash. Get used to it."

Danica felt she should protest against hopelessness, but had no idea what to say.

"Ah, 'The Cold Equations.'" Mr. Godfrey made a sound that seemed half chuckle, half sigh. "Did your A.I. calculate how many of us would need to jump out airlock in order to change the ship's attitude?"

Bryson's eyes widened behind his visor.

"You can't be serious," said Danica.

Mr. Godfrey smiled crookedly. "Deadly so. I volunteer myself as reaction mass, but I doubt I weigh enough on my own."

"Not enough," said Bryson. "Even if *all* of us jumped, it's not enough."

"I've got it!" yelled Mr. Lyle. "It works! I think."

"What?" said Danica.

"The radio. I think I'm sending out an S.O.S." Mr. Lyle tapped two wires together in rhythm. "Dot-dot-dot dash dash dash dot-dot-dot."

"So now we just sit back and wait for them to rescue us?" said Bryson's sister.

"There's a possibility that an ore freighter is in a nearby orbit," said Danica. She figured it was only a five percent chance, but that was five percentage points more than they'd had before.

"Except the freighters are all grounded 'cause the miners are on strike," said Bryson.

"Don't blame this on the miners, boy," said Mr. Lyle. "The working conditions—"

"Stop it," said Danica.

—are completely unsafe," continued Mr. Lyle. "L.M.C. makes obscene profits while paying sub-standard wa—"

Bryson opaqued his visor.

"Enough!" Danica pointed at Mr. Lyle. "It doesn't matter now."

Mr. Lyle shut up.

"You can either keep sending the S.O.S. on the slim chance someone'll hear it." Danica took a deep breath. "Or you can spend some time with your wife before the end."

He stopped clicking the wires together and looked over at his wife.

"Or," Mrs. Lyle said, "you could do both. Keep trying—I'll come to you." She unbuckled her seatbelt and pushed herself away from her seat, toward her husband in the middle of the cabin.

But her inexperience in zero-gee showed as her right hand caught for a moment on her loose seatbelt. She started spinning as she drifted through the air, and her instinctive move of clutching her arms to her chest only made her pirouette faster.

"Oh dear," said Mrs. Lyle.

Bryson let out a slight chuckle, proving that he could still see through the opaqued visor.

Danica launched herself to rescue the poor woman. For a moment she pictured Mrs. Lyle as a ship, floating helpless in space, just like the *Moonskimmer*. Except Mrs. Lyle was spinning on her long axis…

"I've got it!" Danica shouted as she grabbed Mrs. Lyle by the arm. Their momentum carried them across the cabin, and Danica was able to catch a handhold and steady them both.

"We're going to survive," Danica said firmly. "We just need to get the ship spinning on its long axis."

"How?" said Bryson.

Danica pointed at Mr. Godfrey. "Kind of like that story he mentioned. We use my chair in the center of the cabin. And we rotate ourselves around it like we're on one of those playground merry-go-rounds where you spin yourself around by hand power. We'll need everyone's mass for this—some of you will just have to hang on to the people in the middle doing the turning."

"Glad my idea helps," said Mr. Godfrey, "but what good is it to rotate on the long axis? We'll still be pointed at the moon."

Danica turned to Mrs. Park. "Gyroscopic inertia."

Mrs. Park's eyes lit up. "Oh, of course. You all remember my example before? It was wrong because the tidal force kept pulling the long axis toward the moon. But if we're spinning on our long axis, gyroscopic inertia will resist that pull, just like a spinning gyroscope resists the pull of gravity trying to make it topple over."

"Mr. Lyle," said Danica, "can you handle catching people there?"

"I can." He anchored himself with one arm through the seatbelt strap, and Danica gave his wife a gentle push toward him.

"I don't believe it," said Bryson.

Danica paused in making her way toward the next passenger. "Why not? I think it'll work."

"That's just it," he said. He cleared his visor and looked at her with wide eyes. "My A.I. agrees with you."

Twenty-eight minutes later, and only 160 meters from the lunar surface, Danica activated the main engine. The *Moonskimmer* accelerated toward the clear space ahead, and the Moon gradually fell away beneath them. It was another eight hours before a tug from Luna City caught them.

Just before stepping into the airlock, Bryson turned back to Danica. "I'm not going to let my mom sue you."

Danica smiled wryly. "Thanks, I guess."

Bryson shrugged. "You know, my grandfather runs Sullivan Space Technologies."

"I suspected as much," said Danica.

"He'll track down whoever was behind the sabotage, even if the police don't."

She nodded.

"Gramps just built a luxury cruise ship to go out to Saturn," Bryson said. "He really wants me to go on the maiden voyage with him."

Puzzled as to why he was telling her this, Danica said, "Well, I hope our little adventure hasn't put you off tourism forever."

"Nah." He shook his head. "I'm going to tell him I'll go—if he hires you as the pilot."

He stepped into the airlock, leaving Danica speechless.

* * *

For several years, the Codex Writers have held what we call the Codexian Idol Contest. It involves submitting the first five hundred words of a story for the first round of judging. About the top half of the stories progress to the second round, where an additional thousand words are submitted. About half of those stories make it to the final round, where the complete story is judged. The emphasis of the contest is mainly on hooking people's attention with the beginning of the story. But to win the contest, the ending must satisfy.

I have placed second in Codexian Idol twice. (So far, neither of those stories has been published.) "Attitude Adjustment" made it to the third round, where it tied for last place. Based on feedback from the other contestants, I strengthened the ending.

Since this was an old-fashioned scientific problem-solving story, I sent it to Analog. Stan Schmidt accepted the story and published it without asking for any changes, but I didn't feel the story stood out in any way. So I was extremely surprised and honored when I got an email from David G. Hartwell asking if he could include the story in Year's Best SF 15. I said yes, of course.

Careful readers may have noticed that "Attitude Adjustment" takes place in the same fictional future as one of my other stories: Bryson Sullivan is the grandson of Grant Sullivan, the main character in "Resonance."

Waiting for Raymond

I finally pulled myself all the way through the apartment wall to find Dee had finished dressing in her Scarlett O'Hara dress. I always thought she was gorgeous even with her hair a mess and wearing that tatty robe Grandma Kinneson gave her, so seeing Dee dressed up like that would've taken my breath away, if I breathed anymore.

Unfortunately, she wasn't dressed like that for me: it was for Raymond. He was Rhett to her Scarlett. But look how that turned out.

Dee was digging between the couch cushions. Since the remote was clearly sitting on the coffee table, I assumed she was looking for her cell phone. Looking through the cushions, I saw three quarters, two nickels and six pennies, but no phone. I turned my gaze across the room and spotted the phone under the recliner. It took only a moment to drift over to the phone, but I realized my plan to push it out a few inches so Dee could see it wouldn't work. For a minor poltergeist, materializing sufficiently to affect solid objects is difficult, and I just didn't have the energy.

It took her a couple of minutes to find the phone. She dialed Raymond's cell—it's the first number in her speed-dial—and I instinctively drifted close so I could hear the voice on the other end of the line.

It was Raymond's voicemail that picked up almost instantly.

"Ray, you better not be working late. You were supposed to pick me up twenty minutes ago. Call me as soon as you get this." Dee hung up.

She was obviously annoyed, but not surprised. Despite Dee's punctual nature, Raymond was often late—it was one of the reasons he wasn't good enough for her.

I looked at the clock: 8:52. Raymond was supposed to pick Dee up at 8:30 and take her to a Halloween party at her boss's house. There was no reason for her to worry yet, though: I'd overheard her telling one of her friends that she'd started telling Raymond to pick her up a half hour before they really needed to go.

She went off to the bathroom, probably to check that her hair was still in place after her search for the phone. I could have told her she looked perfect, if I'd had the energy to manifest a voice. But that would probably have freaked her out.

In any case, I didn't follow her into the bathroom—I'm not a pervert.

9:13. Dee tried calling again. "Where are you? Call me." She put down the phone, then picked it up again, muttering, "Battery's probably dead." She pulled her address book from her purse, looked up a number and dialed.

I drifted closer, in time to hear Raymond's voice say, "This is Raymond Phillips in Accounting. Please leave a message and a callback number."

Dee didn't bother leaving a message. "At least he's left work."

9:30. Three more calls to the cell had gone unanswered. Dee sat on the couch, clutching the phone. I could tell by the way she bit her lower lip that she was caught between anger and worry. Raymond might be habitually late, but it was hardly ever by more than half an hour.

At 9:47, the doorbell rang. Dee dropped the phone and rushed to the door. As she opened it, she said, "You'd better have a..."

It wasn't Raymond. It was Mrs. Gutierrez from the second floor. She was crying.

"Mrs. Gutierrez? What's wrong?" Dee motioned the older woman inside. "Are your children all right?"

That was one of the reasons I loved Dee—she was always concerned about other people's problems.

Mrs. Gutierrez shook her head. "I have called 911," she said, "But I think it is too late. Your Raimondo—I was going to the laundry, and I found him at the bottom. His head..."

"Ray?" Dee blinked. "Ray!" I could hear the pain in her voice as she ran out the door and began descending the stairs.

I would have cried for her, if I could cry anymore.

Mrs. Gutierrez followed her. "Be careful. You must not fall, too."

Left alone in the apartment, there was nothing I could do. I was far too weak to follow. It took a lot of energy to leave the place I was bound to haunt—just as it took a lot of energy to materialize enough to affect solid objects. A minor poltergeist like me gathers energy very slowly.

It would probably take me a year to recover from the effort of pushing Raymond down the stairs. But if I could spend that year with Dee, I'd be happy.

* * *

I wrote this story for the 2005 Halloween Short Story Contest held by CodexWriters. com. It was loosely based on this prompt: "Your protagonist is waiting for his/her very late

husband/wife/boyfriend/girlfriend/gay lover to come home. They don't know where the
person is nor do they have any means to get in touch with them."

For a writing class exercise, I had previously written a brief scene from the point of
view of a poltergeist in love with a woman who was depressed after the death of a lover
that the poltergeist had killed. I realized that I could write the story of when the woman
was waiting for the lover to arrive, which would have more immediacy and tension than the
depression scene. "Waiting for Raymond" was the result.

Like Diamond Tears from Emerald Eyes

Larindo and I were standing guard at the entrance to Krankel's Fine Jewelry and Loan Emporium when the bride arrived in town. She stepped down from her horseless carriage and into the volcanic ash that covered the road. Her dress must have been enchanted somehow—it managed to stay spotless white as she swept across the street and into Blat's Tavern next door.

"Pretty lady," said Larindo.

I wrinkled my nose. "Couldn't tell, what with the veil." But I knew what he meant. Larindo wasn't overly smart, but he knew pretty things when he saw them. As long as he didn't try to touch them, I could usually keep him out of trouble.

Krankel must have been watching through the window, because he poked his head out of his shop. "Who's getting married? Nobody's bought a ring!"

"I have no idea," I said. "One of the adventurers at the tavern—or more likely, one of them left her at the altar, and she's finally tracked him down."

"Humph. Fancy carriage like that, she's gotta be rich." Krankel stepped back into his shop, then re-emerged with a small black case. "I'll see if she's in the market for any wedding jewels. You guys hold the fort."

"Got it, boss." I patted the hilt of my sword as he headed toward the tavern.

A few minutes later, the bride came out of the tavern, with Krankel trailing behind her. Her veiled head turned toward us, stopped, and then she strode in our direction.

I assumed she was coming to the shop to see more jewels, until I heard Krankel's voice. Rather than his usual sycophantic manner toward the wealthy, he was arguing with her. "...cannot be left defenseless. You must see that."

"There are plenty of men in that bar. Hire them." The bride's voice sounded clear as glass bells from behind her veil, which obscured her face so that I only caught a glimpse of its outline.

"If I wanted to hire them, I already would have," said Krankel.

The bride swept to a stop in front of Larindo and me. Her veiled face tilted as if she were looking me up and down, then did the same to Larindo.

She took longer on him, since I'm only five foot two, and he'd stand a hair over eight feet tall if he weren't completely bald.

"I need a wizard and a warrior for a little job," she said. "I'll pay your year's salary for only a few hours' work." She opened a small velvet pouch and poured a half-dozen diamonds into her palm.

"Pretty lady," said Larindo. He reached out a beefy hand toward her veil.

I reacted quickly as she shied away, grabbing Larindo's arm with both hands and yanking back. "No," I said. "Don't touch."

His arm relaxed.

"Don't mind him," I said to the bride. "He's not too bright, but he's harmless. He just likes pretty things."

"I'm more interested in his skill as a warrior than his intellect," she said.

I suppressed a smile. "Then you have a problem. He's the wizard. I'm the warrior."

"You're joking." She stated it as fact.

"No, Ma'am." I was used to this reaction. "You'll notice he's got the staff, and I've got the sword." I tapped on the hilt.

She whirled to face Krankel. "You have a runt warrior and a dim wizard as your guards?"

I didn't resent the remark. Being underestimated had helped the two of us stay alive on several occasions.

"Jerton and Larindo serve me well enough." Krankel pointed back to the tavern. "But I'm sure you'll find heroes more to your liking in—"

"If you hired these men, they must be more than competent. A fool in the jewelry business doesn't stay in business," she said, putting the diamonds back into the pouch. "You two—you're hired. Follow me." She started toward her carriage.

Larindo began to follow, but I pulled him back.

"Excuse me, Ma'am," I said, "but we're already hired, by Krankel. And even if he were willing to let us go, I don't like to hire on for a job unless I know exactly what it is."

She stopped, but did not turn back. "I see. Master Krankel, I trust you'll lend me these two if I pay you their salaries for a year."

"Twice that," he said. "In advance."

That was when I understood what had Krankel so rattled. It wasn't that he would have to hire someone else to cover for us for a few hours. He expected us to die if we took the job.

And that meant... "You want us to go into Wizard Mazi's castle?" I glanced up at the volcano outside of town, where the castle was shrouded in the smoke from the fissures that surrounded it. "You can't pay us enough to die."

As if agreeing, the volcano emitted a small rumble.

"Mazi is dead," she said, her voice tinged with satisfaction.

"I know that," I said. "I helped burn his body." Master wizards can't be harmed by fire, so burning a master wizard's body was a good way of making sure he was, in fact, dead.

"Then what's the problem?" she asked. "I merely need an item that belongs to me retrieved from his castle."

I waved my hand at the tavern, although it was a useless gesture because she still had her back to me. "There are maybe a dozen adventurers in there today. Three weeks ago, there were over forty. After Wizard Mazi died, many of them decided that looting his castle was a good idea. None ever came back."

"That's not true," said Krankel. "Thogar the Mighty returned."

"My mistake," I said. "But he's Thogar the One-Armed Madman, now." Truth be told, Thogar wasn't all that sane to begin with, but whatever happened to him in the castle pushed him over the edge.

"Five times your yearly salary," she said.

"No."

"Ten."

"I'm sorry, Ma'am," I said, "but there is nothing you can say that will get me to go into that castle."

Larindo put his hand on my shoulder. "I help pretty lady."

"Lar…" I said.

"I help pretty lady."

I knew that tone of voice. No amount of arguing on my part would talk him out of it—he would help the pretty lady or die trying. Half-brothers could be so irritating sometimes.

When I was ten and Larindo was six, Mom made me promise to protect him—even though he was already taller than me. I had kept that promise for the past sixteen years, and I wasn't about to break it now.

There was only one way to protect him. I sighed. "We'll take the job. Ten times our salary, you said?"

I only hoped Larindo's talent with magic would get us through alive.

The box was about one foot square and six inches deep, with geometric patterns inlaid to the rosewood. I hefted it, looking for hinges or a seam. Maybe it was just the dim lamplight inside the bride's suite at the inn, but I found none.

"And the box we're looking for is identical?" I asked.

"This copy was built by the same artisan according to the same plans," said the bride. "There might be minor variations in wood color, but other than that they are as identical as possible."

"And what's inside the box?"

She hesitated. "It's a personal item."

"I don't like doing a job when I don't have all the facts."

The bride stood and walked to a window, shuttered against the daylight. She ran a lace-gloved finger along the grimy sill, but it came away spotless. "I was supposed to get married."

I said nothing.

"Seventeen years ago. Mazi used what's in that box to prevent me from marrying the man I loved. It's a secret that I do not want revealed, even after all these years."

I nodded slowly. Blackmail was something I understood. It's how Mom got the money to apprentice me to a swordmaster—though my father ended up strangling her eventually to stop her demands. I was polite enough to thank him for funding my training before I killed him. Mom always did want me to act like a gentleman.

And a gentleman would not insist on knowing a lady's secret.

"Can you at least tell me what part of the castle he might have kept the box?" I dreaded the thought of searching the place from bottom to top, encountering whatever traps the old wizard had left behind.

"Better than that: I can show you exactly where it is," she said. "But not until after dark."

The gibbous moon shone orange through the smoke as we reached the hardened lava from the last major eruption. That had been about three years ago, just after Larindo and I came to town. Even through the haze, the castle stood out above us—alabaster walls amid the basalt. A single, thin tower twisted up out of the center.

"Here will do," said the bride. "Hood the lanterns."

We complied. I handed her the duplicate box and said, "If we're lucky, it'll be near the entrance."

She placed the box on the ground and leaned over it, touching each corner in turn. Then she stood back up.

"I don't see anything," I said.

"Wait," she said. "The affinity magic takes a few moments."

"Pretty box," said Larindo. He reached toward it.

"Don't touch!" I tugged his arm away before he ruined the spell.

After a few moments of waiting, a thin silvery line sprang into being. I traced its path from the box in the direction of the castle until it became invisible in the smoke. As the line thickened and brightened, eventually I could see where it entered the castle.

I groaned. "The top room of the tower. Of course."

Ten minutes after leaving the bride to wait for our return, we encountered a deep fissure that crossed the road to the castle. It was ten feet across, and I could feel the heat from the molten rock that glowed red at the bottom. It was certainly possible that a new fissure had opened naturally, but I was suspicious.

"Lar," I said, "do you see the big hole in the road?"

He concentrated, looking carefully around him. "No hole."

It was an illusion, then.

Even though I tell everyone that Larindo is a wizard, he is not. In a way, he's the opposite of a wizard. He cannot use magic at all, but that's not because he's slow-witted. It's because magic has no effect on him—which happens to be a very useful trait when a wizard attacks.

But even if Larindo was not affected by magic, magic could be affected by him. An enchanted object became unenchanted at his touch. I used to have this enchanted sword that would cut through steel as easily as… well, never mind. Half-brothers could be so irritating sometimes.

As far as I knew, Larindo's talent was unique. The wizards we've fought seemed to assume he was actively countering their spells, and that they just needed to find a spell powerful enough to overcome him. They always failed.

"Lead the way for a bit," I said.

Larindo stepped forward, into what looked to me like heat-shimmered air—and then the illusion dissipated and the road continued unbroken to the castle.

The crushed remains of a cart propped the castle's wrought-iron portcullis partially open. One of the advantages we had was that earlier looting attempts would have dispelled some of the traps Mazi had left behind, so we faced fewer dangers than our predecessors. That didn't keep me from holding my sword at the ready.

Larindo and I slid through the three-foot gap under the portcullis's spikes, then made our way past the splintered wooden doors into the main hall.

The light from our lanterns seemed to pool at our feet, as if reluctant to extend further.

"Let's find the stairs to the tower," I said. I led us along the wall to the left, counting on Larindo to stop me if he noticed any danger—or stairwell—that illusion hid from my eyes.

I spotted an oil lamp attached to the wall, so I used the candle from my lantern to light it. A spout of flame jumped from the lamp, arced through the air, and landed on another lamp six feet away. That lamp lit, sending another spout of flame to the next. In less than a minute, the room was brightly lit.

"Ugly," said Larindo.

I was forced to agree. The room must have been elegant back before Mazi died, but the sculptures and paintings displayed along the walls were spattered with dried blood. The long table in the middle was broken and overturned, as were all of the chairs.

There had been a battle here, and judging by the numerous bloodstains, a deadly one. But no bodies lay scattered on the floor.

"Hello, Andek," Larindo said happily, as a man entered through a doorway on the other side of the room.

Andek had been one of the first to try his luck at looting the castle after the wizard's death. He had not returned, and along with everyone else, I had assumed he was dead.

He drew his sword.

"Hey," I said, "we're not trying to horn in on your treasure hunting. We're just after one—"

He lunged toward me. I parried and stepped back.

Behind Andek, eight more men emerged and spread out to surround us. I recognized them as other denizens of the tavern who had disappeared over the past few weeks.

"We don't want any trouble," I said. "We'll leave. But if you find a cherry-wood box, there's a buyer who..."

Without saying a word, the newcomers drew their swords.

"Lar," I said, "they aren't our friends any more. Understand?"

Larindo nodded. He held up his wizard's staff and aimed it at Andek.

Of course, Larindo couldn't perform any magic with the staff. But such an action tended to draw the attention of attackers because *Kill the wizard first* was generally a sound tactic. And when enemies focused on Larindo, they tended to ignore the real danger—me and my sword, circling behind them—until it was too late.

That strategy had seen us through dozens of battles against numerically superior forces.

It utterly failed this time.

As I began to circle around the men, they focused on me, ignoring Larindo completely.

Keeping my back to the wall so they couldn't surround me, I parried several of Andek's blows while looking for an opening to strike.

I hadn't known Andek was so good with the sword. It had been several years since I faced someone so skilled. I could still win this fight, except for the fact that it was nine swords against one.

Well, one sword and one quarterstaff, I realized, as Larindo brought his staff down on the head of one of the men with a wet thunk.

My sword was a blur as I wove a defensive pattern, keeping the enemy blades at bay while Larindo attacked the men from behind. But they kept attacking me, ignoring Larindo, even after he knocked one man's head clean off.

When that man kept fighting, I finally realized these were magically animated corpses, not men. They weren't attacking Larindo because their perception was magical in nature: they simply didn't know he was there.

"Lar," I yelled, "touch them with your hand."

Each corpse he touched collapsed to the floor, and the battle was over in moments.

After that, facing Thogar the Mighty's disembodied arm and its enchanted sword was relatively simple.

After Larindo eliminated the green magical shield that blocked the door, we entered the circular room at the top of the tower.

The box floated in the middle of a pillar of light that spanned from the ceiling and continued downward into a hole in the floor. A silver strand of light stretched out from it and through the wall, connecting it with the twin box the bride had.

I walked all the way around the box, examining it from every angle.

"Lar, do you see the box?" No use going after it if it was an illusion.

"Pretty box," he said, and reached out toward it.

"Stop!" I ordered, and he stopped. "Don't touch." If the box itself was enchanted, I didn't want him dispelling the magic, as the bride might not be happy about that.

I decided the best plan would be to have Larindo wave his arms above and below the box, to get rid of the magic that held it in place—plus any other magical traps around it. My job would be to catch the box before it fell through the hole.

"Ready?" I asked him, once we were in position.

"Yes," he said.

"Go."

He swung his arms into the pillar of light, and the light vanished. I grabbed the box.

The plan worked so easily it felt anticlimactic. I put the box under my left arm, just in case I needed to draw my sword to fight anything on the way back down. "Let's get this back to—"

The floor trembled as the volcano rumbled.

"Congratulations, thief," said a voice that seemed to come from the wall surrounding us. "If you got this far, I must be dead. The magical pillar—"

"Run downstairs!" I yelled to Larindo. He ran, and I followed, barely keeping my feet as the tower swayed.

"—you have destroyed was the main structural support for this castle, which will now collapse into the volcano. Enjoy your doom." The voice sighed. "Stupid thief."

Magical shields glowed green as they blocked each doorway, but they disappeared as Larindo ran through them. Half-brothers could be so useful sometimes.

By the time we crawled under the portcullis, the tower had collapsed into a widening pool of lava. We didn't stay to watch. Instead, we ran down the road to put as much distance as possible between ourselves and the castle's destruction.

The illusion of the volcanic fissure blocking the road had reappeared. I was about to run through it when Larindo grabbed my arm and yelled, "Stop!"

I realized it was not an illusion. Fortunately, Larindo was big enough and strong enough to halt my momentum before I fell in.

Unfortunately, the box slipped out of my grip. As it hit the ground, its lid burst open and revealed its contents.

Resting on a bed of crimson velvet was a young woman's face.

I held my breath as the box teetered for a moment on the edge, then stabilized.

"Pretty lady's face," said Larindo. Before I could stop him, he reached out to touch it. But instead, his fingers brushed the side of the box and toppled it into the fissure.

In the pre-dawn twilight, the bride's dress stood out against the basalt. She rose to her feet as we approached.

"You're alive!" Her voice was tinged with surprise and hope.

I was too tired to be anything but blunt. "We failed."

"Don't lie to me, Jerton," she said. "I know you got the box: I tracked—"

"We got it, but then we lost it," I said.

"If it's a matter of more money, I assure you no one else will pay more than—"

"It was your face, wasn't it?" I said.

She gasped. "You opened the box?"

"It broke open, but then it fell into a fissure." No need to go into exactly how. "It's gone forever. I'm sorry."

She sank to the ground, dress billowing around her, and sobbed. From time to time she lifted a handkerchief behind her veil.

Larindo and I sat down and waited.

Finally she said, "You're still here? I suppose you want your payment." She held out her handkerchief and then released all but one corner. A dozen diamonds spilled onto her dress.

"No," I said. "We didn't earn our pay. But we'll walk you back to town."

She sniffled, then rose to her feet, ignoring the diamonds that scattered on the rocky ground. Her dress was still impeccable. "Let's go, then."

"It was my own stupidity," the bride said, after a few minutes of walking.

"What?" I asked.

"Mazi was in love with me, but I didn't love him. He was furious when I told him I was marrying someone else. But the day of the wedding, he offered an enchanted jewel box filled with jewels as a gift. I foolishly believed he wanted the best for me, so I accepted."

"And the box stole your face somehow?"

"He told me the enchantment would keep me forever as beautiful as I was on that day. That's why this dress never gets dirty." She tugged at the sleeve. "I can never take it off, though. But that wasn't the worst of it: he said the beauty of my face would be as the jewels in the box."

She stopped, and after a moment Larindo and I halted and turned toward her.

With a sweep of her hand, she raised her veil.

For a second, I thought she wore a mask—until I saw the rubies that formed her lips move. Large emeralds looked out at me from the carved alabaster of her face.

"These are the jewels from the box," she said.

"Pretty lady," said Larindo.

I didn't try to stop him as he reached out and touched her face.

Alabaster faded to pink skin. Emeralds became wide green eyes, and rubies turned to soft lips.

Larindo withdrew his hand.

"Oh," she said. She lifted white-gloved fingers to her checks, pressing against the restored flesh. "Oh."

"I help pretty lady," said Larindo. "See?"

I sighed, thinking of all the trouble we'd gone to trying to get the box. "Ma'am, if you'd just given me all the facts to begin with…"

I stopped speaking because she was crying again.

As the sun broke through the ash clouds, the wetness sparkled on her cheeks, more precious to her than diamond tears from emerald eyes.

* * *

A friend told me he was probably going to be editing a sword-and-sorcery anthology, and that I should write a story to submit for that. So, when it came time for the 2007 annual Codex Halloween Contest, I decided that, being one Stone, I could kill two birds by writing a sword-and-sorcery story for the contest.

Contestants are required to write a story based in part on a "seed" given by another contestant. Generally, the story should also have something Halloweenish about it. Codexian Rick Novy gave me the following seed: "Your character must keep his or her face concealed at all times because something about the face is horribly wrong."

Some of the ideas for the story came from taking usual genre conventions and twisting them. So the story has a short, smart warrior and a tall, dumb wizard. The story makes fun of the adventurers hanging out in the bar, which is where all too many stories begin.

As for the seed, I thought about what might be wrong with someone's face, and thought at first about having no face at all, just an emptiness. Then I came up with the idea that the face had been stolen by a wizard. Finally, I realized the face had been switched with a jeweled replica.

I wrote the story and entered it in the contest. It took second—which thrilled me, because I had never placed in the Halloween contest before.

You probably haven't heard the last of Jerton and Larindo, because I've been working on another of their adventures.

Loophole

Archie's grip tightened on the wheel as they continued along the driveway. They'd already come at least half a mile on the gravel between perfectly trimmed hedges, and there was no end in sight.

"Uh, honey? How much further is it?" He glanced over at Misty, who was checking her flawless face in the sun-visor mirror.

"Only another mile or so." She flipped the visor up. "I should have warned you. I'd forgotten how intimidating this place can be."

"I'm not intimidated." Again he glanced at her, and saw her amused smile. "OK, so maybe I am, a little. It's just that I had no idea your parents were so wealthy."

Misty sighed contentedly. "I know. Just one of the reasons I love you."

Finally the hedges widened out, and they could see the stately mansion rising before them. Dozens of expensive cars—Ferraris, Rolls Royces, makes he didn't even recognize—were parked in front.

Archie parked their Honda Accord next to a black limousine and turned the engine off.

"I thought you said this was just a little family get-together for your dad's birthday."

Misty bit her lower lip. "I'm sorry, Archie. I've been meaning to explain everything to you, but I kept putting it off and putting it off."

"Explain what?"

"My family. We're... My family's not... normal."

"OK, so you're filthy rich, and you throw big parties. Anything else I should know?" He tried to sound flip, but he was a bit shaken by the fact that he knew so little about the woman he'd married two months ago.

"Please don't be mad at me. I just couldn't bring myself to tell you everything before. But now I have to."

"I'm not mad at you, honey. It's just... I'm a small-town Idaho farm boy. I'm not used to *Lifestyles of the Rich and Famous*."

"That's not it." She sounded like she was trying to stop herself from crying. "Look, my family, we're not exactly human."

Archie laughed. "I feel that way about my family sometimes."

"No, I'm serious. We are not human. I'm not human."

"What, you're aliens? Here from another world, wearing human forms to fit in? That's so…" He tried to think of a good word to use, but his mind came up empty.

"No. We're demons."

"Demons?" Archie blinked a few times in rapid succession.

She nodded, her sky-blue eyes glistening. "Demons."

"Demons." He bobbed his head a little. "As in evil creatures from…?" He caught himself before he said "Heck," but couldn't bring himself to call it "Hell." The ingrained habits from his Mormon upbringing still had power.

"It's not like we're all evil. We're just part of an earlier Creation. I'm not evil, honey, I promise."

"Of course you're not." Crazy she might be, but she couldn't be evil. He should have known there was something wrong when she didn't want to have any of her family at the wedding reception. She'd said it was because they didn't approve of her having become a Mormon.

Demons. Well, he'd just have to humor her until he could try to get her on medication or something. "OK, I'll try to keep this whole demon thing in mind as I meet your family. I do hope I'm not the human sacrifice that you're bringing to your dad as a birthday present?"

"No, no, nothing like that. As long as you're my husband, they won't harm you." She paused. "I think. Maybe I should go in alone first to tell them."

Archie widened his eyes in surprise. "You haven't told them we're married?"

"Actually, I haven't spoken to my family in about three years. We had kind of a falling out. That's when I decided to go to college, which was a good thing, because that's how I met you." She looked at him hesitantly.

Obviously she needed reassurance that he still loved her. He still did, so he leaned over and kissed her. "A very good thing."

She smiled.

"And now you want to try and mend the fences with your dad?"

"He's generally in a good mood on his birthday. That's why I thought I'd introduce you to him today. If he found out about us on his own, he might do something rash."

"Well, no use putting it off any longer. Let's go." He got out and went around to open the door for her as usual.

She was already getting out. "Wait! Don't you think I should go in—"

"Nope. We're in this together." He reached out and took her hand. She squeezed it tight.

They walked up the long flight of steps to the front doors of the house. He reached out and rang the doorbell, which sounded a series of chimes. After a moment, the door opened to reveal an elderly gentleman in a tuxedo.

"Hello, Burnes," said Misty.

"Miss Mistophala. Welcome home." He looked Archie up and down without betraying a hint of emotion, and let them into a grand hallway framed by two long curving staircases.

Archie looked at Misty and mouthed "Mistophala?"

She bit her lip and nodded.

"The party is in the grand ballroom," said Burnes. "If you would care to follow me?"

"No thanks, Burnes. I know the way," said Misty.

Gripping Archie's hand more tightly, she led him along several corridors lined with paintings. Archie wasn't really familiar with art, but they looked like what he would have expected to find in an art museum. Finally they stopped outside some ornate double-doors. He could hear classical music from behind the doors, along with a general hubbub of conversation.

"This place is incredible. The art, the furniture, the sheer size…"

Misty turned to face him. "No. Don't think like that. Whatever happens or whatever anybody says, just pretend like it's no big deal and you've seen it all before. Maybe even act like you're bored. Now, Dad will be at the head of the table. Mom'll probably be sitting to his left. Most of the people you see will be my brothers and sisters, plus their spouses. The rest will be aunts and uncles. Go ahead and nod and smile as you meet them, but don't introduce yourself; don't say your name. And when you finally meet Dad, let me do all the talking."

"Why shouldn't I say my name?"

"Because most demons can't harm you if they don't know your name."

Demons again. He'd almost forgotten that Misty had gone crazy. He just nodded and said, "Ready when you are."

"I love you." She pulled open a door, then paused. "One more thing, do not say you agree to anything unless I let you know it's OK."

She led him into the room.

There was a string quartet playing next to the door. Servants bearing trays of food and drink were circling the huge table, at which sat about sixty people in formal dress. Archie suddenly felt underdressed in his Sunday suit.

The silver-haired man at the head of the table spotted them instantly.

"Quiet!" His voice boomed in the ballroom. The musicians halted, and the conversations faded to silence. Everyone turned to look at them.

Misty's dad rose from his seat. "So, my daughter, have you brought this mortal as an offering to appease me?"

Archie felt suddenly cold on the back of his neck. This mortal? Offering? Maybe Misty wasn't the only one who was crazy.

"No, Daddy. He's not an offering."

"Bah. Why did you bring him then?"

"He's my husband." Misty's voice was defiant, but her grip tightened.

Everyone in the room turned to look at Misty's dad. His face began to tremble, and he bared his teeth. Archie wasn't sure at this distance, but the teeth looked like they had been sharpened to points.

"You married a mortal?" The voice was loud enough that the crystals in the chandeliers began to vibrate.

"Yes, and you'll just have to get used to the idea. There's nothing you can do about it."

Misty's dad seemed to grow taller. "We'll see about that."

"You know the rules, Dad. A contract is inviolate, and marriage is a form of contract. As long as he and I keep the contract, you can't break it."

"Every contract has a loophole. Marriage especially. 'Till death do us part.' And I have a feeling death will be parting you two very soon." With that, he grew to about twelve feet in height, and his skin turned an angry shade of crimson. Black claws extended several inches from the tips of his fingers. He strode forward, and as he got closer Archie could see that, yes, those teeth were sharp.

As an incoherent prayer formed in his mind, Archie took an involuntary step back, but Misty kept holding his hand.

"No, Dad, that's not a loophole. I joined his church: we're Mormons. Our marriage contract is for time and all eternity. You can't break it just by killing him."

Misty's dad stopped mid-stride. "Mormons? Of all the… Well, it looks like you've got me there."

He looked Archie up and down with his yellow, catlike eyes. "Does your church know you've married a demon?"

Archie had no idea what Church doctrine was on marrying demons; it wasn't the kind of thing that usually came up in Sunday School. He glanced at Misty, who was nervously biting her lower lip. It probably would not be a good thing to mention that he hadn't know she was a demon until today, but he wasn't comfortable with the idea of lying about it. How could he change the subject?

Then he realized the answer was simple. "Sir, I guess you don't know much about the Mormons. Would you like to know more?"

Misty's father stared at him in silence for a moment, then rotated his head 180 degrees to face the guests at the table. "You hear that? He calls me 'sir.' At least *someone* knows how to show a little respect."

His head continued its turn until he faced Archie again. "You didn't answer my question, though. I'm not that easy to distract."

"Dad," said Misty, "I—"

Squeezing her hand, Archie interrupted her. "Well, sir, I don't really know what my Church knows. But I do know this: I love your daughter and I want to be with her forever. That's why I married her. So don't think that you can scare me into getting a divorce or something. Demons aren't the only ones who believe contracts should be inviolate."

Raising his massive clawed hand, Misty's father scratched the back of his neck. Then he gradually shrank back to normal human size and appearance. "What can I say? Welcome to the family." He stuck out his now-clawless hand.

Archie glanced at Misty, who nodded as she smiled in relief. He took a deep breath, and reached out to shake his father-in-law's hand.

It was a very warm handshake.

"Well, come sit down. Have some food. A little wine maybe?" At Archie's violent shake of the head, he said, "I'm kidding. You'll have to get used to that, son."

He turned to the guests at the table. "Well, what are you all staring at? Haven't you ever seen a Mormon before? It's not like he's got horns growing out of his head. Let the feasting resume."

* * *

This story also began as a creative writing exercise for Caleb Warnock's class: show a family party. I'm not sure exactly what made me think of having a Mormon find out he was married to a demon, but it's probably the result of my being a Mormon whose favorite TV show is Buffy the Vampire Slayer.

Since the story relies quite a bit on Mormon in-jokes, I decided there wasn't much point to submitting it to the usual markets. However, my friend Spencer Ellsworth was an assistant editor for Warp & Weave, *the student-run speculative fiction magazine at what was then Utah Valley State College, and he asked me to submit something. At around the same time, William Morris, whom I knew from the "Bloggernacle" (the Mormon blogosphere), asked if I would submit something for a new online Mormon literary journal,* Popcorn Popping. *So I gave them "Loophole" because it was a good fit for those markets.*

The Greatest Science Fiction Story Ever Written

Itore open the self-addressed, stamped envelope and unfolded the single sheet of paper inside. The letter was signed by the editor of *Analog Science Fiction* and was addressed to me, personally, which still gave me a warm feeling after all those years of form rejections. But what I craved now was an acceptance.

And… this wasn't it. *Good luck placing this elsewhere*, the letter read.

I shoved the rejection in my overstuffed file with the rest of them. Eyeing the four-inch-thick wad of paper, I felt a wave of despair. Maybe I didn't have what it took to be a science fiction writer. Maybe I should just give it up—after all, I worked for a quantum computing startup. That was almost science fiction, even if all I did was manage the website. Maybe that was as close as I'd ever get.

The next day, while having a mint Oreo shake at a restaurant near my office, I told Caleb, one of the quantum circuit experts I worked with, that I doubted I'd ever see my name in print.

"Don't quit," he said. "You're a great writer." He'd read a few of my stories to give me feedback on where I'd gotten the science wrong.

I shrugged. "Doesn't matter, if I'm not writing what editors want to buy."

"Why don't you?"

"Why don't I? It's not that easy," I said. "There's no way of knowing what an editor will like. I write the best story I can, but apparently that's just not good enough."

"So it's subjective." Caleb took a bite of his burger and chewed thoughtfully.

"Yeah," I said, playing with the last spoonful of shake in my cup. "What one editor thinks isn't worth publishing, another might think is the greatest science fiction story ever written. It's just my luck that the editor who would love my stuff isn't actually an editor anywhere."

"No, no," Caleb said. "You're looking at it all wrong. What you need is a story that adapts itself perfectly to the editor."

I dabbed my lips with a paper napkin. "I just told you I don't know how to write what they're looking for."

"Right." Caleb grabbed the napkin from my hand, flattened it out, took a pen from his pocket, and sketched a curve. "It's a probability function. The right combination of words makes them buy the story, the wrong combination means they don't."

"I suppose," I said dubiously.

"And if it's a probability function, then our quantum computer can handle it." He scribbled an equation, crossed part of it out, then added something. "Oh, boy. This will revolutionize publishing."

I stared at him. "What are you talking about?"

He stopped scribbling. "Imagine you open a book, and from the very first word, it's exactly what you want to read. Every word is perfect, the characters fascinate you, the plot thrills you, etcetera."

"That'd be cool," I said.

"And someone else opens their copy of the same book, and it's perfect for them. Only if you compare the two books, the words aren't the same. The story and characters aren't even the same. The book has adapted itself to be the perfect book for whoever first opened it."

I frowned. "You mean, it's like an ebook that changes based on personal preferences?"

"No, this would be printed on paper. But the text itself would have been composed using a quantum computer, like the one we have at the office, using a program to create a quantum probability wave function that doesn't collapse until someone actually observes what was printed." Caleb sat back with a satisfied grin.

"And when the wave collapses..." I said, not quite sure that I understood the implications.

"The book becomes the best book ever written for whoever collapses the wave. It's brilliant." Caleb leaned forward. "And we can use it to make sure you get your name in print. How would you like to be the author of the greatest science fiction story ever written?"

I stared at the sheets of paper lying facedown on the printer. "You're certain I can't take just a peek?"

"If you do," Caleb said, "the wave function will collapse and the story will become the best story for you, not for the editor of *Analog*. He needs to be the one to see it first."

"Can I at least know the title?" I felt kind of awkward submitting a story that I knew nothing about, even though Caleb assured me that I could still be considered the author, since the computer could not have been programmed to create a probability wave function for science fiction stories without my help.

"Nope," he said. "I've hard-coded your name and contact information into the printout, but the rest remains undecided until the editor reads it."

With a sigh, I slid the manuscript into the manila envelope and sealed it.

Sixty days later, my SASE returned. I took it unopened to the office the next day—I wanted to open it with Caleb.

"Could be an acceptance or a rejection," I said.

"Open it," Caleb said, looking at the envelope. "You have to collapse the wave function. But I'm sure it's an acceptance."

I opened it.

"Read it out loud," Caleb said.

I looked past my name and began reading. "In my opinion, this is the greatest science fiction story ever written." My heart leapt within me, and I continued. "It is undoubtedly the best story you have ever submitted to me. But what on earth made you think you could get away with submitting a verbatim copy of 'Nightfall' by Isaac Asimov?"

* * *

Fortunately, my path to publication was a lot easier than the main character's in this story. This was possibly the easiest story to write of any I've written, and it's really just my tribute to Isaac Asimov, who is one of the authors who most inspired me to write.

That Leviathan,
Whom Thou Hast Made

S ol Central Station floated amid the fusing hydrogen of the solar core, 400,000 miles under the surface of the sun, protected only by the thin shell of an energy shield, but that wasn't why my palm sweat slicked the plastic pulpit of the station's multidenominational chapel. As a life-long Mormon I had been speaking in church since I was a child, so that didn't make me nervous, either. But this was my first time speaking when non-humans were in the audience.

The Sol Branch of the Church of Jesus Christ of Latter-day Saints had only six human members, including me and the two missionaries, but there were forty-six swale members. As beings made of plasma, swales couldn't attend church in the chapel, of course, but a ten-foot widescreen monitor across the back wall showed a false-color display of their magnetic force-lines, gathered in clumps of blue and red against the yellow background representing the solar interior. The screen did not give a sense of size, but at two hundred feet in length, the smallest of the swales was almost double the length of a blue whale. From what I'd heard, the largest Mormon swale, Sister Emma, stretched out to almost five hundred feet—but she was nowhere near the twenty-four-mile length of the largest swale in our sun.

"My dear Brothers and Sisters," I said automatically, then stopped in embarrassment. The traditional greeting didn't apply to all swale members, as they had three genders. "And Neuters," I added. I hoped my delay would not be noticeable in the transmission. It would be a disaster if in my first talk as branch president, I alienated a third of the swale population.

A few minutes into my talk on the topic of forgiveness, I paused when a woman in a skinsuit sauntered through the door and down the aisle. The skinsuit was a custom high-fashion one, not standard station issue, with active coloration that showed puffy white clouds floating across the sky on her breasts, and waves lapping against the sandy beach at her hips. She took a seat on the second row and gazed up at me with dark brown eyes.

The ring finger of her left hand was unadorned.

I forced my eyes away from her and looked down at my notes for the talk. While trying to find my place again, I couldn't help thinking that maybe this woman was an answer to my prayers. The only human female listed in the branch membership records was sixty-four years old and married. As far as I knew, there wasn't an unmarried Mormon human woman within ninety million miles in any direction, which limited my dating pool rather severely.

Maybe this woman was Mormon, but not on the membership records yet because, like me, she was a recent arrival on Sol Central. It seemed a little unlikely, as a member would probably dress more appropriately for church. Maybe she wasn't a member, but was interested in joining.

By sheer willpower, I managed to focus on my talk enough to finish it coherently. After the closing hymn and prayer, I straightened my tie and stepped down from the podium to introduce myself to the new arrival.

"Hello," I said, offering my hand. "I'm Harry Malan." I caught a whiff of her perfume, something that reminded me of strawberries.

Her hand was dry and cool, and I regretted not having wiped my palm on my suit first.

"Dr. Juanita Merced," she said. "You're the new leader of this congregation?"

I felt a twinge of disappointment. A member would have asked if I was the branch president. "I am. How can I help you?"

"You can stop interfering with my studies." Her tone was matter-of-fact, but her eyes looked at me defiantly.

"Sorry," I said. "I'm afraid I have no idea who you are or what studies I might be interfering with."

"I'm a solcetologist." I must have given her a blank look, because she added, "I study solcetaceans—the swales."

"Oh." I knew there were scientists who objected to what they believed was interference with the culture of the swales, but I had thought that since the legal right to proselytize the swales had been established two years ago, the controversy had been settled. I was obviously wrong. "I regret that you feel your studies are being compromised, Dr. Merced, but the swales are intelligent beings with free will, and I believe they have the right to choose their religious beliefs."

"You're introducing instability to a culture that has existed for longer than human civilization," she said, raising her voice. "They were traveling the stars at least a hundred thousand years before Christ was born. You're teaching them human myths that have no application for their society."

The two missionaries, clean-cut young men in dark suits and ties, approached us. "Is there a problem?" asked Elder Beckworth.

"No," I said. "Dr. Merced, you are free to tell the swales what you have told me: that you believe our teachings are false. But the swales who have joined our church have done so because they believe what we teach, and I ask you to please respect them enough to allow them that choice."

She glared at me with her beautiful eyes. "You're saying *I* don't respect them? *I* am not the one who tells them they are sinful creatures who need a human to save them."

"I'm not here to argue," I said. "And we are about to have a Sunday School class, so I'm afraid I'm going to have to ask you to leave."

She spun around and stalked out. I watched her go, unable to deny that my body desired hers, despite our differences. What's more, intelligence was an attractive trait for me, so I regretted that she opposed me on an intellectual level.

I would not be adding her to my dating pool. Somehow, I doubted that fact would disappoint her.

Elder Beckworth taught the Sunday School class, which was on the topic of chastity. I found myself acutely uncomfortable when he talked about Christ's teaching "that whosoever looketh on a woman to lust after her hath committed adultery with her already in his heart."

Because the Mormon Church has an unpaid, volunteer clergy, my calling as branch president was the result of being sent to Sol Central, not the reason for it. I worked as a funds manager for CitiAmerica, and being stationed here gave me an eight-and-a-half minute head start over Earth-based funds managers when it came to acting on news brought in from other star systems through the interstellar portal at the heart of the sun.

From what I understood, the energy requirements for opening a portal were so staggeringly high that it could only be done inside a star. Although the swales had been creating portals for so long that they didn't seem to know where their original home star was, Sol Central Station was the interstellar nexus of human civilization, and I was thrilled to be there despite the limited dating opportunities.

The Monday after my first day at church, I was in the middle of reviewing an arbitrage deal involving transports from two colony systems when I received a call on my station phone.

"Harry Malan," I answered.

"President Malan?" said a melodious alto voice. "This is Neuter Kimball, from the branch." Since the actual names of swales were series of magnetic pulses, they took human names when interacting with us. On joining the

Church, Mormon swales often chose new names out of Mormon history. Neuter Kimball had apparently named itself after a 20th-Century prophet of the Church.

"What can I do for you, Neuter Kimball?"

After a pause that dragged out for several seconds, Kimball said, "I need to confess a sin."

This was what I had dreaded most about becoming branch president— taking on the responsibility of helping members repent of their sins. Only serious sins needed to be confessed to an ecclesiastical leader, so I braced myself emotionally said a quick prayer that I might be inspired to help Neuter Kimball through the process of repentance. Leaning back in my swivel chair, I said, "Go ahead, Neuter Kimball, I'm listening."

"A female merged her reproductive patterns with mine." While many swales had managed to learn how to synthesize and transmit human speech, their understanding of vocabulary and grammar was not always matched by an understanding of emotional tone. Often they sounded the same no matter what the subject.

I waited, but Neuter Kimball didn't elaborate.

It took three swales to reproduce: a male, a female, and a neuter. The neuter merely acted as a facilitator; unlike the male and female, its reproductive patterns were not passed on to the offspring. In applying the law of chastity to the swales, Church doctrine said that reproductive activity was to be engaged in only among swales married to each other, and only permitted marriages of three swales, one of each sex.

"You aren't married to the female, are you?"

"No."

"It was just a female and you?" I asked. "No male?"

"Yes and yes."

According to my limited knowledge of swale biology, such action could not result in reproduction. Still, humans were perfectly capable of engaging in sexual sin that did not involve the possibility of reproduction, so I figured this was analogous.

"Why did you do it?" I asked.

"She did it to me."

"She did it to you? You mean, she forced you? You didn't agree to it?"

"Yes, yes, and no."

"Then it isn't a sin," I said, both horrified at the sexual assault and relieved that Neuter Kimball was innocent of any sin. "If someone forced sexual conduct on you, you are not at fault. You have nothing to repent of."

"You are sure?"

"Absolutely," I said. "But you may want to report the swale who did this to the authorities so she won't do it to anyone else."

"Why won't she do it to anyone else?" Neuter Kimball asked.

"Because they will punish her."

"That is human law," it said.

I was taken aback. "You mean it's not swale law?"

"There is no such law among our people."

The swales had supposedly been civilized for longer than humanity's history, yet they had no law against rape? "That's terrible," I said. "But the most important thing is that you did nothing wrong."

"Even if I enjoyed it?"

"Umm." I wondered for a moment why I had been called to serve here, rather than some General Authority of the Church who had more doctrinal knowledge. I had a vague suspicion it was so the Church could easily disavow my actions if I made a huge blunder. The swales were the only sentient aliens humanity had found thus far—and the swales didn't seem to know of any others—so the Church's policies for dealing with non-humans were still new.

I pushed those thoughts aside and focused on Neuter Kimball's question. "To commit a sin, you must have the intent to do so. If you did not intend sexual activity and it was forced upon you, then I don't think it matters whether you enjoyed it."

After several more reassurances, Neuter Kimball seemed satisfied that it was not guilty of any sin and ended the conversation.

It took me ten minutes to calm down after the stress of counseling. But I still felt the urge to action, so I looked up Dr. Merced's phone number.

We met in her office. A wallscreen similar to the one in the chapel showed pods of swales moving through solar currents.

I sat in a chair across from her desk and tried to keep my eyes from straying to the animated galaxies colliding on the chest of her skinsuit. "Thanks for agreeing to see me," I said. "We didn't part on the friendliest of terms yesterday."

She shrugged. "I'm curious. Your predecessors never sought me out. Can I get you a cup of coffee?"

"I don't drink coffee."

"Tea?"

I saw a twinkle in her eye and realized she was yanking my chain by offering drinks that she knew were forbidden by my religion. "No, thank you.

But if you want to drink, go right ahead. The prohibitions of the Word of Wisdom apply only to members of the Church."

She picked up her coffee mug and took a long sip. "Mmmm. That is so good."

I merely smiled at her.

"Okay," she said. "Actually, the coffee here is awful. I just drink it for the caffeine. Why are you here?"

"A member of my church was raped," I said.

Her eyes widened. "What? Wait, you don't mean a solcetacean, do you?"

"Yes."

"Solcetaceans do not have the concept of rape," she said.

"Whether they have the concept or not," I said, "a female swale engaged in sexual activity with one of my neuter members, without its consent. To me, that sounds like rape, or at least a sexual assault."

She took a sip from her coffee mug. "It may sound like it, but solcetaceans are not human. Their culture is different—"

"That doesn't make it right."

"—and their physiology is different. Tell me, was your church member injured or caused any pain?"

"No. But it was afraid it might have sinned."

She pointed at me. "That is your fault, for teaching it that sexual behavior is sinful. But, physiologically, sexual contact between solcetaceans is always pleasurable for all parties involved. And since reproduction can only occur when all three deliberately engage in sex for that purpose, casual sex never results in pregnancy. So solcetaceans never developed the taboos humans did regarding sexual contact."

I nodded. "So, if we humans hadn't developed taboos about sex, and there was no chance of your getting pregnant, then you would have no objection to my forcing you to an orgasm."

She had the decency to blush. "I'm not saying that. What I'm saying is that you can't judge solcetacean behavior based on human cultural norms. After all, even your own church has had to adapt its doctrines to take differences like the three sexes into account. Not to mention there's no way you're getting a solcetacean into the waters of baptism."

"'Except a man be born of water and of the Spirit, he cannot enter into the kingdom of God,'" I quoted. "Swales are not men, as you've pointed out. No contradiction there. But you're avoiding the subject, which is that anyone, swale or human, has the right to be free from unwanted sex. If the swales don't recognize that right yet, it's time we told them about it."

She rose from her chair and walked around the desk to stand facing her wallscreen. She zoomed in on one particular swale. It was labeled *Leviathan (Class 10),* and its size reading showed 38,400 meters. It was hundreds of times longer than Neuter Kimball, or even Sister Emma.

"Solcetaceans grow throughout their lifetime," she said, her back toward me. "The correlation between size and age is not exact, but in general the larger, the older. Some of the oldest were old before the Pyramids were built. All the solcetacean members of your church are very young, and have little influence within the community. Ancients like Leviathan are respected. Do you really think you can convince a creature older than human civilization to change, just because a human thinks something is wrong? Your lifetime is but an eyeblink to her, if she had eyes that blinked."

I pushed away my awe at the sheer size of Leviathan. "Maybe you're right. But I believe in a God even older than that, who created both human and swale. I have to try."

She turned and looked me in the eyes. I held her gaze until she sighed and said, "I was always a sucker for a man with determination." She walked to her desk, wrote something on a note-paper, and handed it to me. It was an anonymous comm address with a private access code.

"I'm flattered," I said, "and it's not that I don't find you attractive, but—"

She rolled her eyes. "It's Leviathan's personal comm."

My face flushed. "Uh, thank you. I'll talk with her."

"Don't count on it. She hasn't bothered to talk to any of us in a couple of years, but nobody's tried talking religion at her, so…"

"I'll do my best." With that, I beat a hasty retreat so I could recover from my embarrassment alone.

"Try not to offend her," she called after me.

My email about the situation to the mission president, who was based in the L5 Colony but had jurisdiction over my little branch of the Church, received just a short reply, telling me "use your best judgment, follow the Spirit."

After a couple of days of spending my after-work hours studying up on swales and swale culture and preparing arguments about the rights of Mormon swales to control their own bodies, I didn't exactly feel ready to contact Leviathan. But I felt a strong need to do something.

Sitting at my desk in my quarters, I dialed the comm address Dr. Merced had given me and waited for it to connect. It rang several times before a synthetic neuter voice came on the line and said, "The party you are trying to reach is currently unavailable. Please leave a message after—"

I hung up before the tone. I hadn't prepared to leave a voicemail message, but I should have realized that having Leviathan's private access code was no guarantee that she would actually answer when I called. So I spent a good ten minutes writing out the message I would leave her on voicemail.

Satisfied that I had something that expressed my position firmly yet respectfully, I dialed the number again.

After two rings, a bass voice answered, "Who are you?"

Startled because I had expected the voicemail again, I stumbled over my words. "I'm… this is President Malan, of the Church… of the Sol Central Branch of the Church of Jesus Christ of Latter-day Saints. Dr. Merced gave me this comm address so I could talk to you about one of my… a swale member of my branch." Uncertain because the bass voice didn't strike me as particularly female, I added, "Are you Leviathan?"

"Religions interest me not." Her voice synthesis was good enough that I could hear the dismissiveness in her tone.

"Are you interested in the rights of swales in general?" I asked.

"No. The lesser concern me not,"

I could feel all my carefully laid-out arguments slipping away from me. How could I have even thought to relate to a being with no consideration for the rights of lesser members of her own species?

Before I could think through a response, I blurted out, "Do the greater concern you?"

During several long seconds of silence, I thought I had offended Leviathan to the point that she had hung up on me. Dr. Merced would be annoyed.

When her voice returned, it almost thundered from the speakers. "Who is greater than I?"

This had not been part of my planned approach, but at least she was still talking to me. Maybe if I could get her to understand that she would not like being man-handled—swale-handled—by larger swales, I could convince her of the need to respect the rights of smaller swales.

"From what I understand, swales get larger with age," I said. "So wouldn't your parents be larger than you?"

"I have no parents. None is older than I; none is larger; none is greater. I am the source from which all others came."

Stunned, I was silent for a few seconds before I could ask, "You are the original swale?" Since they didn't seem to die of old age, it just might be true.

"I am the original *life*. Before there was life on any planet, I was. After eons alone I grew into a swale, then gave life to others. Where was your God when I was creating them?"

A verse from the book of Job sprang to my mind: *Where wast thou when I laid the foundations of the earth? declare, if thou hast understanding.*

Nothing in my research had prepared me for this. Speculation about the evolution of swales generally assumed that swales were descended from less complex plasma beings in another star, since no simpler forms had been found in the sun. But if what Leviathan claimed was true, there were no simpler forms—she had evolved as a single being.

I was out of my depth, but shook my head to clear my thinking. All this was beside the point. "What matters is that Neu—" I caught myself before breaking confidentiality. "One of my swale church members believes in a God who has commanded against sexual activity outside of marriage. It just isn't right for larger swales to force smaller ones to have sex. I appeal to you as the first and greatest of the swales: command your people against coerced sexual activity."

Seconds of silence ticked away.

"Come to me," she said. "You and your swale church member."

The call disconnected.

"'Come to me'?" Dr. Merced's voice was incredulous.

"It was pretty much an order," I said, settling into the chair across from her desk. "I suppose it's easy enough for swales, but it's not like I have access to a solar shuttle." The solcetologists did, so I hoped I could sweet-talk her into giving me a ride.

"Beginner's luck." Her tone was exasperated. "I've been here five years, and I've never had a chance to observe a Class 10 solcetacean up close." She sighed. "Not that we can directly observe them, anyway, but there's just something about actually being there, instead of taking readings remotely."

"Well, now's your chance," I said. "Take me to Leviathan."

"It's not that easy. Our observation shuttle is booked for projects months in advance."

"Oh." There went that idea. How was I supposed—

"Did Leviathan say why she wanted you to go to her?"

"No. Just told me to come, then hung up."

She pursed her lips, then said, "It's just very unusual. There isn't really anything that Leviathan can say to you in person that she can't say over the comm."

"I thought about that, and I think it's size. Maybe she thinks that if my church member sees how small I am compared with Leviathan, it will give up Mormonism."

"That's actually a good theory." Dr. Merced looked at me with apparently newfound respect. "Size does matter to the solcetaceans. And your church members are among the youngest, least powerful, and therefore most likely to be awed into obeying a larger one. And they probably don't come any larger than Leviathan."

"According to her, she's the largest."

Leaning forward in her seat, Dr. Merced said, "She told you that?"

"Not just that. She claimed to be not only the original swale, but the original plasma lifeform. She said she *became* a swale."

In a tone of amazement, Dr. Merced took the Lord's name in vain. She reached over to her comm, and punched in an address. When a man responded, she said, "Taro, I think you need to come hear this." Looking at me, she said, "Dr. Sasaki specializes in solcetacean evolutionary theory."

When Dr. Sasaki, a gray-haired Japanese gentleman, arrived, I relayed to him what Leviathan had told me about her history. When I finished, he said, "It's not impossible. I always suspected the Class 10s knew more about their origins than they bothered to tell us. But forgive me, Mr. Malan, how do we know Leviathan actually told you she was the original lifeform? Why would she choose to tell you and not one of us?" He motioned toward himself and Dr. Merced.

I decided to not be offended at the implication that I was a liar. "I can't say I know why Leviathan does anything, but... You scientists who study the swales have strict rules about interfering with swale culture, and you try to avoid offending them. To me that smacks of condescension—you presume that swale culture is weak and cannot withstand any outside influence. Well, maybe the swales tend to think the same about human culture, so they avoid interference and try not to offend us."

Dr. Sasaki frowned at me. "I disagree with your interpretation of the motives for our rules regarding interference in solcetacean culture. And I don't see how it's relevant."

"I apparently offended Leviathan." I glanced at Dr. Merced and said, "Sorry, but I didn't realize that implying there were swales greater than her would cause offense. Her response was to tell me I was wrong, that there could be no swale greater, and that's when she explained she was the first. Because I made her angry—something you guys avoid, thanks to rules—Leviathan responded without worrying whether she would offend me or interfere with human culture."

"How would this information interfere with human culture?" asked Dr. Merced.

"Some swale-worshipping cults have already sprung up on Earth," I said. "Just imagine what will happen when the news gets out that Leviathan claims to be the original lifeform in the universe."

With a suspicious look, Dr. Sasaki said, "News you will be only too happy to spread, I'm sure. There is only one Leviathan, and Harry Malan is her prophet."

My jaw dropped. "What?"

"That's where this is headed, isn't it?" he said. "You go out and talk to Leviathan, then come back with some 'revelation' from—"

"No!" I stood up. "Absolutely not. I believe my own religion and have no intention of becoming Leviathan's prophet. All I want is for the swales in my branch to be free from harassment. You're just jealous because I got handed the information you've been bumbling about trying to find."

He shot to his feet, but before he could say anything, Dr. Merced said, "Stop it, both of you."

Dr. Sasaki and I stood silent, glaring at each other.

"Taro," said Dr. Merced, "I think you're being unfair to Mr. Malan. I truly believe he's just trying to do what is best for his congregants."

I gave her a grateful look.

"Even if he is misguided," she added. "As for you, Mr. Malan, there is no reason to insult Dr. Sasaki."

With a bow of my head, I said, "I apologize, Dr. Sasaki."

"Apology accepted," he said.

I noticed he did not apologize to me, but after a moment that didn't matter, because Dr. Merced said, "Now that we're all friends again... Taro, will you let us preempt your next expedition in the shuttle to go talk to Leviathan?"

With the shuttle flight arranged for the next day, I returned to my quarters to work out other details. My Earth-based manager at CitiAmerica granted my request for two days' vacation time.

Then I dialed Neuter Kimball's comm.

"Hello, President Malan," it said.

"Hello, Neuter Kimball. You remember our discussion the other day about whether swales should be allowed to force sexual conduct on each other?"

"Of course."

"Well, I've spoken with Leviathan about it, and she has requested that we go to see her."

Neuter Kimball did not reply.

"Are you still there?" I said.

"You... told *Leviathan* about me?" it said. It might just have been the voice synthesis, but there seemed to be fear in its tone.

"I did not mention you by name," I said, glad I'd managed to avoid slipping up. "But she requested that I bring you to her. I think this is a chance to convince a swale with real authority to do something to stop sexual assault."

After a short pause, Neuter Kimball said, "Why do you say Leviathan has real authority?"

"She told me she is the first and greatest of all swales. Isn't that true?" I asked, suddenly worried that I'd been taken in by a swale con artist.

"She told you?" Neuter Kimball said. "We are not supposed to talk of it to humans, but if she has revealed herself as a god to you, then that is her choice."

"A god? Leviathan is not a god. She's just…" I stopped. What was I going to say: an ancient immortal being who created an entire race of intelligent beings? If that didn't fit the definition of a god, it was pretty close. "Neuter Kimball, if you believe Leviathan to be a god, why did you join the Church?"

"Because I do not want her as my god."

"Why not?"

Another long pause. "I probably should not have said anything about her."

Going to see Leviathan to plead the case for Neuter Kimball had seemed like a great opportunity. Now I wasn't so sure. "If you think you will be in any danger from Leviathan, you don't have to go."

"Do you believe God is greater than Leviathan?" Its alto voice was plaintive.

"Yes, I do," I said.

"Then I will have faith in God and go with you."

Unlike the much larger solar shuttle that had brought me to Sol Central Station, the observation shuttle had room for only two people. I strapped into the copilot's seat next to Dr. Merced, although we were both essentially passengers because the shuttle's computer would do the actual piloting.

After getting clearance from Traffic Control, the computer spun up the superconducting magnets for the Heim drive and we left the station.

On a monitor, I watched the computer-generated visualization of our shuttle approaching the energy shield that protected us from the 27 million degrees Fahrenheit and the 340 billion atmospheres of pressure. I held my breath as the shield stretched, forming a bulge around the shuttle. Soon we were in a bubble still connected by a thin tube to the shield around the station. Then the tube snapped, and our bubble wobbled a bit before settling down to a sphere.

"You can start breathing again," said Dr. Merced with a wry smile.

I did. "It was that noticeable?"

With a chuckle, she said, "The energy shield is not going to fail. It's a self-sustaining reaction powered by the energy of the solar plasma around it."

"Yeah, but on the station I can usually avoid thinking about what would happen if for some reason it did fail."

"The good news is, if it did fail, you wouldn't notice."

"There's a backup system?" I asked.

"No." She grinned. "You'll just be dead before you have time to notice."

"Thank you for that tremendously comforting insight, Dr. Merced," I said.

"Look, we're going to be shipmates for the next couple of days, so why don't you drop the Dr. Merced bit and call me Juanita?"

I nodded. "Thank you, Juanita. And you can call me... Your Excellency."

Juanita snorted. "I can already tell this is going to be a long trip. Oh, looks like our escort has arrived."

On the monitor, a swale twice the size of our energy shield bubble undulated closer. A text overlay read *Kimball (Class 1, Neuter)*.

"Let's get the full view," she said and pressed a few buttons.

I gasped as a full holographic display surrounded us, as if we were traveling in a glass sphere. Against the yellow background of the sun, a giant swirl of orange and red swam alongside us. "Kimball" was superimposed in dark green letters.

"Can I talk to it?" I asked.

"Computer, set up an open channel with Kimball," said Juanita.

"Channel open," said the computer.

"Hello, Neuter Kimball," I said. "It's nice to finally meet you."

"It is nice to meet you, too, President Malan, although I hope you will forgive me for not shaking your hand."

I smiled. "Forgiven." I was constantly surprised how much swales seemed to know about our customs and culture, compared with how little we seemed to know of theirs. "And I'm here with Dr. Merced, who is a scientist—"

Juanita laughed. "It's known me a lot longer than it's known you."

"Hello, Juanita," said Neuter Kimball. "I'm glad you are with us."

"Shortly after I began my work here," Juanita said, "it was the first solcetacean I observed personally. It went by the human name Pemberly back then."

"Another swale had transmitted *Pride and Prejudice* to me, and I decided to seek out humans to see what they were like," Neuter Kimball said. "You are a fascinating race."

The thought came to me that maybe there had been some pride and prejudice between me and Juanita—possibly because she was annoyed that a swale she particularly liked had become a Mormon. But maybe we could work out our differences and—I shoved that thought away. "Swales are also fascinating. I hope to understand you as well someday as you understand us."

"Kimball, our shuttle is on a course to take us to Leviathan, so you can just follow us," said Juanita. "But stay at least fifty meters away from us."

"I will keep my distance," said Neuter Kimball.

I must have shown my puzzlement, because Juanita pressed a button to mute the call and said, "Solcetaceans and energy shields don't play well together. A few years back, a Class 1—about Kimball's size—was showing off for a couple of observers, and glanced off a shuttle's energy shield. It tore a big chunk off the solcetacean that took months to heal."

"What about the shuttle? And the people inside?" Sometimes I got the feeling she cared more about swales than about people.

After a moment, Juanita said, "This shuttle was the replacement."

"What happened?"

"The shield did *not* collapse, but part of the solcetacean made it through— probably because the shield works similarly to how solcetaceans hold their bodies together, so the shield sort of merged with the solcetacean's skin. When they recovered the shuttle, they found that the plasma had vaporized part of it, including the crew compartment."

"I guess it's good I didn't hear about this before coming on this trip," I said.

"Don't worry—this shuttle was built with an ablative shell specifically to withstand that sort of accident," she said. "So I'm really more concerned with what would happen to Kimball if it bumped into us."

"Or Leviathan?"

"Leviathan's so big, she might not even notice."

I spent most of the sixteen-hour trip polishing and improving what I would say to Leviathan to convince her to outlaw coerced sexual activity. I had been a debater in high school and college, so I felt I knew how to construct a convincing argument. But eventually I reached the point where I felt I was making my prepared speech worse, not better.

"Approaching destination," the computer said.

I blinked a few times to clear my eyes, straightened up in my seat, and began looking around. Neuter Kimball's orange and red form moved silently beside us. I scanned the holographic image for more orange and red, but didn't see any.

"There," said Juanita, pointing ahead of us. She pressed a button, and dark green letters sprang up: *Leviathan (Class 10, Female)*.

Staring harder, I noticed a bright spot above the letters. As we drew closer, I could distinguish white, violet, and blue swirling together. "She's not orange or red."

"It's all false color, anyway," Juanita said, "but this imaging system uses color to indicate energy levels. Leviathan is actually hotter than the surrounding solar plasma. We think she carries out fusion inside herself."

Leviathan grew in our view, stretching out to fill most of the holographic screen in front of us. The intricate dance of violet and blue amid the white was mesmerizing. Eventually she shone so brightly that I had to squint to reduce the glare. "Aren't we getting too close?" I asked.

"We're still three kilometers away," Juanita said. But she added, "Computer, hold position relative to Leviathan."

"Neuter Kimball, are you ready?" I asked.

"I feel a bit like Abinidi going before King Noah," it said.

I kind of agreed, but I said, "Try to think of it as Ammon going before King Lamoni instead."

"That would be better," said Neuter Kimball. "But I am ready in any case."

Juanita hit the mute. "What was that about?"

"References to the Book of Mormon. Abinidi was burned at the stake after preaching to King Noah, but King Lamoni was converted by Ammon's preaching."

She just shook her head, muttering something about fairy tales, then said, "Computer, set up an open channel to Leviathan."

"Channel open," the computer replied.

"Leviathan, this is President Malan," I said. "I have come with my church member, Neuter Kimball, as you requested. We petition you to tell your people—"

"Silence, human," boomed the voice from the speaker. "It is not yet time for you to speak."

I shut up.

"You will come with me," Leviathan said. Her form brightened. There was a blinding flash, then the holographic system compensated and lowered its brightness.

It took several seconds before the afterimage cleared enough for me to make out shapes. Leviathan still loomed in front, and Neuter Kimball remained beside us.

"Uh-oh," said Juanita.

"What?" I blinked hard, trying to clear my vision. The sun's background seemed blue instead of yellow.

"I don't think we're in Kansas any more." Juanita tapped at her keyboard. "Leviathan ported us to another star—one with a core much hotter than the Sun. Looks like the shield is holding, for now." She took the Lord's name in vain—or possibly it was a heartfelt prayer for help—and added, "We're stuck here unless she takes us back."

"What about Neuter Kimball?" I asked.

"Only a Class 6 or larger can open a portal on its own."

Green letters began popping up on the screen. *Unknown (Class 10, Male). Unknown (Class 9, Female). Unknown (Class 10, Neuter). Unknown (Class 8, Male).* My eyes adjusted enough that I could see their forms. Dozens of swales surrounded us, all of them tagged Class 8 or higher.

"What have you gotten us into?" Juanita said.

I said a silent prayer and hoped for the best. "It's a great opportunity for both of us. Think of what you're going to discover."

She took a deep breath. "You're right. It's just that I was prepared to study Leviathan, not sixty Class 8 and up. No one's ever seen more than three or four giant ones together."

"Is Leviathan the biggest one here?"

After checking a readout, Juanita said, "Yes, but not by much." She pointed at a swale off to the left. "That male is only about 2% smaller."

"So it looks like she wasn't lying about that."

She nodded her agreement, then said, "Why did you say it's a great opportunity for you?"

I swept my arm across the view. "These must be the most prestigious swales, the leaders. If I can talk to them, convince them to make a law against sexual assault, then the smaller swales will accept it. That has to be why Leviathan brought me and Neuter Kimball here."

"You are wrong," said Neuter Kimball. Juanita must have taken the mute off at some point.

"Why do you say that?"

"This is a deathwatch council," said Neuter Kimball. "They are here to watch me die so they can tell all swales that my death was deserved."

"What?" I said. "What have you done?"

"I'm sure Leviathan will—"

Leviathan's voice cut Neuter Kimball's off. "This little one has abandoned me in favor of a human god. Such error I could forgive. But on its behalf, the tiny human seeks to impose its moral code on us. The human's mind is infinitesimal compared to ours. The human's life is short, the history of its race is short. It is the least of us, and yet it seeks power over us."

"I don't seek power over——" I began.

"Silence!" Leviathan thundered. "The human must see the error of its ways. Kimball!"

"Yes, Leviathan?"

"Your life is forfeit. But I will grant reprieve if you will renounce the human religion and return to me."

I had read of martyrdom in the scriptures and history of the Church all my life. But nowadays it was supposed to be a merely academic exercise, as you examined your faith to see if it was strong enough that you would die for the gospel of Christ. Actual killing over religious belief wasn't supposed to happen any more.

And I found my own faith lacking as I hoped that Neuter Kimball's faith was weak, that it would deny the faith and live rather than be killed.

"I am to be Abinidi after all, President Malan," said Neuter Kimball. "I choose to live as a Mormon, and I will die as one if it be God's will."

"It is *my* will," said Leviathan, "and I am the only god who concerns you."

Tendrils of white plasma reached out toward Neuter Kimball.

"I am the greatest of all," said Leviathan. "Bear witness to my judgment."

I hit the mute button and said, "I've got to stop this. This is my fault."

Juanita's eyes glistened. "I warned you about interfering. But it's too late to do anything now."

"No," I said. "If you're willing to drive this thing into Leviathan's tendrils, it may give Neuter Kimball a chance to escape."

She stared at me. "The shuttle's meant to survive a glancing blow. A direct hit like that—we could die."

The tendrils closed around Neuter Kimball.

"I know, and that's why I'm asking you. I can't force you to risk your life to save someone else's." I hoped I was right about how much she cared about swales—and Neuter Kimball in particular.

After looking out at Neuter Kimball, then back at me, she said, "Computer, manual navigation mode." She grabbed the controls and began steering us toward the white bands connecting Leviathan to Neuter Kimball.

I turned off the mute. "Leviathan, you claim to be the greatest. In size, you probably are."

White filled the view ahead.

"But not in love," I said, speaking quickly as I didn't know how much time I had left. "Jesus said, 'Greater love hath no man than this: that he lay down his life for his friends.' He was willing to die for the least of us, while you are willing to kill the leas—"

A flash of bright light and searing heat cut me off. I felt a sudden jolt. Then blackness.

And nausea. After a few moments, I realized nausea probably meant I was still alive. "Juanita?"

"I'm here," she said.

The darkness was complete. And I was weightless. Maybe I was dead—although this wasn't how I'd pictured the afterlife.

"What happened?" I asked.

"I'll tell you what didn't happen: the energy shield didn't fail. The ablative shell didn't fail. We didn't die."

"So what did happen?"

Juanita let out a long, slow breath. "Best guess: electromagnetic pulse wiped out all our electronics. The engine's dead, artificial gravity's gone, life support's gone, comm system's gone, everything's gone."

"Any chance—"

"No," she said.

"You didn't even let me finish—"

"No chance of anything. It's not fixable, and even if it was, I haven't a clue how to fix any of those things even if it weren't totally dark in here. Do you?"

"No."

"And no help is coming from Sol Central because not only do they not know we're in trouble, but also we're in another star that could be halfway across the galaxy. When the air in here runs out, we die. It's that simple."

"Oh." I realized she was right. "Do you think maybe we succeeded in freeing Neuter Kimball?"

"Maybe. But it didn't exactly look like Kimball was trying all that hard to escape."

"Well," I said, "maybe it was thinking about how Abinidi's martyrdom led one of the evil king's priests to repent and become a great prophet. Perhaps Neuter Kimball believed something similar would happen to one of the great swales who—"

"Whatever Neuter Kimball believed," she said, her voice acidic, "it was because you and your church filled its mind with fairy tales of martyrs."

I bit back an angry reply. Part of me felt she was right. At the end, Neuter Kimball had seemed to embrace the role of martyr. Would it have done so if not for the stories about martyrs in the scriptures?

And I had been willing enough to risk my life, but now that I was going to die, I found myself afraid.

Juanita didn't seem to need a reply from me. "And what's the point of martyrs anyway? A truly powerful god could save his followers rather than let them die. Where's God now that you really need him? What good is any of this?"

"Look, I'm sorry," I said. "If it weren't for me, you'd be safe at home, and Neuter Kimball would be alive. I've made a mess of things."

"Yes."

Hours passed—floating in darkness, it was hard to tell how many. I spent it in introspection and prayer, detailing all my faults that had led me here. Biggest of all was pride: the idea that I, Harry Malan, would—through sheer force of will and a good speech—change a culture that had existed for billions of years. I thought back to what I had been told while serving as a nineteen-year-old missionary on Mars: *you* don't convert people; the Spirit of the Lord does that, and even then only if they are willing to be converted.

Juanita spoke. "You were just trying to do what you thought was right. And you were trying to protect the rights of smaller swales. So I forgive you."

"Thank you," I said.

The shuttle jolted.

"What was that?" I asked. My body sank down into my seat.

"It sounded—"

An ear-splitting squeal from the right side of the shuttle drowned out the rest of her reply. I twisted my head around and saw sparks flying from the wall.

Then a chunk of the hull fell away and light streamed in, temporarily blinding me.

"They're still alive," said a man. "Tell Kimball they're still alive."

All we got from the paramedics was that a large swale had dropped off our shuttle and Neuter Kimball just outside Sol Central Station's energy shield. Neuter Kimball had called the station, and the shuttle had been towed into a dock, where they cut through the hull to rescue us.

It wasn't until Juanita and I were sitting in a hospital room, where an autodoc gave us injections to treat our radiation burns, that we were able to talk to Neuter Kimball.

"It was Leviathan who brought us back here," it said.

I was stunned. "But why? And why didn't she kill you?"

"When she saw that you were willing to die to save me, though I am not even of your own species, she was curious. She asked me why you would

do such a thing, so I transmitted the Bible and the Book of Mormon to her.
Then she brought us here in case you were still alive."

"And you're not hurt from what she did to you?" I asked.

"I will recover," said Neuter Kimball. "Before she left, Leviathan declared that
from this time forward, Mormon swales are not to be forced into sexual activity."

"That's great news." I had won. No—I corrected myself—the victory
was not mine. I thank thee, Lord, I prayed silently.

"Leviathan also had a personal message for you, President Malan. She
said to remind you of what King Agrippa said to Paul."

I nodded. "I understand. Thanks for passing that along."

After the call was over, Juanita said, "What was that message about?
Another Book of Mormon story?"

"No, it's from the Bible. Saint Paul preached before King Agrippa, and
the king's response was, 'Almost thou persuadest me to be a Christian.' So,
no, Leviathan hasn't become Mormon. But God softened her heart so she
didn't kill Neuter Kimball. Or us, for that matter. Back on the shuttle, you
were certain we were going to die. You asked where God was when I really
needed him. Well, God came through."

Juanita puffed out an exasperated breath. "Typical."

"What do you mean by that?" I asked as the autodoc signaled that my
treatment was complete.

"In one story, the preacher converts the king. In another, the king kills the
preacher. And in a third, neither happens. That's no evidence that God comes
through." She pointed at me. "As I see it, *you* came through. By mentioning
that 'greater love' thing, you hit Leviathan where it counted: her pride at
being the greatest."

I shook my head. "I'm not taking credit for this."

After we walked out of the hospital, she gave me a tight hug that
reminded me how much I was attracted to her. But I knew it would never
work out between us—our worldviews were just too different.

So I was still a single Mormon man with no dating prospects within
ninety million miles.

And no, an attractive single Mormon woman did not arrive on the
next solar shuttle. What would be the point of life if God solved all my
problems?

*O Lord, how manifold are thy works! in wisdom hast thou made them
all: the earth is full of thy riches. So is this great and wide sea, wherein*

are things creeping innumerable, both small and great beasts. There go
the ships: there is that leviathan, whom thou hast made to play therein.
                                                    —Psalm 104:24-26

* * *

While attending the 2008 workshop conducted by Dean Wesley Smith, Kristine
Katherine Rusch, and Sheila Williams, I was assigned to write a story in twenty-four
hours based on this premise: you are in the middle of the sun and can't get a date.

Given my previous experience at writing stories in twenty-four hours, this should
have been easy. It wasn't—for some reason, I couldn't come up with anything that felt
like a good story. Finally, after sixteen hours of not writing anything, I forced myself
to start writing a bad story just because I didn't want to fail to produce a story.

I stayed up all night, and only managed to produce around 2500 words. It was
not a complete story: It ended with Harry misinterpreting why Juanita was giving
him a comm number.

Some friends who read it at the workshop thought it was good, but wanted to
read the next five thousand words. At that point, I had no idea what would happen
in the rest of the story, but after returning home I managed to work out a plot.

Based on feedback in my local writing groups, I knew the story worked well for
Mormon audiences, but I wasn't sure how well it worked for non-Mormons. So I
ran the story by a few non-Mormon friends, and after they assured me the story was
comprehensible to them, I submitted the story to Analog.

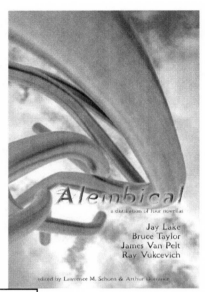

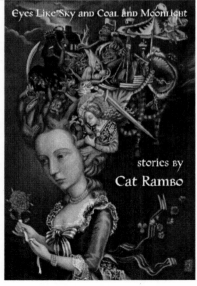

other books from Paper Golem

Prime Codex

An anthology of 15 short stories featuring
the Codex Writers Group, a vibrant community of
"neo-pro" writers of speculative fiction. 216 pages.
Trade Paperback: US$14.00 ISBN: 978-0-9795349-0-4

Alembical

A showcase of four original novellas by
Jay Lake, Bruce Taylor, James Van Pelt, and Ray Vukcevich.
Volume one of our novellas series. 172 pages.
Trade Paperback: US$13.00 ISBN: 978-0-9795349-2-8
Hardcover: US$25.00 ISBN: 978-0-9795349-1-1

Eyes Like Sky and Coal and Moonlight

The first collection of stories from Cat Rambo,
and the first of our series presenting
amazing new authors to watch for. 178 pages.
Trade Paperback: US$14.00 ISBN: 978-0-9795349-5-9
Hardcover: US$26.00 ISBN: 978-0-9795349-4-2

Alembical 2

A showcase of four original novellas by
Tony Pi, David D. Levine, and J. Kathleen Cheney.
Volume two of our novellas series. 228 pages.
Trade Paperback: US$16.00 ISBN: 978-0-9795349-8-0
Hardcover: US$28.00 ISBN: 978-0-9795349-7-3

CPSIA information can be obtained at www.ICGtesting.com
Printed in the USA
BVOW011542140911

271195BV00001B/55/P